The California Book of the Dead

✳

The
California
Book
of the
Dead

a novel

Tim Farrington

POCKET BOOKS

New York   London   Toronto   Sydney   Tokyo   Singapore

POCKET BOOKS, a division of Simon & Schuster Inc.
1230 Avenue of the Americas, New York, NY 10020

Copyright © 1997 by Tim Farrington

Library of Congress Cataloging-in-Publication Data

Farrington, Tim.
    The California book of the dead : a novel / Tim Farrington.
        p.   cm.
    ISBN: 0-671-51960-3
    I. Title.
    PS3556.A775C3   1997
    813'.54—dc21   96-47725
                                                                  CIP

First Pocket Books hardcover printing May 1997

10 9 8 7 6 5 4 3 2 1

POCKET and colophon are registered trademarks of
Simon & Schuster Inc.

Printed in the U.S.A.

for
Margie "Loki" Goldstein
1954–1993

with love

Acknowledgments

Deep thanks to Tom Miller, my editor at Pocket Books, for taking me on in the first place, for challenging me to go deeper, and for shepherding me through it all with such humor and heart; and to Linda Chester, of the Linda Chester Literary Agency, for her grace, guts, style, and the occasional Earl Grey tea. Something beyond thanks, a kind life-gratitude, to Laurie Fox, my text-partner of first and last resort, indomitable agent, poet, dear friend, and general literary angel. And to my wife Claire, my happiness teacher, all my love.

*I approached the borders of the dead: I trod
upon the threshold of Proserpina and I was carried
beyond the spheres of the elements. I saw the sun
shining brilliantly at midnight, and approached
the Gods of the Underworld, and those from On
High; and I worshiped them face-to-face.*

> —Apuleius, on his initiation
> into the Mysteries of Isis

Welcome to the Hotel California . . .

> —The Eagles

Prelude

Jackson

And so I looked and saw a kind of a banner
rushing ahead, whirling with aimless speed
as though it would not ever take a stand;
And behind it an interminable train
of souls pressed on, so many that I wondered
how death could have undone so great a
number.

—Dante, *Inferno*, canto 3

I

An Auspicious Passing

WHEN JACKSON DIED, MARLOWE STEWART REMEMBERED, MONKS HAD come. Everyone had been surprised. Jackson's Buddhism had been characteristically unobtrusive right up to the end, but there was no hiding six guys with shaved heads. The monks just shuffled in, in their sleeveless orange robes and sandals. One of them, the only American among them, had a Buddha tattoo on his biceps, which caused a few giggles and raised eyebrows despite the solemnity of the occasion. They arrived about an hour and a half before Jackson breathed his last, right about at the time that everyone else was beginning to wonder what to do. They seemed so sure of themselves, and so matter-of-fact, like a weird team of pizza deliverymen just doing their job, that no one thought to question their presence. They sat in a semicircle around the outer edges of the room and began to pray. Daa made them tea. Shakti Arguello, ever gracious in matters of life and death, offered them a joint, which they refused.

Jackson just smiled and waved one weak hand to offer them chairs. He was propped up in the bed on three big pillows, as he had been for months when he received visitors; he was obviously still trying to be gracious to everyone, but his gaze kept drifting toward the ceiling, where it tracked movements no one else could see. Marlowe, holding his hand, could hear him murmur from time to time, but she couldn't understand a thing. Jackson was on enough morphine by then that his speech had passed over into a kind of musical babble. At first it had seemed to frustrate him, but at some point he had shrugged and obviously let articulacy go. He had even cracked what was apparently a joke, which no one else got, couched as it was in the weird underwater speech of morphine, because he giggled.

Leave it to Jackson, Marlowe thought, to giggle in the face of death. Even through the muffling drugs and the sharp horror of his skeletal condition, he could find his way to laugh. She was afraid she was going to buckle inward from grief and terror herself; she felt hollowed out, enfeebled. Jackson had been the sanity of California for her, and now he was leaving her with the usual nutty crowd of their common friends, and a bunch of monks. She wanted to scream and run, but she had promised him she would stay.

All around the bedroom candles burned, dozens of them, from every corner and shelf. It made the room seem filled with warm, dreamy light. She could hear Jackson's lungs wheeze; from time to time he convulsed in a hideous coughing. He had fought to die here, not in the hospital, and now he was close to pulling it off.

People kept coming and going behind her, crossing around the bed to make good-byes from the other side, but as the night wore on, Marlowe could see only Jackson's face, his liquid brown eyes wandering, no longer securely attached to objects in the room. His cheekbones, once so elegant they were her envy, protruded now; his skull, shorn the week before, gleamed in the candlelight through a fuzzy bristle of new black hair. He had joked himself, while he still could, about his Auschwitz chic. But he was beautiful, Marlowe thought: in the candlelight Jackson's calm skeletal face glowed with everything she knew of his presence.

Remember, she told herself, remember that even after every feature you loved had been changed, wasted, ravaged, even after the horror of the bones beneath the skin surfaced into cruel transparency, you learned to see his beauty again for a moment. Remember that at the end the blackness turned lucid and lovely. Remember how he slipped away on a wave of peace, the way he wanted it, the way he prayed for.

His hand in hers was cool and limp; it twitched from time to time from the morphine; and from time to time Marlowe thought she recognized a more conscious squeeze, his presence, a communication. The plan had been to read from *The Tibetan Book of the Dead,* but in the end Jackson just shook his head and settled, and the silence filled the room. Through the last hour no one spoke. Marlowe held her breath every time his breath seemed to ease to a stop, but in the end she did keep breathing, and Jackson, with one last long outbreath, stopped. And still she would not let go of his hand; for a long, long time, she just held on.

Around her, everyone stirred into subdued activity. It was a relief, as it turned out, to have the monks there. There were a host of small details to be attended to. No one knew what to do, for instance, with the dozens of candles that had swollen the room with light during the long night of Jackson's dying. The monk who spoke English smiled when questioned and said to just let every candle be what it would, and so some people blew their favorite candles out and took the stubs home as treasured relics, and others let them burn away in degrees of symbolic release.

The monks meanwhile lit fat candles of their own. They were genial and gracious and bowed to the assembled friends and relatives—and there were many, as Jackson had been a beloved man—and then they sat in a semicircle around the emaciated body in the bed and began to chant. They chanted for three days and three nights without much more in the way of explanation, and also without eating or drinking anything except great quantities of Daa's tea.

Nor did they bother to sleep. One of them told Marlowe, who caught him while he was going to the bathroom, that they did not need to sleep because they were caught up in the excitement of this most auspicious passing. It was a great event that reverberated through all the planes. Jackson, it seemed, had been a sort of holy man.

"How do you know that?" Marlowe said; she had long suspected herself that Jackson was a holy man of sorts. But the young monk just smiled at her compassionately, as if she were a little slow, and got back to his chanting.

By the time they were done, some seventy-two hours later, Jackson was well established in the realm of the Clear Light, and his spirit was prepared for its inevitable encounters with the forty-two peaceful deities and the fifty-eight wrathful deities; along with the five wisdom-possessing deities, or Vidyadharas, in tantric union with their Dakinis, or female counterparts; and the wrathful protective deity, Vajrakila or Vajrakumara, who with his three-bladed magic dagger overcomes the three poisons of the instinctual world.

The monks, this excellent work accomplished for the good of all beings, then bowed again to everyone, and to the eight directions, and shuffled off to wherever they had come from, leaving the place redolent with sandalwood. And then Jackson's parents took his sad and ravaged body back to Yuba City and buried it in the family plot, next to the grave of his brother Mark, who had been killed in Vietnam.

No one, incidentally, had chanted when Mark died, although he had been killed defending a strategic Buddhist temple during the Tet offensive of 1968. But ironies abounded in Jackson's family, as Jackson himself had always been quick to point out.

Part I

The Lapidge Street Bardo

The gates of Pluto must not be unlocked—
within is a people of dreams.
                                        —Orphic warning

I

Marlowe and Daa

"Two dorks, a dweeb, a macrobiotic astrologer, a guy on the make, and an ex-Rajneeshie," Marlowe said, leafing through the stack of applications. "A breatharian. A woman channeling Joan of Arc. A man channeling the Buddha—"

"Now *that's* got possibilities," Daa said, perking up. "Maybe we should get them together—hey? What a ménage *that* would—"

"An ac*count*ant," Marlowe went on relentlessly, flipping through the sheets. "A cokehead. A coke *dealer*. A guy into some martial art that involves screaming—"

"Forget it."

"That goes without saying," Marlowe said, and sat back wearily in her chair at the kitchen table, where they had been sitting with their tea to go over the applicants to share the rental of their Lapidge Street house, in the heart of San Francisco's Mission. The fourth bedroom had just come vacant again, when Theresa Gresham moved abruptly back to Canada to be with her boyfriend, on the basis of a three-hour phone call and a tarot reading in which the Lovers card came up. The move in many ways was no surprise—certainly Marlowe had had a sense that it was just a matter of time before the card came up for Theresa—but coming as it did a week before the rent was due, it had left them scrambling to fill the vacancy.

Leafing through the application papers now, Marlowe felt a wave of the familiar despair. The morning's interviews had been the usual fruitless ordeal; and in any case she could not stop thinking of the room they were trying to rent as Jackson's room. This was the third time since he had died in it two months before

8

that she had faced the dreary chore of sorting through people she could never care about, to fill a place that could never be filled.

She was inclined to give herself a hard time about this—it seemed childish and unrealistic not to be able to take life's blows and just move on. It was not even as if Jackson's death had been sudden or unexpected. She could still remember when he had gotten his first sore throat and how they had laughed that off and said he had been singing too much. Then the sore throat had developed into pneumonia that almost killed him, and it was a year and a half before they laughed about much of anything again. By the end, of course, Jackson was laughing about pretty much everything. His brand of realism had been very jolly.

Her own brand of realism, Marlowe thought ruefully, seemed less exemplary. She told herself sternly that she had already had plenty of time to adjust. She had *done* the preparatory grief and the anticipatory mourning. She had been emotionally honest with herself, she had gone through the five Kubler-Ross stages of numbness, denial, anger, bargaining, and acceptance pretty much without a hitch. She had faced her fears and had embraced Lady Death as well as could be expected of any human being. She had accepted, and accepted, and accepted. She had done the work, in a word. She had come to terms.

So it had chagrinned her to find herself laid so low, when Jackson actually died. It had thrown her off, it was *still* throwing her off; it had left her rudderless and adrift, in ways she would never have expected.

"Who else?" Daa prompted now from the sink, where she had gone to begin to wash some vegetables for the lunch salad.

Marlowe turned her attention back to the applications. "A man—oh, here's one for you— a man who insisted on checking our roof to see if it could handle UFO landings."

"Could it?"

"He thought not, but said he was sure they could land in the backyard."

"Not in *my* garden, they can't."

"That's what *I* said." The two women exchanged a brief glance rich with ironic camaraderie. "I suggested he look for someplace a little more suburban."

"How do you know the one guy was a dealer?"

"He offered first and last month's rent, and a deposit, in cash. He just put it on the table, he had it in a paper bag. Small bills."

"Well," Daa said, caught momentarily by the vision of such instantaneous cash, "maybe that wouldn't be so—"

"*And* he had a gun."

"—bad. Okay, it would be bad."

"The breatharian grabbed my ass."

"So the morning wasn't a *total* waste."

"It was no thrill, believe me. For someone technically starving to death, he had a fierce grip. He may have been thinking of me as protein." Marlowe glanced at the last few applications. "A Dharmananda devotee with bad teeth. A serial killer—"

"Oh, come on."

"Or *something*. I swear. A perfectly normal-looking guy, even mildly attractive, certainly charming. It was something about his fingernails. And his haircut. He was holding all his eye contacts at least three seconds too long. Count 'em: one . . . two . . . three . . ."

"All right, all right. Thumbs down. Who else?"

Marlowe tossed the final sheets on the table between them. "An Est type, and a drummer."

"No more Est types. And no more drummers."

"Amen. And no more trumpet players."

"You interviewed another trumpet player?"

"No. I just want that clear on principle." Marlowe sat back in her chair and considered the sprawl of pages before them. "Jeez, Daa, what a *zoo*."

"The usual suspects."

"I don't know. It seems to me it's getting worse."

Daa laughed. "You say that every time. You're in a state, sweetheart, you've had a hard morning and you need some lunch."

Marlowe was silent, feeling vaguely frustrated with her lover. Not for the truths Daa had presented—it was true, she *did* say the same things every time they had to go through the ordeal of renting a room, particularly Jackson's room; she *had* had a hard morning; she did need some lunch. And she had, undeniably, worked herself into a state. She was prone to states. As usual, everything Daa had said was true. But her truths, like gravity, brought everything to earth.

Daa, sensitive to Marlowe's irritations, had been monitoring her obliquely from the sink, where she had started washing some spinach now; and she perceptively relaxed as Marlowe showed signs of mellowing out. Daa began to hum, something vaguely Celtic, and to sway a little to her own music. Soon she had finished the spinach and moved on to the lettuce; and from time to time she would pause in her washing, as at some secret call, and drift across the kitchen to pluck another herb or vegetable from some bin, basket, or shelf. Broccoli, Swiss chard, cucumber, some early cherry tomatoes, and a sprig of cilantro were placed each in their turn beside the sink to wash, in a precisely ordered arrangement. Daa's salads always came together so, with an air of heeding a higher necessity.

She was a formidable presence, even in a large kitchen. There were those who said Daa was built like a linebacker, and Marlowe supposed that this was true, and even that Daa might laugh at it now, embracing it; but there was a lingering trace of cruelty in the formulation. She knew how hard Daa had worked, first to change that square, strong shape, and then to accept it.

They had come together to the Bay Area at almost exactly the same time in the middle seventies, Marlowe from New York, in flight from the Manhattan art scene, and Daa from Minnesota, in flight from her high school sweetheart and imminent maternity. Daa had still been called Sheila then, Sheila Swensen. They had met in a Berkeley women's group, having read the same flyer on different telephone poles.

The group had been a revelation for them both. The shocking extent of their wholesale unconscious concessions, their bondages, their blithe suppressions and distortions and humiliations appalled them, and then enraged them. Marlowe could still recall that rage, its soaring, almost jubilant quality, the exhilaration of finding words, of naming at last a thousand inarticulated burdens. "Rumpelstiltskin," they had called it between themselves, a private code; for a time, for years, it had seemed impossible to relate to men at all, so pervasive was that dwarf's malignant face, and they had naturally gravitated toward each other. They would have coffee together after the meetings, every Tuesday night. No sugar, no cream, for either of them—Marlowe had always taken hers black, as a point of pride, and Daa had been on a perpetual diet, a fierce, unavailing near-fast. It was hard, now, to recall how she had suffered her solidity.

They had made an unlikely pair at best—though all pairs then were unlikely enough: Daa-Sheila big and blue-eyed and frequently mute, her hair for endless months still dyed a painful platinum blond from the last attempts to fit in in Minneapolis; and Marlowe short and dark and sharp, sure in advance she fit nowhere, moody and almost maniacally articulate, or plunged in glooms. But with each other they had been tender, studiously, minutely tender, tender beyond measure, sharing the rawness of freshly discovered wounds. Daa's agony in her body had been searing; she had wept as Marlowe explored it uncertainly, peeling clothes away like charred skin around a burn. For months they had managed little but to hold each other, sometimes warm and yielding, feeling the first flutterings of safety like the most tentative of new butterfly wings; but more often clenched, subtly, maddeningly, against self-consciousness, terror, rage.

They had had to leave town to make love, Marlowe remembered—a weekend in Big Sur, in the fall, in an inn close enough to the sea to hear the waves at night. The room had a huge strange bed, an elaborate canopy bed with no canopy and dark oak pillars sculpted with the faces of gargoyles—a fantastic, silly, incomprehensible piece of work, bulky and cozy and finally safe. At sunset the room had filled with rose light, the walls glowing warmly, and beneath the blind eyes of the grotesques they had settled into each other's skin at last. Sheila's solidity had been a revelation, grounding, homelike, welcoming, a strangely familiar landscape in a country Marlowe had half-expected, even then, to seem alien and cold. She remembered tracing her friend's wondrous languid contours with her tongue, meeting Sheila's eyes across the warm expanse of belly and breast, and smiling. And Sheila's answering tongue, and the firm, confident hunger of Sheila's hands, which surprised them both. Marlowe had not believed such tenderness would ever be possible to her again; she had believed it lost in the sexual wars. But it survived after all.

Afterward, Sheila had stretched, languorously, exposing the length of her body, and fingered one of the gargoyles on the nearest bedpost. "Rumpelstiltskin," she had marveled, and they had looked at each other and laughed.

That night a storm had come in, with lightning and rolling peals of thunder, and they had cozied together in pleasurable burrowing beneath the quilts, listening like contented children to the lash of rain on the windows and roof and reading aloud to each other from "The Waste Land," which they had been plumbing for images of the patriarchy's decayed condition. It had been the next morning too that Sheila had taken the name Daa, to remind herself what the thunder had said. And Marlowe had cut her hair for her, trimming away the last of the shiny, brittle blond, all the way back to the soft, muddier, earthen roots. She had run her fingers through it again and again, thrilled with the clean ease of it, while Daa had arched her head against Marlowe's hands like a stroked cat.

Had it really been over a decade? More than anyone Marlowe knew now, Daa lived in her body with the confidence of home. Watching her friend work at the cutting board, solid and graceful, slicing carrots in staccato strokes, Marlowe marveled again at how lucky they had been in each other then.

"The macrobiotic astrologer was cute," she offered after a moment.

"Oh?" Daa said without looking up. "Well, maybe we should just rent the room to him, then, and get it over with."

"I don't think so. He's broke and wanted to set up some kind of deal where he could pay his rent in life readings."

"Life readings," Daa said, and they smiled at each other.

"Life readings? What's this about life readings?"

They both looked up. Jack Soft Hands, né Wilson, their other housemate, had glided into the kitchen, in his usual smooth fashion, in time to catch their last exchange. Daa, characteristically, was prone to refer to that fashion as greasy, and Marlowe had to agree that it was frictionless enough to suggest the perhaps too liberal application of oil. But that only made sense, in its way: Jack, a masseur—a "body artist," as he said—made a good living on well-lubricated contacts and smelled always of jasmine oil, lavender, sandalwood, eucalyptus. They had rented the attic bedroom to him six weeks before, after yet another scramble to fill a vacancy, and since then he had set up his massage table there and received a steady stream of clients, whom he plied with a variety of scents.

He smelled now of aloe vera tinged with peppermint; Marlowe could see Daa's nose wrinkling in distaste, and she said quickly, to head off a possibly unlubricated remark, "Oh, we're just going over the applicants for the fourth bedroom, and one of them wants to pay his rent in astrology readings."

"Oh, that would be wonderful, wonderful," Jack said mellifluously, apparently believing the situation called for an appropriately supportive response. He was wearing his usual loosely flowing white cotton pants, the drawstring knotted at his waist, and a T-shirt in a somewhat spectacular magenta, on which was emblazoned in yellow, "Go with the Flow." Jack invariably, conspicuously, conscientiously, went with the Flow. "I've personally found that the coordination of a client's physical healing process with her or his chart is invaluable and—"

"Cash," Daa said. "Cash, on the first of the month. We've got to pull thirteen hundred dollars together twelve times a year, and the landlord doesn't give a shit what our signs are, or who's getting transited by what, where."

"Oh, absolutely," Jack agreed at once, smiling and bouncing slightly on the balls of his tanned bare feet. "We have to be realistic." A former philosophy major, he had been born John Wilson and had acquired the name Soft Hands at a shamanic vision-quest workshop a few years before. It had come to him in a sort of waking dream, after he had spent almost a week fasting in the woods. He lost no opportunity now to tell people that his body's hunger had yielded up the spirit's fullness, but it was Marlowe's sense that he should have eaten sooner. Jack's vocation could have used some substance.

Daa rolled her eyes and turned back to her chopping; Marlowe laughed, and Jack, seeing where the sympathies lay, moved at once to stand behind her chair, where he began, with an almost animal naïveté, to massage her shoulders. Marlowe could see Daa stiffen, and the thud of the knife on the chopping board took on an emphatic aspect; but Jack's touch felt good—he *did,* remarkably enough, have soft hands—and she gave herself up to his ministrations.

"Any luck so far?" he asked, indicating the applications, strewn across the table now.

"Not a bit," Marlowe said. "Everyone I've talked to so far has either been useless or crazy, if not dangerous. I swear, it's getting worse every time we interview."

"You say that every time," Daa reminded her from the cutting board.

Marlowe tensed, with the earlier frustration, her reaction inescapably highlighted by Jack's hands at the base of her neck. He felt it too, she knew; she felt his fingers respond deftly, sensitively; and she marveled, as she often did, at a man whose hands were so much more intelligent than the rest of him.

"But what if it's *true?*" she said to Daa. "What if we're really seeing—oh, I don't know—a degeneration. When I came to California—"

"When you came to California, you were a kid," Daa said. "You've grown, your standards, have changed."

"That's exactly what I'm talking about. Ever since Jackson died—"

"That's what all this is really about for you, isn't it?" Daa said. "Life doesn't really quite go on yet for you. And now you're going to blame the world—"

"Not a bit," Marlowe said, knowing perfectly well that it was true. Symptoms of her extravagant disorientation abounded. There were the mops, for instance. Soon after Jackson's death, Marlowe had found herself in a phase of painting mops-heads. Looking out the window of her little cottage studio in the leafy backyard behind the Lapidge Street house, past the jasmine and the climbing bougainvillea she had planted when she first came to the place, she could see Death in the tangled strands of an old mop hung over the rail of the back porch in the yard next door. The image was clear, and vivid, and moved her at once to work. She sketched the mop from every angle for a week, then painted nearly a dozen versions of it in acrylics on cardboard, which was what she often used when she was trying to downplay the importance of a theme that seemed more important to her than to the rest of the world. No one else liked the mops-head series; nor could anyone else among the people she showed the sketches and paintings to see Death in them, even after Marlowe told them what to look for.

Her long pause had left her vulnerable. As Daa smiled indulgently, Marlowe gathered herself. "All right, even granting that Jackson dying may have thrown me for a bit of a loop, I still think I'm seeing evidence of spiritual failure on a massive scale. I *mean,* this woman channeling Joan of Arc, for instance—"

"You interviewed a woman who channels Joan of Arc?" Jack said with ready interest. "How *fascinating.*"

"Maybe," Marlowe said. "But as we were sitting here, Joan herself came in, all *thees* and *thous* and a bad French accent, and she started discussing the esoteric aspects of the rental situation, and I had to ask myself why Joan of Arc was so thoroughly *vapid,* why she sounded like a cross between a bad Coney Island palm reader and my *mother*—"

Daa laughed. "Well, if you're waiting for the new society to come together around someone channeling a better-quality Joan of Arc . . ."

"I think in the new society, *everyone* will be a channeler of sorts," Jack said. "We'll all have access to our higher selves in one way or another."

Marlowe turned to him. "But that's just what I'm *saying,* don't you see? Our higher selves—I'm not *seeing* much of them. This woman's fingernails were bitten to the quick, her hair was ratty, and she needed a *bath.* If she's really channeling her higher self— though she was pretty literal, I must say, she was quite sure it was *really Joan of Arc* speaking through her, I didn't get a sense that she had any perspective or discrimination or even ironic distance on it, or the least bit of humor—and the material was *so shoddy*—''

''You're in a major state, Mar-Mar,'' Daa noted mildly, bringing the salad bowl to the table and gathering up the strewn pile of rental applications to clear a space for them to eat.

''Maybe, but—''

''We've all got a long way to go,'' Jack intoned. ''It's going to take a lot of work, to build a truly new age.''

Marlowe groaned. Jack, taking this as feedback on his massage efforts, lingered over a spot near her shoulder blade. ''Here?'' he said. ''Ah, yes, I've got it . . .''

In fact, he had found some sort of knot. Marlowe straightened involuntarily as he probed, his fingers sinking into the muscle, taking it just, tantalizingly, to a point on the verge of pain before releasing the tension and dispersing it upward in a warm, soothing stroke. Again and again he worked at the spot, deeper each time. ''Oh,'' she said. ''Oh, oh, *oh*.''

Daa, returning to the table with plates, silverware, and dressing, shot her a glance. The look was eloquent enough, though Marlowe, rendered momentarily incapable of anything but small sounds of ecstasy, pretended to ignore it. She knew that her friend tended to look on her lingering attractions to men as the last spasms of patriarchal conditioning. Like smoking, men to Daa were a form of noxious habit, and she could never quite understand Marlowe's recurrent temptations. It was one of the few sore points left between them. At times Daa would urge her to indulge them, ostensibly on the theory that the inferiority of males as human beings and particularly as lovers would inevitably demonstrate itself in practice; but more often—as now—she was openly disapproving.

Not that she *was* attracted to Jack, Marlowe thought. *As* Jack, anyway—he was too stupid, for one thing. Too blithe, too mellow, at once shallow and dense, and hopelessly, comically narcissistic, with his smooth formulas for the world and his perfectly even sunlamp tan and his flat belly and his shelves full of vitamin pills. Jack was frankly planning not to die. He began every day with a dun-colored concoction of soy milk, brewer's yeast, banana, and various magical powders and potions, all mingled noisily and at what was apparently a prescribed length of time in the blender—an unconscionable length of time for a noise of that sort, at seven in the morning, which was when Jack commenced his regimen, all the while softly chanting something in Sanskrit, a mantra for banana smoothies and immortality. And the rest of the day followed in kind.

No, Jack was too ridiculous to be attracted to. And that was without even dealing with his *maleness*, that testosterone heritage of dullness and power. Not that Jack himself had dealt with it either. Politically correct in every utterance, a textbook feminist, a model Sensitized Man, Jack was living, breathing evidence for a theory she and Daa had been evolving for some time: that a little consciousness-raising was a dangerous thing. Confined to the sacred cage of his acquired correctness, Jack was ill-equipped to deal with reality. When genuine issues came up at their house meetings, he could be counted on to make an unimpeachable statement—in jargon—early on, and hold to that throughout, while the rest of them got down and dirty and dealt with the problem.

No, Marlowe thought, it was not that she was attracted to *Jack*. If anything, she was tempted by him as a project, an *idea:* what *if* a man existed who in his wholeness manifested a sensitivity and intelligence, and even wisdom, as sophisticated, as healing, as Jack did in his incongruously wise and healing hands? Civilization would be saved.

Meanwhile, she was grateful for small blessings. Jack, apparently oblivious to the nonverbal commentary between her and Daa, rubbed on. He had worked his way up the shoulder blade now, making a full circle back to the original territory at the base of her neck, and was kneading the tight muscles there deeply. His hands disappeared as hands and became a sort of intelligent heat; Marlowe felt herself melting, pervaded, and she closed her eyes as the heat penetrated, deeper, and deeper.

''*Oh*,'' she said. ''*Oh*, oh, oh . . .''

''Salad's ready,'' Daa said, and Marlowe opened her eyes with a sense of time having briefly lapsed. From the look on Daa's face, it was clear that the two women would be discussing this later. Behind her, Jack had paused, but not stopped, and Marlowe realized that in the face of Daa's implicit demand to stop he was waiting for a word from Marlowe. We could all fight it out, Marlowe thought. In the spirit of the new age.

"Thanks, Jack," she said, and he released her shoulders at once, or almost at once, with just the faintest reluctant lingering, too brief to be taken as more than a possible comment. "That was great."

"Oh, my pleasure, my pleasure," he said cheerily. "We'll have to give you the full table treatment sometime soon—gratis, of course. Hey?"

Daa had sat down already and was dishing out the salad—Marlowe's first, Marlowe noted. Even angry, Daa was scrupulous about such things. "Uh, we'll see," Marlowe said vaguely to Jack, trying to tread a middle path, hoping he would not push it now.

"No, seriously," he persisted. "You'd be *amazed*, what it can do for you. How about this weekend?"

So much for the sensitive new male. Marlowe glanced at Daa, prepared to salvage something from all this, to exchange something of their usual irony at such blatancy; but Daa's face was stubbornly, pointedly turned away; and Marlowe said, on the flash of anger at that, "Well, okay, sure. This weekend would be fine."

"Great," Jack said, pleased, a victor. "I'll pencil you in for Saturday afternoon."

"Great," Marlowe said, feeling sick at Daa's averted face.

Jack went to the refrigerator, inspired, perhaps by the salad, perhaps by his conquest, to make himself a smoothie. Daa and Marlowe ate in silence while he puttered cheerfully around the kitchen, assembling the ingredients, chanting his smoothie mantra quietly to himself—*Udanajayaj jala panka kantakadisua asamga utkrantischa, Udanajayaj jala panka kantakadisua asamga utkrantischa*—without a trace of self-consciousness and perhaps even with a sense of satisfaction in an audience. Marlowe had asked him once what the mantra meant, and Jack had cheerfully confessed that he didn't know. It was the vibrations that mattered, not the sense, he said.

When the blender went on, Marlowe glanced at Daa again, certain that *this* at least could be common ground between them, but Daa refused to meet her eyes and chewed on, stolidly—cowlike, Marlowe thought irritably, hating herself for the thought, and amazed at it. She would have killed anyone who called Daa cowlike, who played on that old wound. God, how quickly they got petty.

"Well, what *are* we going to do about this, sweetie?" she said, gesturing to the stack of fruitless applications in Daa's hand.

Daa shrugged. "The Goddess will provide. She always does."

Part II

Mops

There's not the smallest orb which thou beholdest,
But in his motion like an angel sings,
Still quiring to the young-eyed cherubims;
Such harmony is in immortal souls.
But whilst this muddy vesture of decay
Doth grossly close it in, we cannot hear it.
                                    —Shakespeare

I

The Persistence of Mops

ON THE WORKTABLE IN HER STUDIO MARLOWE KEPT AN EIGHT-AND-A-half-by-eleven-inch photograph of Jackson, in a polished maple frame. It was a striking likeness; Marlowe had taken it herself in that blessed lull between the first, near-fatal flaring of Jackson's AIDS and the later, grueling stages of decline. The photo showed Jackson atop Mt. Tamalpais on a glorious sunny afternoon. The drugs he had been taking for the lymphoma then had made most of his hair fall out; and so he had decided that day to steal a march on fate and shave his head. The last gosling-down remnants of his beautiful black hair, the tufts that had seemed so ironic, surviving the chemicals, were gone, as if they had been burned away; everything dubious and dull had been burned away. Jackson's shapely head was naked, freshly shorn, and his radiant, laughing face was lifted to the blue sky. Almost certainly, Marlowe thought, he was singing. Below and behind him in the picture, San Francisco shimmered across a gulf of blue and gold, like a city in a dream.

Jackson had used to say the city *was* a dream: that all of California was a dream. And, laughing, that the rest of the country was a nightmare. In either case, the point was to wake up.

They had had lunch together every week for more than five years; it had become a deep and cherished ritual in both their lives. At their Thursday lunches, Jackson would order endive salad and flirt with the waiter and discourse on the need for compassion amidst such painful unreality. When he still had all his rich black hair, he would comb it twice during a typical lunch hour, slipping off to the bathroom and returning groomed and sleek and smelling slightly of rose water.

22

Marlowe wondered what Jackson would have made of the mops she was painting. Probably he would have laughed, she thought. It had been Jackson's gift, that remarkable talent for laughter that saw through it all, and yet was kind. Marlowe mourned her own more cynical nature. All she seemed to have a talent for was morbidity.

As for the mop paintings themselves, her friends were beginning to worry. Many of Marlowe's friends believed her painting acted as a crystal ball, and they followed its subtle indicators the way some people follow the exclusive bulletins of certain Wall Street savants, or tarot cards. Marriages and job changes, moves and breakups and recommitments, deaths and healings and the courage for journeys, had all been discovered in Marlowe's work by various people at various times, and the legend of its oracular qualities had grown with the years.

Marlowe herself found the belief amusing, and even at times alarming. She believed her reputation was inflated and had noted that people generally found only what they had needed or expected to find in her paintings anyway. Most of what they saw, indeed, could as easily have been discovered in a crumpled washcloth. Still, she knew her art *did* occasionally seem to show a certain prescience. Months ahead of the big earthquake of '89 she had painted a series of cataclysmic urban landscapes, including horrific collapsed freeways and a trembling baseball stadium that was uncannily anticipatory of that autumn's disturbed World Series. Unfortunately, she had interpreted these images at the time as signs of personal upheaval, as shifting emotional plates, and tremblers portending imminent catastrophe in her relationship with Daa. This had led to no end of needless fights with her lover, for Daa had insisted stolidly as always that they were on solid ground together, that they had always been on solid ground together, and would be until the end of time, and that the only shaky thing in their relationship was Marlowe's courage and capacity for commitment.

The anticipated earthquake played on Daa's nerves so roughly that the actual 7.1 shake that had rocked the Bay Area that October was a great relief to them both. They had laughed together over the broken glassware and china, the spilled bookshelves and crashed houseplants and the shattered plaster, and played among the debris like children—better the china than our relationship, Daa had said.

It had become a sort of policy statement for them, a mantra, repeated anytime their priorities came into question—*better the china than the relationship*, meaning, first things first. First things being: love.

What mops had to do with love was clear to no one. Daa in particular disapproved. She didn't see Healing in a single one of the works, which was what Daa always looked for. She didn't see a positive, life-affirming statement, and it made her edgy.

"I liked it when you were doing the nobility of the female form," she told Marlowe. "All those bold, lusty torsos, those gorgeous fleshy nudes—I loved that, that was beautiful. Celebrating breasts, and thighs, and hips. And the variety of body types—very healing. That was good for the world. I don't see how this is good for the world."

"It's just what's catching my eye at the moment," Marlowe said. "Like this one. See that skull? See how Death just sort of jumps out at you from the most unexpected—"

"It's gray, it's tangled," Daa said stolidly. She was still wearing the earth-brown uniform from her waitress job at the Constellation Cafe, a vegetarian place in the Haight. Her name tag read CAPRICORN—it was the restaurant owner's idea that all his waitresses display their astrological signs. "It's a dirty mop, with birds picking at it. It's a morbid Rorschach."

"The birds are Healing," Marlowe said, feeling it to be a sop even as she said it, and a sort of betrayal. But it was hard for her when Daa didn't like her work.

"I liked those birds you did for the Freedom series better. The spirit soaring free. And I thought you were going to work on the tarot deck next."

"I was. But then Jackson died."

"Jackson wouldn't have wanted you to get hung up on morbid

images for *his* sake. Jackson would have told you, life goes on. The celebration continues. Beauty is *here*, joy is here, and now—only the names have been changed, to protect the innocent."

"That's true."

"I really think you should consider giving this mops-and-death stuff a rest for a while, Marlowe. It's got you all grim and tied up in knots. Why don't you work on something that will help you process Jackson's death in a healthy way?"

"Like the goddess Isis and a circle of dancing priestesses welcoming his soul into the pure realm, or something? Their bounteous breasts bouncing freely? The whole scene bathed in golden light, and happily ever after?"

"That sounds great," said Daa, earnest and impervious to irony, as always.

For a time, then, Marlowe set aside the sketchbook full of mops-heads, the cardboard, and the acrylics. She tried instead to work on something life-affirming and compassionate. She did a series of portraits of Jackson and spent almost a week sketching out a picture of him at a table in the Constellation Cafe. His hair gave her fits—contrary to everything she knew about Jackson's careful coiffure, it kept coming out long, and wild, and went through several stages before she settled on a kind of dreadlocks look. So absorbed was she by the process of the stylized hair that it was some time before she realized that the figure was not Jackson at all, but simple Death, eating an endive salad. Death with hair like a dark, dark mop.

Beyond her window, across the backyard fence the mop still hung from the neighbors' porch rail. It hadn't been used in weeks. She kept hoping the neighbors would take the damned thing away and clean their floor with it or something, but it just sprawled there, day after day. Birds occasionally landed on it, tugging gray threads free with their beaks and flying off to use them in nests.

Marlowe fought the specter for another day and a half, then sighed and gave it up. And then for a while, for quite a while in those months after Jackson's death, she painted mop after mop on cardboard, helpless before the mystery of fascination; and each mop had a sort of Death in its tangled strands, for those with eyes to see.

II

A Theme in a Minor Key

ONE DAY IN LATE OCTOBER, DANTE PRUITT ARRIVED AT THE LEAFY LAPIDGE Street backyard early in the afternoon, whistling a blues version of the *Inferno*'s eighth canto, and carrying a portable synthesizer keyboard and a paper bag laden with burgers and fries. He found Marlowe in the cottage hard at work on her latest effort to plumb the metaphysical depths of mops. Her original model, on the back porch next door, had by now been picked almost clean by birds, and Marlowe was working from memory.

She gave Dante only the briefest of nods as he came in, preoccupied as she was in mixing yet another, ever-subtler shade of gray on her palette. Dante McDonalds Pruitt was always dismissable, more or less: it was hard to imagine anyone named after a medieval Italian poet and a hamburger chain who wouldn't be. Burdened by his parents' unrealistic hopes for a magnificent synthesis, he was an endearing eccentric, a sort of self-conscious throwback to the troubadours, who was constantly wandering the Bay Area in search of places with good musical vibes, seeking the resonant nodes of truth and love, and frequenting fast-food places. The course of such musical meanderings often took him to Marlowe's studio, which he apparently found an endless source of inspiration. He had had a hopeless, distinctly platonic crush on her for as long as she had known him; while Marlowe saw Dante, for the most part, as a sort of bright, large species of songbird, who came around to perch nearby from time to time, harmless but entertaining, if occasionally a little too loud.

Dante, unperturbed by the cool welcome, sat down on the room's only chair. He was almost thirty but he had a smooth, handsome face, boyishly unlined, Marlowe had always thought, untouched by life; and a cherubic tangle of curly brown hair. He made and repaired musical instruments for a living and gave lessons from time to time, barely scraping by, but he really lived for his eccentric brand of performance. The place where he went to play his music varied from day to day. Sometimes it was as simple as walking into his studio and sitting down, but more often he was moved to seek a different setting. He might go into his backyard or to the beach or into the reaches of the park. Sometimes he went north, as far as the spirit took him along the coast, across the Golden Gate and through the green hills of Marin, until he came upon a spot that seemed to speak his name. Dante believed that the universe was threaded through with strands of true music, and that only by aligning himself with these—by tuning himself, as it were, to the true song's perfect notes—could he avoid making what most of the rest of what passed for reality seemed to him to make, which was the most awful noise.

"Would you like a cheeseburger, Marlowe?" he said now, opening his bag.

"I'm a vegetarian, Dante," Marlowe said without looking up. "You know that. I refuse to contribute to the ongoing destruction of the rain forests, and the slaughter of innocent beasts. Not to mention polluting my body with carcinogens and fat." She considered her palette unhappily. "Damn, I can't get this gray right to save my life."

"Purple," Dante sad, taking a bite of cheeseburger.

"What?"

"Try a touch of purple, in that. It will jazz it right up."

"Don't be ridiculous, Dante. I want gray here. *Gray*. I want to convey the full grim truth."

"Suit yourself." Dante shrugged equably. "How about some fries?"

Marlowe hesitated, resisting an urge to wildly scratch her legs.

She had blundered through poison oak on a walk in the hills the week before and had been miserable ever since. Daa had been feeding her some kind of anti-itch Indian tea, monitoring her diet closely to keep it particularly yin, and dressing her in blues, to soothe the inflammation.

Daa, she knew, would have shuddered to know she was even considering eating french fries.

"Maybe just a few," she said, and squatted beside him to accept the entire bag.

As she applied ketchup, the two of them considered the painting on its easel. Marlowe's early tentative efforts on cardboard and paper were long past; the image had swollen by now to dominate a four-by-five-foot canvas and was being given a full treatment in oils. Sprawling across the entire surface, the mass of gray swirls looked grimly cosmic, like a dirty galaxy in flux.

"A circle of hell?" Dante suggested after a moment.

"A mop."

"Ah. A mop. Well, it's very suggestive."

Marlowe glanced at him, suspicious. "Really?"

"Oh, yes. I always find your work suggestive." Dante's hands moved vaguely in the air. "You know—the *music* of it, the, uh, contrapuntal—"

"Can you see anything particular in this?" Marlowe interrupted hopefully.

"Death." Dante set aside his burger and, wiping his fingers carefully on his napkin, picked up his synthesizer and laid it across his lap. His slender fingers hovered briefly over the keyboard, then struck a chordal organ note that sounded to Marlowe like something out of *The Phantom of the Opera*. "It's sort of fugal," he said apologetically.

"Death. I love you, Dante. I always have and I always will."

"Death, and rebirth."

"No," Marlowe said firmly. "No rebirth. Just dying, dying, death—a gray that ends in black."

"Suit yourself," Dante said, and began to develop the musical notion quietly. Marlowe listened for a while, eating her fries, amazed in spite of herself. She would not have expected this precise and classical response, but then Dante was a more or less constant source of surprise to her. His father, Donald, an unsuccessful visionary entrepreneur, had believed wholeheartedly in Franchising and Mass Marketing; to him, the greed and speed and swift propagation of fast foods were metaphors for the spread of truth. Everyone, after all, was hungry for truth; the real challenge was in packaging. Donald Pruitt longed for a radical integration. He saw the deeper processes of the universe reflected in video games and the durability of Styrofoam and was perpetually on the lookout for a notion that might sweep the world as Big Macs had, while conducive also to contemplation of eternal values.

Dante's mother, Elizabeth, from what Marlowe understood, had endured all this as part of an ongoing purgatorial project. A stately, serene woman who refused her entire life to be called Liz or Betty, a student of classical Florentine verse, she believed so imperturbably in love's redemptive nature that she felt it could heal even American popular culture. She saw an angel in her husband, struggling to get out. To her the twists and turns of his delusional thinking were the whorled fingerprints of the divine— smudged, visible traces of God's mysterious ways—and she could not help but love him for it. Elizabeth had nurtured Donald's dreams of vast and replicable success through a dozen spectacularly failed ventures, hoping all the while that he would see the light and dine more often at home. But Donald Pruitt, while he aspired to the most extravagant syntheses, had never achieved simplicity and died relatively young, in his late forties, of complications arising from what should have been routine gallbladder surgery. The notepad beside his hospital bed was filled with notes for a Heroes of the Renaissance Video Arcade, which in accordance with his last wishes his wife generously offered to the San Francisco Chamber of Commerce. Elizabeth in the immediacy of her grief had considered joining a convent; but eventually she remarried, to a poet twenty years younger than her, and she lived now in Paris, where she was the center of a fervent neoclassical literary circle.

Fruit of such marital disparities, Dante had remained resolutely single; to Marlowe it was obvious he had devoted his life to the pursuit of a god who reconciled vivid opposites more deftly than his father had. Finding all available gods too locked already into either thesis or antithesis, and feeling himself to be desperate, Dante had struck out at seventeen for the Orient and gotten as far as California, where he pursued a renunciatory meditative path so extreme that he lost forty pounds. He took a vow of silence, to avoid speaking in conflicting voices, and did not utter a word or indeed make any sounds, except for sneezes and coughs and the occasional bit of flatulence, for three and a half years. At last, however, while waiting for a bus, he picked up a discarded plastic pipe that lay on the bench beside him and began to play; and he was hit by a vision of higher harmony. He went at once to Mc-Donald's and broke his vegetarian regimen with three cheese-burgers and a vanilla shake. That same day he began setting the *Divine Comedy* to the most eclectic possible music, in the service of his new god.

This god required none of the feverish and spectacular com-promises that in Dante's view had plagued his parents' attempts even to inhabit the same household, much less to embody peace in the world at large. This god needed only a three-piece band and resided, Dante firmly believed, in rock and roll.

Still, the threads of his heritage could not help but show. While Marlowe listened now in amusement, Dante gave her *Phantom of the Opera* mop motif the full classical treatment, building and de-veloping, fleshing it out, darkening here and deepening there; at length he took it to some wild Beethovenian height and let it crash; then let a beat pass before he lifted it again, liltingly, play-fully, in deft, light-footed sound like the most playful Bach.

Recognizing the theme reborn, Marlowe smiled in spite of her-self. It was almost always so with Dante—ridiculous but true. On the night of the first new moon after Jackson died, she remem-bered, Dante, sitting on a hill facing west to honor Jackson's de-parting spirit, had seen seven shooting stars, in rapid succession. He almost died himself, Dante had said, after the fourth star. Three shooting stars he could have handled. But *four;* and then five, and six—*Jesus.* By the time the seventh meteor arced across the entire sky, from north to south, and faded, Dante was in a state of pure stunned exaltation, and subject to suspicions of even wilder things. He believed firmly that he had heard a chorus of angels singing ceaseless songs of praise. He had even been able to make out Jackson's clear tenor among them, and he would tell this to anyone who would listen, for as long as they would listen. Even now, he was working on setting the heavenly songs to music for his band, the Holy Rose Parade. From the early versions Marlowe had heard played in Dante's garage, it appeared the angels had been much influenced by Lightning Hopkins, Elvis, and the early Rolling Stones.

Abruptly she rose and went back to the canvas.

"How's your love life, Dante?"

Dante stopped playing at once and looked uncomfortable. "What?"

"Your love life, sweetheart," Marlowe persisted. "You know—*girls*. Sex. Romance. Are you getting any?"

"Uh, no," Dante said, more uncomfortable than ever. "I'm not really, uh—that is, I mean, I don't—well—"

"Oh, come on, Dante. An attractive guy like you? Women must be throwing themselves at you all the time."

Dante contemplated his keyboard. "Not really. Not that I notice, anyway."

"You're not gay, are you?"

"No."

"Well, then?"

Dante looked tormented. "Well, it's just that—" He hesitated again. "It's just that sexual love is much too complicated," he said at last with an air of having been unduly provoked to frankness. "Too complicated, and too—you know—*messy.*"

"You can always shower afterward."

He flushed. "That's not what I mean. I mean, uh, that too, I suppose. But really—it's too *involved*, you see? Too—"

"Intimate?" Marlowe suggested, feeling cruel.

"Much, much too involved," Dante repeated. "I don't think I was meant to be a lover, to tell you the truth. I think I was meant to be a musician."

31

"And never the twain shall meet?"

He looked down. "Apparently not."

"I suppose that's why I love you so, Dante. You're so *safe*. You know? You're such a safe goddamned exquisite dead end."

"I'm sorry if I've made you angry," Dante said with feeble dignity, and picked up his keyboard and fled.

Marlowe watched him hurry across the green backyard and up the alley like a man pursued, and shook her head. She could not imagine what had gotten into her. It was like teasing a retarded child or something; it was a perversity in her.

She turned back to her palette and added some black to its tortuous gray; and then, almost as an afterthought, some purple. The result, unexpectedly, pleased her. Dante had been right about that, at least—it really did jazz it up. A glob of french-fry ketchup had found its way onto the canvas as well, which gave her a moment's pause; but with the purple, she thought, it worked just fine.

Part III

Go West, Young Woman

And when the queen of Sheba heard of the fame of Solomon concerning the name of the Lord, she came to prove him with hard questions.

—I Kings 10:1

I

A Timely Arrival

THE CRISIS OF THE EMPTY FOURTH BEDROOM IN THE LAPIDGE STREET HOUSE
had grown acute by the end of the month, but Daa's faith in
providence had been well placed, as usual. The day before the
rent was due, the Goddess provided Sheba McKenzie. Marlow's
cousin, whom she had not seen since junior high school, arrived
unannounced on a bus from Indigo Falls, Virginia, with a backpack and a well-thumbed copy of Krishnamurti, who she apparently believed was still alive. Her avowed purpose was simple:
she wished to have her kundalini awakened, and to become enlightened. It was Sheba McKenzie's understanding that this sort
of thing was more or less rampant in California.

Marlowe, unnerved at this apparition from her familial past,
would have sent her back on the next bus; she was certain her
mother had sent Sheba to spy on her. Daa, however, quickly
determined that Marlowe's cousin had undertaken her spiritual
journey prepared to pay rent; and her vote, with that of Jack—
who was never averse to another attractive female presence in
the house—carried the day. Sheba's cashier's check for first and
last month, and cleaning deposit, cleared just in time to avert
catastrophe with the landlord, and she settled into residence at
Lapidge Street with an air of matter-of-factness, as if she had
known it would work out so well all along.

II

Cousins

THE EVENING SHEBA MOVED IN, MARLOWE SHOWED HER TO HER ROOM. Jackson's old bedroom was the smallest in the house, an angular little cell with a single curtainless window facing Lapidge Street and its traffic. Here Jackson had lived for five years as a sort of sensualist scholar-monk and freelance agitator for higher values. The walls had been hung then with Tibetan tapestries and mandalas, David Hockney prints, and a poster of Mark Spitz in a brief red-white-and-blue U.S. Olympic team bathing suit. The room had always smelled of champa and wine and resounded with Ralph Vaughan-Williams and Madonna, Benny Goodman and Rossini and John Lee Hooker; the shelves had been filled with books on everything from the decline and fall of the Roman Empire to Lauren Bacall.

Marlowe had never thought of the fourth bedroom as shoddy in those days. Jackson's presence had transformed it; it had seemed like the very hub of a thriving microcosm of civilization. It was only as the miracle had passed that she could appreciate what he had wrought. For half a decade, Jackson's sense of style had affected them all. He had cooked and mothered and sung and danced; he had gotten them out to vote and planted the bright red bougainvillea that framed the front porch now. He had kept up with the international news and known who was singing *Carmen* in that season's opera. When things got slow, he would read aloud from the late Henry James, whom he worshiped, as a kind of comedy routine, rolling out the endless intricate thread of the master's compulsively subtle prose in an unctuous, reverent Anglophonic monotone until it passed into hilarity and every nuance and inflection and qualification deepened their laughter.

The space now was barren of furniture and decoration, and the scuffed walls, once yellowish but dimmed to a colorless drab, were scarred and studded with the nail holes and leftover nails of dozens of transient hangings, and with the lingering bits of tape from posters long removed. The single naked lightbulb in the center of the ceiling gave a flash and a pop as Marlowe turned it on when they came in, and expired. But the light from the hallway and from the streetlight outside was more than sufficient to establish the room's minimal merits.

"Oh, it's *perfect!*" Sheba exclaimed, setting the backpack on the bare wood floor.

"It's sort of neglected," Marlowe said. "And a little shabby, I'm afraid—"

"No, no, I *love* it! Really, I can do whatever I want with it. My old bedroom, in Virginia, was *pink,* you know."

"I know. It was *really* pink." It had been almost fifteen years since she had seen Sheba McKenzie at all, but her clearest memories were even older ones—for some reason she had been most impressed by her cousin in the second grade. Of Sheba at eight she remembered little more than a white dress and a well-scrubbed look, and black patent leather shoes, with white knee socks. Sheba had taken her to her room, which was so immaculate that Marlowe had been contemptuous, unable to imagine anyone living in it with any pleasure. It had indeed been pink, deeply pink, obnoxiously pink.

"Really pink," Marlowe said again.

"Exactly. And all full of heavy furniture and lacy curtains and pictures of Snow White, and about a hundred teddy bears and stuffed animals."

"I remember those stuffed animals."

"Yeah, my parents were always giving me stuffed animals. And later, my boyfriends would. I swear, sometimes I felt like the stuffed animals were the ones who really lived in that room, and I was just there as an afterthought, or a caretaker, or something. Yes," Sheba declared, looking around with what appeared to

Marlowe to be an unjustified and unsustainable enthusiasm. "Yes, this will do just *fine*, just fine. It's a fresh start, a new beginning, not a stuffed animal in the place."

Marlowe smiled. She was on the verge, undeniably, of a *state;* but she nevertheless had the presence of mind to be amused by the incongruity of her memories and her cousin's reality. Reality in such cases was almost invariably a relief. Sheba McKenzie was not an obnoxiously angelic second-grader anymore, nor did she show obvious signs of a sinister commission from Bernice. She was an attractive young woman with auburn hair and green, intelligent eyes, and a large, ready smile, which she bestowed on everyone she encountered, it seemed, with an indiscriminate benevolence. Sometime since the last time Marlowe had seen her, Sheba had managed to get beyond the white frilly dress with bows, and the patent leather shoes—she wore blue jeans now, and a T-shirt that was probably her father's hand-me-down, a baggy white thing without message or decoration. Similarly, her shoes were well-worn canvas tennis shoes—not the flashy athletic footware prevalent in California, with stripes and a brand name emblazoned on them, but, well, *sneakers,* Marlowe thought. Her cousin was wearing sneakers. It was oddly endearing.

"I was always jealous of those stuffed animals, to tell you the truth," she said, leaning on the doorframe. "My parents never gave me stuffed animals."

"Oh!" Sheba said, solicitous in retrospect. "I wish I'd known then! I would have given you some of mine."

"You did. You gave me a pink elephant named Ellie, a yellow bear, and a kangaroo. I still have the elephant and the kangaroo, but my mother put the bear through the washing machine, and it came apart. I could have killed her. But she was always doing things like that—helpful, destructive things."

"Your mother?"

"Yes. Whatever I have managed to keep, of any value at all, has had to pass through my mother's washing machine at least once."

Sheba laughed. "Well, while we're true-confessing—*I* was always jealous that you got to live in the big city."

"Ah, the big city."

"Yes, and that you were such a terrific artist. Did you know we had a painting of yours on our living room wall?"

"Oh, God," Marlowe groaned. "Painted when I was in junior high school, no doubt. Probably out of my simpering landscape phase. Or was it a horse?"

"It was a horse. A *beautiful* horse."

"My mother would give those to everyone we knew. And they'd all feel compelled to put them up. I think that's one of the reasons I had to leave New York—everywhere I went, I was confronted with framed figments of my adolescence."

"I thought it was a great painting. I wish I could paint like that—shoot, I wish I could do *any*thing that good."

Marlowe smiled perfunctorily and scratched at a little bit of wax on the room's single remaining shelf, a stubborn glob left over, almost certainly, from the night Jackson had died. Leave it to Jackson to go out in an unelectric blaze of serene glory. They had been peeling wax off every wooden surface for weeks afterward.

"I don't paint horses anymore. I left all that in New York."

"That's a shame."

"Hardly. I think of it more as growing up." Marlowe paused, recognizing with frustration and chagrin that her tone had sharpened. Daa would no doubt have noted by now that she was verging on a *state*.

But Sheba, it seemed, was more forgiving—more naive, at least, and less acute: she was still listening earnestly, wide-eyed with the light from the hallway falling across her face. Marlowe said, "Oh, I don't know. Daa is always after me to paint pretty too, to tell you the truth—she thinks I should be painting pictures of the Goddess, or tarot decks. She's been after me to do a tarot deck with her for years. It's funny, how she doesn't understand."

"Understand what?"

"Well, *shit*, I don't know. I mean, look—I make earrings for a living, right? Jewelry. And I'm good at it, I make nice stuff. I'm a craftsman—craftswoman, craftsperson, whatever. And everyone says, 'Oh, you're *so* artistic.' But it's not the same. It's not the same at all, as painting something *true*." She hesitated, aware of a kind of vertigo; Sheba's naive listening, like a precipice, allowed a dangerously fresh view. Marlowe was aware that she had not talked about anything like this since Jackson had died; it was not a line of thought she would have pursued with any of her other friends. Jackson, who had dabbled in watercolors himself, had been a kind of second art school for her; the two of them used to talk for hours, they had talked whole nights through on topics like the psychic weight of yellow and whether style could seriously be said to be organic. Civilization, the nature of perception, faith, the modern mind—they had covered it all. Not that they had agreed on anything. For Marlowe the point was substantiality, the postmodern ground: it had seemed to her that the whole world had dissolved into surface, and she was trying to find a new place to stand. While Jackson had believed that style was all. He was always bringing Buddhist notions in—form is emptiness and emptiness is form, and things like that. He had wanted in his gentle, refined way to dissolve the illusion of substance into perfect flux. It made for lively dialectic, especially as the wine bottles continued to be opened.

Marlowe caught herself now, shook her head, and laughed. "Oh, forget it. It's the same old story, girl meets void. It's been like this since I was seventeen. I wanted to catch things as they came into being, the creative instant, the emergence out of chaos—out of *nothing*. And I was reading Nietzsche and Heidegger, God was dead, and I was fighting with my mother, who was always saying things like, 'But it was so *nice* when you were painting horses! I *liked* the horses.' "

"I liked the horses too," said Sheba, who was doing her best to follow.

"Well, of course you did," Marlowe said impatiently. "That's the point. That's the *point*. I liked the horses too, to tell you the truth. But I wasn't *at* the horses anymore, I was somewhere between those horses and the real world, and I didn't feel like I was getting any closer to the real world, and I sure as hell wasn't going *back* to those horses, just to please my mother. So I came to California. And I paint what I *see* which is not that pretty at all."

"Well, I can understand it I guess," Sheba said tentatively, frankly striving to. "I mean, well—if you really feel about your pretty painting the way I feel about those stuffed animals . . ."

Marlowe laughed. Sheba smiled back, pleased, and turned to survey her room again. "And *now* look at me. Home sweet home!"

"We can get a lightbulb for you tomorrow."

"Oh, no hurry," Sheba said, and rummaged briefly in her day pack. Marlowe noted that it was stuffed mainly with books on reincarnation, rebirthing, and other forms of radical renewal. Her cousin, it seemed, had been doing her homework on California.

At last Sheba came up with half a candle in a cheap glass holder. She set this in the middle of the room and lit it with an unself-conscious air of ceremony.

"There we go!" she said, stepping back and looking around. "It really *is* better than cursing the darkness, isn't it?"

"I don't know. I'm just as often inclined to give the darkness a piece of my mind, personally." But Marlowe's arms had risen into gooseflesh; there had been no candlelight in this room since Jackson had died. She almost resented being moved so, by such a trivial gesture. She could still recall the rich quality of the room's light that night, the buoying warm glow of all the candles, the rich tapestries making stray glints of gold at the edge of the shadow where the monks sat, hushed and attentive. But the stripped-down room at this point was hardly improved by illumination. Jackson had taken it all with him, serenity included, when he went.

Still, the small glow was the first the place had seen in months. Marlowe hesitated, then said on the strength of it, "Look, Sheba, I'm sorry if I was rude, earlier."

"Oh, don't mind that. I can understand how you must have felt, hick cousin dropping in out of the blue, and all."

"Well, I just want to get it clear between us, to make sure we understand each other. You came to California on your own, right? I mean, nobody put you up to it, you're not here to—"

"Spy on you for your momma?" Sheba said, and laughed. "No, no, rest easy, Cousin Marlowe. I came to California to *find my-self*—is that a corny way to say it?"

40

"Well . . ."

"Well, however you say it. Just like you, though, from the sound of it. I came here to find out who I *am*, aside from all those stuffed animals."

"All right. Just wanted it to be clear." And Marlowe left her cousin to her unpacking in the candlelight. Back in her own room, she surprised herself by bursting into tears. It had been a little traumatic every time, renting Jackson's room.

III

Udanajayaj Jala Panka Kantakadisua Asamga Utkrantischa

SHEBA HAD ARRIVED ON A WEDNESDAY, AND ON THURSDAY MORNING SHE awakened at first light and lay still in a delicious anticipation. What she expected she could hardly say, except that she knew that it would be spiritual, revelatory, *deep*. She had come to California for meaning as frankly as the forty-niners had come for gold.

Outside the window an empty hummingbird feeder hung. As she watched, a bright green bird whirred close to it and flitted away in disappointment. Sheba resolved to fill the feeder before the day was out. There were a million things to do, in fact. She wanted to meditate, for instance. She wanted to have visions. And there was toothpaste to buy. Sheba reached for the little pad she kept handy to make lists—she prided herself on her organizational skills—and began to note the things she would need to get to that day:

KOOL-AID FOR HUMMINGBIRD FEEDER
KUNDALINI? CREST
PEANUT BUTTER TAMPONS DRIVER'S LICENSE

All at once she was startled by a dull roar from the kitchen, below her room. The noise was so incongruous, and the hour so early, that at first Sheba didn't recognize it; she wondered briefly if she might be experiencing some sort of psychic phenomenon already. But when she descended the stairs in some haste and alarm, she found Jack Soft Hands running the blender at full speed, chanting his mantra pleasantly over his usual smoothie combination: *Udanajayaj jala panka kantakadisua asamga utkrantischa, Udanajayaj jala panka kantakadisua asamga utkrantische* . . .

He waved to Sheba cheerfully as she came in. "Hello. You're up early too, I see."

"I'm sure that everyone in the house is," Sheba said with what she felt was great subtlety. But her relief and disappointment that no demonic force was involved in the noise was already giving way to sociability and curiosity. She sat down at the kitchen table in her long sleeping T-shirt and bare feet, noticing Jack noticing her legs. It was not an unpleasant ogling, she thought. "I'm Sheba McKenzie, by the way. I just moved in to the bedroom upstairs."

"Jack Soft Hands." He reached out to shake her hand. "Welcome to Lapidge Street."

Sheba laughed, taking his hand. "Well, now, it *is* soft, isn't it? Lord, where'd you get a name like that?"

"On a vision quest," Jack said modestly, unruffled. "It came to me in a dream, actually."

"Wow," Sheba said, impressed in spite of herself.

Jack returned to the blender. Always delighted with an audience, particularly a female one, it was not long before he had launched into an earnest explication of the basis for immortality in the perfect circulation of unimpeded pure energy through the physical form.

Sheba listened willingly enough. It all sounded spiritual enough to her, though the idea of physical immortality struck her as vaguely blasphemous, and certainly absurd. But Jack himself was genial and visionary and thoroughly sincere, which appealed to her; and he was also—she could not help noting—very attractive in his smooth, tanned, supple way. In response to his questions, she confided several of her own energy impediments, and he promptly volunteered to lay hands on her in the locations indicated. One thing led rapidly enough to another, and before long he was leading her up the two flights of stairs to his attic room for a full massage.

IV

A Taste of Eternal Life

JACK'S ROOM WAS STRIKING. HE HAD GONE TO GREAT LENGTHS TO MAKE it into a proper Immortality Environment, a phrase Sheba could not hear at first without giggling. She entered, shoes off, through a curtain of dangling Indian beads interspersed with protective and filtering crystals and was struck at once by the altarlike quality of his state-of-the-art mechanized massage table, which was draped in white and located—partly of necessity, for the low slant of the attic ceiling made it impossible to stand upright anywhere else—at the precise longitudinal center of the room. At the far wall was a smaller altar, a real one, draped in red satin cloth and loaded with candles, crystals, gems, and a gold-framed picture of a man who to Sheba looked something like a used-car salesman or a television evangelist, a man with a denture-commercial smile who Jack said, with a reverence that again brought her to the verge of giggling, was the man who had taught him everything about the science of Eternal Life.

Most of the Environment, indeed, was keeping her close to mirth. The room was liberally crisscrossed with strings of multi-colored lights that Sheba thought at first were simply Christmas lights hung charmingly out of season, but which Jack hastened to explain were actually sophisticated color-therapeutic Arrays. He showed her the console with some pride, his fingers lingering over a panel of dials and rheostatic knobs, by which he could program any desired frequency of flashes and mixture of color—thus, he said, setting up a Specific Emotional Resonance.

While Sheba marveled at this, still containing her urge to laugh, Jack set the machine to a slow beat of soft pink laced with languid yellows and the occasional red. He also set a tape of flute music going in his excellent quadraphonic sound system; lit a stick of incense and murmured something else in Sanskrit; then stood upright at last—most business in the room had to be conducted in a slightly cautious hunch—beside the massage table and smiled that all was ready.

Here was the first awkwardness. Sheba wondered if he expected her to take off her T-shirt. She suspected that he did, but she certainly was not going to do that: the T-shirt, a big baggy white one, once her father's, was what she used as a nightgown and it was all she had on. It seemed beyond imagination that she should simply get naked in front of Jack. She climbed onto the table as she was, with a slight, self-conscious air of preemptive defiance. Jack, however, did not miss a beat; he continued unruffled, genial and smooth, and even draped a clean white towel over her bare legs, as if to reassure her of the chasteness of the proceedings.

Then he laid his hands on her back, working at first in long, slow strokes along the length of her spine; and Sheba almost instantly succumbed, first to pleasure and then, as he continued, deepening the strokes, to bliss. She was astonished at her body's unsuspected readiness to dissolve, to melt before the warm pressure of Jack's hands, which were not soft at all but rather absolutely firm: it was her body that was soft, softer and softer, yielding its accustomed definition and arranging itself like stirred water around the single imperative of those hands. Each long stroke seemed endless, a long wave rolling in; and when it crested in a tingling curl at the top of her spine, she would groan in a collapse of delight, certain that such a culmination must be a conclusion, and find herself freshly astonished when the next stroke started at the base of her spine and began the same gathering wave anew. Moving, Jack's hands seemed to awaken things she had forgotten; they left a trail of vague intimations of well-being glowing after them like the phosphorescent trail of a boat in a warm night sea. Ceasing, even briefly and tantalizingly, to move, she was certain that his hands left her at a horizon-like brink of insight, an instant away from the clear vision of glory, before tilting her back through the long pendulum swing to the other horizon.

So delighted was she, so immersed in the ebb and flow of the sensation, that Sheba took it only as a deepening of the pleasure when Jack slipped his hands under the T-shirt; and soon she lifted herself briefly to aid him in taking it off completely, then lay again on her belly with a sigh, her breasts flattening against the warm terry cloth, her skin alive to it. Jack poured warm oil on his hands and her back. Freed of the encumbrance of the shirt, and lubricated, he ranged more widely now, and with a surer touch, moving over her lower back to her hips and buttocks, then down, discarding the towel, down her legs in circular, deepening strokes, until he reached her feet and toes; and then working his way up again, patient and firm. She tensed as he drew near her genitals, but he seemed oblivious to anything but her musculature, matter-of-fact and attentive without suggestiveness. Indeed, his concentration had a kind of scrupulous precision now. Sheba sensed the poise of an ethic: Jack had placed the sexual at a safe distance; and as she realized this, a depth of relief opened in her. Her thighs relaxed, then her loins, and she gave herself up to the pleasure again more deeply than ever.

Jack worked his way up her back again, and then again, taking his time, finding tensions and heightening them deftly, then caressing them away, squeezing them up and out as if she were a toothpaste tube, with thoroughness and patience. It went on, and on, until time was forgotten, and when he ceased at last, she realized for the first time that the music had stopped. The room was filled with a live hush; her body seemed buoyant, as if in a new supportive medium, a friendly sea. Jack gave her back the towel, and she wrapped it around herself and sat up slowly.

"Well?" he said.

She felt a little disappointed, to be required to return so quickly to the ordinary world. Speech seemed an effort, and its results distant and irrelevant, compared to the fullness and glow of her body; but she said, hearing her voice as something new and different and far away, "Oh, it was *wonderful*. I feel like I'm floating. *Thank you* so much."

"We can feel like this all the time, you know. We can feel like we're floating always, and live forever."

The lights were still flashing languidly, the room was gently pulsing with mild pinks and gold. Sheba sat contentedly watching them, feeling the flashes as a pleasant throb in herself, and the color as a caress. So *this* is what it's all about, she thought. It all made sense now.

"I feel like I'm *already* living forever," she said, luxuriating in it.

"Exactly!" Jack said, pleased.

Part IV

All Hallows' Eve

*Six kinds of existence are identified in Buddhism:
gods, demigods, humans, animals, hungry ghosts,
and hells.*
—Sogyal Rinpoche, *The Tibetan Book
of Living and Dying*

I

Toni and Pesky

ON THE FIRST HALLOWEEN AFTER JACKSON'S DEATH MARLOWE AND DAA were invited to an intimate and respectful gathering in his name at the Mendocino County ranch of Antoinette Lafontane and Persephone Prescott-Bowers. Old friends of Jackson's, Toni and Persephone—a tiny, indomitable woman known to her friends as Prescott-Bee, or Pesky—ran the Tyger Lady Bar and Barbeque in Willits, originally a lesbian vegetarian establishment but one that had softened its stance and expanded its menu with time to embrace a broader clientele. The regular crowd by now included truckers and lumberjacks and workers from the local mills, as well as painters and poets and marijuana farmers, and one renegade Dominican priest who was letting his hair and beard grow to John the Baptist dimensions and who could be found at any time of the day or night drinking very strong tea and writing his memoirs in the corner beneath the cruciform head of a great moose.

There had been some resistance when they had first opened the place; there were incidents and accidents and letters to the editor, and even the occasional vandalism. But Toni and Pesky had stuck it out and more than held their own, and the early wars with the local rednecks had ended in mutual respect. The Tyger Lady's Wednesday-night feminist-poetry readings, Thursday-night chants to the Goddess, and Saturday-afternoon drum dances and Mythological Potlucks had been mainstays of the town's cultural life for years. Also, as Toni liked to point out, the Tyger Lady coed softball team, the Pink Flames, regularly kicked butt in the county intramural league. This added immeasurably to their status in the rough logging town. Toni was the pitcher, and her fastball was universally feared. A powerful, burly woman, once a dancer against the grain of stereotype, she kept a wad of tobacco in her left cheek. Checking coolly for the catcher's sign, she spat dark streams onto the ground at her feet, between pitches. She had once struck out twelve batters in a row, against the Georgia-Pacific team, which was composed entirely of burly men, who had not enjoyed the experience. They were breaking their bats against the dugout wall in frustration, by the time somebody managed a pop-up. She had pitched a no-hitter that day and made the front page in all the local papers, and the Georgia-Pacific team was buying the drinks for weeks afterward at the Tyger Lady happy hour. High and tight, low and away, as Toni always said: she could throw that brushback pitch with the best of them, to keep those suckers from digging in at the plate.

II

Amazon Ranch

Amazon Ranch, Toni and Pesky's eighty-acre spread, was some miles north of Willits, and east, back into the mountains. It was a hard place to get to even in good weather, and all but impossible to reach in bad. Just off the main highway was a locked gate with a combination lock—6-20-80, known to everyone important in their lives as Toni and Pesky's anniversary—and beyond the gate lay five miles of winding dirt road susceptible to washouts, avalanches, and axle-breaking potholes. Marlowe and Daa made the drive that Halloween afternoon without incident, passing through the watershed's main creek twice, and braving a ridge road crumbling away at its edges into the Eel River valley, before arriving at the arched wooden gate, emblazoned with a hand-carved image of a double-bladed labrys, that marked the entrance to Amazon Ranch proper. Toni and Pesky believed that the journey to the ranch was a sort of initiation rite, and that only those favored by the Goddess could possibly make it so far, and so this second gate was never locked and swung open on its greased hinges at the slightest touch.

Within the gates, they were greeted at once by Pesky, a dynamo of a woman, tiny and vibrant, who wore her jet-black hair Medea-style in serpentine tendrils and had painted the lids of her huge dark eyes lavender, with a hint of green, for the occasion. Dressed in a loose blue velvet robe and sandals, with a pentacle at her throat and a Budweiser in her hand, she bustled about, welcoming them twice, and offering refreshments, then retreated to the kitchen again, where she was making some kind of spectacular surprise dessert with a Day of the Dead theme. Marlowe and Daa passed on through the house, a ranch-style place that both of them had helped Toni and Pesky to build ten years before. Every rafter told a story here, Marlowe thought; they'd spent the best part of three summers and dozens of weekends working on this place from the ground up, learning their construction skills more or less as they went. But it had been fun. She still noticed every spot where her carpentry had failed, though. It was part of the pleasure of Toni and Pesky's place, indeed, sitting back in a chair with a glass of wine and looking at the places where she had failed to make the ceiling lines meet in 1983, or stumbling on that bit of flooring she had never quite been able to make lie flat. The history of their apprenticeship in self-sufficiency showed in the amateur lines of this house as tree rings showed rough seasons in the life of trees.

One of Jackson's watercolors, an impressionist view of the Eel River valley, hung on the wall opposite the fireplace. The mountains and trees seemed insubstantial, as they did in many of Jackson's works; the summer landscape dissolved almost into abstraction, while the sky might have been a looming blue barrier, split capriciously, subverted with light. To Marlowe's eye, Jackson took great risks structurally. None of it held together without the river—the silver-green movement of the Eel here unified every element almost as an afterthought, streaming play-fully, making every stone part of its flow. It was water that Jack-son had loved; he had often enough said it was the only thing he really understood.

His signature at the bottom was painfully familiar, almost like hearing his voice: precise and stylish, with the *J*'s loop sharpened and the rest of the letters running past, it was playful as the river water, almost blurring before the clean finishing flourish. The work was dated, as well, August of 1988—a week before Jackson had been diagnosed, Marlowe noted with a pang. She paused over that a moment, then moved on through the house, ignoring the paintings of her own that decorated several of the other walls.

Daa was already out back, in full conversational flow with Toni, who was wearing a floppy chef's hat and an apron that said PINK FLAMES KICK BUTT, cooking tofu burgers and zucchini squash on the barbecue. The boom box beside them was playing something by Black Sabbath. Toni waved a spatula at Marlowe cheerfully. She had her T-shirt sleeves rolled up to show off her triceps and her Kali tattoos, and she was pouring beer onto the burgers every few moments, ostensibly for flavor but actually just because she liked to hear them flare and sizzle.

Marlowe waved back, then went to the cooler and opened a beer of her own. She was not feeling particularly social; Daa had had to twist her arm to get her up here, and if the occasion had not been specifically to honor Jackson, she would not have come at all.

She sat down on the porch's railing to sip the beer, looking out over the downslope of the mountain. The view from here was more or less the view Jackson had painted. She loved the silence and the vastness here; the landscape always dwarfed every tiny conversation. Aside from Daa and herself, the only other guests for the dinner party were Shakti Arguello and her latest boy-friend, who came out of the house just then.

"Ah, Maaaarrlowe!" Shakti exclaimed. She hastened across the porch to give Marlowe her usual extravagant hug. Shakti was a vivacious woman, with elegant cheekbones, shining eyes of mild brown, and a tremendous white smile, less ostentatious than lavish. Her hair was bleached golden blond in streaks that suggested sunlight, with endearing glimpses of the original soft drab to suggest an organic process; and her skin was smooth and perpetually glowing in a rose pink flush. All her movements were graceful to the point of flourish—in general, she burst upon one like a benevolent wind, in swirling, genial gusts. She had been Jackson's astrologer and, to the awe of everyone, had predicted the time of his death to within three hours, a year before it happened. Marlowe was not inclined to give her too much credit for this; it had been obvious even then that it was just a matter of time for Jackson, and anyone could get lucky. It was like an office pool, someone had to win. In her weaker moments Marlowe even suspected Jackson of dying on the date Shakti had predicted as a kind of private joke, an irony that no one would ever appreciate. Jackson's belief in astrology had run more to camp. But Jackson had had a real fondness for Shakti, Marlowe knew. He had felt she was a sensitive soul, the madness in her method aside.

Shakti's boyfriend stood by grinning supportively while the women hugged. Marlowe could not recall his name, though she had met him twice. Her general feeling about Shakti's boyfriends in any case was that there was no real need to remember their names—Shakti ran through men so quickly, one love for the ages after another, that to get emotionally involved with any of them only led to confusion. Shakti had met this one the previous July in Mexico, at a particularly rare sort of analunar eclipse that happened only once every twenty thousand years. She had been fresh from Bali, where she had gone to learn to dance. Shakti did not believe that any other place sufficed for such a thing. But she had rushed to the Pacific coast of Mexico upon learning that the eclipse would be visible there. Unfortunately, her timing had been such that she had had no time to procure protective glasses. As it began to get dark at midday, she had rushed out onto the beach and gaped up at the sky, risking blindness. The present boyfriend, then a stranger, well equipped for the awesome event himself, had given her a piece of film to cover her eyes.

"I've been waiting for this moment for ages," he told her, with such tenderness and conviction that she fell in love with him instantly and was sure that they must have met before, in a past life. Perhaps, she thought, they only met at analunar eclipses, every twenty thousand years. He had turned out to be a Taurus as well, which clinched it for Shakti. She'd been waiting for a Taurus for months, if not millennia. The stars did not lie; there were serious issues to be worked out in her seventh house, and only a Taurus would do.

"I dreamed about Jackson the other night," she told Marlowe now.

"Oh?" Marlowe said politely.

"Oh, yes. He came to me in white."

Marlowe nodded; she sipped her beer and studied the river valley. Jackson, it seemed, was always coming to Shakti in white.

"Dinner's ready!" Toni called just then, to Marlowe's relief. She promised Shakti she would hear all about this latest vision later and went to grab a paper plate. As she did, she finally remembered Shakti's boyfriend's name. It was Gerard. Somehow that only made Marlowe feel worse. Everything, it seemed, was making her feel worse. It was going to be a very long night.

III

Concerns

"WHERE'S MARLOWE?" TONI ASKED DAA SOME HOURS LATER. THE TWO of them were sitting on the deck, their chairs angled to include the moonlit river valley below in their view. A bottle of red wine stood between them, and from time to time one of the women would reach over and refill her glass. Pesky was doing the dishes inside; it was often impossible to keep her out of the kitchen. Shakti and Gerard had disappeared into a bedroom not long after dinner and not been seen since, although occasionally little cries of ecstasy could be heard. Marlowe, however, was simply gone.

"I don't know," Daa said. "She could be anywhere—hiding out, I suppose. She's been so moody lately."

"For a change," Toni said dryly.

Daa smiled, acknowledging. "Yes, but it's worse, it's definitely worse since Jackson died. I think Jackson used to be able to mellow her out."

"Jackson mellowed everyone out."

"Yeah. But some of us need it more than others."

They considered the valley for a moment.

"God, I miss him," Toni said at last, pouring herself more wine. "I keep dreaming about him. I keep expecting him to call up and say, 'What's cooking, cookie?' "

"Me too. I keep thinking I see him on the street." Daa hesitated, then confided, "Marlowe's been painting mops for almost two months now, you know."

Toni glanced at her uncertainly. "Mops?"

"Yeah, you know, those old stringy mops—all loose and gray and tangled. God, she's so gifted, you'd think she could paint something gorgeous. I keep trying to tell her she's wasting her talent. I mean, can you imagine Georgia O'Keeffe painting mops? These monumental, archetypal, numinous . . . mops."

"I remember when she was painting the cracks in sidewalks."

"At least she had flowers pushing up through those, once in a while. I took that to be her creativity coming through the patriarchal conditioning, and all. But these mops are awful. Marlowe says you can see Death in them, if you look right."

Toni laughed. "Marlowe could see Death in a piece of chocolate cake." She paused. "You know, Daa, speaking of chocolate cake—"

"I'm worried about her, Toni."

Toni sighed. "It's just her grieving process, sweetheart. Marlowe needs more space than most people. And *you*, my dear, need to take better care of yourself. You're letting yourself get all caught up in Marlowe's trips. You always give too much, that way. And Marlowe just laps it up, without ever giving back."

"I know all that. I try not to get all codependent about it, and all. But I just wish—oh, I don't know. The basics, you know? That she could just open up a little more, share it with me."

"Yeah," Toni said, and sipped her wine. The two of them considered the moon. Below them, the river glinted in the silver-gray landscape; the night was so bright they could see the shapes of individual trees.

"It's so beautiful, here," Toni said.

"I know it's all in the hands of the Mother. I know it's all just Marlowe's cycles and rhythms, and that she'll come back around, like spring. But it scares me, you know? When she gets so far away."

"It's always been like this, you know, with the two of you. You've been saying the same things to me for almost ten years. It's just the way Marlowe *is*. It will be okay, Daa."

"I just love her so," Daa said, and looked at her wine. Toni took her hand, and the two of them sat in silence for a while. From time to time, in spite of herself, Toni would glance across the deck to the food table, at the chocolate cake. Pesky had made it in the shape of a skeleton, for All Hallows' Eve, and it was delicious. The bones were traced on in white frosting, in an anatomically correct configuration that tasted like licorice.

IV

Miracles Abound

MARLOWE, IN FACT, WAS LOST IN THE WOODS. SHE HAD FLED FOR A WALK after dinner, along the ridgeline above the ranch, and lost her way when she started back down. The moon was no help here, halfway down the forested slope; from time to time it lit the way for perhaps half a dozen steps before the canopy of trees blocked its light again. For the most part Marlowe stumbled along in the dark, feeling her way step by step through the pitch-black woods. After an hour of failing to find the house by simply walking in the direction in which she thought it lay, she had decided to try working her way down the mountain. Surely, she reasoned, if she just followed the slope she would come upon the ranch below one way or another.

The brief exhilaration she had felt earlier upon escaping from the dinner party had long since leaked away into the night. Marlowe tried to recall what kinds of animals in this area were large enough to kill her. It seemed to her that she could see eyes gleaming from time to time in the dark and hear breathing other than her own. Unseen branches scraped across her face and grabbed at her clothes; her nerves jangled at every crackle of leaves nearby. Stepping unexpectedly into a knee-deep stream, she soaked herself to the waist and slashed her hand on a sharp rock as she scrambled out in a near-panic.

She couldn't remember crossing that stream on the way up to the ridge, and now she began to worry that she had strayed off course and would miss the ranch entirely if she kept going downward. She started cross-slope, her ears straining for sounds of the party, her eyes seeking the glimmer of the barbecue fire or the ranch house lights. When she didn't come upon anything she recognized after what seemed like a very long time, she reversed her direction; and then she started uphill again, gripped by a deepening fear. She was lost, there was no question about it. In six months they would find her bones picked clean, in these endless woods. Like Jackson, it was her time to die.

And what a shame to die so ridiculously, Marlowe thought, and in such a foul mood. Dinner had been as much an ordeal as she had expected. Everyone had raised their glasses in toast after toast to Jackson and told insipid inspirational stories and said spiritual things. His presence this and his spirit that, and the journey of his soul through so-and-so to such and such, bardos and heavens and realms of light. It was as if Jackson had not died at all, but simply gone on some extended New Age vacation, a package deal to some Atlantic City or Disneyland of the soul where he was having a wonderful time and sending regular postcards. Certainly anecdotal miracles abounded; the dinner guests had each recounted their breathless share. Aside from the appearance of the monks, which everyone took to be divinely arranged, and Shakti's moment-of-death (more or less) vision, there were a host of other phenomena associated with Jackson's death that had passed into the general lore. Trees had split in three counties, and clocks had stopped; water pipes and pillows had burst; and dreams were recorded. Shakti's mother, Gabriella, had also had a vision of Jackson, in her living room in Orange County. Jackson, resplendent in a natty medieval tunic, tights, and robe, had interrupted the late movie and scared the cat. He had told Gabriella that love would always find a way, and that true love was the most powerful force in the universe. Gabriella agreed with him wholeheartedly. She had jotted down a few of his more pertinent remarks on the yellow notepad she always kept around to transcribe whatever channeled material might "come through," as she said, and then spent some time consoling her cat. Her fifth husband, Herb, was in the room with her the whole time and didn't see a thing.

That was typical, of course. Shakti's mother had always felt cursed, in her luck with men. But it confirmed her sense that the marriage had failed, and she cited Herb's obliviousness to spiritual realities, among other things, when she filed for divorce a few weeks later. It amounted to irreconcilable differences, she told the judge; a lifeless marriage was a dungeon to a woman's soul, and Gabriella noted for the record—it was duly transcribed by the court stenographer—that Jackson's spirit had set her free.

There had been so many reported sightings of Jackson at and around the moment of his death that the concern arose that it was impossible for Jackson's spirit to have appeared in such a diversity of places simultaneously. Shakti had reported at dinner that Albert Nerdowsky, who was interested in the mathematics of such things, had calculated that to have covered its entire reported itinerary on the night of his death, Jackson's free-flying soul would have had to travel at least three times the speed of light. To be more or less precise, 3.1416—the phenomenon appeared to have some relation to the value for pi. This was intriguing, though later Nerdowsky, known to his friends as Nerdo, could not explain to anyone's satisfaction how he had arrived at his figure. He had returned to his computer and arrived at a different number. An awkward aspect of the new calculation was that all the events ended by having taken place in the twelfth century. It was plain that the math would need some work. Nerdo did say, however, that it was all quite clearly a result of one of several frontier-of-physics kinds of things—parallel-universe dynamics, perhaps, or something to do with tachyons. He said Bell's theorem covered such phenomena nicely, and pretty much everyone was content, by then, to leave it at that.

An owl abandoned a branch not far above Marlowe's head and swooped down the mountain, its great wings briefly shadowing the moon. Marlowe, her nerve endings crackling, stopped in despair and said a Hail Mary, something she had not done since she was twelve and told her father she did not believe in God. Her father, typically, had hit her twice, once for her defiance of him, and only as a sort of afterthought, for the sin against God. He had made her continue to go to mass for another year and a half anyway, until the parish priest in his wisdom had suggested one Sunday that belief could not be compelled or coerced, and that Marlowe must be released to find her own way to the Lord. And even then, when they got home, her father had hit her one last time, for the embarrassment.

Holy Mary, mother of God, pray for us sinners, now, and at the hour of our deaths. Amen.

The trees all looked the same; every step in this darkness looked the same. It reminded Marlowe of a Buddhist teaching story Jackson had used to tell. Imagine, the Buddhists say, a blind turtle, swimming freely in the depths of an ocean the size of the universe. On the surface of that vast sea floats a wooden ring. Every hundred years, the turtle rises, once, to the surface. To be born a human being is said to be more difficult and more unlikely than for that turtle to surface accidentally with its head poking through the wooden ring.

And even among those who do manage to poke up into humanity, it is said, those who have the great good fortune to encounter the teachings of wisdom in their lifetime are rare—as rare as if wisdom itself were another wooden ring, floating on the surface of another universe-sized ocean. And those who really take the teachings to heart and embody them in their actions are rarest of all—as rare, the Buddhists say, as stars in broad daylight, as rare as a blind turtle finding yet another ring by chance, on yet another vast, unlikely sea.

Jackson had been the ring, Marlowe thought; and she had missed it. It was going to take another universe for that ring to come around again.

She noticed just then that she could see the moon for the first time in what seemed like hours, bright through a break in the trees. Apple trees, Marlowe realized—she was in the orchard, closer to the house than she could ever have imagined in her terror and despair. Apparently she would not be joining Jackson as soon as she had thought.

Five steps away, in a shaft of silver moonlight, a deer munched contentedly on some fallen apples. Marlowe marveled at the animal's nonchalance—once it even lifted its head and looked right at her, its great floppy ears cocked, before apparently deciding she was harmless, and returning to its feast.

There seemed a sort of permission in its acceptance of her. Marlowe cautiously stooped and felt around on the ground at her feet; finding an apple, she picked it up and straightened; and she took a bite. It was ripe and crisp and sweet; it seemed to Marlowe a kind of miracle of its own.

Still, she knew she wasn't going to tell anyone about all this. An apple was an apple was an apple; and besides, somehow to make a big deal out of it would cheapen her own quiet silly sense that it was a gift from Jackson.

Part V

Growth and Change

CALIFORNIA WATCH: *How conscious are Californians of the biorelative, essentially psychoid nature of the California landmass? Or is the whole state a holograph generated by UFOs?*
—featured in *The Archaeus Project Newsletter,* vol. 2, no. 4, July 1983

I

In Which Sheba Commits Herself to a Deeper Exploration of the Principles of Immortality

SHEBA CONTINUED TO SETTLE EXUBERANTLY INTO RESIDENCE AT THE Lapidge Street house; she felt that the West Coast had welcomed her with open arms. Everyone was so nice, and everything was falling into place. It had been her impression that California was something like a third-world country, and she had arrived anticipating difficulties of adjustment comparable to a stay in Kashmir or Uzbekistan; but she had discovered that Bay Area stores did carry tartar-control Crest, allaying a vague but real concern she had had, and that dental floss and Kleenex and Ragu and indeed most brand-name products were readily available, at prices comparable to those in the rest of the United States.

The hummingbird feeder outside her bedroom window was filled now with sweet red Kool-Aid. Working from one of her books, Sheba had begun to try to wrestle her legs into a lotus position, and for twenty minutes every morning she tried to meditate. Usually she just ended up making lists of things to do that day in her head, but sometimes something seemed to flutter near the edge of her awareness, and if it was not a hummingbird at the feeder or the wind through the lacy pink curtains she had put up—not *too* pink, Sheba thought, though Marlowe had wrinkled her nose in distaste—then Sheba was fairly sure it was the spirit stirring. And who was to say that the hummingbird and the wind in the curtains were not the spirit as well? Though she had yet to have an unambiguous experience of her kundalini awakening, many encouraging signs of progress were along the spiritual path.

There was Jack, for instance. On the strength of Sheba's first massage, Jack had offered to take her to the Institute for Health and Immortality, an organization with which he had been actively involved for five years. They had made the pilgrimage to Berkeley on a Tuesday morning, which was vaguely disappointing to Sheba—Tuesday seemed just too mundane a kind of day for such a deeply spiritual event, though when she tried to think of a day that would have been better, she could not, really. Sunday, after all, had been taken.

The IHI—or "*Ee*-hee," as those in the know were prone to refer to it—operated out of a former sorority house near the campus of UC-Berkeley and indeed was still subject to occasional panty raids by fraternity brothers under the mistaken, generally beer-fueled, impression that the IHI logo denoted the continued presence of sororal women. Often after a party weekend the stately green lawn that had been a factor in the original decision to acquire the place—for the note of dignity it lent—was marked by tire tracks, condoms filled with water, and the empty kegs of frustrated young seekers after underwear. But IHI had endured these and other indignities for the better part of a decade, and if it was not quite the internationally renowned center of a burgeoning world movement that one might have imagined from Jack's description, it had weathered the years better than many of the scores of similar institutes and aspiring spiritual centers in the Bay Area, which opened with the frequency and rapidity of new restaurants, and suffered a rate of failure at least as high.

Certainly the place was impressive to Sheba, prepared as she was by Jack's soft hands to be awed. She could not, of course, help but notice the condoms and beer cans; as they got out of Jack's Toyota and walked up IHI's driveway, the front lawn looked a little like a beach after a peculiar high tide.

Jack led her inside, where they were greeted by a weary, somewhat preoccupied receptionist. After some searching through drawers, a three-fold pamphlet was produced, which listed all the activities and classes offered by the Institute. Sheba, it appeared, was in luck: an introductory class was beginning that very evening, "Immortality: The Science of Eternal Life." The paperwork proved extensive, and the cost exorbitant, but Sheba was at last properly registered and rejoined Jack with some relief. He beamed at her with a congratulatory air and took her arm, leading them down the hallway to continue her introductory tour.

"Lord, that woman was *something,*" Sheba said, laughing, when they were out of earshot. "Wasn't she?"

"Uh, 'something'? " Jack said cautiously.

"Yes, well, I *mean*—she wasn't exactly *friendly,* was she? What's she doing sitting there if it's gonna ruin her day every time anybody comes in?"

"Well, we're all responsible for our own feelings and perceptions," Jack said, looking a little pained. "Really, it's all a matter of right thinking. We can experience people as anything we want, it's in our own power. Our lives are completely under our control. That's one of the basic premises of Immortality Thinking."

"Did *you* think she was friendly? You were eager enough to get away from that desk, I noticed."

"I didn't think of her as friendly or *un*friendly," Jack said with a trace of loftiness. "I thought of her—well, I thought of her as a being of light."

"No *shit.* A being of light?"

"I try to think of everyone as a being of light," Jack said modestly.

"Well, she lit up when it came down to accepting my traveler's checks, I'll give her that."

Jack looked dubious and seemed inclined to continue to press for a higher view, but they had entered the working heart of the building now, and he was obliged to exhibit its wonders. The Institute, in addition to its classrooms and a full floor of residential suites—"for those who want to *immerse* themselves in Immortality Thinking," Jack said—had a fully equipped weight room, sauna, and hot tub, as well as workout rooms for yoga and aerobics, a meditation room, and a common dining facility.

The dining room occasioned a lecture on Eating for Eternal Life. The Immortality Diet as Jack explained it for her benefit was extraordinarily principled and intricate; Sheba retained few of the details but was impressed with the passion of the presentation. It appeared that everything she had consumed up to this point in her life was lethal.

The tour culminated at what Jack reverently called The Founder's Room. They paused in the corridor outside the closed door for him to prepare her for its full import. The founder of the Institute for Health and Immortality himself, Jack said, had dwelt in this very room for years.

"And where is he now?"

"Well, he died."

Sheba rather ungraciously laughed. "Died! But I thought the whole *point* of immortality was—"

"It *is,*" Jack said hastily. "But you have to understand, there are a lot of other factors involved. The establishment of this center, for instance, took a lot out of him. And also, he was a prophet ahead of his time—in our modern culture, we are *constantly* exposed to a *tremendous* amount of Mortality Thinking. His life was a *constant battle* against the almost over*whelm*ing negative tendencies of the culture in which he found himself, and yet *still* he managed to establish the principles of the Science of Eternal Life on the soundest basis of research and made it possible for *us* to reap the benefits of Immortality Thinking."

"You'd think he could have reaped a little more himself."

"It's exactly that kind of doubt and negative thinking that kills us," Jack said, and opened the door to usher her in.

The Founder's Room proved to have been scrupulously maintained in precisely the condition in which the founder had left it on his demise. It was temperature-controlled at a greenhouselike warmth and equipped with special fluorescent lights and a series of humidifiers, dehumidifiers, and air conditioners. The bed was similar to a hospital bed and equipped for traction and mechanical variations of posture. A large cabinet of faithfully preserved vials and bottles testified to the founder's faith in vitamin pills. Crystals were placed at strategic points to filter out negative vibrations. And at the far end of the room, there was an altarlike arrangement, with a large marble-plated box set before it. The box looked like a coffin.

In fact, as Jack informed Sheba, leading her over to it, it *was* a coffin—or rather, a Life Box, as those at the Institute preferred to call it.

"Oh, come on," Sheba said, certain that she was being teased.

"No, really," Jack said, and leaned over to raise the heavy marble-covered lid. And there, under a sheet of sturdy bullet-proof glass, looking faintly, unnervingly shriveled and parchment colored after the embalming and drying but otherwise perfectly preserved, was the founder himself.

"He's a mummy!"

"We prefer to refer to it as a State of Deferred Decay," Jack said, the slight note of pedantic pride mingled with a trace of defensiveness. "It's a crucial element of Immortality Thinking, you see—the maintenance of the bodily image. If we can retain a clear conception of our physical form, we can maintain it indefinitely."

"I reckon you can."

"A lot of people find this a little hard to stomach. Or even *weird.*"

"Oh, no, it's okay. It's *weird,* all right, but it's, um, interesting too." It appeared, however, that she was going to be unable to linger long without giggling; and Jack was at last forced to hasten them out.

II
One Thing Leads to Another

DESPITE HER UNORTHODOX AMUSEMENT AT THE FOUNDER'S CONDITION, and her Negative Perceptions of the receptionist, Sheba was primed by her ongoing massage experiences to look kindly on whatever institutional structure supported Jack's soft hands, and

IHI's illuminating agenda apparently was it. She marveled at it, a little; she found the place in its particulars often silly, venial, and even foolish—at times she found Jack himself so—but she could not forget the light that had poured into her on the massage table. As Jack said, the new age would no doubt take some time in the making, but Sheba felt that she had glimpsed—had *felt*, in her very nerve endings—what that promised land might be. The hope of a world lit with that vision was after all what had brought her to California. It had not occurred to her since she was a child that religion could be so thrilling—and that IHI amounted to a religion, she had no doubt. She picked up at once on the subliminal apocalyptic fervor of the place, the deep sense of a chosen few on a mission of divine revelation. That she should have come upon the new revelation, and its agents on the planet, so quickly and with so little fuss seemed to her only right.

Nothing in her early, somewhat heady experiences at the Institute for Health and Immortality did anything to dissuade her from the notion that she had arrived at the height of her aspiration. She quickly branched out from her weekly beginner's class on Wednesdays to take advantage of IHI's other offerings, including an ongoing Tuesday workshop on "thinking for immortality" and a class on massage and "intuitive healing" taught by Jack himself on Wednesday and Friday evenings, where she hoped to learn how to soften her own hands.

The cost of all this was spectacular. Sheba fretted occasionally at the depletion of her savings account, which she had originally calculated would see her through a full year or more of spiritual seeking, but which now in the light of California reality seemed good for about six months. She wondered if she could manage to squeeze the entire process of enlightenment into such a shortened interval. But it took only the occasional massage from Jack to renew her conviction that that holy glow her body took on was the pearl of great price itself, and she was ready enough to sell everything for its purchase.

The classes themselves were a canny blend of challenges to her old assumptions—which were invariably revealed to reflect some aspect of Mortality Thinking—and emphasis on the saving tenets of the Science of Eternal Life. Sheba, indeed, was increasingly amazed that she had managed to survive to such an advanced age, given the fatal mispresumptions that had riddled her former life. It was not long before she was rising at seven to breakfast with Jack on banana smoothies and to discuss, even at that hour, the radical requirements of Immortality Thinking, and the urgency of change; nor, perhaps inevitably, was it long before she went from sharing his massage table to sharing his bed.

III

Strains

IN THE WEEKS FOLLOWING HER COUSIN'S ARRIVAL, MARLOWE BEGAN TO feel overwhelmed. The blender now ran twice as long at seven in the morning; the weird singsong of the Immortality Mantra could be heard at almost any hour of the day or night; and all their house meals had become long discourses on Immortality Thinking. The bathroom floor was always wet now, and the mirror steamy, with Sheba and Jack's latest purificatory bath; they invariably found occasion to take these together, and the sounds of their sloshing and giggling set Marlowe's teeth on edge.

And then there were the phone calls—since Sheba's advent at IHI, the house phone had been ringing off the hook with a steady stream of earnest fellow seekers eager to assist her on the spiritual path. Her cousin's "spiritual blossoming," as Jack obnoxiously persisted in calling it, was drawing a lot of bees—mostly men, Marlowe could not help noting sourly—and the house seemed filled with their buzz and persistent hum.

Meanwhile, the mailbox was filled with cards, letters, and packages from Sheba's family, who were treating their youngest daughter's pilgrimage to the West Coast as if it were her first time

away at a slightly dangerous summer camp. Cookies and underwear and long missives of advice and admonition arrived almost
daily. Sheba's mother seemed to feel that a broad range of certain
basic elements of civilized living could not be acquired in California. She had sent some exquisite handwoven Peruvian place
mats, and silverware and cookware; she had sent a shower curtain, and a lovely bath rug; and a white rosebush, in full aston-
ishing bloom, had been delivered onto the Lapidge Street front
porch by UPS, causing the neighbors to gather and gawk.

Apparently the bush was some kind of historically significant
relic of Sheba's maternal lineage, for it arrived with a cover letter
and a copy of an old document in Sheba's great-grandmother's
elegant hand, a sort of pedigree tracing the history of this particular strain of roses, the Virginia White, back through colonial
Virginia to Elizabethan England. Marlowe was prepared to mock
Mrs. McKenzie's apparently talismanic hopes for the gift, but to
her dismay, Daa was delighted with the roses and promptly
helped Sheba plant the bush in the backyard. It ended up right
outside Marlowe's studio window, next to the brown-edged concrete pool and dry fountain with the sculpture of Aphrodite at its
center. There its richly scented blooms irritated Marlowe as
she tried to paint. It was almost like having Sheba, or Sheba's
mother—or, by an easy association, her own mother—standing
there while she worked. Also, the vivid roses seemed to Marlowe
to make the fountain and pool look shabby and sad by contrast,
and that pained her soul. She had sculpted the Goddess figure
herself, when they had first moved into the house, and rigged the
statue to shower water in a constant arc into the double-tiered
pools below. For the better part of a decade the sight and sound
had delighted and inspired her in her studio, but the pipe to the
fountain had been broken in the earthquake of '89 and never
repaired, and cobwebs hung now in the arc of Aphrodite's arm,
where water should have streamed.

That seemed appropriate enough, suddenly. The abandoned
fountain reminded Marlowe of everything left undone, and everything allowed to fall by the way—all the failures, every exhausted hope and dream of her California life seemed gathered

like the dry brown leaves in the empty pool, beneath the hollow arms of the dusty Goddess. Painting her mops-heads every day, Marlowe contemplated the depth of her neglect. She had failed Aphrodite, she thought, as she suspected she had failed Jackson, and failed herself, in ways she could not even enumerate; and dozens of live white roses had arrived, courtesy of her vivacious cousin Sheba, to mark the funeral rites.

IV

Jack Calls It Tantra

CONTRIBUTING FURTHER TO MARLOWE'S GENERAL SENSE OF MISERY AT this time was the sudden spectacular presence of Sex in the Lapidge Street house. The old heating system apparently centered acoustically on Jack's bedroom, and every murmur of passion from that quarter, every giggle and moan, every rocking of the bed and thump against the headboard, reverberated in perfect clarity throughout the building. Conducted and even amplified by the ancient tin vents, the frolics of Jack and Sheba poured into every room in the house as part of their new shared air.

It was unbearable; it seemed to Marlowe that the two of them were at it eight or ten times a day. And there was no escape. She tried shutting all the vents, but that just made the house stuffy and did not diminish the racket in the least. Jack and Sheba even discussed their passion at the breakfast table, in maddening spiritual terms; Sheba giggled shyly while Jack held forth on the virtues and challenges of the tantric path.

Daa, infuriatingly, took it all in stride and even seemed to approve. It was Daa's belief that good sex was good for everyone no matter where it took place. All pleasure, she said, was praise of the Goddess. Marlowe, however, lay awake at night, and awoke early, to the same ongoing assault. She even dreamed one night that Jackson had returned: ignoring Marlowe entirely, despite her joy at seeing him, he went straight to Sheba's room. Marlowe woke in a sweat from the dream, to the sounds of a fresh bout of mortal passion emanating from the vent above her head. It seemed to her that she could see the noise in the air like a kind of smoke.

Part VI

Another Untimely Demise

Die and Become—till thou hast learned this
Thou art but a dull guest on this dark planet.
                                        —Goethe

I

A Sacrifice to Pele

AUMAKUA PARKER DIED THAT THURSDAY NIGHT IN HAWAII VOLCANOES
National Park, when the shelf of still-hot, freshly hardened lava
on which he was peddling his unicycle exploded and collapsed
into the sea. The tragedy occurred at 10:02 P.M. Hawaiian time—
after midnight on the West Coast—but it was not until late Friday
afternoon that the news began to spread among Aumakua's
friends and acquaintances in California. Typical of many of Aumakua's stunts, the event had been videotaped; footage of Aumakua's death arrived on the West Coast within days. A dozen
high-grade copies of the tape were made for friends and family, as
Aumakua would have wanted it, and the following Tuesday a
number of the people who had loved him gathered at the Lapidge
Street house for a combination first-run showing and wake.

II

Some Things Are Fated

EVERYONE AGREED THAT IT WAS AN EERILY APPROPRIATE DEMISE. AU-
makua's passion for Pele was well-known. After seeing a television special on the Kilauea eruptions, he had moved to Hawaii

74

five years before to live, as he said, "on the edge." He had changed his name from Terry and let his hair grow. He had studied the Huna religion and opened the Aloha Fuck-You Firing Range and Rebirthing Center, to further the development of will and compassion; but his main interest had always been in the volcanoes. He believed it was his calling to live with fiery intensity, and he was drawn to the lava as to something kin. He would dance up to live flows, so close that his eyebrows and hair would singe off; once he had lost a whole roll of pictures because it turned out that his camera lens had melted.

No one had been able to dissuade him from his passion, Jack Soft Hands, as host for the wake, told his assembled friends: Aumakua felt that he had been called to dance on the edge by the Goddess herself. There had been no stopping him, and he had gone out the way he would have wanted, alive to Pele's will.

Jack, who had made organic popcorn and mai tais for the occasion, wept then and turned down the lights. The tape was set in motion; and a hush came over them all as the screen flickered to life.

III

Into the Arms of the Goddess

FOR THOSE WHO HAD NOT SEEN IT ALREADY ON THE EVENING NEWS, THE video was a spectacular piece of work. Aumakua, in perfect focus, teetered and cavorted on the smoking rock, between streams of live red lava, his unicycle's tires aflame. He waved and mugged for the camera; he grinned, his fine white teeth showing against his tanned face. Above the background hissing as the hot lava hit the water behind him, he could be heard chanting one of the love poems he had written for Madame Pele:

Goddess of flame and birth
Goddess of the red fresh earth
Goddess of the new-born world
Into your arms I am thrown
By my love
By my love
Into your arms I am hurled.

All at once the ground heaved, and the edge of the lava shelf behind him blew out toward the sea in dazzling streamers. The camera shuddered and tilted, but held; the cameraman's voice could be heard exclaiming in the background.

Aumakua too kept his balance, on the unicycle. He stopped peddling and remained poised and upright, his face a mask of placid concentration as he made the little adjusting movements required to keep his balance. He did not appear to be distressed by the turn of events; he appeared intrigued, and even weirdly pleased. All the rubber had burned off his tires by now; he was resting on the rims, which were also beginning to melt.

And then a second explosion occurred, a bigger one, hurling hot lava balls and boulders into the air, and the whole shelf collapsed into the sea in a boiling tumult of white steam.

The camera tilted slightly then; or perhaps it was the earth itself beneath the tripod that tilted. In any case, the long, lingering final shot, steady after the rain of flaming rock had ceased, was of the night sky above the ocean, the sparkling stars obscured from time to time, but less so as the night went on, by fresh bursts of smoke and rising steam, and a low red glow.

IV

The Relevance of the Major and Minor Arcana

IT WAS AUMAKUA'S DEATH THAT FINALLY MOVED MARLOWE TO PAINT something besides mops. Aumakua had lived in the Lapidge Street house—in the bedroom that Jack now occupied—for a year and a half in the late eighties: he was, in fact, the last man with whom Marlowe had had sex. He had still been going by "Terry" then; he was fresh from Baltimore, wide-eyed and well-groomed and reading Alan Watts and the *Tao Te Ching*. He had had a tremendous and flattering crush on her, and he had been a sweet and naive lover, which had suited Marlowe fine—he was such a nice change from the slightly cynical hipness of the California men who had been hitting on her for years.

Still, it had been a terrible time, Marlowe remembered. The affair had almost sunk her and Daa. Terry had wanted for a while to marry her, and she had been shocked to find herself considering it. She had felt sheepish and stupid and confused, afraid her swings of attraction indicated a lack of character, a lack of seriousness, a lack of substance. All those years to liberate her sexuality, to get in touch with her feelings for women and be what she truly *was*, and now she was going to throw it all away on some kid from Baltimore who would have delighted her mother, if he just got a job?

Jackson, she recalled, had told her not to fret.

"But you've been with Josh for *years*," Marlowe had said. "For years, steady as a rock."

"And for years before that I was a confused kid from Yuba

County. It took me years to figure out that loving men wasn't twisted or perverse, that it was just the way I am." He smiled. "It's not such a bad thing, you know."

"What do you mean?"

"Loving men. For some people it's the most natural thing in the—"

"Oh, I don't think it's *men* I love, necessarily. I don't think that's the great revelation here. I don't even think it's *Terry*. God, I don't know. Am I crazy? Am I insincere? Maybe it's just marriage itself—the great white way. I'm a sucker for the movie moment or something. I'm a sucker for the idea of happily ever after."

"So marry Daa."

"Daa says I haven't got the courage of my sexual identity."

Jackson had laughed. She had loved that laugh of his; it always made her feel safe and lucid and free to be herself.

"I don't think courage will ever be your problem, sweetheart," he had said.

In the end, only Jackson's timely observation that Terry still had all of California to go through had saved her. And in fact Terry had proven to have more "California" to go through than any of them: more, finally, than even the West Coast could supply. Marlowe had actually been relieved when he took off for Hawaii on a mission from the volcano goddess so obviously crazy that she felt no temptation to follow him. It had taken her and Daa another six months to get back to normal, and the whole experience had been so painful and disconcerting that Marlowe had not tried anything similar since.

Now in the wake of his silly death she found herself working on her tarot deck again.

The tarot project was going to make them a bundle, Daa had long insisted, as well as making a positive, life-affirming statement. It was a healthy gesture in a world that needed it. Marlowe was less sure, and less and less sure as the years went by. But certainly the deck she was designing with Daa, card by card and image by image, had saved their relationship at many points, as well as Marlowe's sanity, and never more than when she had first conceived it some nine years previously.

It had been born of their first big fight, which had come about a month after they had begun living together. They had gone that night to a show of works by one of Marlowe's old painter boyfriends from art school, Greg Sturmmacher—a very sick guy, as she herself had warned Daa in advance: sexist, ambitious, crazy at times and even perverse, an edgy man given to existing on coffee and licorice and existential bile for extended periods while he painted his dark and jagged works. But, Marlowe said, for all that, a terrific talent.

Daa had not even wanted to go, but she had done so out of a sense of partnerly duty: she wanted to share as much of Marlowe's "creative life" as she could, to be as supportive as possible. Predictably enough, she had found Sturmmacher's work ugly and pointless, if not misogynistic. It had made her want to go home at once and take a bath. Marlowe, however, was not only taken with the paintings, she had stayed for hours, passionately arguing arcane painterly doctrine with Sturmmacher, a pompous, slightly bloated man with small black eyes and a way of talking out of the side of his oddly lush mouth that seemed obscene somehow, to Daa. There was a light in Marlowe's eyes that Daa had never seen either, as if she were on drugs; it was like seeing a manic stranger. After drinking four glasses of cheap white wine in plastic cups, Marlowe had ended up making out with Sturmmacher on the roof of the gallery. Daa found them there when she climbed out for her own breath of fresh air, and it had been touch and go for a week afterward, with Marlowe alternately pleading that it had been an aberration and insisting that Art needed the occasional shot of wildness; that Sex fed Creativity; and that nothing, least of all a *man*, could alter her relationship with Daa.

None of this could mollify Daa, who believed in true love. True love conquers all, she always said; but also—you can't fuck around with true love. And if you *do* fuck around, the love is not true.

They tried everything to get the relationship back to center—

walks and chants and prayers and saunas, and long drives out into the country; silence and argument, and every interpersonal technique that either of them knew. Nothing had worked. It was after their third or fourth failed attempt to do a healing tarot spread that Marlowe, brought to a sense of ultimate frustration with inadequate means, was struck with the idea of creating her own spread, with her own cards: a tarot made to order. If the cards could not heal their love, she had said, perhaps it was up to their love to heal the cards.

And so Marlowe set about designing a reading that fit her sense of what *could* heal the two of them. To do so she began to make a deck from scratch. She sketched each card initially on drawing paper and then transferred the image to laminated cardboard for its final painted version. First she made a Two of Cups, showing Marlowe and Daa dancing as two mermaids beneath a limpid aquamarine sea. This was ominously crossed in the spread she made by an Eight of Swords, Disillusion, on which a bent figure suspiciously reminiscent of Greg Sturmmacher sat before an empty canvas, beyond which lay a wasteland view. Marlowe interpreted this for Daa's benefit as the spiritual emptiness of the postmodern art project as embodied in her old boyfriend, and its culmination in hollowness and soul-death.

For the spread's outcome card she painted a glorious Ace of Cups, with a torrent of healing crystal water streaming from a golden grail held by the Goddess Minne.

The tarot magic had worked its wonder. Daa wept and forgave and embraced Marlowe, who wept as well; and the True Love Goddess Deck was christened in healing tears.

Through the years, the deck had slowly grown, in organic spurts—as oysters generate pearls around intruding grit, the images tended to form at sore points in Marlowe and Daa's relationship with each other and with their world. Often the seed incidents were quite specific, and they would giggle over them later, leafing through the half-completed deck like a long-married couple over their photo albums. The Wands suit commemorated a series of artistic crises, disputes, and breakthroughs; and the Cups sequence held a secret history of their evolving love: the Nine of Cups, for instance, Happiness, showed Marlowe and Daa in the garden on a summer day, immersed in healing green, and had been painted as the fruit of a particularly idyllic period. The Swords, a crowd of women warriors, had come more easily—the dynamics of battle appealed to Marlowe's combative streak; and the Pentacles suit was a celebration of grounding images such as the Three, Work, on which Marlowe had depicted the table where she made the jewelry she sold, and herself as craftswoman. The images were generally modern, and even immediate—Marlowe took them from the world around them, stylizing their friends and their problems, their powers and their prayers, their beauties and their fears, and trying to distill some archetypal essence.

Certain significant cards, particularly among the Major Arcana, remained undone, and others had appeared in multiple versions. It unnerved Daa, for instance, that Marlowe had never managed to complete a single Lovers card, while she had painted six or eight versions of the Hanged Man, and another half dozen Hermits, Death cards, and Devils. Daa wished her lover would paint the life-affirming cards more often. But she had come to accept the quirks of Marlowe's artistic process as part of the price of love. And Daa was nothing if not patient. She firmly believed the deck would change the world, when it was completed.

V

A Card for Aumakua

MARLOWE'S FIRST ATTEMPT TO PAINT A TAROT IMAGE FOR TERRY PARKER was what seemed to her the obvious one, the Eight of Wands—Fall. She sketched out Aumakua, Icarus-like on his bicycle, teetering at the edge of a fiery abyss, riding for a fall. But this didn't satisfy her. Next she tried a spacey Seven of Cups, with Aumakua after he had let his hair grow crossing a beach toward the sea where seven mermaids were singing, the heat waves rippling off the sunny sand blurring everything toward dream. But this too seemed to miss the essence of what she felt: it had not been hubris or ambition, nor a siren song, that got Terry killed, Marlowe thought; it had been an exorbitant playfulness.

She finally settled on the Prince of Wands—the card of youthful exuberance and passion, in the suit of creativity. And so Aumakua danced in her tarot deck as he had danced in life, barechested and tanned between the fiery mountain and the sea, a gentle, joyful man, a lover of the Goddess, and almost certainly a fool.

At last Sheba exclaimed, "Oh, for God's *sake!*" and headed for the stairs. "Come on, then. You want to talk, we'll *talk.*"

Victor Morris smiled at Marlowe, without smugness but with a definite air of having known it all along; and followed. Marlowe watched them ascend to Sheba's room, then returned to her own room, shaking her head.

II

A Blast from the Past

SHEBA'S ROOM HAD EVOLVED CONSIDERABLY FROM WHAT IT HAD BEEN when she moved in. Aside from the new curtains, she had painted the walls a vigorous yellow, so that the immediate effect upon entry was of moving into a cheerful and caressing glare. The walls' radiance was less dimmed than complemented by the posters she had tacked up, dazzling, vibrant images of whales, mountain peaks, elk, some sort of angelic being, and a cabala diagram superimposed upon a human body, which Jack had given her, with the various aspects of energy flow illuminated suggestively in Day-Glo colors. Crystals dangled everywhere from dental floss, turning gently at the least inducement and occasionally gleaming red or blue or gold as they caught the light. A Zen meditation pillow was in the corner, flanked by candles; and a bronze Buddha overlooked the room from a high shelf, one hand raised. Sheba had intended to make the room a sort of nursery of the spirit, a greenhouse of the soul, purged of stuffed animals and other karmic accumulation, devoted entirely to the cultivation of higher values. And now here was her old boyfriend with a panda bear, banging against the dangling crystals and eyeing the cabala diagram dubiously, a bull in the spiritual china shop. Victor Morris wouldn't have known his chakras from a Firestone tire. She had gone out with him all through high school and she knew. He still thought God was that God at Sunday school with a long white beard. Vic had proposed to her six times before they were eighteen, and Sheba had accepted once, after four beers, an act she would always regret: even though she had come to her senses and broken the engagement off to come West, he had persisted in believing they were supposed to mate. Victor Morris had a very simple mind.

Sheba's bed was a cloth-covered futon that she folded up when it was not in use; she sat on this now and tossed a pillow on the floor for Vic Morris to sit on. He accepted it without ceremony, arranging his strong, thick legs into a cross-legged position made a little difficult by blue jeans and cowboy boots. You would never have caught the Buddha wearing jeans and cowboy boots, Sheba thought; it seemed more obvious than ever to her now that spiritual men wore cotton.

They stared at each other for a long moment. At last Vic extended the panda bear, as she had known he would. "Here. This is for you."

"I don't want your damned stuffed bear."

Vic shrugged and set the bear gently on the floor beside them; it slumped a little, and he carefully rearranged it into an upright sitting posture, so that it added a strange silent third to their conversation.

It *was* sort of cute, Sheba thought; and to counter this weakness in herself she said aggressively, "Well? You wanted to talk. So talk."

"You're looking good."

Sheba rolled her eyes. That was so like Victor. "You drove all the way across the country to tell me *that?*"

"No," he said steadily. "That's just God's truth. I drove all the way across the country, as you know damn well, to bring you home with me."

Sheba stood up abruptly and went to the window. In the street below, a battered Oldsmobile was driving by, with rap music pulsing from within it like a heartbeat. Teenaged boys were hanging out the windows on either side, hollering at a pedestrian. It was oddly reassuring somehow. There were no gangs in Indigo Falls. This was definitely California.

"I thought that's what this was all about," she said. "Well, you might just as well have saved yourself all the gas and aggravation—"

"It weren't no aggravation. It was a real pretty drive. A little much the same, through the middle there."

"I'm glad you enjoyed it. You can enjoy it on the way back too. I'm not going home with you, Victor Morris."

"You'd rather stay here with what's-his-name? With *Stan?*" Sheba laughed. "You see? That's just *you,* that's you all over. King of the hill. It's the only way you can think of things. It would never *occur* to you that what I'm doing in San Francisco has nothing to do with *you* or *Stan* or Jack or—"

"Jack! Who's *Jack?*"

"—or anybody," Sheba finished firmly. "It has to do with *me.*" There was a silence. For once she had shut him up, Sheba thought, a little amazed; it was a new and somewhat disorienting experience. Apparently she'd already grown more here than she had thought.

At last Victor said, "Well, I can respect that. And truly, I reckon Stan and his like ain't the problem. He don't *amount* to enough, to particularly problemate anything. I know that."

"Well, that's real gracious of you."

Victor shifted on the pillow and straightened his legs, then stood up. He certainly was taller than Jack, Sheba thought; she had to give him that. Not that height mattered, of course.

"And what *is* the problem, as you see it, Mr. Smarts?"

"The problem is you want magic," Vic said readily enough. "You want a house you didn't have to build, with a lawn and garden you didn't have to grow and don't have to water. You're out here chasin' after some phony God on Wednesday nights, when you never figured out how to act rightly by the real one on *Sundays.* Much less Monday mornings. You didn't like the decent church you had, and the decent work you had, and the decent guy who loves you. You want fairyland and magic wands, and guys who don't sweat."

89

"You've been giving this a lot of thought, I can see."

"You know I have."

"Well, then, think about this: there's a whole world you don't have the least idea of. There are people who've realized there's more to life than the church you were born to and the job you got stuck with and the sweaty guy who took you to the senior prom." Sheba paused, in the irritated awareness that her accent was coming back strongly; she had been whittling that drawl away for weeks. She saw in its return more evidence of the retarding influence of Victor Morris in her life.

"I thought the senior prom went right well."

"Victor, I never asked you to drive out here. And if you'd asked *me*, I'd have told you not to. I don't owe you anything. I know I made it plain enough to you when I left Virginia that—"

"You made it plain to me that you was bent on droppin' something and tryin' out nothing. I figured then that the only thing to do was to give you your head for a while, but I never intended for a minute to just let you go permanent."

"You never *had* me. I was never yours to let go or not."

"I ain't goin' back without you."

"Well, then, you'd better get yourself some California plates for that truck of yours, because I ain't—I'm *not*—going back. With you or without you. I have a life here, and it's a better life. I'm learning things. I've got room to grow now."

Victor Morris considered this for a moment, then shrugged. That shrug made Sheba nervous; it was not a gesture of resignation, in Victor. Far from it. She had seen that same shrug once before when he slugged some guy in a bar. "I was hoping you'd have come to your senses by now."

"No. You were hoping I'd have come to *your* senses."

"California's a big old fluffy place. Like a state full of cotton candy. I expect it might take you some time to get down to the bottom of it, at that." And he turned without giving her a chance to reply and walked out, his boots thumping on the stairs.

III

A Sympathetic Ear

He had not been gone long when Marlowe appeared at the door of Sheba's room, laughing.

"My *God*. Who on earth was—?" But Marlowe broke off as she saw that her cousin's eyes were red, and her cheeks wet. "Oh, Sheba! What is it?"

"It's nothing," Sheba said, straightening, and wiping her face. "I'm okay. I'm *fine*." She was upset with herself for crying at all. But she consoled herself that the lapse had been brief and that she had not given way in Victor Morris's presence. "It's just— what do you call it?—one of those California words for old *stuff*."

"Karma," Marlowe supplied automatically. "But who *was* that guy?"

"An old boyfriend. *The* old boyfriend, I guess. My high school sweetheart. We were engaged once, he gave me a beer-can pull-top as a ring. And he's never stopped acting like we still are."

"What a savage. God, the way he handled Stan! Though of course Stan didn't take much *handling*."

"Victor's a redneck. I'm ashamed I ever loved him. That's the only reason I was crying at all—pure shame. And frustration! Lord, I just wanted to leave all that stuff *behind*."

"Well, you *have*." Marlowe's heart, unexpectedly, had gone out to her cousin, aided in part by the habitual reaction to these atavistic calls from the East. "You have, you've just got to hold firm. You didn't give *in*, did you?" she added in sudden horror, looking at the panda bear. "What did he want?"

"What do you *think* he wanted!" Sheba laughed. She was recovering rapidly. "He wanted to toss me in that pickup truck of

91

his and haul me back to Indigo Falls, put an apron on me, and get me pregnant! Of *course* I didn't give in, it's not a question of *that.*''

"Just making sure. You'd be surprised, the effect an old boy-friend can have. It's like a form of posthypnotic suggestion, or something." Marlowe shook her head, fondling the panda bear idly. "God, it's men like that that drove me to women in the first place. But he *is* sort of cute, isn't he? And such a *type.*''

"You're welcome to him," Sheba said, and hesitated. "You really think he's cute?"

"Well, in a primitive sort of way," Marlowe said cautiously. "Sexy, I guess, more than cute. I mean, it's pretty visceral, but he's got the *thing*. You know?"

"Oh, yeah."

"But of course all that macho bullshit is a complete turn-off." Marlowe hesitated, inclined to pursue it, then shrugged. "Oh, well. As Daa says, sexuality is wasted on males."

Sheba laughed. "It ain't wasted on Victor Morris, I'll tell you that. He's gonna give some poor God-fearing woman eight or ten little God-fearing redneck babies someday. But not this woman."

"Well, good for you." Marlowe wished her goodnight, then, and went out, before her sudden sympathy for her cousin moved her to do anything foolish.

IV

A Conversation with Bernice, or The Lord Works in Mysterious Ways

THE ARRIVAL OF VICTOR MORRIS DID NOT, IN FACT, SHAKE SHEBA'S FAITH. If anything, it spurred her on to a deepened involvement with Jack, with IHI, and with Immortality Thinking. She was at the center now four nights a week or more, with an intensified devotional energy that Marlowe recognized well—a passion for liberation that was one part spiritual aspiration and one part historical exorcism.

Sheba's vocabulary, inevitably, was affected; she strove to acquire the IHI dialect, and before long her faithful, frequent letters home reflected this. Communicating her enthusiasm for her new discoveries as well as certain heavy-handed hints that her family might do well to consider the consequences of their present, wholly degenerate way of life, she set off alarm bells among her kinfolk. Soon after the receipt of the third of these letters, Sheba's mother called her sister Bernice, full of concern that her daughter had succumbed to a cult, and inclined to blame this on the influence and long-established deviations of her cousin Marlowe. Bernice, sympathetic to her sister's concerns, and chagrined if not completely unsatisfied that the evil climate of California had claimed another victim, promptly called her own daughter.

So it was that Marlowe's original fears for the situation were to some degree realized. Bernice reached her on a Sunday morning, having forgotten, as she always did, the difference in time zones between the two coasts, with the result that a wholly reasonable hour in New York translated to 5:30 A.M. in San Francisco. Marlowe, never a morning person, much less a predawn one, was typically rude.

"It's none of *my* goddamned business what Sheba does with her life!" she told Bernice when they had completed their usual, by now somewhat ritualized exchange of fury and broad apology to open the conversation.

"Don't swear, dear." Bernice retained a naive faith in such admonitions despite years of contrary evidence from California, knowing at heart that her daughter was a good girl. "And I certainly think you *should* take an interest in what's happening with your cousin. I mean, she *is* your cousin."

"I'd only seen her ten or twelve times in my life before she showed up here. And I didn't like her *then*. She's a grown woman, she's perfectly capable of leading her own life, and if she wants to piss her life away at the Institute of Living Forever, or whatever the hell it is—"

"*Marlowe!* Your *language.*"

"All I'm *saying* is that it's none of my business. Sheba is renting a *room* here—that's all. And I didn't particularly want to do *that.* I've hardly seen her since she's arrived."

"Family is family," Bernice said firmly.

"That's not how it works in California, Mother. Family is *history.* We live in the present here. We form our relationships through free *choice,* and mature affinity."

"Yes, I know all about your mature affinities, thank you."

Marlowe rolled her eyes at Daa, who was lying in the bed beside her listening with a sleepy, amused sympathy. "We don't really need to get into all that again, do we?"

"I certainly hope not."

"The point is, Sheba and I have not *chosen* each other."

"Her *mother* is very concerned," Bernice said, still intent on developing the case for family. "This is the first time Sheba has been out of Virginia, you know—except for a couple of trips to the beaches, of course, and that *hardly* counts and besides it was only for a day or two."

"You don't *get* it, do you, Mother? *I am not my cousin's keeper.* I am *not.* I am *not.*"

"Easy, spud," Daa said languidly. "Don't get yourself all worked up into a state."

There was a pause at the other end of the long-distance line. In the background crackle, Marlowe could hear faint music, a hymn of some kind bleeding into the line from a Sunday-morning radio service. At last Bernice said, a little plaintively, "I don't know *what* I'm going to tell her mother."

"Tell her that Sheba is doing *fine.* As cults go, IHI is not a bad one at all. They're too *inept,* for one thing."

Daa laughed.

"I'm sure her mother will be glad to hear that," Bernice said.

"Oh, Mother, I'm just kidding. Really, it's *okay.* Sheba is doing *fine.* She's a grown woman, with a good base of common sense. This happens to a lot of people when they first come to California, it's sort of like, uh . . ."

"Malaria," Daa suggested.

"Malaria," Marlowe said.

"Ma*lar*ia!"

"Or *some*thing like that," Marlowe said. "A local fever, you know, that's all I mean. You show up in a tropical place and you get all the diseases. It will pass."

"Hmm," Bernice said unhappily. There was another pause, and then, by a relatively transparent association, she said, "So, how *is* Daa?"

Marlowe covered the mouthpiece. "Speaking of malaria, she wants to know how you *are*. Can you *believe* the nerve of—"

"Oh, be nice, Mar-Mar," Daa said. "The poor woman is doing the best she can. Tell her I'm fine, thanks."

"She's fine, thanks," Marlowe said dutifully, returning to the mouthpiece. "All's well in the den of iniquity."

"I'm glad to hear that," Bernice said, taking the sarcasm in stride. There was another pause, and then she sighed. "Oh, well. I guess I'll let you get back to whatever you were doing."

"I was *sleeping*, Mother. It's five-thirty in the morning."

"Yes, yes, I *am* sorry about that. It always seems like it will be so *pleasant* to just give you a call on a Sunday morning, but it never works out. I've never really under*stood* why California has to have a different *time*. . . . Well, anyway," she said brightly, "try to look after your *cousin* a little, will you, dear? It would mean so much to her mother."

"Mother, I thought I had made it perfectly clear that I—"

"I love you, sweetheart. Bye-bye."

Marlowe glared at the receiver a moment in frustration, then slammed it down. "I *hate* it when she does that. She's like a kid in the schoolyard getting in the last tag and then running away. 'I love you, sweetheart.' "

"She *does* love you," Daa said. "In her way. Give her credit for *that* much, at least."

"It's a funny kind of love. She *doesn't* approve of my life, she *doesn't* care for who I really *am*, and yet she—"

"She *did* ask about me."

"Only when she was prompted by the thought of tropical diseases!"

"You're too touchy. You're still fighting battles that should have been over a long time ago."

"So I should just let her have the last word? Is that what you're saying?"

Daa laughed. "Well, if the last word is 'I love you, sweetheart'! You could do worse."

"Oh, she didn't *mean* that she loved me. That was just her way to get out of the conversation one up. She *meant* she had just successfully ignored *everything* I had said throughout the *entire* conversation—"

"You're in a state, Mar-Mar."

"—and told me to look after my *cousin* again, which was the only reason she *called*. And having slipped *that* in, one last time, she got off before I could tell her—"

"What you had already told her half a dozen times. You're not mad that your mother is playing one-up games with you. You're mad that she *won*."

"But—"

"But nothing. You're playing the same game. What's the big *deal* if she got in the last word? She was paying for the call."

Marlowe was silent a moment, fretting. She herself felt her *states* as a sort of ignominy. Ten years of Jungian therapy, endless work on her dreams, feminist circles, Goddess worship—a decade of the most determined efforts to raise her consciousness, and her mother still drove her crazy. It was appalling.

The sky to the east was just beginning to gray. Marlowe thought of Bernice in full sunlight at that same moment, on a New York autumn morning, puttering around the house humming to herself, preparing to go to church. She knew the reason her mother always called at such an ungodly hour was because she wanted to make it to nine-o'clock mass.

The thought made her smile in spite of herself, and Daa, seeing that her *state* was subsiding, took the opportunity to say, "Besides, your mother's right—we *should* do something for your cousin."

"Oh, come on," Marlowe said, laughing.

"No, really, I'm serious. I had already been thinking that she's a sweet kid, and that she could use a little influence beyond Vapid Jack and that necrophiliac crowd at IHI."

"You get what you're ripe for," Marlowe said, conscious both of a certain uncomfortable brittleness in the formula and of the fact that she was not on entirely sure ground in her own feelings on the vapidity of Jack. The promised Saturday massage had never materialized—the coming of Sheba had occupied his massage table extraordinarily for weeks—and she had told herself she was lucky to be off *that* hook, but she had dreamed twice recently of having sex with Jack—once in the garden, wreaking passionate havoc among Daa's young cabbages; and once, as if her unconscious had a perverse sense of humor, in a girl's locker room. "It all comes out in the karmic wash."

"Sure it does," Daa agreed easily enough. "But I'm as much a part of the karmic wash cycle as anybody else. And so are you. Why should we leave all the initiative to places like IHI? It's the fast food of spirituality—Sheba shows up hungry and Jack takes her out for burgers."

"Well, if she's satisfied with hamburger—"

"Who knows *what* she would be satisfied with, if she gets half a chance. Sheba's no idiot, she's just naive, and overly inclined to believe the best of things. All she needs is a little more seasoning, a little more perspective—"

"To become as jaded as the rest of us."

"Speak for yourself, old lady. I think we should throw a full-moon party."

Marlowe groaned. "Oh, Daa, no."

"Why not? We haven't had one since—God, when was the last one?"

"We haven't had one since Jackson died."

"All of the more reason to have one now. It would be a perfect opportunity for Sheba to meet some different types, get a better sense of what's out there, see what she's *really* ripe for. At least then if she sticks with IHI and Mr. Soft Hands, we'll know it's because she likes spiritual hamburger and banana smoothies, and not just because no one ever took the trouble to let her taste anything better."

"Well, who would you *invite?*" Marlowe said, inwardly wincing at the thought that she did not seem wholly immune herself to the hamburger-like attractions of Mr. Soft Hands.

"*Every*body," Daa said with some satisfaction. "I'd invite *everybody.*"

Part VIII

Beneath an Autumn Moon

The idea of the journey to the moon after death is one which has been preserved even in the more advanced cultures. . . . It is not difficult to find themes of the moon as the Land of the Dead or as the regenerating receptacle of souls.
    —Fred Gettings, *The Book of Tarot*

I
Party!

DAA WAS AS GOOD AS HER WORD, AND THE PARTY TOOK PLACE ON A Saturday night a week and a half later. The moon was not quite perfectly full—it would technically not fill out until the following afternoon, but a Sunday party would have conflicted with a long-scheduled peace march on the weapons laboratory in Livermore. Still, it was close enough for the crowd they had assembled: if not *everybody*, at least a lot of them.

Daa and Marlowe had thrown their first full-moon party a decade before, conceiving of them then as the ritual gatherings of the seed of a new civilization. At that time, the parties had been all-female affairs, honoring the Goddess, reveling in their liberation, and in no small measure despising the absent sex. Ten years of organic (Daa's word; Marlowe said *messy*) development had blurred those original clear lines, however. The Goddess was still much honored, but it now appeared that the new civilization too would be stuck with men. The present guest list was loaded with lovers and ex-lovers of the original separatist circle, and even with husbands and ex-husbands; and in general the diverse invitees reflected the hectic course of everyone's history in northern California. Daa's most radical lesbian friends condescended to mingle here, if somewhat warily, with actual men; witches met yogis, leftists, Dharmananda devotees, anarcho-herbalists, artists, musicians, neo-Reichians, Tibetan Buddhists, aikido black belts, Earth Firsters, Muslims, color therapists, two members of the Berkeley City Council, and a host of other organic offshoots and spiritual variants too intricate to easily name.

Antoinette Lafontane and Persephone Prescott-Bowers were

down from their ranch in Mendocino County; and a number of other out-of-towners had made the trip. But the real surprise guests were Jackson's parents, an almond farmer and his wife from somewhere just south of Gridley, in the Sacramento Valley, who had crossed the state on the strength of Daa's invitation in their red Ford pickup truck and showed up without warning just after noon. They had just been looking for an excuse to meet a few of Jackson's friends, they said, and to visit the Bay Area. They were ripe for a vacation; Jackson's father had just retired and they hadn't been out of Yuba County, except for one wild trip to Shasta Lake, since 1973. Daa, who had sent the invitation in a spirit of reconciliation without ever suspecting that they would take her up on it, quickly determined that Jackson's father, Mark Sr., drank his Jim Beam straight and was partial to beer and smoked almonds. She set him up in the deep green easy chair by the fireplace, where he argued politics for much of the afternoon and into the evening with a series of bemused and generally re- spectful anarchists, artists, and ecofeminists. Jackson's mother, Trina, had brought a casserole. She helped in the kitchen, in any way she could, and later bonded with Daa and Antoinette over the big memorial quilt they were making for Jackson. She started in on the celebration's huge pile of dirty dishes shortly after that, singing the Twenty-third Psalm; and she could not be persuaded away from the sink until the chore was done. The best that any- one could manage was to dry for her.

The party began in midafternoon, according to custom, and by early evening, when the moon made its appearance—to scat- tered cheers and greetings—over the housetops to the east, it was in full wild swing. The Holy Rose Parade, Dante's rock band, blasted out their cheerful apocalyptic lyrics from a small stage near the back fence, and a small crowd was dancing in front of the enormous speakers, which were pointed, at Daa's insistence, away from the garden. A food table stood nearer to the house, laden with the fruits of a potluck as varied as the party's constit- uency—macrobiotic casseroles and raw vegetable salads, tofu cheesecake and sprouted six-grain bread and some phenome- nally potent curry, meatless lasagna, soy steaks, cauliflower stew, and every kind of bean cooked in every imaginable fashion. A long loaf of French bread had a black tire track across it—Shakti Arguello and her new boyfriend had had a tremendous fight on the way to the party, about the meaning of perfume, and Shakti in a fury had thrown the bread out the car window. A Buick behind them had run over it. Shakti and the new boyfriend, whose name no one could remember, had been so delighted at the gesture—Shakti was working on access to her Anger—that they had stopped the car and retrieved the bread as evidence of a healthy expression of rage and brought it to the party as their part of the potluck. The tire track made it a wonderful conversation piece.

There were ice chests of beer and a card table sagging under the harder liquors, which many people were forgoing or supplementing with the good Humboldt County hemp that was making the rounds. Bobby Van Knott, who had been in Oregon collecting mushrooms, incommunicado, when Jackson died, and who had had a dream just three days before this party in which Jackson informed him of his demise and directed him to return to California by way of the third circle of hell, was circulating through the throng like an attentive butler—albeit in bare feet and a colorful Sufi robe—carrying a silver tea service and a teak bowl filled with greens. He had made mushroom salad and mushroom tea, also on the advice of Jackson in the dream, and in keeping with the potluck spirit. Bobby was proud of his Jackson dream; it was a very fashionable way to have learned of his friend's death, and everyone at the party had been appropriately impressed. Bobby was not sure what the third circle of hell part meant, but he thought it might have been referring to the agricultural check he had had to undergo at the Oregon border of California.

Inside the house, the stereo was cranked up in the living room, and another crowd was dancing there to a tape of sixties music someone had put together. There was more food and drink in the kitchen. The stairs were strewn with conversational clusters as well; everywhere was an energetic din, and Marlowe, who had refused the mushroom tea but not the sinsemilla, found herself not long after the moonrise sitting on the back steps with a sense of happy immersion. She recognized in the clamor the music of a successful mix, an achievement by no means guaranteed at these gatherings. For all that she fretted about these parties in advance, certain of catastrophe, bemoaning the tensions, the feuds and the cliques brought into risky proximity, the accumulation of slights, snubs, and historical outrages, when it did finally all come together, she was invariably delighted, and for a period her faith in civilization's advance was renewed.

In this contented frame of mind, she nibbled on a piece of Shakti's tire-tracked French bread, which people were consuming ceremonially by now as a sort of forgiveness ritual, and amused herself with watching Sheba make the rounds, approving almost in spite of herself. Her cousin, true to Daa's prediction, was mingling exuberantly. Marlowe, observing her in a succession of absorbed conversations with Buddhists, feminists, ecologists, and convincingly sincere freelance fanatics, could almost see the IHI influence thinning moment by moment, diluted like a backwater channel opened abruptly to the river. Sheba looked radiant, fluid and colorful in the gypsy skirt and blouse Daa had picked out for her; with a bright yellow scarf in her hair and two miniature silver skulls dangling fashionably at each ear, and thin black Chinese slippers on her feet, one would never have suspected she was so recently off the bus from Virginia. Only her accent told— Marlowe could hear it, and Sheba's rowdy laugh, through the party noise at times like a trumpet through oboes.

At last, after still another animated exchange, with a man Marlowe knew to be a longtime practitioner of tai chi and a preeminently sane soul, Sheba circled around to the back porch and approached her cousin with an excited grin.

''*Mar*lowe!'' she exclaimed jubilantly. ''Isn't it fan*tas*tic!''

''Oh, yes,'' Marlowe agreed, scooting over to make room for Sheba to sit beside her.

''Ah *mean*—'' Sheba said, settling, and moving an encompassing hand almost helplessly, so badly did words fail to do it all justice.

''So you're having fun?'' Marlowe laughed.

''*Fun?* Ah believe Ah've *dahd,* and gone to *heaven!*''

103

"Hmm," Marlowe said, trying to introduce a balancing vector, recognizing that Sheba's enjoyment of the party—not to mention her accent—had almost certainly been enhanced by one of the available intoxicants. She hoped, for everyone's sake, that it had not been the mushroom tea, the farther reaches of which could take exotic behavioral forms even for those accustomed to it. "You've been meeting some interesting people?"

Sheba nodded happily, once, twice, three times; it amounted to a sort of rough calibration, and Marlowe noted, relieved, that the nodding stopped at three. "Oh, yes. My head's all full! That man I was just talking to . . ."

"Brian?"

"I didn't catch his name. But he was telling me all about this tai chi—he's been doing it for fifteen years!"

"Yes, there are actually some serious people around. Thank God."

"It sounded so great, and he was so nice. I think I might try it myself. Or something like it—somebody else was telling me about this meditation stuff. I think I'm ready for something *serious.*"

"How are you going to fit anything serious into your schedule at IHI?"

"I don't know." Sheba lowered her voice. "That guy said IHI had ripped off some ancient Chinese principles and trivialized and dis*tort*ed them! Can you i*mag*ine?"

"Yes."

"It's all so con*fus*ing. And somebody else was telling me that too many banana smoothies will put your yin out of balance with your yang, or something like that." Sheba brooded over this a moment, then brightened. "And this other woman wanted to do an aura reading for me! How about *that?* She said she could see my astral body beginning to stir!"

Marlowe laughed. "What does *that* mean, I wonder?"

"I don't know," Sheba said earnestly. "She said she doesn't do full readings at parties, but she gave me her card. And *another* man was telling me all about some kind of *screaming* he does."

"Primal screaming?"

"That's it. He said if you scream loud enough, and long enough, you can let out all the pain that's clogged up inside you."

"That's the idea. It never worked for me, to tell you the truth. I just lost my voice. Too much pain, maybe."

"Oh, you've tried it?" Sheba said, looking at Marlowe with heightened respect.

"Oh, I've tried quite a bit of this stuff. And look at me!"

"You mean it hasn't *helped?*" Sheba said, a little aghast.

"Far be it from me to say *that.* But . . ."

But Sheba had already relaxed. "I feel like I've been asleep my whole life, until *tonight.* I swear, I feel like I've been a *zombie,* just walkin' around in a daze." She turned suddenly to face Marlowe directly and took her arm with a fierce grip. "I want to *love!* I want my life to be *filled with love,* nothing but love! I don't want to waste any more time, Marlowe—I *want* love. All the time!"

"Me too," Marlowe said; and she was filled, abruptly, with sadness.

II

The View from Above

LATER, SHEBA RETURNED TO CIRCULATION, HER JUBILANCE UNIMPEDED; but Marlowe found that her own mood had been pricked like a balloon. As the party went on, a deepening melancholy settled on her; she felt less capable of the simplest social niceties, and at last, near midnight, she retreated entirely, wandering aimlessly at first through the house in search of haven. Finally, on a desperate whim, she climbed out through Daa's bedroom window onto the roof. Here, at least, was solitude, and she squatted gratefully on the flat, shingled ledge above the backyard, looking down on the celebration with a sense of helpless distance.

She might have been on another planet. Below her almost everyone she knew in California was dancing in the floodlights, to the genial rock music of Dante's band; or they were off in any of the dozens of cozy nooks and special crannies that graced the Lapidge Street house and grounds, sipping wine and talking or singing or making love. It was much the usual scene, except that at the northeast corner of the house's redwood deck, where Jackson had always used to hold forth at parties like this, leaning on the rail with a hand-rolled cigarette between his fingers, eyeing the garden below and talking a blue streak, Daa had set up the eight-and-a-half-by-eleven-inch photograph of him instead, in its polished maple frame. The altarlike little table on which the photograph had been placed was inches deep in flowers and pinecones and bits of mystical stone, and flanked by banks of candles glowing golden in their sooty jars in the cool night air. But the setup was not exactly having the healing, unitive effect that Daa had intended when she had ceremonially erected it that afternoon. Even from the rooftop Marlowe could see the cautious distance everyone kept from the makeshift shrine, the little island of uneasy awe that it created. No one quite knew what to do with this jutting, sharp reminder; the party broke around it like waves around a rock.

Marlowe had not known what to do with it herself, of course; it was a good part of why she was up here, observing the antic ebb and flow of the rites below her like an alien anthropologist. This tribe, above all, danced—the Holy Rose Parade was playing one of the songs Dante claimed to have received from angels, a straightforward rocker called "Jackson's Goin' Home," all major chords in the key of G, and everybody seemed to be on their feet. On the deck, Antoinette and Pesky and Daa were all dancing with each other, sloshing wine from their chalices; Shakti and her boyfriend gyrated in a trance of two at the yard's far edge, their eyes locked together, their hips synced as if they were part of the same magnetic field. On the band platform, Dante had climbed atop one of the amps for his guitar solo, and his eyes were rolling back in his head as he vanished into the rapture of the riff.

Marlowe sighed. The moon above her floated in the vast black sky; the silent rooftop, lit with silver, seemed a world apart. She was on a level with the taller trees here, and the leaves nearby stirred in the cool night breeze. Unexpectedly, she could hear crickets from the quiet yard next door, and as she sat listening to them, Marlowe felt a peace beginning to steal over her, and a quiet sense of strength.

The feeling crept up softly, as if from the buffering dark trees below. She almost held her breath, for fear of scaring it away, but it stayed, as delicate and as stable as the moonlight. Jackson had used to climb out on this same roof with her to sunbathe. They would talk about everything, Marlowe recalled—plumbers, angels (pro and con), Hollywood, minimalism, meditation techniques, and who was sleeping with whom. What was it about Jackson that had made everything seem more profound when he said it? Marlowe wondered. He had been as silly as any of them. He followed the stock market closely, an odd habit in someone who lived on six hundred dollars a month. Jackson, sleek with oil, bronzed and slim and beautiful in the sun, would bring the *New York Times* West Coast edition up to the roof with him and exclaim over the previous day's NYSE results; he rooted for certain stocks the way some people rooted for baseball teams. He kept orchids, faithfully, frivolously, right up to the end, spending money on plants that he should have spent on—well, on *something*. There must have been something more important than orchids. But that was one of the things about Jackson, he had made you feel that money spent on orchids was well spent in any case. Marlowe's studio now was crowded, ringed with orchids; she fed and watered them faithfully according to the instructions he had written in a shaky hand during the last weeks of his life. And from time to time one would burst into bloom and astound her. Just that morning, she had come in to a stunning fuchsia-colored blossom that had opened overnight; its fragrance had made the air heavy with sweetness.

Recalling it now, Marlowe felt heartened. Around her the silver light glittered on every possible surface. Perhaps this was what Daa always meant when she talked of drawing down the moon—Marlowe could believe for an instant that Jackson's soul had found a home in this fullness of unearthly light, and even that his passing was part of a larger journey, a round in a cyclic dance. He was gone only as a waning moon was gone, or gone as an orchid blossom faded while the bulb lived on, lost to sight by a trick of cosmic rhythm, before some inconceivable waxing of the spirit into new flesh.

Everyone she knew had been saying more or less exactly this, of course, for months now: it was the "spiritual" view. But the spiritual view had been ringing painfully false to Marlowe; it had seemed like the nervous babbling of children. For this instant, however, for just this instant buoyed by the silver light, the note rang true; and it seemed to her to redeem the dance below. It seemed to redeem all of California, for that matter; it redeemed the world. *This,* just this sense of the spirit's enduring presence, was what the party was all about; they had come together to sing the praises of this.

Marlowe stirred. Unexpectedly, she was eager to join her friends again, and she crept backward, crablike, toward Daa's open bedroom window.

III

An Unexpected Encounter

ON THE MAKESHIFT STAGE, THE BAND HAD PAUSED BETWEEN SONGS TO regroup. Dante had his guitar out and was tuning up for the next effort. Daa and Toni Lafontane were sitting on the back steps with a bottle of wine. Jack Soft Hands and Pesky were deep in conversation on the other side of the deck, both of them wearing red-and-white aprons after the last round of dishes. They appeared to be exchanging recipes. Shakti Arguello appeared to be doing an astrology chart on a napkin for Jackson's mother, who looked dubious but not entirely averse. On the backyard's grassy expanse, people were beginning to stir again, in anticipation of the band's starting up. Almost everyone was dancing now.

The music began again just as Marlowe was climbing back in through the window, and she smiled to hear it. The reassuring wail of Dante's lead guitar was quite distinct, and the low lilt of Stan's electric oboe, and Martin's mandolin. Marlowe even recognized the song they were playing, though she had heard it previously only on Jackson's acoustic guitar. The Holy Rose Parade was playing "Bridge to the Other Side," a song that Jackson had written when he was seventeen.

> *And I'll see you there, I'll see you there—*
> *we've been there all along—*
> *there, where the world is a lover's face*
> *and its voice is a perfect song.*

As she paused in the darkness of the bedroom, getting her bearings, Marlowe could hear shuffling footsteps on the stairs. Someone was making his way upward, wheezing and comically clumsy. Marlowe tensed and stayed back in the shadowed doorway, out of sight, unwilling, after all, to be returned too soon to the human world.

It was Jackson's father. She recognized the stooped shoulders, and the John Deere cap. He had apparently wandered away from the party in search of a toilet. Marlowe watched him stumble down the hall and into the open bathroom at the end; he left the door open, and for lack of anything better to do she watched him unzip his trousers and saw the long arc of urine sparkling in the moonlight through the window.

Some odd humility in the act surprised and touched her. She remembered that earlier she had avoided the man, knowing that while Jackson was alive, he had condemned his son as perverse. Sitting in the chair by the fireplace all afternoon, and into the evening, drinking steadily and holding forth, he had seemed as rigid and limited to her as her own father, as fortified against life by alcohol and prejudice, and as out of his depth. Only here did he seem human for the first time. He had Jackson's nose, Marlowe realized, seeing it in moonlit silhouette—or rather, of course, Jackson had his.

As she watched, he zipped up his pants and started back; and then, three steps from the stairs, he paused and sank abruptly to his knees. The movement had the air, almost, of a collapse. Marlowe started toward him instinctively, then caught herself and waited, hushed, still hidden in the doorway's shadow.

The upstairs hall grew quiet once more; the band outside had finished the song, and then a second song, before Jackson's father finished his prayer and got back to his feet and lumbered back down the stairs toward the party; and even then Marlowe waited a while before she went back herself, for fear that he might feel shamed somehow in having been seen.

Part IX

In the Stars

I hear the aged footsteps like the motion of the sea.
—Bob Dylan

I

Shakti Arguello

NOT LONG AFTER THE PARTY, SHEBA WENT TO HAVE HER ASTROLOGICAL chart done by Shakti Arguello, whom she had met over the punch bowl. Shakti lived in the Berkeley hills, in an enormous angular house with a great westward facade of tall glass sheets that caught the sun and made the house through the late afternoon appear to be a source of glaring light. To Sheba, glimpsing it repeatedly as she drove the old laboring Datsun she had recently purchased up the winding road to the ridge, it seemed auspicious to have spotted the house from so far off. Shakti's directions had been breathtakingly simple—her place, she had told Sheba, was "the highest thing in sight." Though this did little to help Sheba through the maze of contorted lanes an actual arrival necessitated, it did convey a stylish truth. She chugged up the steep driveway only fifteen minutes late.

Shakti met Sheba at the door with an extravagant hug. She was a hostess gracious almost to the extreme, so much so that Sheba was slightly unnerved, and even dubious of her new acquaintance's sincerity. But as time passed and she saw Shakti's energy to be consistent, she began to relax, to accept and even to relish Shakti's phenomenal vitality. She was a kind of gracious force of nature.

The first order of business was a tour of the place. Shakti exhibited her exquisite domain with an air of deferential apology that became a subtle mutual flattery: pointing out this or that fine touch, she seemed to imply that her guest had probably noticed it already and was accustomed to better.

The very ground beneath their feet proved holy—each carpet

seemed to have its own numinous tale. This Persian rug woven by a Sufi saint over a period of years; that afghan created by a master even amidst the tumult of the Soviet invasion and smuggled out through the mountains by the same route along which arms to the freedom fighters were being smuggled in; and so on, until Sheba could not help but feel honored to walk about, with her shoes carefully removed.

She could also not help comparing this place with Jack's Immortality Environment; and the comparison crystallized a sense that had slowly been dawning on her since the party, of Jack as a cheerful primitive. Shakti Arguello didn't need flashing lights synchronized to the seven chakric frequencies to belabor the spirituality of her domain; dozens of subtle touches proclaimed it without the least effort on her part. Here was a horn acquired on pilgrimage to Tibet, bestowed on her by a lama now imprisoned by the Communists; and there a hand-carved ivory Buddha figure, acquired in 1964 by her first husband on his own pilgrimage to the East. It had been made by a Vietnamese monk who later that year had immolated himself, sitting serenely in lotus posture in the fire, to protest the corrupt regime and the war itself.

Every object in the house seemed similarly radiant with hard-won meaning. Sheba was awed at how many people seemed to have died or been imprisoned or tortured to produce such assembled magnificence. The ambitions of IHI seemed a braying in comparison, a crass rough draft of this quietly realized spirituality; and for all her gratitude to Jack, Sheba decided now, on the spot, that she was done with Immortality Thinking and the Science of Eternal Life and banana smoothies. It was time to move on, to deepen herself. It was time to grow up.

II

An Auspicious Conjunction

THEY SETTLED AT LAST IN THE LIVING ROOM, WITH INDONESIAN TEA. BEyond the solid wall of high windows the sun was setting across the Bay, backlighting San Francisco with red and gold. Sheba became aware for the first time of the delicate scent of champa pervading the room and could again not help but compare—even Shakti's incense was a reproach to Jack's olfactory assault. The carpet here was a mere deep pile, cream colored and so lush that Sheba longed to roll around on it and run her hands over its surface for the pleasure of changing the grain. She contented herself with sinking into the vast off-white sofa, amid a tasteful scatter of plump blue pillows patterned with a Matisse print. Shakti settled opposite her in a matching cushion chair, curling her shapely tanned feet up under her and smiling a down-to-business smile more dazzling than ever, as if her earlier displays of teeth had been the merest warm-up.

"So," she said. Having taken Sheba's natal information at the party, Shakti produced now an exquisite hand-drawn and hand-colored birth chart. She slid this over the big glass coffee table between them, and Sheba accepted it with some awe, holding it cautiously between her fingertips and marveling at the artistry and the alien, inscrutable symbols.

"I took the liberty of superimposing your progressed chart, which indicates the current alignment of planets relative to the position of the planets at your birth. Your natal planets are in blue, and the present configuration is in green."

"And the purple?" Sheba said, savoring the colorful mandala pattern.

114

Shakti, to Sheba's amazement, blushed a little. "Well, it's odd, I know, it may sound strange—but the purple is *my* chart. For some reason while I was doing yours, I was inspired to see how it meshed with mine—and lo and behold!" Shakti's slender fingers made a motion like a hula dancer's, indicative of delight.

"It's real pretty."

"We *fit.* We're simpatico. I was *thrilled*—I mean, I'd already had a sense from your aura, at the party—but *this.*"

"Uh-huh," Sheba said uncertainly.

"Look at the Venuses, for instance, it's a very pure sextile, and the Marses are trined. The moons are in opposition, but that can be a blessing in disguise . . ." And Shakti went on at length, singing the praises of the various conjunctions, commonalities, and complements with a relentless, if highly technical, enthusiasm, until even Sheba, who understood only the smallest fraction of what Shakti was saying, had to agree that the degree of karmic coincidence was extraordinary. Sheba was flattered, moreover, that this beautiful, glamorous, and accomplished woman should be so frankly delighted to find their destinies intertwined.

Shakti then proceeded to sketch Sheba's childhood and youth in surprising detail and depth, noting significant events, relationships, traumas, turning points, with an accuracy that Sheba first resisted inwardly and then surrendered to as a kind of miracle. The recent history in particular was unnervingly apt—the move to California, it seemed, had been inevitable for a number of spiritual and planetary reasons. Victor Morris showed up, in the guise of an overactive Mars. Her Uranus, activated by a passing Mercury, would prove decisive, however. Everything made perfect sense, more or less. And when Shakti launched into Sheba's near and distant future, barely pausing to sip her tea, the air cleared entirely. The road ahead held certain spiritual trials and tests, but for the most part the forecast was for glory.

"You're blessed," Shakti concluded a little breathlessly, falling back in her chair in happy marveling. "Coming and going, you're blessed. You brought tremendous spiritual gifts to this incarnation; this is the chart of a very old, very advanced soul. The only problem has been expression, which has been blocked by the Saturn factors I mentioned, and the afflicted Mercury and hyperactive Mars. But I think that with Jupiter's influence in the creative house beginning to predominate now, you'll find that all that will change. It will be a time of great spiritual expansion—things are going to take off for you in a big way." Shakti flashed her brilliant smile; in the much-darkened room, it was all of her face that was visible, and Sheba realized that the sun had set while they talked. As if in response to her thought, the room's three lamps all clicked on at once. Sheba jumped, startled; and Shakti laughed.

"Well, that's synchronistic, isn't it?" Shakti said. "Let there be light . . ."

"How—?"

"It's the automatic timer. It's set for this time of day. And your life is going to do the same thing now, Sheba—the time has come. You're going to click on like a lightbulb and shine the way you were always meant to shine."

Sheba looked at the glass wall behind her. At the center of it was a small altar, of such simplicity and taste that she had not noticed it before. It held only a gardenia floating in a china rice bowl, and a small picture of a man with a shaved head and orange robes. The window itself had gone opaque when the lamps came on: she could see only their reflection in it now, a cozy image that closed them off from the night outside; and she was filled with happiness at the sight.

"Wow," she said, feeling the inadequacy of words, and then she flushed.

But Shakti only laughed kindly. "Wow is right."

III

Conflicted Aspects

JACK TOOK THE NEWS OF SHEBA'S DECISION TO BREAK WITH THE INSTITUTE for Health and Immortality with grace, for the most part, mingled with a pathetic resignation. He had seen it coming, he said mournfully, as other, lesser influences entered her life. It was even to be expected—many were called, as he said, but few were chosen.

Jack was in any case preoccupied with larger troubles of his own. It appeared that the mummified body of the founder, only recently discovered by city health officials, was a gross violation of any number of local ordinances, and the authorities were insisting that it be removed and disposed of properly. IHI had taken the case to court, arguing that their constitutional right to freedom of religion was being abused; and a district judge had issued a temporary restraining order, allowing the founder to remain for the time being in his state of deferred decay. But the case was to be heard before the state court soon, and Jack, along with the rest of the IHI congregation, was in a state of nervous expectancy.

The stress was affecting his health—the day Sheba broke the news of her spiritual departure to him, he was snuffling and red-eyed from a lingering, galling cold, and drinking such quantities of carrot juice in his attempt to turn the tide that his skin had taken on a faint orange tint. He implied without actually saying so that Sheba's abandonment of the principles of Immortality could not have come at a worse time and was akin to a rat's fleeing a sinking ship. Sheba for her part was surprised to find herself feeling guilty, an emotion she resented under the circumstances as just too ridiculous; and for some time afterward she avoided Jack.

IV

A Profusion of Oracles

THIS PROVED EASY ENOUGH—SHE WAS, SUDDENLY, ALMOST NEVER HOME. Shakti's delight in their mingled destinies showed no sign of cooling; Sheba spent most of her evenings at the house on the hill, and in the weeks that followed the first astrological session, more and more thorough readings followed. There were tarot readings, I Chings and runes, tea leaves, and palms—Shakti, it seemed, read everything. The universe was a book of meaning to her, in subtle code. All texts continued to proclaim a new era in Sheba's soul.

The tarot deck and its symbols in particular fascinated Sheba; unlike her birth chart and its attendant foreign vocabulary, the cards made a sort of intuitive sense to her, so much so that a pleased Shakti gave her her own deck and began teaching her its ways. Before long, Sheba was doing readings of her own, for herself, and for everyone who would sit still for one. One night she laid a spread for Marlowe that seemed to indicate the approach of the man of her dreams, which gave them both a good laugh, only slightly uneasy on Marlowe's part. Sheba did a spread for Daa that showed nothing but happiness ahead for her. She did a spread for Jack that was dominated by awkwardness—the Hanged Man came up prominently, as did the Tower, indicating the destruction of hubris-suffused human institutions. Jack just nodded gloomily, as if he had known it all along, and went back to his room. He was spending a lot of time in his room, thinking about death. It had occurred to him, amidst all the recent difficulties, that he might not be immortal after all.

V

The Persistence of Victor Morris

SHEBA EVEN DID A SPREAD FOR VICTOR MORRIS, WHO CONTINUED TO show up at the Lapidge Street house regularly, with ritual stubbornness. The cards said that he should go back to Virginia.

Vic had gotten a studio apartment in the Mission, and a job as a carpenter on a nearby construction site. He seemed in no way deterred by either the tarot's advice or Sheba's unrelenting refusals to consider their relationship as anything but a historical item. He maintained an air of confidence and cheerfulness that perversely endeared him to Marlowe, and even to Daa—with whom, to everyone's astonishment, he would have far-ranging and remarkably good-natured arguments on every topic imaginable. Daa and Vic would sit in the kitchen for hours, discussing American foreign policy, the merits of organic agriculture, and the role of women. Vic would even ask Daa's advice on what he should do about Sheba, to which she would invariably reply that he should show his faith in true love by leaving her alone. If Sheba came back to him, Daa said, it was meant to be; and if she did not, it was also meant to be. True love, Daa said, was the simplest thing in the universe. If love was real, nothing could change it in the long run, and so in the short run he should just relax.

Vic took this advice, for the most part, to heart. He pushed nothing; he bided his time; he waited. He seemed to feel he had made his position clear enough, and he was prepared to watch Sheba go through any amount of "that spiritual stuff," as he called it, while the inherent strength of his true love dawned on her. He was fortified in his patience by his inability to take anything that happened in California seriously. Only Sheba's stubbornness, which he seemed to consider with pleasure to run a close second to his own, did he take seriously; and in recognition of it he did in fact get California plates for his truck. He never tired of reminding people that love was a long road.

Sheba noted the new plates on the Chevy with amusement only—she could as little take Victor Morris seriously at this point as he could take California. Lounging in the evenings in Shakti Arguello's backyard hot tub, looking up through the gently rising steam at the stars that had shaped her life and relieved her of Virginia, she was immensely grateful. Shakti was making it a point to introduce her widely in her broad circle of friends and activities—there were, in addition to the hot tub, the astrology and the tarot tutoring, evening programs at the Dharmananda ashram, Saturday drives to the wine country in Napa Valley, picnics at the beach and walks in the hills, and the pleasures of the frequent "spiritual soirees" for which Shakti was known, attended by a host of various devotees and evolved beings almost as gracious and sophisticated as Shakti herself.

Her life, Sheba thought, had never been fuller, nor more imbued with a sense of vibrant and significant expansion. Certainly she had no time to regret the loss of a career as Mrs. Victor Morris, or to be more than occasionally irritated at the persistence of the option.

VI

Dante Too

ANOTHER OPTION THAT PERSISTED WAS, TO EVERYONE'S ASTONISHMENT, Dante Pruitt. He had, it turned out, been smitten by Sheba's beauty at the party, and though he was characteristically obscure and ineffectual about his courtship, Marlowe's friend had taken to showing up at the Lapidge Street house at odd hours with a little portable sound system. He would plug in his guitar and play love songs at a reduced volume. Aside from the music, he was so skittish and oblique that no one knew what to make of him, least of all Sheba. Generally he got no farther than the backyard—he would slip in along the side alley and set up near the fountain and sing his odd lilting songs; and then he would flee. Apparently he was ransacking Guillaume De Lorris for his lyrics; he kept offering up bits of the *Roman de la Rose* in four-four time, with a bit of a backbeat on his synthesizer's automatic drum.

> *My longing drew*
> *Me towards the rosebush and then flew*
> *Through all my soul its savour sweet,*
> *Which set my heart and pulse abeat*
> *Like fire. And were it not for fear*
> *That I the scot might pay too dear,*
> *I surely should have dared to seize*
> *A rosebud, seen nought else could please*
> *My senses equally.*

Sheba, more bewildered than flattered, appeared to view Dante as some strange species of California songbird. She would go to the kitchen window to chuckle over his performances in much the same spirit as she might have gone to get a better view of a hummingbird at the hanging feeder. As Dante appeared incapable of bearing even the slightest bit of more personal attention from her anyway, this arrangement had a certain stability.

Marlowe suffered Dante's bizarre courtship of her cousin with mixed feelings. She was mortified for him and pained to see him make such a fool of himself. Sometimes she would be in her studio when he showed up to sing. In the old days he would have come in to see her and done Mozartian jams on the theme of her latest painting, but now he went right to his spot beyond the fountain and sang to the kitchen window, whether Sheba was there or not. Marlowe, unable to concentrate on painting her mops then, would find herself sketching him, as a troubadour, or as a fool. And she would sometimes surprise herself with tears: her heart was wrung with sharp poignancy. Dante's naïveté and ineffectuality tore at her. He had not a ghost of a chance with Sheba; that was clear. She did not take him seriously, and she never would. He could only get hurt. Marlowe tried to tell him so, as gently as she could. But she could not dissuade him from his futile efforts. She had never, indeed, seen him happier.

Nor had she ever seen Jack unhappier. Marlowe came upon him one afternoon in the kitchen making a listless smoothie. Since the Institute for Health and Immortality had begun to unravel into scandal, Jack had hardly gone out of the house, but he continued to live on smoothies and spirulina. Instead of the potent immortality mantra issued him by IHI, though, he kept a secular silence while the blender ran.

Jack's hair was uncombed, his cotton garb was rumpled, and his brown eyes were bloodshot; to Marlowe it looked suspiciously as if he had been drinking, but she doubted that this was so. More likely he was drunk on disillusionment. She knew that he was still reading books about death.

He actually looked good, Marlowe thought, with a three-day growth of beard. Of course, with Jack, a three-day growth of beard took several weeks to attain.

Preoccupied as he was, it took Jack a moment to notice her entrance; when he did, he froze briefly, like a wild animal, as if he might flee.

"You look like hell, Jack."

Jack relaxed. "I know," he said with a faint trace of satisfaction.

"Undeferred decay. It's actually sort of appealing, in a rough way."

"I think I have a tumor."

Marlowe's heart went out to him. He reminded her, actually, of Aumakua, who had gone through a similar disillusionment when his tai chi teacher was arrested for statutory rape and possession of cocaine.

"I'll bet you don't," she said.

"The body can crystallize its stresses, you know. And I've been thinking so many negative thoughts lately. Maybe—"

"Jack . . . Jack, sweetheart, relax. It's just a bad phase. It will pass."

He hesitated; she noticed that his lower lip was trembling. Oh, God, Marlowe thought, please don't let him start blubbering. But she moved toward him instinctively and put her arms around him, and sure enough Jack started to cry.

"I've been taking extra B complex and neg ions for strength," he said. "But I don't feel very strong at all."

Part X

A Difficult Thanksgiving

Up from Earth's Centre through the Seventh Gate
I rose, and on the Throne of Saturn sat,
    And many knots unravelled by the Road;
But not the Knot of Human Death and Fate.
                                        —Omar Khayyam

I

A Posthumous Fifteen Minutes of Fame

BY AN ODD TURN OF EVENTS, JACKSON MADE THE COVER OF *NEW NEW York* magazine's mid-November issue. Marlowe's onetime boyfriend Greg Sturmmacher had done the portrait for the slick weekly as an exquisite parody of everything Californian—in a faux-Manet style, the painting showed a group of people picnicking in the manner of *Le déjeuner sur l'herbe*, surrounded by the remnants of a fast-food lunch. A serene figure, recognizably Jackson, sat at the heart of the little group, in a full-lotus posture with an expression of fatuous bliss on his beautiful face. The rest of the picnickers, including the naked ones, were suitably insipid. The Golden Gate in the background, through the trees, established the location.

Sturmmacher had caught the beauty, all right, Marlowe thought ruefully, studying the Jackson figure. After her first clear impulse to kill her old boyfriend for the presumption and violation had passed, she was afraid her heart might break, so perfectly had Sturmmacher captured a quality of Jackson's that she herself had been trying to paint for years. Sturmmacher's contempt had freed him to use the truth: Jackson radiated loveliness and peace, serene as any caricature wise man; with the deftest touch, Sturmmacher had made him ridiculous. The cover story was entitled "Twilight of the Idle: California's Empty New Spirituality," and the lengthy text spent a great deal of time establishing that too many people on the West Coast had nothing better to do than dabble in meaningless spiritual fads that distracted them from the essential vapidity of their lives.

True enough, Marlowe thought. She could have written the article herself; the usual suspects from auras to past lives to self-indulgent tantra had been rounded up, and she didn't begrudge the writer, whoever he was, his target practice on such sitting ducks. He got paid by the word, after all; it was nothing personal. But the accompanying artwork was something else. Looking at the picture of Jackson on the *New New York* cover once more, Marlowe wanted to kill Sturmmacher all over again. It was so like Greg to unerringly defile the only genuine thing around.

She even knew when he had done his sketches for the work. Sturmmacher had visited the Lapidge Street house in 1987, at Marlowe's invitation. He had been in San Francisco on the closest thing to a vacation Sturmmacher was capable of, a spasmodic flight from his real life, a sort of mobile mental breakdown conducted in motel rooms. He had been at the low point of his career; his vicious paintings were not selling, his last show had been savagely panned by the New York critics, and he was doing advertising graphics and T-shirt designs to pay the rent—and making good money at it, which only galled him more. Marlowe had felt sorry for him, for once, a big mistake in retrospect. Sympathy was no protection; like Mexican water, Sturmmacher in even the smallest doses could make her sick. But she had felt superior in her own poverty; selling out seemed to have made Sturmmacher vulnerable. She had invited him over to the Lapidge Street house, and Sturmmacher had showed Marlowe and Jackson his commercial portfolio one night over a big bottle of wine, mocking himself cruelly. He could actually be entertaining briefly, when he turned his venom on himself.

It had been a odd evening. Daa had left the house early, in disgust; she could not bear Sturmmacher's presence. But Jackson had stayed. He had—not *liked* Sturmmacher, exactly, Marlowe thought, but seen through him in a way that had come across as kindness. He had found Sturmmacher interesting, as a sort of pure phenomenon; he could apparently appreciate Greg's desperation. Marlowe remembered the two of them talking at some length about emptiness, a theme they shared in surprising depth. Jackson's emptiness, of course, was the Buddhist void, the essential insubstantiality of samsaric existence; for him, to see through the painful grasping at vanities that was the human condition gave out into compassion, in the end; while for Sturmmacher, as far as Marlowe could tell, seeing through the obvious illusions got him only as far as a kind of stylish, slightly sadistic wallowing in the suffering. To Sturmmacher the rest of Buddhism's Noble Truths were for the birds. He despised the notion of transcendence as escapist, and he thought the Eightfold Path was a feudal remnant of archaic social power dynamics.

Still, Marlowe knew, Greg had been impressed with Jackson. He had told her afterward that Jackson understood the ground of his painting better than anyone else he had met. Marlowe had had to laugh at that. What Jackson had understood, she thought, had been Sturmmacher's abyss; he was prepared by temperament and philosophy not to flinch before the corrosive blackness in which the painter made his home. Buddhism, after all, even in its facile escapism, allowed for any number of hells; and in any case Jackson had been watching his friends die one by one of AIDS for years by then. His serenity had been tempered by fires fiercer than Greg Sturmmacher's unhappiness with iconic inadequacy and the failures of painterly surface.

Greg had also been taken with Jackson's features; he thought Jackson had an absolutely classic face. He had come back the next day with a sketchbook, and Jackson, amused, had sat for him for a series of studies. The drawings had been good, Marlowe recalled, uncharacteristically sensitive—not tender, that would have been too much to expect of Sturmmacher, but delicate, cool, and elegant. They had lacked the spite that almost invariably tipped Sturmmacher's portraits over into subtle caricature. She had marveled then at what seemed like Jackson's taming of the beast; like Saint Francis, he had gentled the wolf, at least temporarily. Sturmmacher had gone back to New York a couple days later refreshed and renewed, and that had been the last Marlowe had heard from him for years, which suited her just fine. She hated fighting with Daa every time the man came to town.

Now, almost five years later, Jackson was dead, and the sketches Sturmmacher had done of him had apparently ended up as grist for the mill of spite after all. Marlowe stared at the magazine cover. The Manet parody was perfectly rendered; there was no doubting the skill this thing had required. Few people on the planet were talented enough to accomplish such vileness so deftly. She wondered how much Sturmmacher had been paid.

On an angry impulse, she called New York. Despite the time difference that made it nearly midnight on the East Coast, Marlowe knew her old boyfriend's habits. Sure enough, he answered his studio phone on the second ring, sounding preoccupied. "Hello?"

"You're lower than I ever thought possible, you mean-spirited piece of shit," she said without preamble.

"Marlowe?"

"It could be just about anybody, at this point, couldn't it?"

"No one quite has your style, dearest. And, ah, that voice, that voice. O sweet abuse, so achingly familiar. Do my ears deceive me? Can it really be you, darling?"

"You know goddamned well it's me. And I think you probably know why."

"I actually don't. But anything that got you to call me is good—whatever it is, I'm grateful."

"Fuck you, Greg. I'm looking at the cover of this week's *New New York.*"

"Oh? Did that come out already?" He actually sounded offhand.

"You *shit.*"

"Now, now, I thought it was rather good. Clever, you know. Manet is hard to *do,* it was really quite a challenge."

"I'm moved by your devotion to your art."

"Well, *art*—that's another matter altogether. But we all have to pay the rent, don't we? This was more a technical exercise, a tour-de-force kind of thing. They wanted something tasteful and zippy—a kind of satire haute, you know. Really, I'm surprised that you're so upset. It's not like you to lose your sense of humor—certainly not about something as harmless as a little tweaking of a few New Age noses."

"You're not that stupid, Greg."

"Didn't your friend like it? What's his name? Jason?"

Marlowe hesitated, unwilling, suddenly, to let Sturmmacher have any more of Jackson than he had already taken. But Sturmmacher had gone on: "No, right, right, *Jackson*. Smart guy, actually. A perfect face. Good sense of humor, too, as I recall—and of course, so very *sensitive.*"

"Is that the latest code among your crowd for homophobia?"

"Now, now, Marlowe. I meant spiritual sensitivity. Some of my best friends are gay. Some of them are even Buddhists."

Marlowe considered just hanging up. This wasn't accomplishing anything. Jackson didn't care; he would never have cared, he would have laughed. Sturmmacher *couldn't* care. But she was too angry to stop now. "You had no right, Greg. *No right.*"

"He sat for the sketches, as I recall. I think he might even have been flattered."

"He was humoring you."

"He might have been condescending. But the moment was deeply shared. Look, if he's pissed off, just remind him it's all maya anyway, it's all illusory, the play of emptiness. He'll know what I mean."

"He's *dead*, Greg. You fucking ghoul. He died last summer."

There was the briefest of pauses at the other end of the line, and she thought for an instant that Sturmmacher might slip and let some human quality show. But apparently not, for he just said, "Then certainly he'll understand that it's all illusory. I thought the likeness was rather flattering, actually."

Marlowe hung up the phone. Her hands were shaking with rage and frustration. She felt nauseated, literally physically sickened. Sturmmacher always made her feel that way. And what was worst of all, she thought, was not the sense of violation, not the mockery, not the posthumous insult: what was worst was the knowledge that Sturmmacher in his inhuman way was right. Jackson would have laughed. He would have laughed and laughed and put the goddamned picture up on the refrigerator.

II

The Swensens

As the holiday season came upon them, the tensions in the Lapidge Street house grew more pronounced. Sheba had been invited to a spiritual Thanksgiving bash at Shakti Arguello's, complete with a tofu turkey, pumpkin wine, and Native American dancing. Jack continued to stay in his room most of the time. Dante continued to sing under Sheba's window, and it was driving everyone a little nuts. Daa, ever alert to Marlowe's stresses, suggested some time away; and so the two of them flew to Minnesota and spent Thanksgiving with Daa's family.

Bob and Karen Swensen always cheered them up—over the years, Daa's parents had come to accept their daughter and her partner wholeheartedly, and holidays at the Swensen home in Minneapolis were for Marlowe small miracles of happy domesticity, time in a nurturing family atmosphere she had never found among her own clan. Thanksgiving in particular was a joy. Karen Swensen baked three kinds of pie and a mammoth turkey every year; she made her own cranberry sauce and dressing from ancient family recipes and baked yams and potatoes and pepper biscuits and pulled out all the bottled beans and corn from her summer garden. There was homemade ice cream to top the pies, cranked out in front of the various football games by Daa's father; and homemade Swedish-style beer after dinner, drunk from big weathered metal mugs, in front of the great stone fireplace. The house was filled with cooking smells and laughter from early in the morning, and Daa's siblings and their own burgeoning families arrived all day long from every corner of the state to add to the cheerful hubbub.

Daa was the only child who had actually left the confines of Minnesota, though her youngest brother, Danny—"the *other* wild one," as the Swensens had it—had gotten as far away as Duluth, where he operated a wilderness hunting and fishing guide service that often took him as far away as Montana and even into Canada; and so whenever Daa and Marlowe came to visit, they were treated as a great event. Both of Daa's parents still called their daughter Sheila, though they did not mind when Marlowe called her Daa. Daa's mother always put them into the best guest bedroom and took out the best quilt for their bed. Marlowe had wept in astonishment, the first time Karen had draped the big queen-size bed in her grandmother's quilt. The casual ceremony had seemed like an extraordinary blessing, an unimagined acceptance.

Aside from the frankness of the bedroom arrangements, Karen treated them both as daughters, gossiping and giggling with Marlowe as she did with Daa, always including and embracing, exchanging recipes and confidences and shared womanly looks when the menfolk got out of hand. And Daa's father, Bob, would always treat Marlowe respectfully and affectionately as Daa's husband—or Daa's wife, if it seemed to be going that way for the moment, shifting easily as circumstances demanded to give her status according to his ways of defining the human world of relationship. Marlowe was "the little woman," while Bob and Daa watched the football games together, as they had done since she was young; or, on visits when Daa helped in the kitchen and Marlowe would watch the football games instead, Bob Swensen would treat her with rough camaraderie and humor as one of the guys, as a member of the husband clan. He would ask her studiously about her painting, which he could not comprehend but honored as an awesome activity; or he would joke with her as he would have joked with any son-in-law about getting a *real* job and supporting his daughter in the manner to which she had grown accustomed.

At first this slightly strained overlay of incongruous roles had struck Marlowe as oppressive, but over the years she had come to recognize Bob's sincerity even when he seemed to her to play the buffoon; and she could appreciate his awkward tenderness toward Daa, the cautious heartfelt affection he showed, the way he labored to make his categories bend to include his daughter. Daa's father had always said he only wanted for Sheila to be happy, and it was his accomplishment to have seen that she was happy in a way he could not have imagined. His imagination still failed him regularly with regard to Daa and Marlowe; but in all the years they had been visiting Minneapolis, his love had not failed him at all.

III

Bad News

THIS THANKSGIVING WAS DIFFERENT FROM THE MOMENT DAA'S PARENTS met them at the airport. Daa's maternal grandmother had had a stroke the night before; she was at the hospital, on a respirator. The doctors said her brain had been hopelessly damaged, and that she would die if she was taken off the machine. Karen Swensen obviously had not slept. Her face was stretched and gray, and her eyes were red-rimmed. It had been a family joke, half-believed, that Daa's grandmother, who was ninety-three, would live forever.

Daa, to Marlowe's surprise, let out a wail at the news and began to sob uncontrollably. They stood awkwardly at the arrival gate, making a little island amid the stream of disembarking passengers, Karen with her arms around her weeping daughter, and crying herself now; Bob, unshaven, looking pained, patting both of them self-consciously; and Marlowe off to one side holding both their carry-on bags and trying desperately to recall Daa's grandmother's name. Edith? Edna? She had only the feeblest image of a broad white face floating above a tiny form swathed in blankets, in a big stuffed chair in the wing of the Swensens' house that Daa's father had added on when her grandmother was widowed in the late seventies. The old woman had not left her bedroom, except to go to the bathroom, since 1981. On all the major holidays everyone would do a ritual stop-in to say hello, but otherwise she had been a quiet, unobtrusive aspect of the house, alone with her crossword puzzles and her little bowl of Cheerios, which she nursed all day, and the soap operas on the television. Marlowe realized that she had thought of Daa's grandmother, when she thought of her at all, as something akin to a houseplant.

The thought provoked a stab of guilt. She felt oddly lacking in any emotion other than a sort of disappointment that their Thanksgiving would be spoiled, and dismay at her own peevishness. She was a selfish monster, there was no doubt about it. And it was snowing outside the big plate-glass windows of the Minneapolis airport terminal. Marlowe hated snow. She had gone to California in the first place, at least in part, in the explicit hope of never seeing snow again.

Daa continued to weep; Marlowe had never seen her lover so undone, and it made her uneasy. Daa had taken Jackson's death, and half a dozen other significant deaths, soberly, and in a balanced fashion, with dignity. She had celebrated them as passages. She had shaken her head over the mysterious ways of the universe. She had called down the moon and wished her friends well on their way. For Jackson, whom Marlowe knew Daa had loved deeply, she had read the *Tibetan Book of the Dead* aloud weekly, for seven weeks, to help his spirit through the bardos. But never before had she seemed to grieve with such spontaneous ferocity. Was her real life still here, then, in Minnesota? Did death in California somehow not count? Marlowe realized that she was irritated, as if her lover had kept something back. No one had wailed like this in public for Jackson.

And suddenly, to her surprise, Marlowe began to sob too. She was mortified to know that it was for Jackson and for her own loss and had nothing whatsoever to do with Daa's grandmother, whose name she could still for the life of her not recall—Emma? —but it still felt wonderful to let it rip. She cried and cried, as the airport attendants tried gently to ease the whole grieving group out of the direct flow of traffic; and she even took a perverse pleasure when Bob Swensen took her in his arms to comfort her and murmured that he understood, he really did, that he had come over the years to love dear Alva too.

IV

A Snowy Night

THEY DROVE DIRECTLY TO THE HOSPITAL. DAA HAD MORE OR LESS CALMED down by the time they got out of the airport parking lot. She sat in the backseat with her mother, the two of them, side by side, looking almost identical in their stolid pain. They talked in low tones together, square faces bent close, discussing respirator decisions. Karen had already resolved to have the machine turned off, after all the children had arrived; but Daa—again, to Marlowe's eyes, uncharacteristically—was arguing gently to leave it on. Bob Swensen drove in silence, attentive to the snow-slick road. An unlit cigarette dangled from his lips. Marlowe knew that he had been trying for years to quit smoking. From time to time he would lean forward and push in the car's cigarette lighter; then, moments later, he would pull it out again and leave the cigarette unlit.

Marlowe herself continued to cry quietly. She was amazed at the expanse of grief that had opened up in her; it seemed disproportionate, even to her feelings for Jackson. Perhaps it was the satisfaction that Daa and her parents were obviously taking in her response that was egging her on—to them her tears made her more deeply a part of the family. They were surprised and moved, gratified by the force of her reaction. Marlowe, knowing this, felt like a fraud. But it felt so good to let go. Jackson had told her once, quite late in his illness, not to be afraid of anything—not sadness, no matter how deep, not love, and especially not death. "Death is easy," he had said. "It's comedy that's tough."

She had laughed when he had said it. Jackson made everything seem easy. Now the memory made her cry harder. Every movement of her consciousness was making her cry. She felt that she must have been false since the day she was born, to have so much grief stored up: everything, it seemed, had made her sad. She had not taken a single thing, a single loss, a single disappointment, in stride. Jackson was wrong; they all were wrong. Death was not easy at all, it was impossible. She could not get it right— even now, crying at the right time, she was mourning the wrong death.

At the hospital, they were ushered at once to the bedside in intensive care. Daa's brothers and sisters were all there, and several aunts and uncles, each square Swensen face at once singular and similar. This only made Marlowe cry harder, all those variations on the same theme of a grief she did not share. Alva lay on the bed beneath a landscape of tubes, inert and gray, an afterthought to the mechanisms. The doctor came by and in low tones reaffirmed the impossibility of revival. Daa sobbed afresh and conceded; the machine was turned off. They all gathered close around the bed, but minutes passed and Alva did not die. Her breath was inaudible, her heartbeat weak. But she hung on.

Half an hour went by; chairs were brought. Daa had settled in with her siblings, and Marlowe slipped away. Down the hallway was a little waiting area with a television set, and beyond it through a glass door, a patio. Marlowe pulled her inadequate California coat around her and went outside.

It was twilight. The snow continued to fall steadily. The hospital grounds were swathed in soft white beneath the low gray sky, and the dark branches of the pine trees drooped beneath accumulating loads. She was alone on the patio, but after a few minutes the door opened behind her and another figure emerged and crossed to stand at the far rail, where he lit a cigarette. By the match's flare, Marlowe saw that it was Daa's youngest brother, Danny. She hesitated a moment, then went over to him. He glanced up as she approached.

"I should have known you'd be out here," he said. "Cigarette?"

"No, thanks."

Danny smiled. "That's right, I forgot, you're from California."

Marlowe laughed and settled her elbows on the rail beside him. It had a little of the feel of a ship's railing, looking out over a snowy night sea. "I'm from Long Island, actually. Everybody smokes on Long Island. It starts in junior high."

"But not you."

"I'm not on Long Island anymore."

Danny conceded the point by looking back out into the night. The patio was protected by an overhang, but at the rail they were exposed to the falling snow, and Marlowe watched the flakes gather and flatten and melt in his dark hair. That black hair was unique among the Swensen children. Danny was also the only other Swensen child besides Daa who had not married yet—the last, really, as Daa's family treated her for all intents and purposes as married to Marlowe. Danny in his early thirties still arrived with a different woman every Thanksgiving, unless, as this year, he came alone. His ongoing bachelorhood was an edgy family joke, and Danny could be defensive about it, though generally he took the teasing in stride. He was Marlowe's favorite among the clan. He had taken Daa and her out several times on camping trips into the north woods, which really seemed to be his element—among the pines, beside a chilly blue lake, he was at ease in a way that never came through in Minneapolis. One trip in particular, Marlowe thought, she had glimpsed him in a unique way. They had fished from a canoe all afternoon and cooked a delicious dinner of pike and bass and sat by the campfire late into the night talking and drinking beer. Daa had gone to bed first, and Marlowe and Danny had talked on quite late. It had been easy and warm and intimate; and when they had stood up to go to bed, they had both paused, and he had kissed her. She had not been surprised at all, she remembered; everything in their conversation seemed suddenly to have led up to it. She could still remember the feel of his mustache, the smell of wood smoke on his flannel shirt, and the taste of beer on his breath. His hands had been surprisingly tender. Uncannily, he had Daa's pale blue eyes, right down to the amusement crinkle that showed at their corners. She had never told Daa about the kiss, and she and Danny had never spoken of it afterward. She supposed that he felt as she did about it, that it had been an odd moment out of time, beneath a different sky, far from anywhere they knew.

"What do you mean, you should have known I'd be out here?" she said now.

Danny shrugged. "It doesn't take a rocket scientist. You're as out of place here as I am, in your way. And this is as far away as you can get."

Marlowe hesitated, resisting it obscurely, then shrugged herself. They looked out at the falling snow together for a moment.

"I guess I'll have one of those cigarettes after all," Marlowe said.

Danny laughed and held out the pack. He smoked Marlboros, Marlowe noted; all the boys in junior high had smoked Marlboros. Jimmy Jameson had smoked Marlboros. For a time, in eighth grade, the sun had risen and set around Jimmy Jameson. She drew a cigarette out and put it between her lips, and Danny lit it for her, leaning just close enough to make her wonder if he was thinking of that moment in the woods. She drew the smoke into her lungs and coughed until tears came to her eyes.

"It was snowing when my maternal grandmother died too," she said when she had recovered her breath.

"Oh?"

"I was six. She spit on me, when she died."

Danny looked at her. "You're kidding."

"No, she really did. It was very formal—she called me to her bed. She looked horrible, I remember. All I wanted to do was run away. But I went in. She was like an old wild woman, my grandmother—like a gypsy or something, like a druid witch. She gestured for me to bend close, and then she spit right into my hair. I just ran away—right out of the house, and into the snow. It was a regular blizzard, I remember—I almost froze to death. Literally, they found me in a snowbank with my legs all blue. But nothing would have made me go back in there. She died right after she spit on me, they said."

"Why did she spit on you?"

"It was her blessing, I think. She was that sort. It was her way of passing on her spirit. But I didn't even begin to understand that for about twenty-five years. Even now, sometimes, it feels more like a curse. I suppose I'll never know for sure."

"That's a crazy thing to do, to a little kid."

"Yeah."

They were silent for a time, a comfortable silence. At last, Danny flicked his cigarette butt over the rail, and they both watched it fall with the swift snow and disappear into the dark below.

"I suppose we should get back in there," he said, and looked at Marlowe; and she was sure, suddenly, that he remembered.

"I suppose we should."

Part XI

Season's Greetings

May I recognize my own mind
in the terrors that arise
May I know all this to be
like smoke, in the Bardo.
—Bardo Thodol
(The Tibetan Book of the Dead)

I
Merry Christmas

IT WAS A DIFFICULT DECEMBER. DAA'S GRANDMOTHER DID NOT DIE UNTIL Christmas Eve, and Daa stayed in Minnesota for the whole month, spending her days at the old woman's bedside, reading aloud to her from *The Arabian Nights* and Kipling's *Just So* tales, as her grandmother had done for her when she was a child. Alva was lucid only at two- or three-day intervals, floating to the surface of consciousness according to some rhythm of her own to open her pale blue eyes and blink, and smile, and possibly remark on something that had happened in the 1920s, or on some subtlety of Rikki-Tikki-Tavi's behavior with the cobra. She also mentioned the presence of her ancestors in the room at times—her mother and her grandmother and some woman she didn't recognize but loved nonetheless were apparently as real for her as Daa was. She would chat with them all for a bit—"a decent visit," as she said—and would then sink gently back into her peaceful fading state, and Daa would wait for her goose bumps to settle and then read on, drinking Swedish beer and eating potato chips with sour-cream French onion dip. She gained twelve pounds before her grandmother died, and after the funeral she came back to San Francisco changed in other ways as well. She had a sudden patience for everything; she was very serene, even in the face of Marlowe's usual holiday frenzy. And she was overflowing with generosity. Four days late, Daa bought Christmas presents for everyone she knew, something she had not done in a decade and a half, since they had decided that Christmas was a patriarchal Christian rip-off of the pagan solstice.

Every present was eerily on the mark. Sheba got a kitten, an actual live kitten, and burst into tears. She had dreamed a few nights before that all her stuffed animals had come to life and were speaking Californian. She called the new kitten, a brown-and-white female with one black ear, Rebirth, on the suggestion of Shakti Arguello, who was given to corny names; but everyone called her Reebie, or Re-Bop.

Jack got a basketball from Daa, a seemingly goofy gift that made them all laugh until he put up a backboard and hoop over the garage door and began spending hours in the driveway shooting baskets. It turned out that Jack had been a passable point guard in high school, with a nifty jump shot from the top of the key and a good driving move to the basket. Marlowe marveled, watching him—there was a grace and truth to Jack on a basketball court that she had previously believed resided only in his hands during massages. All his phoniness fell away. It only made it more unbearable, of course, when he put the basketball away; but the glimpse had been revelatory. These glimpses through the cracks showed that there was always hope.

Daa gave Victor Morris a set of her own tarot cards, an exquisite Wicca deck that he used to play a modified game of solitaire, and gin rummy. She bought Dante a Kashmiri flute and a gong from Tibet that was said to be able to summon the dead. She sent one of her grandmother's best handmade quilts to Toni and Pesky, in Mendocino, and gave two silver spoons from Alva's wedding set to Shakti Arguello, who Daa thought needed to get married.

To Marlowe, Daa gave the diamond engagement ring her grandfather had traveled to Chicago to buy for her grandmother in 1921. Alva, in one of her last lucid moments, had taken it off her own finger and given it to Daa. Marlowe, speechless and unnerved, contained an urge to give it back. She had spent the month that Daa had been in Minnesota in her studio, painting snowstorms, blizzards that obliterated all trace of landscape, in cold, cold colors; and she felt chilled to the bone inside and out. Daa's warmth only made her feel a kind of failure in herself. But she did her best, she put the ring on and wept. She'd never seen Daa so beautiful.

II

Ring In the New

SHEBA FELL IN LOVE THAT NEW YEAR'S EVE, WITH BODHICITTA SCORICH, known to his friends as Chris. She met him at Shakti Arguello's New Year's Eve party, not long before midnight. He was standing in one of the little spotlights that Shakti placed around her house, peering at an old Tibetan prayer wheel that was said to have been turned by the master Jikme Lingpa in the eighteenth century. As she watched, the prayer wheel turned by itself—once, twice, three times. Sheba looked at Scorich in astonishment, and he looked back at her, perfectly calm.

"Did you *see* that?" she said.

"Just pretend that you're dreaming," he said, "and everything will be fine."

She suspected at once that he was an extremely advanced being. She would have checked this out with Shakti, but Shakti was absorbed in conversation with Victor Morris, whom she had invited to the party at Sheba's request, out of compassion for his loneliness during the holidays. Victor at that moment did not look lonely at all; and neither did Shakti, for that matter. She was laughing at everything Victor said.

Sheba watched Scorich closely for the rest of the night, alert to new miracles. He was drinking Evian water and eating rice cakes, a tall, thin man with rich black hair and blue eyes that seemed to take everything in. He reminded her of a panther—perhaps it was his black sweater and slacks, or the sleek cat's grace of his movement; but he seemed dangerous, lithe and poised. He was a student of the Tibetan master Dak Dzin Rinpoche, Shakti told her, when Sheba was finally able to catch her friend away from

Victor Morris. Shakti herself seemed a little awed by Scorich. He had been meditating for almost twenty years, she said; he had studied in Nepal and knew Sanskrit and Tibetan. One of Dak Dzin Rinpoche's translators, Scorich had rendered a number of his written works into English.

"Does he have a girlfriend?" Sheba said.

Shakti sniffed. "I believe he's more or less transcended all that sort of thing," she said, and went off in search of Victor Morris. Sheba, feeling chastised and crude, spent the next interval of time resolutely avoiding Chris Scorich's eyes; but when the count-down to midnight came, she found that he was standing beside her. They looked at each other, and it seemed to her that he understood everything. The whole room faded away and there was nothing but his face, and he smiled. No words were neces-sary. As the New Year struck, he kissed her, once, and then, like the prayer wheel turning, a second time. *Just pretend that you're dreaming,* Sheba told herself, *and everything will be fine.* And sure enough, he kissed her a third time, and they laughed together, at how silly it all was, and how easy.

III

Happy New Year

SHEBA CAME BACK TO THE LAPIDGE STREET HOUSE THAT NIGHT JUST AFTER 3 A.M., singing to herself. Chris Scorich had given her a ride home, and they had talked all the way, about dzogchen and Padmasam-bhava and the luminous Ground of Being. Sheba felt that she had never met anyone so dedicated and so wise and so sexy. He had kissed her goodnight and touched her tongue lightly once with his, and she had been sure that the luminous Ground of Being was as plain to her at that moment as it had ever been to anyone on the planet Earth.

The lights were on in the kitchen. Sheba came into the room still singing and found Marlowe sobbing, across the table from a stony-faced, angry Daa.

"Oh, Marlowe!" Sheba cried, rushing to her. "What is it?"

Marlowe only shook her head and continued to sob, burying her face deeper in her arms. Sheba, pained, looked across for help to Daa.

"She's pregnant," Daa said curtly.

"Pregnant! But how—I mean, who—?"

"Jack," Daa said, the syllable clipped with contempt; and she rose abruptly and left the room.

Sheba, marveling, pulled a chair up beside Marlowe's and sat close to her, draping her arm ineffectually across her cousin's shoulders. Marlowe resisted comfort and sobbed on for some time, her body heaving pathetically. At last, though, she began to calm a little and raised her head. Sheba promptly offered paper towels, and Marlowe accepted one and even managed a wry, wet smile.

"What a mess, huh?" she said, and blew her nose.

"You look okay," Sheba said weakly.

"The hell with my looks," Marlowe said with more of her usual bite. "I'm talking about my goddamned *life.*"

"What *happened?*"

"What do you *think* happened? You're a big girl, Sheba. Use your imagination."

"No, I mean—well, I thought—"

"Well, you thought wrong. It's never as simple as you think." She banged her fist on the table, so sharply that Sheba jumped. "*Shit.* Shit, shit, *shit.*"

"Did he *seduce* you?" Sheba said, unable yet to progress much beyond the shock of Jack's involvement. She felt vaguely violated herself.

"Sheba, this is not a Jane Austen novel, this is consenting adults. Do you think I'd let an idiot like Jack seduce me? If anything, I seduced *him.*"

"*When?*"

"Oh, God, I don't know. November, sometime before Thanks-

giving. The first time, anyway. He was like a little puppy dog or something, with all that stuff about IHI falling apart. I felt sorry for him, I guess. And I was feeling lousy too and thought it might help.''

Sheba was silent, reviewing the past two months in the light of this fresh information. She couldn't help it, and she was sure it showed her lack of sophistication, but there it was: she was shocked.

"It's ironic, I suppose," Marlowe went on. "You think of it as the male thing, to use sex that way. I even remember being sort of impressed with myself that night, that I had turned the tables, reversed the roles. But ha-ha, the joke's on me. It's my oven the bun's in. I suppose that's why the roles were what they were in the first place.''

"Does Jack know?"

"Oh, yes. Why do you think Daa's so mad? I told him first.''

"What did he say?"

"He wants me to have it, of course, the typical macho thing. He wants to *marry* me.''

"No!''

"Yes. Can you i*mag*ine?''

It was framed rhetorically, but there was a vulnerability to it, and Sheba had an inkling all at once of why Daa *was* so mad. "You're thinking about it, aren't you?''

"No! Of course not. No *way.*''

"But you are.''

Marlowe met her gaze angrily for a moment, then rose abruptly and went to the window at the sink. She leaned on the enamel edge of the sink and looked out into the night, her back to Sheba.

"You don't even know what you're saying. To even be *tempted,* at this point, is degrading. Don't you see? I didn't come to California and spend ten years working on myself, trying to liberate myself, just to end up a New Age hausfrau. And what about Daa?" Marlowe said, turning. "Have you even *thought* of *her?*''

"Did you think of her when you slept with Jack?''

"Oh, great, now you're starting to sound like my mother. Well, look, Miss Moral Majority, Daa and I have an understanding. We've always had an understanding. We're not bound, we're free. We've always agreed we could see other people, that that doesn't have anything to do with our love for each other.''

"Then why *is* Daa so mad? Surely not just because you told Jack first. I think she's mad because you're not being honest. Not even with yourself.''

"And what do *you* know about it? It's all fun and games to you—come to California, try this, try that, get your chart done, throw a tarot, the future's all aglow. You don't know *shit* about what it all really means, it's all done in soft pastels for you. And until you *do* know, until you stop playing the spiritual dilettante long enough for life to catch up with you, you can keep your Pollyanna-pink moralisms to yourself.''

"You can holler at me all you want," Sheba said steadily. "It ain't gonna change nothing.''

"Oh, God, don't get all huffy and Southern on me *now*,'' Marlowe said, relenting at once. She came back to the table, sat down, and put her head in her hands again. "Christ, Sheba, what am I going to *do?''*

"Well, what does Daa think you should do?''

"She thinks I should just *have* the kid and raise it with her. We've talked about it before, a lot, how great that would be, but of course there was always the problem of the father. Which we appear to have solved.''

"Well?''

"Oh, God, I don't *know*. I'm so confused. I can't *imagine* actually raising a kid with *Jack,* of all people—but, well, there he *is,* right? He's saying he wants to be the father—I mean, he's *already* the father, of course, damn him, but you know what I mean.''

"Maybe all three of you could raise it.''

Marlowe laughed. "Now *there's* a California idea. Happily ever after, right? Just me and Jack and Daa, and baby makes four.''

"Well, why not? Stranger things have happened. With enough love—''

"Love is one thing. Don't even get me started on love. But

raising a child together is something else entirely. Besides, Daa can't *stand* Jack."

"I thought *you* couldn't stand Jack, mostly. But—"

"I *can't*. There, you see? Maybe I *should* just marry him!"

They laughed. Sheba said, "It would make your mother happy, anyway."

"Actually, it wouldn't," Marlowe said, sobering.

"Oh? You've talked to her?"

"I talked to her *first*. Funny, huh? Reverse order of what it should have been—her, then Jack, then Daa. It's bizarre. But there you are—when it came down to the crunch, ten years of liberation didn't mean shit. My first impulses have had all the profundity of a sophomore's at Saint Veronica's who got herself knocked up by a football star from Saint John's."

"What did your mother *say?*"

"You'd never guess. She thinks I should get an abortion. I couldn't believe it myself—she was so soft, and so concerned. She just wanted me to be happy, she said, she didn't want to see me forced into anything. It almost killed me, I cried like a baby. I'd been so sure she would take the hard line. But at this point, strange as it seems, she's the only one who *doesn't* think I should have the kid. Jack wants a New Age Magical Child, and Daa wants a Sensitive Infant Woman raised on Sound Matriarchal Principles—"

"And you?"

"I'd probably be happy if it had ten fingers and ten toes," Marlowe said, and shook her head. "God, what am I *saying?* Sheba, I don't *know*. It scares me, that I would even *think* of having it, much less having it with *Jack*. It'll probably be some monstrous California hybrid, it'll be born speaking mellow nonsense and giving strokes. And it scares me, too, how much saner Daa has been about it all—I mean, for her, it was just like we've always talked about, take the sperm and run. She was *glad*, she was even amused at first that it was Jack—that didn't even matter to her, she said, 'Well, at least she'll be pretty.' She hasn't got a doubt in the world that it would be a gorgeous, little perfect baby girl and that she and I could raise her neopagan and witchy-wise. She only got mad when she realized I had told Jack before her—you were right about that. To Daa, it was all clear."

"So what *are* you going to do?"

"I don't know. I've got a month at least, before the first trimester. Daa's already mad at me, and I don't think she's going to get any madder, or at least not much, so there's no hurry there. And Jack's not going anywhere. His Immortality Institute is about to get sacked by the authorities, they've started looking into the books now too, so *he's* preoccupied with that. I suppose he'd want to get married in a redwood grove, or on a hilltop overlooking the ocean, at sunrise or something, some ungodly hour, with flutes."

"Marlowe, you can't seriously be considering marrying Jack," Sheba said with sudden conviction.

"Can't I? You were just saying a minute ago—"

"That you should at least admit you were tempted! It was so clear you were thinking about it. But to actually go *through* with it—God, Marlowe."

"Oh, don't fret, cuz. I'm not that desperate, or that crazy, yet." Marlowe rose, putting an end to the subject, and ran a glass of water for herself at the sink. "Oh, well, happy New Year, I suppose," she said, raising the glass in a mock toast. "Eh? Old acquaintances should be forgot, and all that. How was the party at Shakti's, by the way?"

Sheba shrugged, then smiled, remembering. "Oh, it was fine. It was, um—fine, yeah, great."

"Did Victor behave himself? Or did he punch some poor New Age type out?"

"He seemed okay. I didn't pay much attention to him, to tell you the truth. Though Shakti did."

"Ah! Will wonders never cease. I suppose I should have known that Shakti would have a secret taste for grade-A American beef. Those conspicuous vegetarians often do."

"There were a lot of interesting people there. I met this one guy, Chris, uh, Scorich, I think his name was . . ."

"Ah, the great Bodhicitta, Dak Dzin's right hand in America."

"You know him?"

"Hardly. I'm afraid the air he breathes is a little too thin for me—he's always struck me as enormously arrogant, you know, the worst of this whole new breed of smart-ass-American-kid-from-the-suburbs-gets-Eastern-religion. Very intellectual and all-is-one and quotes from the original Tibetan. And *very* holier-than-thou. We only used to invite him to our parties at all because he was so tight with all our Dak Dzin friends—*they* all thought he was seated at the right hand of God, and that it was a privilege to be on the same planet with him." Marlowe peered suddenly at Sheba. "You didn't fall for him, did you?"

"Well . . ."

Marlowe laughed. "Oops. Never mind. I think he's a great guy. Very *spiritual*, you know. Very pure."

"He seemed nice enough. He's a good kisser."

"So's Jack, the son of a bitch," Marlowe said, and sighed. "Oh, well, I suppose you can take care of yourself. Happy New Year, sweetheart." And she went out, and up the stairs.

After she was gone, Sheba sat for a long time alone at the table, digesting it all as best she could. As she sat, the sky to the east began to gray, and then to redden, and Sheba watched the year's first dawn with a feeling of odd deep peace. Probably, she thought, she should be upset, for Marlowe and her predicament; probably she should be concerned for the larger tumult of the suffering world. Probably she was shallow, to find it so, but it seemed to her that she had never seen such a beautiful sunrise, even in Virginia.

IV

An Apparition

ALBERT NERDOWSKY GAVE A NEW YEAR'S PARTY OF HIS OWN A FEW days later, which was such a strange, rare thing that everyone decided to attend. Nerdo seldom took time out from his usual preoccupations, which included formulating a scientific Theory of Everything, establishing the reality of the immortal soul, and contacting extraterrestrial intelligences, to which purpose he had tuned a satellite dish atop his warehouse laboratory south of Market Street to the Andromeda galaxy. The dish was equipped to both transmit and receive; a constant stream of messages went out, and Nerdowsky was expecting an answer any day. He had the dish linked to his car radio as well, and to the telephone answering machine at his apartment, so that there was no chance of missing any incoming communications. Every time he came home and the message light was blinking, it could be Andromeda galaxy calling.

Nerdo was beloved, though no one knew quite what to make of him most of the time. He had been hit by lightning when he was six years old and it had melted the bottoms of his tennis shoes and burned his teeth. He said that in that moment his destiny had been made clear to him. He had been in hot pursuit of that destiny ever since, mastering calculus by junior high and building a rocket in the sixth grade that had attracted the attention of the local Air Force base, which had scrambled three fighters to shoot it down. He had been thrown out of the physics doctoral program at UC-Berkeley for untenable speculations, though this had not fazed Nerdo much, as he had never particularly noticed that he was *in* the physics Ph.D. program at UC-Berkeley. Even now it was unclear to his friends whether he was a genius or just someone whose brain had unfortunately been fried at an early age.

He made great mixed drinks, though—everyone was agreed on that. Apparently certain alchemical principles were employed—Nerdowsky, if asked, would go into a deep explanation of the correlations between the phases of construction of a good margarita and the various stages of the transmutation of elements as described in the ancient texts. The key was in the neo-mercuric properties of tequila, Nerdo would say, to anyone who would listen; at the subatomic level the parallels were perfect. No one knew what he meant, but the cocktails were unsurpassed.

The gathering took place on a Saturday afternoon at Nerdo's laboratory. He had billed it as a cosmic event, and he had the place set up in advance for magic. The skylights were covered with black felt, and a sky full of projected stars and galaxies covered the ceiling, as if the place were a planetarium. A number of great gray papier-mâché pillars had been placed strategically to create a Stonehenge effect. Sitar music wafted gently through hidden speakers, and the air smelled faintly of frankincense and myrrh—Nerdowsky was nothing if not eclectic. The warehouse floor was a maze of mirrors and lasers, beam splitters and diffusing lenses. There was no food because Nerdo had forgotten to mention that it was a potluck, but the drinks were exceptionally potent and were served in Egyptian goblets. Nerdo himself wore a wizard's robe and a pointed, tall cap and spoke only Latin as he greeted all his guests and directed them to the folding chairs that ringed the center of the pseudo-Stonehenge.

As everyone settled in expectantly, he dimmed the lights; there was a long, dark hush, and then Dante Pruitt struck his Tibetan gong. The sound reverberated uncannily; it rose to the stars on the ceiling and seemed to seep up through the floor into the soles of their feet; it made the pillars quiver. It went on and on; and just as it began to finally ebb, Dante hit the gong again, and Nerdo flicked a switch on his laser array. And there, suddenly, in the center of the room, stood Jackson, smiling affably in three eerie dimensions, a little brighter, perhaps, a little more vivid than he had been in fleshly form; but undeniably *there*.

Nora Jane Hathaway screamed and fainted. Everyone looked at her a little enviously; it seemed like such a heartfelt and appropriate response. No one else seemed prepared for the moment in the least. Nerdo hastened to explain that the image was holographic, but even so, everyone treated it for a while as if it might explode. They circled it cautiously, like animals. It was all very simple, actually, Nerdo said. The image was a result of interference patterns.

While Nerdowsky talked about Fourier transforms and the mathematics of waveforms, Jackson stood there placidly, sparkling at odd moments, but otherwise unmoving. He was wearing hiking boots and khaki shorts, and a T-shirt that said *Fiat lux!* With a red bandanna tied at his throat, he looked a little like an unearthly Boy Scout. He would disappear and reappear in an instant when someone passed across the laser beam. The first time this happened, everyone jumped and exclaimed; but then it seemed that people found the phenomenon reassuring, and every once in a while someone would break the beam intentionally, as a child will throw a stone into a still pond, just for the effect.

Marlowe stared at Jackson's image and waited for the goose bumps to settle back into her skin. Nothing Nerdo could say about the technology of it all could dilute the moment's eeriness for her. She was dizzy with Jackson's presence. At the same time, she wanted for some reason to hit the holographic Jackson with a chair. She wondered guiltily if the intensity of her desire had summoned this weird counterfeit: she had longed so to ask Jackson what to do about this baby in her.

Nerdowsky was saying that everything, actually, was holographic—that all of what was thought of as the objective world of matter was a kind of illusion similar to this. "Reality," Nerdo explained, was nothing but a resonating sea of waveforms, a frequency domain that was transformed into the world as we know it by the selective interpretive functioning of our brains. It was a play of subatomic maya, an illusory dance without substance. In this sense, Nerdo said, the Buddhists were correct.

Marlowe stepped toward the ghostly Jackson and put her hand

out. It went right through, and Jackson's face remained frozen in the same stupid smile.

"Are you all right, Marlowe?" Daa said, beside her, and Marlowe turned to her and smiled.

"Oh, Daa, I love you so."

That night Marlowe dreamed that Jackson came to her, laughing. He was pregnant himself, he said, and showed her his swollen belly. He was wearing the same silly Boy Scout outfit that his hologram had worn. Marlowe teased him about the look and kissed him; and she knew he was not a hologram because he kissed her back. They were in a garden somewhere, a green, leafy place suffused with sunlight. Jackson told her that the land of the dead was a cheerful enough place; there was an Illusory Dance every Saturday night. He said he appreciated all those paintings of mops, no matter what anybody said; he felt they were a form of prayer. And he said that she was lucky because her baby would be born on the Fourth of July. He thought that if it was a girl, she should name it Jacksonetta, and Marlowe woke laughing, in Daa's arms, feeling lighter than she had for years.

Part XII

The Path of Wisdom

With mind far off, not thinking of death's coming,
Performing these meaningless activities,
Returning empty-handed now would be complete
*   confusion;*
The need is for recognition, the spiritual teachings,
So why not practice the path of wisdom at this very
*   moment?*

—Bardo Thodol

I

A Rose, and a Dull Glow

THE REST OF JANUARY PASSED WITHOUT MUCH FURTHER DRAMA. MAR-
lowe having decided to have the baby with Daa, the air in the
house cleared somewhat. The two of them went away for a week
at Big Sur and ate grapes and figs and drank good brandy, and
they came back glowing with a private glow; for weeks afterward, they kept to themselves.

The officers of the Institute for Health and Immortality, meanwhile, were arrested for tax fraud and health-code violations;
several of them were found to have accounts in Swiss banks,
swollen with diverted funds, and IHI collapsed into a rubble of
scandal. Jack began to shoot baskets night and day in the driveway. He was working on his foul shooting and a crossover dribble
move, and he apparently maintained the delusion that he might
yet turn pro. He said that basketball was a mental game, essentially. He said that stranger things had happened than a guy like
him making a late career. He was letting his beard grow in, and he
looked like hell.

At Chris Scorich's invitation, Sheba began attending meditation sessions and lectures at Dak Dzin Rinpoche's center in Oakland. She was given a fifty-seven-word mantra and told to
visualize a shining lotus blossom at the top of her head. The best
she could do was a rose, and a dull glow; by February, she still had
not memorized the Sanskrit mantra, and she still had no clear
image, really, of what a lotus blossom looked like. But Scorich
assured her that she was doing fine. After all those kisses the first
night, he was busier than she had supposed he would be and had
less time for her; Sheba began to fear that Shakti had been right,

that Scorich had in fact transcended that sort of thing. But from time to time they would go out for "coffee" on a Saturday afternoon (Scorich always drank water, whatever they went out for). Then she would feel encouraged. They always talked deeply of spiritual things, and he always held her hand. He said that they had no doubt shared past lives and told her of a dream he had had, of the two of them in ancient Ireland. They had been priests together, Scorich said. Sheba felt a mild disappointment at their being the same sex in that past life, but she kept this to herself. Her own dreams of Scorich were decidedly less collegial.

II

An Incarnation of Compassion

ONE AFTERNOON ABOUT A MONTH AFTER THEY HAD MET, CHRIS SCORICH telephoned Sheba in some excitement: it appeared that his spiritual master, Dak Dzin himself, was going to bless a soiree the next evening at the private home of one of his devotees with his divine presence, and Scorich had arranged that Sheba was invited to attend.

"Oh, Lord!" Sheba exclaimed. "What will I *wear?*"

Scorich laughed and reassured her—such gatherings were by no means unprecedented; they were generally intimate and even casual; and, if past occasions were any indication, the Teacher in his enlightened informality required little more than that she bring a towel in case the evening's events required the imparting of wisdom in the hot tub. Sheba marveled at this; but she agreed to arrive early to help with the dinner preparations. Unlikely though it seemed to her that anything mundane could suffice to feed the forty-seventh embodiment on earth of the Bodhisattva of Compassion, Scorich said the hostess would be making quiche.

The soiree was being held at the Nob Hill home of Gloria Demonde, an elegant blond woman with a trenchant and even at
times mordant wit. Sheba arrived early the next afternoon, bearing daffodils and irises, which Gloria promptly threw out—it appeared that Dak Dzin's allergies forbade live floral offerings.
Gloria's living room was filled instead with silk roses and tasteful
plastic lilies. She was going over the evening's wines when Sheba
got there—several French labels, for the Master, it seemed, would
drink nothing Californian, a piece of information only slightly
less surprising to Sheba than the fact that he drank at all. But
Gloria informed her that Dak Dzin's path incorporated elements
of tantric practice as if that sufficed for explanation; and Sheba
nodded, not wishing to seem prudish or ignorant. It had been her
previous impression, from Jack, that tantra meant sex; but no
doubt the correct translation was something closer to "license."

After examining the wine labels with some concern, Gloria
pronounced the collection for the most part adequate to the
Teacher's apparently sophisticated palate. One bottle was set
aside, being of a vintage known to have failed the divine test; and
Gloria wasted no time in opening this herself.

"No sense letting it go to waste," she said, and toasted Dak
Dzin's health with her slightly edged laugh. She had been a dev-
otee for twelve years and allowed herself liberties that astounded
Sheba.

The afternoon passed swiftly in the kitchen and in watching
Gloria make imperceptible tidyings and adjustments to her already—to Sheba's eyes—immaculate domain; before Sheba was
quite prepared for it, the evening's guests began to arrive. The
soiree would be more than usually exclusive, Gloria had told her,
and only the select members of an inner circle whose circumfer-
ence was still relatively vague to Sheba had been invited. The first
to show up were Gurudas Lapham, the manager of Dak Dzin's
ashram in Berkeley, and his wife, Prema. Gurudas was a young
man in his early thirties with a distinctive British accent; it came
as a surprise to Sheba to learn from the irreverent Gloria that he
was actually from Long Beach. Towheaded, lanky, and self-
important, Gurudas had a perpetually distracted and harried air,

as if he were privy to constant concerns far exceeding the situation in which he found himself, an air that was much enhanced by the electronic beeper he wore on his belt at all times to facilitate the ready communication of the latest crisis—Gurudas called them, without perceptible irony, Spiritual Tests—at Dak Dzin's hectic main facility on the West Coast. To Sheba, he was unfailingly condescending, an attitude she was prepared to accept on the grounds of his spiritual advancement and exalted position. His wife was a short woman with tough red hair, built a little like a bantamweight boxer. She played the harmonium at the ashram's chants and seemed always to be irritated with her husband; and, like Gloria, she consumed wine at a rate that made Sheba marvel. After the second glass, she began to call Gurudas "Henry," or even "Hank," which was apparently what he had been called in Long Beach.

The last two guests in the evening's select circle were Shanti Messerschmidt, a sturdy blond German woman with a ready laugh and steady blue gaze, a devotee since Dak Dzin's early days in Kashmir; and Rebecca Tomlin, a sweet-faced, almost completely silent young woman with great liquid brown eyes and cascades of walnut hair. Like Sheba, she had only recently arrived in California, from Wisconsin, to seek her spiritual fortune, and Gloria had taken her under her wing. Rebecca made her greetings to everyone with lowered eyes and went at once to the sink, where she began without ado to do the dishes.

They were all assembled by just before seven, the appointed hour for the Master's appearance, and the group sat around the living room amid the profusion of artificial flowers in desultory conversation, with half of everyone's attention poised toward the arrival of the guest of honor. Sheba listened to the talk without contributing more than an occasional appreciative murmur, amazed by the glibness, brightness, and devastating analyses of these spiritual veterans. Gurudas went on wittily at some length about the failings of his ashram staff, the dullness of the general population, the impossibility of a true spark of divinity doing anything but fizzling amidst such soggy tinder; and Gloria was scathing and hilarious in detailing an encounter with a former friend who wanted nothing more now, it seemed, than to get married and lead a quiet life of conventional piety and children. (Sheba took some justifiable quiet pride, here, at her own stout resistance to Victor Morris's similar aspirations for her.)

At seven-thirty the sound of a powerful motor was heard outside; Dak Dzin's white Rolls-Royce limousine was pulling up the steep driveway, and they all leaped at once to their feet and hurried to the front door to greet him.

Gurudas and Gloria had both crowded in front of Sheba, but peeking between them and through the open front door, she could see the car as it stopped in front of the house. The Master's driver got out first, followed by Chris Scorich, looking serious and spiritual, in a business-like way, in a jacket and tie. Sheba thrilled at the sight of him, but Scorich was too preoccupied with his official duties to acknowledge her. The arrival was a complexly orchestrated event—a series of other people were pouring out of the other doors of the enormous car, more and then incongruously more, until Sheba could not help but have the unpious thought of circus clowns coming out of a trick vehicle. At last the unloading entourage had run its course, and Dak Dzin himself emerged from the plush purple depths of the velvet backseat, to the bows and prostrations of the imported throng. Nodding benevolently, the Master made his way toward the house, where he was greeted at the threshold by Gloria, radiant, graceful in her dignified humility, and just a little bit sloshed.

"Rinpoche, welcome to my humble abode," she said, bowing.

Dak Dzin beamed, showing big, white regular teeth. He was a large man, with a prominent belly that perceptibly strained at his silk gown, a sort of pale orange robe that to Sheba looked unfortunately like her mother's second-best bathrobe. But she restrained her urge to giggle. The occasion was too solemn. And Dak Dzin otherwise was perfectly impressive, dark and heavily browed, with a sharp nose like a hawk's and rapid brown eyes that jittered back and forth almost constantly as if to take in everything. Scorich had said that Dak Dzin could see people's karma in their auras. On his smooth shaved head the Master wore a soft woolen cap of fuzzy maroon with a round logo that said REDSKINS.

"Ahh, Gloria," Dak Dzin said in a surprisingly chirpy voice, and began to speak to his hostess in Tibetan. Gloria listened attentively and even breathlessly, her face shining. Scorich, a step off Dak Dzin's elbow, translated in a low, modest voice, so smoothly that he was all but invisible to the process.

"You are more beautiful than ever," he told Gloria for Dak Dzin. "No one is so beautiful as you. Your beauty is like that of the Goddess of the World. It defies description. And your home is lovely too."

Gloria bowed again, pleased. Dak Dzin passed on into the house, followed closely by Scorich, and then by the other debarkees from the limo, a smooth group of courtiers with uniformly solemn, knowing faces, who paused and nodded at all the right places. The Master paused to say something to Gurudas, joked briefly in Tibetan with Shanti, nodded to Prema. For Sheba he had barely an indifferent glance; the rapid eyes passed over her with an impersonality for which she was grateful, and she just hoped his auric-detection mechanism had not registered her thoughts about the bathrobe. She was trying her best to understand what it could mean that this man had realized his God-nature. At the evening programs she had attended, it had not seemed so impossible from afar, that his being was divine: sitting on his thronelike orange chair and speaking over the professional sound system to an adoring audience of hundreds, he had been impressive indeed. But now, up close, the incongruity of his sheer physical reality was confusing her. He was just too obviously a *man;* he smelled at several yards of garlic and incense; and when he cleared his throat, Sheba was reminded, unwillingly, of her uncle Mel with his postnasal drip, which had always irritated her. Combined with the unfortunate robe, it was eroding her sense of the sacred. Not that Dak Dzin himself was diminished; Sheba rather felt her perceptions as a failure and a lack in herself. It was to her shame that she should be so petty and hung up on mortal details and unable to respond instantly, deeply, gratefully, as the others were, to the divine in this man.

When Dak Dzin reached Rebecca, who had been hanging back behind the others in the entry foyer, he stopped abruptly and turned his full gaze upon her. Confused, Rebecca looked down; she still had her apron on and was clutching a damp dish towel between her hands. Gloria, who was trailing the Master, said quickly, "Rinpoche, this is Rebecca Tomlin, one of your newest devotees."

"Ahhh," Dak Dzin said approvingly, looking Rebecca up and down, and then he took her hand and led her on with him into the house. Gloria exchanged an unmistakable glance with Prema Lapham; and they followed with the others. In the living room, everyone settled into their places; there was some subtle jockeying for positions close to Dak Dzin's, with the result that Sheba found herself at the back of the small assembly, which suited her well enough in any case. Rebecca, she noted, had been installed on Dak Dzin's right hand.

When everyone was seated, Dak Dzin closed his eyes and began to chant the mantras he always chanted to open a gathering. The others joined in, and the sound of the singing swelled to fill Gloria's living room. Sheba joined in as best as she could, her eyes still wonderingly on Dak Dzin, still trying to comprehend her proximity to the avatar; and, occasionally, on Rebecca beside him. The younger woman had her own eyes closed, and her face was lit with transparent ecstasy as she chanted in the Master's presence; and, Sheba couldn't help noting, Rebecca continued to twist the dish towel quietly in her hands.

III

The Nature of the Ego

AFTER THE CHANTING, THERE WAS THE USUAL MEDITATION. THE LIGHTS were dimmed in the living room, and a deep hush fell over them all. Sheba sat cross-legged, as quietly as the rest, but her mind was uneasy and no effort she made could still it. Something about

Rebecca's elevation troubled her. She told herself that it was probably only the most petty jealousy that she herself had not been similarly singled out by the Master; but she knew this wasn't true. She didn't, in fact, envy Rebecca; the other girl's sudden spiritual prominence was the last thing Sheba wanted for herself. If anything, Sheba thought, she was embarrassed for the other girl. Dak Dzin's attentions had seemed only too plainly those of a powerful man picking his new mistress. Gloria's glance at Prema, while it was happening, had even seemed to acknowledge as much—to Sheba it had been a shockingly secular look, filled with irony and dry, cynical amusement.

Sheba was horrified by her thoughts, but she could not escape them. While the others around her meditated in apparent serenity as usual, she seethed. Was it only her impurity that led her to such suspicions? She told herself it must be so, but the thoughts and images persisted. Dak Dzin's eyes had gone up and down Rebecca's body in a way that had seemed blatant to the point of parody. Sheba couldn't help it, she despised herself for it, she felt it as almost certainly a failure of her spirituality—but she wondered.

The rest of the evening did little to relieve her agitation. After the meditation, Dak Dzin gave a short talk on the nature of the ego. The ego, he said through Scorich as his translator, resented purity, resented even God, because the ego understood that in God's triumph was its own demise. Therefore the ego, brought into contact with purity and light, would do everything it could to maintain its power and position; it would celebrate its vices with fresh rationalizations and disparage virtue by every means possible. It would find fault with all that was holy to justify its own low nature.

And so on. Sheba could not help but feel the talk was directed uncannily at her; and indeed Dak Dzin's jittery eyes seemed to rest on her disproportionately; and his voice seemed sterner and more emphatic as he looked at her. So obvious did it seem to Sheba that she was sure everyone else had noticed it too, and that her shame was already a matter of public knowledge to this spiritually sophisticated group. She flushed and lowered her eyes, squirming in her place.

At last the talk ended, and they went in to dinner. Here was more cause for chagrin. Sheba and Gloria had made four different kinds of quiche that afternoon; and Gloria had made a great point of having Sheba make one entirely on her own, in order that Sheba might have the honor of offering it herself to the Master. The three quiches of Gloria's manufacture were done now to a golden perfection, but Sheba's quiche, at the back of the oven's lower shelf, had somehow burned black on the bottom. She still, however, had the honor of offering it to the Master, although to Sheba, disposed by now to see evil in practically everything, Gloria's insistence on the point seemed almost malicious.

She brought the quiche to the table, as per Gloria's instructions, on a ridiculous silver tray. Rather than showing his earlier indifference to her, as Sheba had hoped, Dak Dzin accepted her quiche with an almost theatrically heightened consideration that inevitably drew everyone's attention. He tasted it, chewed broadly, and made a face.

''*Burned*,'' he said in English, to everyone's delight. It was always a great occasion when the Master spoke in English, and his comment was repeated and recounted for the rest of the evening. Sheba, her face deep red, suffered her new notoriety with a painful smile that she maintained as best as she could throughout dinner. She felt quite burned herself.

Rebecca seemed particularly struck by Dak Dzin's pronouncement on the quiche. Glowing under all the new attentions and relieved by now of the dish towel, she repeated the comment again and again from her place at his right hand, imitating the Master's accent saucily: ''*Burned!*'' Each effort drew a fresh burst of hilarity from those around her. Dak Dzin himself beamed approvingly; Gloria exclaimed that she had never seen her protégée so radiant and so lively. To Sheba, it was the most painful part of all, to find herself resenting Rebecca bitterly; the emotion undermined any chance of clarity about it all. Perhaps, she thought miserably, she *was* just jealous.

Later, however, her suspicions were aroused again. After dinner, they did all retire to the hot tub, but Dak Dzin did not join them there. He stayed in one of the house's bedrooms, with Rebecca—for a *darshan,* as everyone seemed careful to call it, a spiritual audience. But Sheba noted that Chris Scorich was in the hot tub with the rest of them.

"Won't Rebecca need a translator?" she asked him in lowered tones, trying to be discreet.

Scorich looked distinctly uncomfortable, but Gloria, on the other side of him, snickered.

"Not likely," she said. "It will all be plain enough, I'm sure."

"There are teachings that go beyond words," Scorich said in a tone of mild corrective. "It's enough just to *be* with the Rinpoche."

Sheba nodded dubiously and leaned her head back on the redwood edge of the hot tub. The steam rose around her in the cool night air. She was conscious that in some sense this was the moment she had been waiting for all evening; Scorich, relieved of his official duties, was beside her at last, and obviously somewhat eager for her company, despite her burning of the quiche. Sheba had already noted that he had a marvelous body; in this advanced group, no one had bothered with clothes. But not even the pleasure of unclad proximity to Scorich in warm water could completely dispel her sense of malaise; and for the rest of the evening, while the others talked of elevated things and gossiped, Sheba was preoccupied with her own meditations, on the nature of the ego.

Part XIII

Love, Love, Love

Oh, that my heart would not stumble and sag!
That I were able to love more intensely,
That I had more than myself to give
To that measureless light,
That sweet splendor.
—Jacopone da Todi, *The Lauds*

I

The Effect of Budweiser on the Third Chakra

SHEBA WAS DEPRESSED FOR DAYS AFTER HER EVENING WITH THE DAK Dzin group; she was sure her spiritual future was blighted, not to mention her relationship with Chris Scorich. She would have liked to discuss what it all meant with Shakti Arguello, to do tarot spreads and throw I Chings and consult the stars, but Shakti was busy herself, suddenly, with Victor Morris. She went to movies with him two or three times a week—and not even art movies, or anything uplifting, though Shakti claimed to be slowly reforming his taste. They saw action movies and comedies—Schwarzenegger and Stallone and Clint Eastwood, and Chevy Chase. Once Shakti even went to the rodeo and came back wearing a big brown cowboy hat, which she modeled for Sheba with much giggling. She found Victor a perfect savage, she said; she believed the relationship was doing wonders for her third chakra. Victor teased her for her "leaf-eating" and fed her cheeseburgers and french fries and chicken fried steak; they went out on Sunday mornings for omelets with ketchup. Shakti had begun to drink Budweiser, and to watch sporting events on television. It was clear to Sheba that her friend was in love, though Shakti denied it. It was just a fling, she said; and when Sheba warned her that Victor Morris did not believe in flings, Shakti just smiled.

"California has changed him," she said. "As it changes us all. He's grown."

Sheba doubted that, but there was nothing to do but let the

thing run its course. She was not jealous, at least—she had examined herself closely and found no symptoms. A brief pang, maybe, at the sight of that bridge burning at last behind her, more poignancy than anything else. But mostly she was relieved that Vic had turned his relentless attentions elsewhere. She just didn't want to see Shakti—or Victor, for that matter—get hurt.

II

Victor Sets His Sights

SURE ENOUGH, VICTOR MORRIS PROPOSED TO SHAKTI ON VALENTINE'S Day.

He had a somewhat sheepish lunch with Sheba the day before; he felt that he owed her that much. His analysis of the situation, to her astonishment, included references to a tarot spread he had done the night before. Apparently Daa had helped him lay the cards out and had interpreted the results for him. Cups had predominated, an abundance of fluid love energy. Victor reminded Sheba self-consciously that Arguello meant "water." He was uneasy on this new ground; the literalism of his new taste for synchronicities was touching to her. He referred several times to notes he had taken of what Daa had said. The Lovers card had come up in the Past, crossed by the Five of Cups, Regret. He believed the image of spilled chalices signified the course of his love for Sheba. Beyond the Hanged Man, however, was Renewal: the World card, symbolized in the Wicca deck Daa had given him by a dancing goddess, juxtaposed suggestively with a Prince of Pentacles. The robust Prince card emanated truth, honor, patience, and determination; Victor, suddenly shy, refrained from mentioning Daa's interpretation of the Prince card as an archetypal horned god, a potent phallic consort of just the sort that Shakti Arguello needed to keep her honest.

In a nutshell, the signs pointed to a union of female and male at the highest level. It was all very auspicious. Daa had given the thing her blessing, Victor told Sheba at lunch, and spilled his beer. While the waiter scrambled to mop it up and bring him a new bottle, Victor studied his big rough hands. He looked miserable, and apparently expected Sheba to berate him. Sheba felt far from this. She was touched, in fact, by Victor's clumsy efforts to temper his love with mystical gallantry, both for Shakti and for her. It was like watching a Labrador trying to do math.

She reached across the table and took one of his hands in hers. "Well, Victor, you've got my blessings too. I think it's wonderful."

Vic looked relieved. "I know I said I'd wait for you forever."

"I never wanted you to do that."

"I know. I always knew, I guess. I just kept hoping, like the mule I am."

"You're not a mule. You're just a good old marriage plow horse, all yoked up and ready to go. All you ever needed was a field to till."

"Do you think she'll go for it?"

"She could do a lot worse than a good man like you. I just hope you invite me to the wedding."

"I'd be willing to have it in whatever church she wants," Victor said earnestly, "if I could just figure out what the hell church that *is*."

III

Heart Stomps

SHAKTI SAID NO TO VICTOR THE NEXT DAY, WHEN HE PRESENTED HIS PRO-
posal along with an enormous red, heart-shaped box of chocolates, thirty-six red roses, and an antique can opener he had
found in a little shop in the gold country, which symbolized to
him everything enduring and domestic. She not only said no, she
panicked and threw him out and told him she never wanted to
see him again. Almost as soon as he was out the door, she broke
out into hives and began to run a high fever. The smell of the
roses pervaded the house for weeks. Shakti could not bring herself to throw them away, and all her tabletops lay deep in fallen
petals, like some weird autumn, well into March. It was all so
corny and so heavy-handed she could barely stand it. The chocolates lay unopened on the floor where she had thrown them;
she felt that to touch them, even to throw them out, would de-
molish her credibility.

Victor phoned regularly, leaving poignant messages. He wrote
numerous songs in a bluesy country vein and played them on her
answering machine:

> *And I will always love you,*
> *though it always will be pain.*
> *You took my heart and stomped it,*
> *and left it in the rain.*

Sheba was no help. She was even a little smug and told Shakti
that she should not have led poor Victor on.

"Poor *Victor!*" Shakti cried. "What about poor *me?* My answering machine has been turned into a country radio station!"

"I think it's real sweet that he's writing songs for you," Sheba said.

Shakti tried to meditate her way out of it all, but even in the lotus position she was plagued by images of Victor Morris. She kept thinking in particular of one night when they had driven up the winding road to the top of Twin Peaks and parked beneath the clear starry sky. The city had glittered below them like a dense net of bright jewels; everything had been so vivid. They had made love on the Chevy's wide front seat, as if they were high school kids; and afterward had peeked over the dashboard tentatively, giggling, looking for cops, and had seen the moon, huge and bright, almost full, rising over the hills of the East Bay.

Shakti found herself eating the chocolates one night, and re-playing "You Stomped My Heart" on the answering machine. She had saved the entire collected works into the machine's memory. She managed to get through this unnerving lapse, but when she found herself weeping one afternoon as she used the can opener on a can of olives, she knew she was in real trouble. She packed two bags and canceled all her astrology appointments and took the next available plane to the British Isles. Phoning Sheba from the airport as her flight was boarding, she said that she had been called by God to investigate the druidic mysteries. She'd always known she had a lot of past-life stuff to work out, on the Celtic side.

IV

If You Can Feel It, You Can Heal It

VICTOR MORRIS TOOK THE REJECTION BADLY. HE DRANK HIMSELF INTO A stupor and got into a fistfight with a rebirthing expert from Palo Alto, at a seminar on men reclaiming their wild natures, which Vic had signed up for at Shakti's urging.

"Wild nature *this*," Victor said before he hit the man.

Apparently he blamed California. The motion of the Pacific plate along the San Andreas fault could not take the state to Alaska fast enough for him, he said. The whole damn civilization was a house of cards in an earthquake zone.

Sheba called him a couple of times, but he scorned her sympathy. His only comfort came in listening to Willie Nelson tapes and hanging out with Daa. The two of them would go for walks in Golden Gate Park and end by eating ice cream together at a little Chinese place near Ninth Avenue. They both loved vanilla, as it turned out. Victor would pour his heart out to Daa over a two-scoop sugar cone. He felt that Shakti was using her so-called spirituality to cover an abyss of longing, and an incapacity to commit.

"Marlowe's the same way," Daa told Victor. "Completely out of touch with her need for intimacy most of the time, and terrified of what a real relationship requires."

"Love, love, love. That's all Shakti talks about. And then when some real love is looking her in the face, she runs like a deer."

"That's all anyone around here talks about. Love. Mostly they have no idea what it means."

"I hear *that*," Victor said morosely.

These conversations could go on for hours, and Victor took great comfort in them. Daa, he said, was the only person in California with any sense at all. It was just too damned bad she wasn't into men.

V

An Alternate Proposal

DANTE PRUITT, SECRETLY INSPIRED BY VICTOR'S BRAVE EXAMPLE, PROposed to Sheba on the first of March.

This was crazy, of course—they had not exchanged a dozen

words of actual conversation, though he had sung thousands of lines of love poetry in the backyard. Apparently Dante believed this sufficed.

He rented a tux for the occasion and showed up with a lute and a forty-seven-verse song of courtly love. The proposal itself was oblique at best and was couched in an allusive scene within the song's narrative structure. Sheba, in fact, never fully understood that it *was* a marriage proposal; and during the instrumental bridge that Dante had thoughtfully left for her to mull her reply, the phone rang. Hoping that it was Chris Scorich, who had not called since the night at Gloria Demonde's, Sheba excused herself and took the call in the kitchen. To her disappointment, it was not Chris, it was another friend from her old IHI days. Sheba chatted with him for a while, then hung up the phone and came back to the living room to find Dante, inexplicably, profoundly downcast.

"Sorry to keep you waiting. Now what was it you were . . . ?"

"Nothing," Dante said manfully; he had actually caught a glimpse of his futility while Sheba chatted on the phone in the other room, and not long after that he took his sorrow home. Sheba looked after him, a bit surprised at the abruptness of his departure but otherwise with affection. The unfinished song had a catchy little refrain, and she found herself humming it later, cheerfully unaware that she had refused yet another formal offer.

VI

Love Is a Rose

MARLOWE, SECLUDED IN HER STUDIO, PAINTED ROSEBUDS ON A SAVAGED bush—tightly knotted little buds, clenched against a late-spring snow. The bush had risen from some depth in her psyche to the surface of the canvas, surprising her as her best work always did.

She had painted it standing beside a weathered brick wall, in a garden that had gone wild some years before. Beyond the wall, deeper into the painting, Marlowe felt, were fields and trees, and horses, perhaps. And ravens. Perhaps it was her grandmother's place in western New York State, a seedy, old, sprawling farm, neglected after the early death of Marlowe's grandfather. Her grandmother had kept up a little herb garden and a patch of kitchen vegetables, and a birdbath shrine to St. Francis of Assisi. The land had been beautiful and mysterious to Marlowe as a child, all green hills and oak forest, the old fields succumbing to grass and brush and birches. What roses her grandmother had kept had all gone wild—it had been Sheba's mother, Marlowe's aunt Lucy, who had kept up the pristine strain of Virgin Whites— and there had been no bush that Marlowe could remember like this one she was painting, storm-stripped and lonely. She felt that the buds might be the child in her, or ten thousand things that had never bloomed.

VII

Distractions

IT WAS HARD TO CONCENTRATE ON PAINTING. SHE WAS SICK EVERY MORN-ing. Also, as spring approached, the Lapidge Street backyard out-side her studio was suddenly a hectic place. Victor Morris, working under Daa's direction, was digging a trench and laying new plastic pipe to the Aphrodite fountain. Daa was in a great phase, bursting with energy, getting her garden tilled and planted, arranging new compost heaps, painting the kitchen. She had cleaned all the leaves out of the fountain's basin and was planning a celebratory ceremony for when the water could be turned on again. In anticipation of Aphrodite's new glory she planted a ring of bulbs around the pool—irises and daffodils and gladiolas. These would be blooming, she was sure, by the time Marlowe's baby was born. Daa was certain the baby would be a girl, and she wanted to name her Gaia.

Victor Morris, digging only on weekends, took almost a month to get the trench in and the pipe to the fountain laid. Marlowe watched him through the studio window while he worked one Saturday afternoon toward the end of the job. He dug carefully near the flower bed around the fountain, shirtless in the mild March sun, sweat gleaming on his broad back. His arms and neck were dark, a construction worker's tan neatly defined by the lines of the T-shirt he had shed; his thick, strong chest had a rose tattoo that rippled with his pectorals. He worked cheerfully, singing and whistling to himself. When Marlowe took him iced tea, he accepted the glass, but sniffed it warily.

"Don't worry," she said, smiling. "It's Lipton's."

"Oh, I don't mind those weird teas much," Victor said, relieved, and drank. Marlowe watched the line of his throat and shoulders in spite of herself and realized she was picturing him in bed. She almost left, but stood her ground; Victor drank off almost half the glass, then lowered it and found her eyes on him. He blinked and looked away, disconcerted; then raised the glass and finished it off in a few long gulps. He wiped his mouth with his forearm.

"Well, I thank you kindly, ma'am," he said, handing the glass back to Marlowe.

"Iced tea brings out your accent, I see."

He glanced at her, startled; she saw that he had not expected to be teased and was not primed for banter. They stood for a moment in silence, then Victor cleared his throat and said, "I, uh, hear that congratulations are in order."

"Congratulations?"

"Daa says that you're going to have a baby."

"Oh, *that*."

He looked so uncomfortable that she laughed.

"What's, the matter, Victor? Do you think I've got a bad attitude? I should be knitting little booties or something? Or is it that you think I ought to run out and round up a husband for myself before I have it?''

"I reckon you have a right to do whatever you please," he said stolidly. "I know that Daa's real pleased. I just wanted to say I sure do wish y'all the best."

"Why, thank you, Victor," Marlowe said, feeling vaguely frustrated. He was treating her as a hired hand might treat the mistress of the house. She turned and would have gone, but as she did, he said, "It's pretty girls, by the way."

Marlowe stopped. "What?"

"It's pretty girls that bring out my accent. When I'm all by myself, I sound just like Walter Cronkite."

And he turned back to his digging. Marlowe hesitated a moment more, feeling zinged; then said, "Pretty *women*, you mean."

Victor Morris looked up. "What?"

"Not girls. Pretty *women*. It's a California thing, I suppose—girls grow up. I'd have thought Daa would have taught you that much by now." And she turned on her heel and strode back into the studio, closing the door behind her. Her pulse was racing; her face, she knew, was flushed. She had not found so cheap a thrill in such shallow stuff since junior high. It made her more certain than ever that she was cracking up.

Later, that night as they sat in bed with their books, she told Daa that she thought Victor Morris had come on to her, a little.

Daa just laughed. "Yeah, he can't help it, the poor guy. He comes on to every female in his path. He even comes on to *me* once in a while, just to let me know he respects me as a woman, I think."

"So I shouldn't take it personally," Marlowe said, embarrassed to note that she was disappointed.

"I don't," Daa said, and turned back to her reading. She was reading Hemingway, whom she liked a lot, and gleefully marking every sexist inflection in pink.

VIII
De Signatura Rerum

THE GODDESS CRACKED WHEN THEY TURNED ON THE WATER A FEW DAYS later—the old pipe, as it turned out, had rusted shut near the hand, and the backup burst the pipe within the statue's body. An arm and breast fell off, and the jaw cracked open; water seeped out weakly at the armpits, knees, and ears.

Daa, shocked, put her hand on Marlowe's belly protectively. "It's just plumbing and concrete, sweetie. It doesn't mean anything."

"I know it doesn't," Marlowe said, though she knew it did. Everything meant something; she had learned that much in California. It was just a question of what.

Part XIV

Spring Cleaning

God is always incomprehensible to the knowing power. But to the loving power, he is entirely comprehensible in each one individually.
            —The Cloud of Unknowing

I
Out of the Closet

THAT SPRING SHEBA CLEANED HER ROOM IN A SORT OF FRENZY, WASHING the windows inside and out, scrubbing and waxing the floor, thrashing cobwebs out of the high corners and dusting every crevice. She recognized the frenzy with a sense of chagrin: she was cleaning as her mother had always cleaned. Had her mother always been this shaken by life? Chris Scorich had not called since the dinner debacle at Gloria Demonde's house, and Sheba was sure he had given up on her in disgust. Whether it was the quiche (which hadn't really been her fault, Sheba longed to explain—it had been the oven); or her no doubt obvious doubts and blasphemous reflections about Dak Dzin; or whether it was just that she didn't look good enough in the hot tub—though Sheba felt that she had held her own there—she had been found wanting somehow; and now, like her mother, she was turning disappointment and anxiety into cleanliness. It was a little frightening that it worked that way.

Still, it felt good. The room was really shaping up. She had not given the place such a thorough going over since she got to California. Sheba scraped up the last of the ancient wax that was still scattered around the room in odd little islands and washed the walls, where months of accumulating incense smoke had left a fragrant, sticky layering. She moved the bed and the dresser; she banged the panda bear free of dust—despite her rejection of Victor Morris, she had kept the stuffed animal, which was cuter than he would ever be—and she vacuumed her pink curtains.

She even began to clean out the closet, and it was here that Sheba found Jackson's journal. The simple spiral-bound school notebook had been lying unnoticed on a small shelf above the closet door, undisturbed, apparently, since his death. Sheba brushed off the dust and examined the document warily. It was almost filled with a closely written, lovely script, which toward the end loosened somewhat, sprawling into larger loops and trailing off.

Sheba didn't know what to do with the notebook at first. She had not known Jackson, of course; she had only heard him mentioned occasionally, with a kind of reverence or regret. Marlowe would not talk about him much. Shakti Arguello said that Jackson had been a very spiritual being; he apparently still came to Shakti regularly during her meditations, a fact that Sheba no longer mentioned to Marlowe, aware that it made her cousin angry. Sheba knew that Jackson had lived at the Lapidge Street house for years; her bedroom had been his, and she had even imagined several times, with a little chill, that his spirit lingered somehow. She had even dreamed of him once—he had come to her in a Model T Ford and beeped a little comic horn, inviting her on a drive. She had refused, Sheba recalled; even in her dream she could not help but feel that Jackson represented a kind of danger, a warning: he was a casualty, somehow, of California— the opposite of a success story, as it were. But on the whole, she had not given him too much thought. He had died of AIDS, which made her nervous.

Now, with his journal in her hands, her first impulse was to throw it out. She knew this was not a spiritual urge, but coming upon the notebook like that on her closet shelf had shaken her. It was as if he had somehow been in her closet all that time. It gave her the creeps, a little.

Still, she knew what she should do; and at last Sheba rose. She padded down the hall to Marlowe's room and knocked on the door.

"I thought you might want to see this," Sheba said when her cousin answered, and she handed her the notebook.

II

A Message in a Bottle

HAPPY EASTER, MARLOWE THOUGHT. SEASON'S GREETINGS FROM THE grave. It was almost funny. She had dreamed for three nights straight that Jackson was trying to call her on the telephone but couldn't get through, and she had assumed some Freudian or Jungian or Reichian aspect of her psyche needed expression—that her animus figure or her superego was frustrated with the waking self's obtuseness, that her deep energy was stymied by the failure of daylight connections. No doubt it was. But here was Jackson himself, decidedly unsymbolic, person to person.

The familiar handwriting, so strong and so sure, was like the promise of his voice. Marlowe had quickly flipped through the whole journal already and been relieved to see that almost every page was filled. After the initial thrill of contact, she was not sure she could have endured a fragment. This gift would be a feast, not a snack.

Sheba had fled back to her room after delivering the notebook, so obviously unnerved that Marlowe felt sorry for her. A message from the dead was not exactly what Sheba had bargained for, cleaning out her closet, tidying up her aura: she was still in that early phase of California honeymoon spirituality when death and damage seemed distant things that happened to other, insufficiently enlightened people; she felt invulnerable and pure, protected by her innocence and her good intentions. And Marlowe knew her cousin to be squeamish about AIDS. She'd seen it before—people came to San Francisco half-afraid to breathe the air.

Marlowe opened the notebook again, gingerly. The first entry was dated August 13, 1988, the day after his diagnosis. *I am not ready for this,* Jackson had written that day, beginning the journal of his dying. *I am not ready for this at all.*

III
August 13, 1988

I am not ready for this. How could I be? And what am I to do now? Live, to be sure: I know the facile answer. The Four Noble Truths apply. Live lightly, lovingly, compassionately. I have studied all the proper texts, listened to the proper lectures, sat in the proper postures, and said the proper words. I see now how much I prided myself that my spirituality was deeper—deeper than the perfunctory Sunday performances of my parents, deeper than the banal God of the heartland. I had come to San Francisco and met the East—I had renewed my spirit in the Buddha's wisdom, while the rest of America languished. Funny how utterly useless it all seems just now—my bastardized California Buddhism, all my go-with-the-flow wisdom: it rings so amazingly hollow. Embrace the moment, I would always say: it is the fluid process, not the product, that matters. The wisdom of life is acceptance without attachment, enjoyment without greed, love without grasping. Etc., etc., and so on. But what does it mean to live in the moment, when the moment is being torn from my embrace? And what does it mean to flow with a process whose product is my annihilation? My bitterness now, my sudden rage—this savage resentment like that of a child interrupted at play: I see now that I have accepted nothing without attachment, enjoyed nothing without greed, loved nothing without grasping and clinging. And even now it is no nobility in me, no wise exercise of discrimination, that will break my grasp on the world—it is no skillful playing of the game. The things I love and clutch will simply be torn from me one by one. My acquiescence in the process is not required.

IV

A Broken Rosary

M<small>ARLOWE REMEMBERED THOSE FIRST DAYS SO CLEARLY—THE RAWNESS</small>
and shock, the unreality. Perhaps it should not have been so surprising—there had been signs, after all. And they had nursed and buried enough of their friends, already. But Jackson, wise, clear-eyed Jackson, Jackson the spiritual realist, had had his head in the sand for once. He had been so sure it was just a cold, the news had taken him by complete surprise. His rage at first had dismayed her, Marlowe remembered now, reading the journal. Funny, how she had not wanted to remember that. It had seemed to invalidate everything they had been saying and doing for years. His first day back from the hospital, Jackson had yanked his mala, the Buddhist rosary of rudraksha seeds he fingered while he meditated, from around his neck. The string had burst, the one hundred and eight beads had flown all over the floor, and Jackson had kicked at them in a frenzy, scattering them farther in every direction. Later, he had regretted it, she recalled—they had been down on their hands and knees for hours, too grim to laugh, trying to find all those tiny rudraksha seeds, so they could re-string the mala. Jackson, usually the most casual of ritualists, had uncharacteristically placed an intense magical value on the complete recovery of all the beads. But that first day they had only found eighty-seven.

They were finding the damned things for months, Marlowe remembered; thank God it had eventually seemed funny. Someone walking barefoot would suddenly wince and hop, and everyone in the room would cheer. It even became a small ritual of its own, and a kind of running joke: they would celebrate every

fresh find of a prodigal rudraksha with laughter and a mock ceremonial restringing. Some of the seeds had found their way
somehow as far away as the kitchen—maybe the mice were moving them. But by the time Jackson died, they had found one hundred and three of the things. Marlowe had no idea what that
meant, that they had not found them all.

The afternoon had fled; the room had darkened while she
read. While she ''read,'' that is—in an hour and a half, she had
not gotten past the second page. Outside, a spring dusk was
gathering. Rather than turn a light on, Marlowe set the notebook on her drawing table and went to the window. She felt
sad, and emptied; she could go no further, for the moment. She
didn't know what she had expected from the journal. Wisdom,
perhaps—great, sweepingly wise statements of perfect equilibrium, the keys to life and death and love. She had, it seemed,
needed Jackson to be wiser than he was, even in her memory—
certainly she had conveniently forgotten his unpreparedness,
the collapse of his spirituality like a house of cards in those first
weeks after the diagnosis. How had she managed to remember
him as so serene, so wise, so perfectly accepting? Because it was
easier, maybe, than remembering the terror. *I am not ready for
this.* And he *hadn't* been. It seemed she was not ready, either,
even now.

Small green buds showed at the tips of the oak tree by the
driveway. Jack was on the pavement with a basketball. In the
twilight the methodical thunk-thunk of his dribbling was oddly
poignant. At least someone had something to do with himself
that seemed meaningful, Marlowe thought: faced with mortality,
Jack had barricaded himself for the moment in some unassailable
fantasy involving twenty-foot jump shots, and as long as he kept
dribbling, he would be okay. Was it a step up, or a step down,
from the similarly unassailable fantasies of the Institute for Health
and Immortality? The emphasis on physical preparation in both
seemed to suit Jack's nature.

And it would not last. That much, at least, was very clear: no
fantasy was really unassailable.

And so I must begin now to try to say what it means to me—must make my own apologia pro vita sua, and my own—Californian—book of the dead. It's funny how little the other ones help, after all, when it comes to this . . .

V

If Ye Have the Faith Even of a Grain of Rudraksha . . .

WITH ONE THING AND ANOTHER, IT WAS NOT UNTIL THREE DAYS LATER that Sheba got around to cleaning out the rest of her closet. Chris Scorich had called in the meantime and, miracle of miracles, had sheepishly asked *her* forgiveness! He hoped, Scorich said, that Dak Dzin had not freaked her out; sometimes new people found him a little odd. Scorich had even asked her out, to someplace besides a coffee shop for once—he had taken Sheba to a Tibetan puppet show, where he had spent most of the evening putting the Master's actions in a context of nonattachment and spiritual illustration. As they watched the little, grotesque hand puppets battle through some ancient Tibetan saga of gods and demons, Sheba's doubts about Dak Dzin had been laid to rest; Chris had explained everything. The point was to see through the game, he said—Dak Dzin could play at wine, women, and song, the lures of the world, because they meant nothing to him. The Master had no need for such things, but his disciples were still susceptible to the pull, so from time to time Dak Dzin took on the karma himself and acted out the emptiness of indulgence, just to illustrate for his followers' sake that it was meaningless and led nowhere. In any case, too much of spirituality in the past had been based on repression and the harsh denial of the body and its desires; Dak

Dzin's unique synthesis of Theravadan Buddhist nonattachment and Shaivite tantric practice had been specifically formulated with the Western psyche in mind: one escaped from the wheel of rebirth not through the suppression of desire but through seeing it through to the very end. Like a sacred flame, Dak Dzin's practice allowed indulgence in, only to burn it up in the fire of enlightenment.

And so on. It all sounded good to Sheba, who was relieved to hear that Dak Dzin's apparent lasciviousness had a spiritual context. And she was not without a certain appreciation of what the Master's unique synthesis of Theravadan Buddhist nonattachment and Shaivite tantric practice might imply for her relationship with Scorich.

Seeking Theravadan nonattachment, in the days that followed, Sheba pruned her mother's white rosebush back fiercely. She wanted to put a blossoming lotus in the fountain's pool, once it was filled. She cut her hair short because Chris Scorich seemed to like it that way: with her trim little bangs she looked like a fresh-faced nun just starting her novitiate. After their date at the Tibetan puppet show Scorich had taken her home to his spartan little apartment in North Beach, and they had meditated together, which Sheba was inclined to view as a kind of foreplay. She was much encouraged—Scorich had even asked her out again, to a documentary film on the Dalai Lama, and she felt that with her own uneasiness about the relationship to the lures of the world clarified, things were progressing nicely, Shaivite tantric practice–wise. Their goodnight kiss had gone on and on.

When Sheba did finally get around to finishing off the closet, the work went fast. She dusted the shelf where Jackson's journal had been, twice; she threw out most of the last of her East Coast wardrobe, and on a second thought put the panda bear on the high back shelf. Finally, she swept the closet thoroughly, then wiped the floor with a damp rag and some Murphy's wood soap.

In the course of this final wipe on her hands and knees, she came upon two little wrinkled, reddish beads in the far back corner of the closet. Sheba was struck by the odd things; they looked as if they had come off some kind of necklace. She happened to show them that night to Scorich, who said they were rudraksha seeds and had probably come off someone's mala. A mala was a kind of rosary, it seemed. These seeds, then, had been fingered in prayer.

Impressed, Sheba put the rudrakshas in a little bowl on her altar table, figuring she would start a collection and maybe even make a mala of her own someday. She'd found two already, after all. According to Scorich, she only had one hundred and six beads to go.

Part XV

Gold Country

For an extremely large percentage of the history of the world, there was no California. That is, according to present theory. I don't mean to suggest that California was underwater and has since come up. I mean to say that of the varied terranes and physiographic provinces that we now call California nothing whatever was there.
—John McPhee, *Assembling California*

I

May Day

At the end of April, Toni Lafontane and Persephone Prescott-Bowers hosted their annual White-Water Beltane, on the American River. The event, a combination camping trip, river-rafting expedition, and pagan holiday, was always looked forward to by everyone in their circle. They all gathered at the same site every year, a little campground near Placerville. Toni and Pesky came early to prepare, and by the time everyone had arrived on May Eve the clearing was ready for the first night's celebration. A maypole stood at the center, crowned with orange gladiolas and streaming with a rainbow of multicolored ribbons. The branches of all the surrounding trees were hung with apples and pears and nectarines, with strings of nuts and popcorn, with fragrant peach-blossom leis and lavender orchids, with round breads and ginger cookies baked by Pesky in the shape of entwined lovers, with doughnuts and bagels and pomegranates. A bonfire burned at the clearing's south side, just beyond the reach of the maypole's longest ribbons, and bottles of Mendocino wine chilled in the little snow-fed stream to the east, along with several six-packs of Budweiser and Red Tail ale, and some diet Cokes.

By late afternoon everyone had arrived and set up their tents. They gathered near the maypole, and slowly conversation died away and a hush came over them all. They stood together, breathing quietly and listening to the birds in the trees, and to the river to the west. The silence deepened, until at last Toni stirred and said formally, in her capacity as priestess, "This is the eve of May, when sweet desire weds wild delight."

"Oh, *baby*," Pesky said, and everyone laughed.

192

"What we weave tonight with a dance of love is life's renewal," Toni went on, and they all chose their ribbons, in colors appropriate to their desires. Dante and the Holy Rose Parade started in softly on an upbeat version of "Greensleeves," with a building lead guitar and a mean bass line; and they all began to dance, slowly at first, smiling at each other and weaving gently in and out; and then more swiftly, and faster and faster, whirling and weaving, laughing as they went. By the time the ribbon cone was woven, they all were breathless and Dante was standing on top of his amplifier with his eyes rolled back in his head, making his guitar scream. Every year they were all amazed by what you could do to "Greensleeves" with a decent amp and a good drummer.

II

Wishes

AFTER THE MAYPOLE, MOST PEOPLE CONTINUED TO DANCE. THE HOLY ROSE Parade swung into a rock-and-roll rendition of "Froggie Went A-Courtin'," and everyone hopped and boogied, jumping over the fire and calling out wishes. Tristan Sussman and Nora Jane Hathaway jumped over the flames together and wished for a happy marriage of true minds and hearts. As they leaped, Nora Jane's scarf caught fire, and she was compelled to roll on the ground to put it out. Tristan, alertly, rolled with her; and they got up laughing and announced that the incident was auspicious. The scarf had been given to Nora by a former lover, and its unresolved karmic weight was no doubt what had been holding them back. It was a message from the goddess of spring. They tossed the scorched remnant of the scarf into the flames, to cheers.

Marlowe jumped carefully and wished for truth in her life and a healthy child. Toni Lafontane wished for a new pickup truck; and Pesky for a composting toilet. Daa wished for Marlowe's wishes to come true, and Victor Morris, invited on the trip by Daa and amused at all the ceremonial fuss, jumped the flames three times and wished for peace on earth, cold beer, and a pennant for the Orioles. He said, though, that he would settle for the beer and peace on earth. The Orioles just didn't have the pitching, they hadn't in decades, and they probably never would.

Sheba jumped the flames once and wished for love; and moments later she was able to catch the eye of Chris Scorich, who had not jumped at all, and led him away from the clearing for a walk.

"Why didn't you make a wish?" she said as they reached the river's edge and turned north. Across the water to the west, the sun was just going down, and the sky was orange and pink. The river was high with the spring melt-off and ran swiftly here. Downstream they could hear the roar of the first rapids.

Scorich shrugged. "What would I wish for? Right View, I suppose—the lucidity to watch the dream arise and fall away, without suffering attachment."

"I wished for love."

"Uh-huh," Scorich said carefully, and fell silent.

They walked without speaking for a while after that. Sheba was chastising herself internally for pushing too hard. It was a miracle that Scorich had agreed to come on the trip at all. These pagan extravaganzas were not his style. It was just that much more fuss and transitory illusion to him. Still, he was being a good sport about it. He had taken a black ribbon at the maypole, for emptiness. She knew that he had come for her sake, that he would have preferred sitting at home in the hushed little sanctuary room in his apartment, meditating on the essential unreality of the phenomenal world.

When they reached a little clearing farther up the river path, however, Scorich stopped and took her in his arms. They stood entwined for a long time, watching the sun set. Back in the main clearing, the music went on, as in a distant world. Sheba could feel the warm solidity of Scorich's body against hers. It always surprised her how firm he was, after all that talk of insubstantiality.

"It's beautiful, isn't it?" she said, of the sunset.

"Yes," Scorich said with an air of concession. He hesitated, then said in a sort of rush, "Listen, Sheba, I've been wondering for some time how to tell you . . ."

"Tell me what?"

"You may have gotten your wish." She glanced at him, startled. "I think I'm in love with you, is what I'm trying to say. I think I've gotten, um, attached."

Sheba smiled. *"Uh*-oh."

"But I've got to be honest with myself. I think about you all the time."

"Just pretend it's a dream, and everything will be all right," Sheba said, and put her arms around his neck. Their eyes met, and they smiled.

"Then again, maybe it's just the wine."

Sheba laughed. "You haven't had any wine."

"Maybe it's the thought of the wine," Scorich said, and kissed her.

III

An Emanation of Exuberance

THEY MADE LOVE ON SCORICH'S JACKET, IN A CLEARING BY THE RIVER. THE spring evening was still warm; in the twilight Sheba could see the insects winging above the water at the river's edge, and the darting movements of birds among them. Beyond this the stream's surface broke occasionally at the rising of a fish. The woods behind them were alive with the sounds of crickets, and the new leaves of the oaks stirred in the slight breeze. A great peace and certainty had descended on her, and everything unfolded placidly. Sheba believed that she was finally understanding just what Scorich was getting at when he talked about his meditative states—surely, she thought, this was what he meant when he described the ground of being, and how the phenomenal world arose from it spontaneously, as an emanation of exuberance; surely this was what he meant when he said that one could rest content beyond what was usually taken for reality.

Scorich himself might have been lighting the lamp at his altar. He seemed awed, and tender and attentive; and, when it came down to it, surprisingly deft. His tongue stirred her, his hands traced arcs of warm light, and his lips were sure and firm. They smiled at each other as he entered her, and she stroked his shoulders and hips and marveled at his clear eyes; and then as the pulse of him in her grew and deepened, she closed her eyes, and the river sounds faded. The world grew simpler and simpler, resolving into the firm, warm weightlessness of meeting, until even his presence as rhythm and heat blended into a kind of silence. Her mind grew still and calm, and when she opened her eyes at last, she could only smile and shake her head at the sight of his face and marvel that words would eventually have to be used again.

They walked back to the party hand in hand, still without speaking. The music had stopped now, and the moon was up. Everyone was feasting on the food from the trees. On a log at the far side of the clearing, Toni and Pesky fed each other cashews and bits of bagel. Albert Nerdowsky was trying to explain quantum physics to a woman who specialized in past-life readings. Victor Morris had gotten his cold beer and was drinking it with Daa. Marlowe sat off to the side, sketching the gathering, her face serene.

Sheba sat with Scorich and split a pomegranate with him, smiling as he opened a bottle of wine. She felt lit from within. Maybe this soft glow was the compassion that came in the wake of insight, she thought: it seemed so poignant, and so sad in its way, that they should have to assume again the mortal disguise and act as if fear had any meaning at all. It made her want to be kind to everyone she met.

IV

A Strong Brown God

THE NEXT DAY ALMOST EVERYONE GOT UP EARLY FOR PESKY'S POTENT coffee and buckwheat pancakes, then prepared themselves for the rafting. A small ceremony convened at the water's edge; salt was strewn, for purification, the quarters were called; there were impromptu baptisms and bathings, and poetry:

> *I do not know much about gods; but I think that the river*
> *Is a strong brown god—sullen, untamed and intractable,*
> *Patient to some degree, at first recognized as a frontier . . .*
> *Keeping his seasons and rages, destroyer, reminder*
> *Of what men choose to forget.*

Sunblock was applied to every pagan nose, and the life preservers were donned. Toni, who would steer one raft, pored over a map of the river's major rapids with Daa, who would be guiding the second raft. Each of them wore the traditional hermetic baseball cap, with little silver wings and the logo of the Grateful Dead on the front. Victor Morris labored on the hand pumps for an hour to inflate the rafts, hauled the rafts to the water's edge, alertly saved the paddles when they threatened to float away, and in general impressed the lesbians as a handy guy to have around.

Sheba, who would have preferred to pass the day in Chris Scorich's tent, where she had stayed the night, spent most of the morning untangling fishing lines. Jack Soft Hands, still moping over the fall of IHI and his rejection by every woman in his life, had gone off by himself before dawn to fish for trout and had entangled himself with the multiple lines of Marianna Swift. An intense young woman who believed in the imminent demise of Western civilization, Marianna kept three poles working at all times on these annual trips, to stay ahead of starvation in the event of catastrophic failure of the normal food supply. In her view, Jack's blundering into her array constituted a survival threat; and so Sheba, who had a known gift for intricacies, was called in to deal with the emergency. Marianna would not let Sheba simply cut the lines—the nylon fishing line was too precious a resource, and you never knew when you would be able to get more. They must be teased apart just so. The four lines were a tangled mess, and the unraveling took hours; but by the time Sheba was finished, Jack and Marianna had both calmed down and had even discovered a mutual taste for shiitake mushrooms and the channeled teachings of the Course in Miracles. Sheba left them deep in conversation, with the distinct sense that Jack's moroseness was passing.

V

Regarding the Essenes

AT LAST THE RAFTS WERE LAUNCHED, AMIDST HUBBUB, SPLASHING, AND song. Toni's rottweilers, Managarm, Anubis, and Diogenes, bounded around on the shore, barking and yelping and plunging in and out of the water. Toni and Daa called cadence as everyone paddled hard toward the center of the stream; and then the river's current took them off.

Those who had remained behind in the quiet camp went on about their business. Sheba had gone on Toni's raft, but Chris Scorich was still in his tent, absorbed in the most intensive meditations. He had awakened that morning in a panic, certain that two decades of spiritual work had been squandered on passion like coins at a fair. Only the sight of Sheba's face had kept him from returning at once to San Francisco and going into deep retreat. As it was, he prayed for guidance in the dark waters of corporeality. From time to time he would recall the night's delights and smile. He was hungover from the wine and it was affecting his concentration.

Many of those who stayed behind went for walks. Albert Nerdowsky sat by the still-warm embers of the previous night's bonfire and read from the Dead Sea scrolls, making notes as he went. It was Nerdo's suspicion that the Essenes had been in contact with the Andromeda galaxy, and he was finding confirmation for this theory in almost every line of the Nag Hamadi texts.

Marlowe had remained behind too, for the baby's sake. She had Jackson's journal with her; she had been reading it a few pages at a time for weeks. By now she had worked up to the spring of 1989. After his initial rage Jackson had been seized by a furious practicality and filled page after journal page for months with lists of symptoms and treatments, drugs (legal and black market), and doctors, legitimate and crazy. Faith and chemicals ran neck and neck. Jackson was on top of his white cell count and platelets, and doing visualizations; he was meticulous on diet and exercise. He was going to beat this thing.

March 19. Greens, greens, greens. Greens!

April 23. If I ever see another plate of greens I'm going to run screaming to the nearest surf-and-turf and eat a cow and two lobsters. But I have to say it seems to be helping—certainly my energy is up. Ironic if getting diagnosed turns out to be the best thing that ever happened to my health.

May 19. In the hospital again. So much for the greens. Maybe I should have eaten that lobster while I could.

The return of the humor reminded Marlowe of how things had turned that spring. Jackson's initial zeal had subsided eventually—the disease was so very obviously one thing after another that the phases of faith in the various magics passed quickly. There was always news of somebody surviving wonderfully on some new thing, and, it seemed, almost inevitably a few days later news of somebody dying on it too. Some things helped and some things didn't, but nothing helped entirely. The programs came and went. They had begun to develop a different balance. Jackson had in fact had three bites of lobster and a symbolic bite of medium-rare steak on Memorial Day; a little bit of eat, drink, and be merry was coming into the thing by then.

June 17. Will I ever be married in white?

June 19. Probably not, thank God.

Dante came over to where Marlowe was sitting just then. He could not swim and would not go near a raft, and so he always stayed back at camp on these trips and played his guitar. He had been hanging out for most of the morning at the picnic table beneath the camp's big oak trees, alternately strumming a tune or two and eating leftover pancakes dipped in honey. But now he had had a wonderful idea. He had come up with a couple of frying pans and wanted Marlowe to go with him to look for gold.

"Gold?" Marlowe said.

"Oh, it's everywhere around here," Dante said.

Marlowe laughed. It was a typical Dante idea. No doubt all the gold in California was long since gone, but after the briefest hesitation she put the journal in her day pack and went along to humor him. Why not? she thought. A little adventure, a little foolishness. They were none of them getting any younger.

VI

Aurum Nostrum Non Est Aurum Vulgi

ONCE THE IDEA HAD TAKEN HOLD, THE QUEST BEGAN TO ABSORB THEM.
Marlowe and Dante panned at the river's edge for a while, then
began to work their way up a rocky little inlet stream, back up
into the hills, sifting the sand and gravel in the swift-running
water without result. Marlowe found a quarter, lost perhaps by a
previous seeker; but there was no gold.

At last, after about an hour, they rested in the sun on a big flat
rock beside the stream, half a mile up from the river. Marlowe
leaned back and sighed and cupped her belly in both hands. She
could feel the baby kicking.

"He's all fired up," she told Dante, and placed his hand on her
stomach. Dante's eyes widened in awe.

"How do you know it's a boy?"

"Because everyone wants it to be a girl. There's such contrari-
ness in his genes, he can't help but be a boy, just to piss everyone
off."

"Ah," Dante said, as he always did when he found her incomprehensible. Marlowe laughed, and they sat for a while in silence
in the sun, watching the dragonflies flit above the stream and
listening to the breeze in the foothill oaks. Marlowe took her
sketchpad and charcoal pencil out of her day pack and began to
sketch Dante as a forty-niner, with a beard and boots and sus-
penders. Dante watched her, languidly amused. He seemed to
have recovered from his disappointment with Sheba, Marlowe
noted; he was his old imperturbable musical self. This silly search

201

for gold was a lark for him—he wouldn't have known what to do with riches had he found them. At this thought, she turned the sketchpad page and began to draw him as an alchemist instead.

A hawk circled above them in the bright air, riding the rising heat above the ridge; far below they could see the broad bend in the river, and the beach near the camp. A lizard scampered across a nearby rock and stopped abruptly, its mottled sides flexing like a bellows. Marlowe sketched him into her drawing as a salamander in the retort's flame and smiled.

"Maybe if we don't go back, the world will stay like this," she said. "Quiet and warm and beautiful. Wouldn't that be something? I wouldn't feel like such a fool, having a baby in a world like *this*."

"So let's stay," Dante said.

Marlowe laughed. "Oh, sweetheart, you're nuttier than anyone I know."

"Seriously. We'll build a house with the gold we find."

"And eat music, I suppose."

"Sure. We even have frying pans. We can live on music and lizards and acorns, and fried sunbeams."

"I could never eat lizards."

The lizard fled, as if on cue. They laughed. Marlowe turned the page on her sketchpad and started on a drawing of the tree across the stream.

"Would you really have married Sheba, Dante?"

"Oh, yes," Dante said serenely. "I would still marry her, if she'd have me. It's just not meant to be."

"You don't seem too broken up about it."

"Well, it lets me off the hook in a way, if you know what I mean," Dante said, and looked puzzled when Marlowe laughed. "It *does*."

"Oh, don't I know it. You just never cease to amaze me."

"I mean, what terror to be in an actual relationship. What *torment*. Always having to be here or there at a certain time, and say certain things, always having to worry about the person dying or getting bored—this and that, this and that, one dense realist thing after another, and no time left for art. Unrequited love is best for people, by far. I believe it's the next step in evolution—uh, present company excepted, of course," he said quickly with a glance at Marlowe's belly.

"Oh, for God's sake, Dante, this baby isn't the product of requited love."

Dante looked horrified. "It's not?"

"Of course not. It's *Jack's.*"

"Yes, I know, but—"

"Well, I don't love Jack. I never did. And Jack never loved me. Neither of us, to be perfectly honest, is *capable* of love."

"That's not true."

"The hell it's not."

"You love Daa."

"No. Daa loves me. Deeply, truly, faithfully. Daa is capable of that kind of thing. She's a modern miracle, a mature human being. But I'm not. I'm a monster, a freak of nature—or a product of my times, I suppose, depending on which side of it you want to play up."

Dante, flustered, reached into his pocket and drew out a harmonica. He gave it a tentative puff.

"And now I've made you uncomfortable too and ruined a sweet moment," Marlowe said. "You see, though, it just proves my case. I'm a loveless, hideous monster, a blight on the earth."

"You shouldn't talk like that, Marlowe," Dante said reproachfully.

"Oh, I know, I know. I'm a fountain of wrong thinking, I know I'm doing great damage to my inner child, even as we speak. I'm an Inner Child abuser—you should call the authorities and have me locked up."

Dante, looking miserable, blew a blues chord on the harmonica, then considered the instrument sadly, as if it had let him down.

"I'm going to go look for gold," he said, and clambered down off the rock with his frying pan. Avoiding Marlowe's eyes, he moved a few steps upstream until he found a sandy patch, where he dipped the pan to scoop some material up and began to shake and sift it. Marlowe watched him morosely. She could hear Dante humming to himself, and she found an odd comfort in the sound. It was like a night-light.

"Do you love me, Dante?" she said, raising her voice slightly to be heard.

"Of course," Dante said at once.

"No, I mean *really* love me."

"I've always loved you," Dante said, and met her eyes across the stream.

Marlowe marveled at that look; it was as shocking as if the tree across from her had suddenly spoken. She would never have imagined Dante capable of such a look.

"You're serious," she said. "Crazy as a loon, of course; dangerous even, maybe—but serious."

"And I'm going to find gold too. You just watch me."

VII

All That Glitters

AFTER THEY GOT BACK TO SAN FRANCISCO, MARLOWE TRIED TO RECAPture that look of Dante's, in a bookful of sketches and in several paintings. She spent a week and a half on the drawings and studies, and another week each on two canvases, working with acrylics and failing completely to catch what she had seen, until at last the image faltered and ceased to haunt her.

In a way, she was relieved; it was like the passing of a fever. She had used to see that look in Jackson too—a gaze of utter certainty, the look of a love she could believe in. The end-of-the-movie look was how she thought of it; the one that rang true. With Jackson she had just begun to settle into what a love like that might *mean* when he was diagnosed, and she had followed that look like a thread into the labyrinth of his illness. Every twist, every change for the worse, every momentary obscurity and fumbling had held such terror for her. But the thread had held. On his deathbed Jackson had glanced at her and winked, and she had recognized the look afresh, changed of course to accommodate his wasted features, transposed like a piece of music to a different key, for a different instrument, but for all that clearly recognizable. She had even had a sense after he had died that the look somehow went on, like the Cheshire cat's smile, just waiting for Jackson in some different form to materialize around it again.

It had not meant sex, of course, that look, it had meant nothing of the usual love. Not with Jackson, and certainly not with Dante, with all his blathering about unrequited love. Glimpsing it now in Dante, indeed, Marlowe was inclined to doubt the phenomenon entirely. It was all just projection on her part, a crystallized wish, a mask of longing laid over the world's usual face. It was a failure of maturity.

Daa came in while Marlowe was finishing the second painting. "What in the world is *this?*"

"Oh, just something from a dream I had."

"Is this *Dante?*"

"Sort of. I dreamed that he was an alchemist, see, and that he somehow made gold."

"Not bloody likely. Dante couldn't make change on a dollar. All that guy can make is music, and God bless him for *that.*"

"I know." Marlowe put the last touches on the salamander, dancing in the flames, and laid the painting aside.

It would have been nice to be able to leave it at that, but Dante *had* found gold. Not a lot, the merest scattered handful of dust and a few grainy nuggets, panned out of a spot just up the stream from the boulder they had sat on. He had given it all to Marlowe, in the blue velvet bag he normally used for his harmonica. She had taken it to be assayed, at a jeweler's she knew in the city, feeling sheepish even to bring it in.

"I know it's probably just fool's gold and all," she had told the man as he tested it with acid.

"No," he said cheerfully. "No, it's the real thing all right. Not much, of course." He glanced at her and winked. "Maybe enough for a couple of wedding rings, though—hey?"

"What the hell is that supposed to mean?" Marlowe demanded.

The jeweler held up his hands placatingly. "No offense meant, lady. It's your call. Hell, I could make a Saint Christopher's medal out of it, if you want. I could make a gold chain. I could make a set of gold toothpicks—hey, there's an idea. I just had a guy in here last week, wanted a whole goddamned set of gold toothpicks."

"Forget it. I was just curious."

Marlowe put the gold back in the harmonica bag and took it home and put the bag in a box, and she put the box at the bottom of her closet. Silly, silly, silly, she thought; silly. All gold was fool's gold, it was nothing but trouble.

Part XVI

Journey to the East

Men come and they go and they trot and they dance, and never a word about death. All well and good. Yet when death does come—to them, their wives, their children, their friends—catching them unawares and unprepared, then what storms of passion overwhelm them, what cries, what fury, what despair!

To begin depriving death of its greatest advantage over us, let us adopt a way clean contrary to that common one; let us deprive death of its strangeness, let us frequent it, let us get used to it; let us have nothing more often in mind than death. . . . We do not know where death awaits us: so let us wait for it everywhere. To practice death is to practice freedom. A man who has learned how to die has unlearned how to be a slave.

—Montaigne, Essais

I

Colin

Marlowe's father had a stroke in June. Her mother called her at two in the morning, California time, edgy and apologetic, and spent the first five minutes of the call reassuring Marlowe that she had in fact known *exactly* what time it was on the West Coast. Marlowe's irritation swelled; she thought it was all just Bernice's usual dither. But at last her mother came out with it: Colin was in intensive care, and lucky to be alive at all.

Marlowe hung up the phone as if she were putting an egg back in its box and looked at her hands in the lamplight for a long time. They were big, strong hands, supple and graceful—her father's hands, everyone had always said. An artist's hands, her father had said. She had been ashamed of them for years because they were not delicate; even now she found herself hiding them sometimes, from old habit, as she had in junior high. But she had grown into them, as Colin had always said she would. Marlowe wondered now if he would ever know that—she and her father had not spoken for almost seven years.

She realized that she was not surprised at the news. In some odd way she had known this was coming. Looking back over the series of her mop paintings recently, she had been startled to find her father's face in several of them—his blue eyes, pale and cool, had jumped out at her, and the whimsical sprawl of his gray, unmanageable mane, and the smile he offered the world, precise and ironic. She had wondered what he was doing there, where Jackson should have been.

And she had dreamed of him lately as well. In one dream he had been walking with her on a beach at sunset. She had been surprised because the only beaches they had ever walked on together were the Eastern beaches of the Atlantic seaboard. But this had been the Pacific. The tide had just turned; it was starting to go out, and her father had commented on this. In another dream, it was Father's Day, and she had been shocked to find a pair of perfectly good shoes in a trash can. Someone had told her they were worn-out, and she had replied, "Nonsense—look at the soles. They're fine." And then, just the week before, she had dreamed her father was a tiger chasing his tail. He had gone around and around a tree, faster and faster until he was a blur, and she had been sure that he would turn into butter, like the tiger in *The Jungle Book*. But instead the tree had blossomed. It was the apple tree in their backyard on Long Island, and in the dream she could smell the sweet, light flowers. A shower of white petals fell steadily, like spring rain. "There's still the question of the covenant," someone had said, and Marlowe had awakened, in inexplicable tears.

"What are you going to do?" Daa said now. She was sitting up in bed in her T-shirt, having listened to Marlowe's end of the phone call.

"I don't know. Pray, maybe? He may die, Bernice says. He's still unconscious."

"You should go back."

"Hah."

"You *should*. You should be there."

"Like he's been there for me?" And as Daa set her jaw stubbornly and said nothing, Marlowe said, "Well, what would I do anyway, once I was there? Watch him lie there with tubes in him? Or, worse, have him wake up and snub me on his deathbed? I'd rather cherish the bad memories I've got, thank you."

"For God's sake, Marlowe. Grow up and get real. It's your father."

II

A Sense of Style

SHE TOOK THE FIRST PLANE EAST, AS SHE HAD KNOWN SHE WOULD. HER mother met her at the airport. Bernice looked like hell in a rumpled cotton summer dress and sandals; Marlowe was shocked to see her with her hair neglected and no makeup. In a way, it delighted her. She had a sense of catching her mother backstage at last, between acts.

They embraced briefly.

"My God, look at you. When is it due?"

"In about a month. What a cow I am, huh?"

"I was twice as big with you, and you were born early," Bernice said, attempting to take Marlowe's carry-on bag.

Marlowe shifted the bag deftly to her other hand. They walked away from the gate in silence. Bernice reeked of some sharp, expensive perfume; she appeared to be trying to compensate for everything with an impenetrable field of fragrance.

"So, how is he?" Marlowe said at last.

Her mother sighed. "Still not awake. The doctors say it could go either way. But I don't think they know what they're talking about, to tell you the truth. It wouldn't be like your father, not like him at all, to die like this."

"Jesus, Mother. How the hell *would* it be like him to die?"

"Oh, you know what I mean."

"I don't, actually." Marlowe did, though. Bernice's capacity for denial was showing clearly. Her mother believed with the force of dogma that a man's sense of style held through everything he did. It would have been uncharacteristic of her father to do anything abrupt or jarring. It would have amounted to rudeness.

Colin would never stoop to rudeness; therefore he would not die. It was a faith almost too sad to contemplate, and certainly too flimsy to examine.

Bernice took Marlowe's hand in both of hers. "It's so wonderful of you to come out here like this. It does my heart good. And I know your father will be delighted."

"If he wakes up, you mean," Marlowe said, and felt cruel as her mother's face fell. She had never seen her eyes so tired.

"He'll wake up," Bernice said. "If only to make a proper goodbye. He's that kind of man."

III

The Perils of Reconciliation

THEY DROVE STRAIGHT TO ST. JOHN'S IN BERNICE'S BUICK, A MASSIVE sedan of olive green that she had had since Marlowe could remember. Bernice drove erratically, but this could not be attributed to the current stress: she always drove erratically. Marlowe sucked in her breath as they changed lanes without signaling in front of an eighteen-wheeler and nearly grazed a guardrail. Her right foot was jammed to the floor against a phantom brake, as it always was when she rode with her mother. A St. Christopher's medal dangled from Bernice's rearview mirror, slapping against the windshield at her wilder maneuvers.

"What bothers me most, I think, is that Colin would not have wanted you to see him like this," Bernice said, narrowly avoiding a pickup truck. "He would have preferred a reconciliation with more, um . . ."

"Dignity?"

"Exactly," Bernice said, pleased.

"He had seven years to come up with a dignified reconciliation.

And besides, I'm not sure reconciliation is the point here. In fact, I'm not sure *what* the—Mother, you're drifting left, you're *drifting*, Mother."

Bernice steadied the Buick in the center lane of the expressway. Cars flowed past them on either side, the drivers glancing over at them uneasily.

"Of course reconciliation is the point," Bernice said.

Marlowe reached into her purse and came up with a cigarette. Reconciliation, however unlikely, was always the point with her mother; Bernice's failures were not in good intention but in her reality sense. Marlowe lit the cigarette with a snap of the lighter, breathed deep, and blew smoke toward the St. Christopher medal. Since her childhood she'd hated that medal whacking at the windshield every time Bernice took a corner or slammed on the brakes. She hated it now. Perhaps there was comfort in the unchanging verities after all.

"I thought you'd stopped that years ago," Bernice said reproachfully as the smoke filled the car.

"I only smoke when I'm away from California, if you must know. I think the East Coast is bad for my health."

"That's right, blame it on me."

Marlowe laughed. Bernice wanted credit for everything. "Oh, Mother, I'm not—"

"Besides, it's bad for the baby. Are you thinking of the baby?"

Marlowe sighed and stubbed the cigarette out. "There. Okay? Happy?"

"It's only common sense," Bernice said, and crossed three lanes to make the exit, the medal banging on the windshield.

IV

Last Rites

St. John's hospital kept two priests on call at all times for the administration of last rites; it had been Marlowe's impression since childhood that this stately granite building with its chronically inadequate parking and leafy grounds was where all Catholics came to die. When she had been brought here in fourth grade to have her tonsils out, she had been terrified the entire time, and uneasy that she had not been given extreme unction. Now she knew from Bernice that her father had already received the sacrament twice, which was typical of the hospital's efficiency in that area.

The place had not changed much since her youth, though it seemed less sinister now, and sadder. Nursing nuns sailed up and down the halls like gulls, in simple white habits, and every waiting room's silence was punctuated by the click of rosary beads. The hospital gift shop still did its brisk business in laminated prayer cards, illustrated surreally with bright and gory images of the Bleeding Heart of Jesus and doe-eyed Virgins. There were crucifixes everywhere. Marlowe realized with some amusement that even she was wearing a crucifix—she had made the rosary of her childhood into several pieces of jewelry at some point, and its cross dangled from her left ear now. Her other earring was a miniature Kali figure dancing on a skull. She had not thought her accessories through before she got on the plane, but it seemed to her that in this case at least her usual California practice carried over well enough into St. John's. This place, armored against death with ritual and talismans, could use a touch of the Goddess who swept it all away like a house of cards.

213

Her father was still in intensive care, his bed screened by a ring of drawn curtains. The nurse, who obviously knew Bernice, paused to confer with them. There had been no change in his condition, she said. Marlowe stepped inside the curtain while the two women talked and felt her throat clench in dismay. Colin lay enmeshed in a web of tubes and wires, hooked up to intravenous units and a heart monitor, with an oxygen tube up his nose. His arms were black-and-blue from needle entries, and his cheeks were sunken. His hair was a mess, which Marlowe found oddly comforting. It had grayed completely and gone wild in his late twenties, and Bernice had been trying for three decades since then to keep it combed.

Her father's eyes were closed, and his ashen face gave no flicker of response at her arrival. The ridge of his brow stood out, and she could easily imagine the skull beneath the skin. On the other side of the curtain, the man in the neighboring bed was receiving his last rites. Marlowe could hear muffled sobs, and the priest's voice droning low: "In the name of the Father, and of the Son, and of the Holy Spirit, may there be extinguished in thee every power of the Devil by the imposition of our hands . . ."

"He looks awful, doesn't he?" Bernice said, beside her, and Marlowe jumped a little, startled.

"Yes. He does."

"He needs a bath. These nurses are terrible. I'd asked them to bathe him and give him a shave and do something about that hair, before you arrived."

Marlowe glanced at Bernice incredulously. Beyond the curtain, the priest murmured on. She could smell the *oleum infirmorum*, the consecrated olive oil that was smeared in the sign of the cross on the eyes, ears, nose, mouth, hands, feet, and thighs of the dying; she could still see traces of the same oil on the closed lids of her father's eyes.

"By this holy unction, and by his most tender compassion, may the Lord forgive thee in whatsoever way thou hast sinned by sight . . ."

"I'm sure the nurses are doing the best they can," Marlowe said. "This isn't a beauty salon, after all."

"Your father never went a day in his life without shaving. Most

days he shaved twice. He would even shave when we went camping.''

"I remember that."

"Still, I suppose I can understand it. Them not shaving him, I
mean. With the tube up his nose and all. Now, his *hair* on the
other hand . . .''

*"By this holy unction, and by his most tender compassion, may the
Lord forgive thee in whatsoever way thou hast sinned by hearing . . ."*

"I'm sure the nurses are doing the best they can," Marlowe
said again, and went to the bedside to take her father's hand. Her
first memory was of her father's hand in hers. She must have
been three years old at the time. They had been in a sunny
meadow in the Catskills, and he had been painting—an oak tree
by an old stone wall, she remembered even that, or at least she
believed she did. This memory was so vivid that it was suspect;
she felt that she could have re-created every hue from his palette
that day, and she could not be sure how much of the detail was a
later addition of what she knew now, and how much was real
memory. But the basic elements were clear: it had been sunny
and warm, and they were surrounded by greenery. The world
was enormous and peaceful. She held her father's left hand while
he painted with his right, and she could still see his wedding ring,
and a smear of green paint across the knuckles of his second and
third fingers; she could see the easel's silhouette and hear birds.

*"By this holy unction, and by his most tender compassion, may the
Lord forgive thee in whatsoever way thou hast sinned by speech . . ."*

She had asked if she could help him paint, Marlowe recalled,
and she remembered daubing some of the oak tree's green onto
the canvas and feeling very proud of the effect. No doubt her
father had worked that green blob deftly into his landscape. He
had never let her believe her work was anything but lovely.

His hand lay limply now in hers, cool and bruised. The oxygen
hissed a little in his nose, and his heartbeat registered on a green
screen across the bed from her. The beat seemed fine to Marlowe,
regular and strong; she marveled that Colin didn't simply wake
and smile at her and ask her to fetch his pipe. Jackson, in just
such a posture, had opened his eyes unexpectedly and gazed at

her, toward the end; through the morphine and the flickering candlelight, he had unmistakably winked.

Her father, of course, was not the winking sort.

Beyond the curtain, the priest had begun the litany for the dying man in the neighboring bed, calling on the Mother of God, the angels, patriarchs and saints, to pray for him.

"We shouldn't stay long," her mother said. "We'll tire him." And, as Marlowe said nothing, she prompted again, gently, "We should go, dear."

"Not just yet, Mother, please."

"But—"

"I think he's glad to see me."

Bernice fluttered a little, pleased and flustered, like a preening bird. "Well, I suppose that it's all right, at that, if you want to visit a bit. You always had a better sense of him, actually, than I."

Marlowe pulled a chair up beside the bed and sat down, taking her father's hand again in hers. She could feel his pulse now, weakly, beneath her fingers. Bernice took out her rosary and sat at the bed's other side, her lips moving as she murmured the Hail Mary. At the neighboring bed, the priest had cut to the chase.

"Go forth, Christian soul, from this world in the name of God the Father Almighty, who created thee; in the name of Jesus Christ, the son of the living God, who suffered for thee; in the name of the Holy Spirit, who was poured out upon thee; in the name of the holy and glorious Mother of God, the Virgin Mary . . ."

And so on, through the entire elaborate hierarchy of angels, archangels, thrones, dominions, principalities, powers, cherubim, seraphim, patriarchs, prophets, apostles, evangelists, martyrs, confessors, monks, hermits, virgins, and saints, while the women wept.

V

Intensive Care

FOR A WEEK COLIN'S CONDITION REMAINED UNCHANGED. HE LAY COMA-
tose in the same bed in the ICU, while a succession of people died
in the beds around him or moved on to regular care. Marlowe
and her mother soon evolved a routine that suited them both.
Bernice would wake her early and they would go to morning
mass at the chapel of Saint John of the Cross, and then they
would go by the hospital and visit Colin. They would sit on either
side of the bed for about an hour, and Bernice would chatter to
him. She believed it was important to keep her husband informed
of daily events. She even read parts of the newspaper to him at
times, to keep him current. Marlowe sat across the bed from her
with her drawing pad and charcoal pencil and sketched, as she
once had at the grown-ups' parties, when her parents let her stay
up late. She drew her mother and her father, and the big chestnut
tree beyond the window, with its broad, heavy leaves and spiky
nuts; she drew the flowers on the bedside table, and the nurses
and doctors.

Mostly she drew Colin's face, again and again, in the changing
lights. She drew his hands too, bruises and all. She had never
been able to draw him so much; he had never liked to pose. He
could not happily sit still for long, and he often joked that there
would be plenty of time for portraits when he died. Sketching
him now, Marlowe would think of that sometimes and find herself in tears, which made Bernice uneasy. Her mother persisted in
treating Colin's condition as something akin to a long nap.

Afterward, the two women would go home for lunch and drink
iced tea in the big backyard, beneath the sprawling apple tree.

Bernice would continue to chatter, and Marlowe would nod lazily, savoring the summer afternoon, with images of Colin turning over and over in her mind's eye like clothes being tumbled in a dryer. Her mother was catching her up on every local event of the last decade. The world according to Bernice seemed very simple to Marlowe. All Marlowe's friends from high school had married and bred by now and were leading blissfully happy lives. All of their parents had divorced and remarried, or died horribly or become alcoholics. Bernice seemed to approve of the alcoholism, if only because it kept the marriages together.

"Oh, Millie Preston called, by the way," Bernice said one afternoon. "Millie Miller, I mean—she's married now, of course, with three lovely children."

"Of course," Marlowe said.

"She'd heard you were in town and was eager to get together."

"Fat chance."

Bernice hesitated, "She, um, wants to give you a shower."

"A shower?" Marlowe said, confused for a moment by images of bright Millie Preston from junior high, in braces and shorts, soaping her up in a stream of hot water.

"Yes, a baby shower. I thought it was so thoughtful of her. And Millie's just the person to—"

Marlowe groaned.

"I told her I didn't think you'd feel it would be appropriate, of course, with your father and all," Bernice said quickly.

"That was brilliant, Mother. I'm forever in your debt."

"Still, it *is* a nice idea, and if you *did* think it might be something you'd like, I'm sure we could—"

"Forget it. That's the last thing I need right now, some kind of weird pink ordeal."

Bernice sipped her iced tea. "You should give Millie a call, at least," she said after a moment. "She was so eager to catch up with you. And she's such a nice girl."

"Mother, Millie Preston is an insipid twit."

"Her mother is very nice too," Bernice said blithely, unfazed. "Though she's got all she can handle, I must say, with Albert's drinking."

After lunch, they would go back to the hospital and repeat the morning's routine; then they would eat a light supper in the hospital cafeteria and spend the evening at Colin's bedside as well. The routine, though grueling in its way, had an odd monastic simplicity that appealed to Marlowe. Stripped of inessentials, constrained to contemplation of her father and herself, she was, unforeseeably, making her peace.

And she was grateful for the opportunity. Bernice had been right about that much, at least—it was not like Colin to end anything abruptly. This drawn-out departure, if such it was, was more his style. Marlowe and he had fought for seven years before they had stopped talking to each other.

The issue, ostensibly, had been artistic. Colin, a minimalist of great precision, had felt that her West Coast work failed to sustain a necessary irony, that she had succumbed to the creeping blight of "meaning." He had not given up an inch of ground to the "narrative myth" of California without a protracted battle, and even when they had exhausted the dialogue, he had still continued to send her articles and clippings advocating a return to painterly surface. It was hard for Marlowe to conceive, looking at the wasted man in the bed before her now, that they had ceased to speak over such a hermeneutical point. For her part, she had always suspected that Colin's attempts to deconstruct her West Coast work smacked more of a father's failure to maintain control than of disinterested concern for the purity of her painterly surface.

"You don't give a shit about my 'meta-narrative,'" she had said to him more than once. "You just want me to stop sleeping with women and go back to art school to get my spirit properly crushed."

"I want you to stop painting insipid New Age fairy tales."

"The Goddess is not a fairy tale, she's real," Marlowe said, aware of the irony. Within her circle of friends in California she was widely regarded as a cynic. "The sacred is real, the sublime is real. You can't declare a whole range of human experience off limits to art just because it exceeds your dried-up little conception."

"It's a false sense of communion, it's like an intoxication that's gone in the morning. And you're capable of such substantial work. I loved that series you did on the chromatic lattices, for instance."

"And Mom loved my horse pictures. I'll paint whatever I damn well please, Father. And sleep with whomever I damn please too, which I still think is really the point."

"You always take it to the crudest literal level."

So the arguments had circled. And somewhere along the line they had both thrown up their hands and ceased to speak. Now, faced with her father's prostrate form, Marlowe felt that their alienation had been a foolish waste of time, a squandering fed by pride. All she could recall of her father now seemed colored with love alone—failed love, admittedly, confused and battered love; but love, for all that. Every memory, every image, found its place in that light. They had squabbled and debated and minced every word and phrase and notion into a contradictory hash, and none of it—he had been right about that much—had meant a thing. What survived all the confusion and the hurt was just this tenderness, this soft, mild longing to reach out and heal, this peace. Sitting by his hospital bed, Marlowe felt she could pray for her father at last with an open heart. It was an irony he alone might have appreciated that her deathbed portraits of him promised to be some of her best work yet. He would have liked that a lot, she thought, though he might still have felt she had strayed from a surface without depth into the hazards of communion.

VI

Boxes

ONE NIGHT TOWARD THE END OF THE FIRST WEEK, MARLOWE CLIMBED TO the attic of the Long Island house to look for baby clothes. Her mother had said several boxes of Marlowe's infant wardrobe were up there somewhere, though she could not recall precisely where and had no energy to rummage. The hospital routine was visibly wearing on Bernice; she came home more haggard every night and made herself a knockout cup of blackberry tea laced with vodka, which she took to bed with a book on the afterlife by a Jesuit theologian who held that sin incurs both an eternal and a temporal punishment. The eternal punishment was wiped out by the sacrifice of Christ, provided that its effects were mediated to the particular soul through the sacraments. But the temporal punishment remained due in any case: the soul must suffer for its sins. The Jesuit, apparently influenced by Brueghel, painted a vivid picture of the purgatorial fires in particular. Masses and prayers offered for the departed had the effect of shortening the stay in the flames, and Bernice was gearing up, for Colin's sake. Though she knew at heart he was a good man, she had always feared his postmodern views would serve him badly in the hereafter.

The attic was lit by a single bulb. In the bad light, Marlowe climbed the ladder and scattered the mice and began to sort through the packed cardboard boxes her mother had assiduously collected over the decades.

All Marlowe's history was here; Bernice threw nothing away. Every old doll and plaything, all her books and games, leaf collections and pressed flowers, traces of keepsake spiderweb preserved in some kind of spray; *Misty of Chincoteague* and *An Otter's Tale*, and porcelain horses and unicorns and bears, fairies, warlocks, and maps of the stars. Here was her high school life in a layer of boxes labeled in gray pen, in Marlowe's own handwriting—she'd affected for a while to write only in silver ink, and it had not aged well. Here was her grade-school era, a mass of flattened butterflies and jars of pebbles collected for some forgotten reason, duly saved by Bernice; a Brownie's cap, almost new—she'd quit after two days—and a magnifying glass cracked across the face.

Mostly there were drawings, sketches, paintings—box after box of paper dating back to her first crayon scrawls and loops. As Marlowe paused over a crayon drawing she'd made at the age of eight, of a big blue, happy whale spouting a spray of rainbow, the baby kicked within her, and she felt a wave of déjà vu. The day she'd made that drawing had been gray and cool, and she'd made herself a cup of tea and spent the afternoon beneath a lamp, in a magical pool of yellow light. She'd always meant to paint that whale in watercolors too.

"What?" she said to the baby now. "Do you want to come out and play?"

At last she came upon a stack of boxes that held old baby clothes. She sorted through them, smiling at the accumulation of incongruities. Bernice had always said Marlowe would find a use for these; they'd fought about it often enough. And now her time of need had come around. It was a humbling thing.

The bottom box in the stack held not infant clothes but a satin wedding dress, her grandmother's, and her grandmother's billowy wedding veil. Bernice had offered these to her once as well, no doubt in the hope that she would use them properly. Now Marlowe hesitated a moment; and then put the box with the veil and the gown aside, with the rest of the baby clothes she intended to take back to California.

VII

A Fresh Palette

COLIN WOKE ON A THURSDAY AFTERNOON, MAKING HIS REENTRY INTO THE land of the conscious with so little fuss that it took Marlowe a long moment to register that he was awake. One instant she was sketching him with a streaming backlight of afternoon sun in his hair like a frazzled halo, and the next she was aware of him looking at her quietly, with a faint quizzical smile.

He did not speak for quite a while, for long enough that the doctors feared brain damage. But to Marlowe it was clear from the start that he was all there, and even that he'd changed. They sat for hours holding hands, savoring the luxury of silence. When Colin did begin to speak on the second day, it was with a sort of wink, as if to acknowledge how silly all these words were.

Bernice was thrilled to have her husband back among the speaking. She and Colin discussed a wealth of world events and domestic details—apparently Colin had registered everything from his wife's briefings, and he was prepared to talk intelligently about the latest developments in the Balkans, and how to handle some recommended car repairs.

He was walking almost right away and went home within a couple days. Marlowe stayed another week and went for strolls with him as far out into the neighborhood as he could handle, a little farther every day. They still spoke of almost nothing but the beauty of the summer and the way the vegetation had changed while he was out. Most days they would paint as well, in the backyard, as they had when she was six and seven and eight. She told him about her dreams of him, and the way he'd shown up in her mops, and she was not surprised to find he could relate to that. He said the world between was a vivid, vivid place. And he laid his hand on her belly and said he'd seen her child, a remark so casual and wild that she had no idea what to say. Mostly they laughed and joked and ate Bernice's new low-cholesterol meals with a sodium-free salt substitute and a kind of giddy glee.

Marlowe flew home smiling to herself, chasing a sunset across most of the United States. The rose clouds and golden traces in the western sky lay glowing below her. The baby kicked and played, and she felt for the first time that they would know each other someday. That seemed miracle enough; but there was the knowledge too that Colin was in a brand-new phase. They had painted together every day, and there could be no doubt: his palette had completely changed. Her father was painting angels, in his wry, ironic way.

Part XVII

Meanwhile Back at Home

> It seems that those whom the gods wish to destroy
> they first send to California.
> —Shiva Naipaul, *Journey to Nowhere*

I

A New Resolve

SHAKTI ARGUELLO RETURNED FROM THE BRITISH ISLES FEELING THAT SHE was fully recovered from Victor Morris's marriage proposal and bent on giving away everything she owned. Her plan now was to retire to the north woods to live a life of pure communion with the nature devas that had contacted her.

Her experience in Ireland had been profound. She'd stayed in a stone cottage in an ancient forest glen south of Knock, near the western coast, living on oatmeal and potatoes, and walking and walking in the cool summer woods. The spirits of the greenery had left her serene for weeks on end, and all her past had resolved itself one day into a stone she had tossed into a stream. Every night she'd dreamed of the same elegant elf, Arturo, and a fairy who resembled a playmate named Jessie she'd had when she was young. No one had ever seen Jessie but herself, and Shakti was ecstatic to see her again, albeit somewhat changed— Jessie wore veils now, trailing freely, a definite concession to an archetypal look, where once she had worn a kind of sweatshirt. And she had matured in myriad other ways; she no longer seemed quite so involved with frogs, for instance, and she had forgiven Shakti's mother for things that Shakti herself had long forgotten. The two of them had used to spend quite a bit of time, Shakti recalled now, griping about her mother. It all seemed so silly in retrospect. But the continuity was clear enough, the fairy was as Jessie as ever, and Shakti felt thrilled that such a long-lost aspect of her psyche had been reemerged from the depths.

Her future had become clear to her as well. It had nothing of the human realm in it; she would live her life out as a priestess and attendant to the trees, listening to the whisper of their eternal song.

The flight home had been flawless. Shakti cultivated a meditative poise through every connection and maintained an unruffled calm amid all the intricacies of baggage and in-flight movies. When anything threatened to disrupt her equilibrium, she'd sniffed at a sprig of lavender and, rubbing a stone from the riverbed near Knock, said a prayer to deities that predated civilization. Even her usual fear of flying had disappeared into the psychic green; her mind had flown beyond the reach of any machine, and no mere prospect of a 747 crash could shake a serenity so ancient.

She'd also taken a vow of silence, which lasted until the cabdriver had overcharged her for the ride from the airport. They haggled ignominiously; she lost the argument, but gave him no tip, and lugged her baggage up the driveway to her house herself, with his abuse ringing in her ears. The phone machine was full, and weeks of mail were spilled all over the hallway inside the front door, a flood tide of neglected obligations and enmeshments. Shakti could feel her hard-won peace and the wisdom of the woods slipping away second by second. To combat the erosion she took a tab of LSD that she had been saving for a sacred emergency and picked up a golden seated-Buddha figure from Thailand, which she took out into the street, intending to give it away to the first person she met. It seemed to her that if she could just get the process of material abnegation firmly in motion, all would be well. The Buddha was not much, compared to all she had, but it was her favorite piece.

II
No Business in the World but Love

THE FIRST PERSON SHE MET, UNFORTUNATELY, WAS THE MAILMAN, WHO refused to take the statue on the grounds that he already had enough to carry. Shakti longed to tell him that the Buddha was worth thousands of dollars and had been blessed by a saint, but the acid, just beginning to make its presence known in heightened colors everywhere and in a keen awareness of the mailman's past lives as a medieval cobbler and an Iroquois woman who'd died in childbirth, had given her a renewed sense of conviction; she held once more to her vow of silence.

She proceeded downhill and had the statue refused in turn by a bicyclist, a motorist at a stop sign, and three teenagers who asked her for cigarettes instead. Shakti marveled that no one could recognize the treasure she offered. Everyone's auras showed that they were good at heart, but ignorant, sunk in the bog of illusion.

By the time she reached the flatlands and wandered across a shopping district and onto the U.C.-Berkeley campus, she was peaking, and the Buddha in her arms had turned into an X-ray lamp, irradiating everyone, exposing them to their karmic depths. Shakti wept at what that light made plain. All the pain of living was etched inwardly on everyone's soul; she saw how it had crippled them psychically and blinded them to their true nature, which was joy. She felt that she was roaming like Diogenes, searching for a single happy person. She longed to tell the masses that truth and peace were as close at hand as their next breath, that beauty lay in every glimmer on every leaf, and in the kindness of sunlight, that the Buddha was within each of them as well

as in her arms, that God was merciful and the universe was benevolent and eternity was now, that there was no business in the
world but love. Unfortunately, her vow of silence made it necessary to conduct all preaching by telepathy. Still, Shakti could see
that people were responding to her message, turning mutely to
the statue in her arms, like plants turning their faces to the sun.
Everywhere around her the universal mind stirred, just beginning to wake to the jubilant recognition of itself in every being on
these urine-stained streets.

It being Berkeley, she caused little alarm to the populace. A few
people even gave her coins. Shakti wandered past the library and
toward Sather Gate, savoring the songs of birds and nodding ceremonially to the trees, who seemed to her to be the only crea-
tures who fully grasped her point. The architecture around her
was blossoming like time-lapse photography, in cascades of swell-
ing stone. The humble brick and concrete of the sidewalks held
all the truth of the spiritual path—it was a matter simply and
eternally of putting one foot after another in a world that was
wholly God.

And still no one would take the statue from her. The Buddha
had begun to weigh quite heavily in her arms—a cross, Shakti
thought gleefully, her ecstasy deepening: a burden to bear. She
staggered and almost fell, caught herself, and staggered again.
The stations of the cross had lit the campus up like streetlights. It
was all so clear, so clear. The nature of fallen society itself made
the walk to Calvary necessary in every generation.

Reaching the southern border of the campus, she hesitated before the spectacle of Telegraph Avenue. That it was a circle of hell
was clear. But she plunged in gamely and made her way down
the crowded street, past the beggars and the sidewalk peddlers,
the pizza shops and the winos and the music stores, into the loud
heart of the world. She could smell incense and excrement and
hear seven kinds of music by actual count. The people's faces
seemed grotesque, subhuman, frenzied. Shakti prayed aloud for
the world to be redeemed, ignoring her vow of silence, humbled
into speech. Who was she to feel superior to this degraded realm
of greed and pain? She too lusted and grasped. For years she'd

shopped this stretch of street almost every weekend, looking for two-for-one sales and averting her eyes from the dying in the gutters.

Now she was pregnant with the Buddha statue; her body felt swollen with its presence in her. She wept at her unworthiness and staggered on, looking for a stable. There was no room at the inn. There never would be. That was the way of the world.

Near People's Park a filthy man in a green plastic poncho grabbed at her, and she flinched backward and fled. Everything seemed to have speeded up and grown sinister; even the stunted bushes seemed to snarl. Farther down the street, another figure loomed in front of her, blocking her way, and Shakti began to wail in terror and despair. She should never have come into the demonic realms in her condition. It could be lifetimes before she escaped these clutches.

But it was Victor Morris, who had pulled his pickup truck to the curb beside her and gotten out.

"Shakti? I didn't know you were back."

"I'm not," she said frankly.

"Are you all right? What's going on?"

Shakti could see by his aura that his intentions were pure, that she was safe again; and she began to weep.

"Oh, Victor, Victor, Victor. It's so hard, it's so very hard to say it all in English. But it has to do with love."

Victor smiled. "Sweetheart, you're drunk."

"I'm sober as an angel," Shakti said, composing herself. "It's a virgin birth, you see, darling. It's absolutely essential that you understand that."

"Uh-huh," he said, and took the statue from her arms and set it in the front seat of his truck.

Shakti's arms, relieved of their burden, rose by themselves. She watched in awe as they floated in front of her, just above shoulder height, as in some weird new salaam.

"The body lit with light spontaneously prays," she told Victor, who nodded again and put her in the truck beside the Buddha. He buckled the seat belt around her and the statue and took them home.

III

True Friendship

SHAKTI SUFFERED VISIONS WELL INTO THE NIGHT AND FELL ASLEEP NEAR dawn. When she woke, the room was filled with golden sunlight, and Victor Morris was dozing in the chair beside her bed. He had tucked her in with all her clothes on, removing only her shoes.

She felt an instant's panic; she had no memory, briefly, of anything after 1610 B.C. But slowly everything came clear again. Victor snored slightly. He made her feel at ease; he might have been a guard dog. She watched his chest rise and fall in the late-morning sunlight, utterly content. The Buddha was back on its table by the window, she noted; it seemed she would have to give nothing away after all and make no spectacular gestures to find peace.

"Did we make love, Victor?" she said when he woke.

"No. How are you feeling? Would you like some breakfast? Toast, at least? Orange juice?"

"I can't marry you. No matter how good you are. I'm sorry, I truly am, it's just not right."

"I know."

"It's not in the stars. It's not in *me.*"

"I know. Would you like some orange juice?"

"I loved those songs, though, Victor. I truly did. They were so beautifully *bad.*"

"I'll take that as a yes," he said, and went to fetch her drink. When he came back, Shakti saw that the juice was freshly squeezed, a skill she'd taught him in her kitchen over dozens of mornings, against the grain of his profound resistance to the

231

idea that anything but frozen was real and American; and she smiled.

"I suppose this means that now we'll always have to be friends," she said, and gulped her juice.

IV

A Tragedy

SHEBA MCKENZIE'S KITTEN RE-BOP WAS RUN OVER BY A CAR ON THE DAY before the summer solstice, which also happened to be her birthday.

She was sitting on the front porch of the Lapidge Street house when it happened, chatting and drinking wine with Jack's new girlfriend, Marianna Swift, and watching Jack and Chris Scorich play basketball in the driveway—"boys being boys," as the two women put it to each other, each of them secretly pleased. Marianna had been over to the house a lot since the May Day rafting trip, and she appeared to be making Jack forget his woes. His jump shot had never been sharper; he was hitting effortless twenty-footers over Scorich, smiling and winking toward the women on the porch after every shot.

Scorich, characteristically unperturbed, was holding his own. To everyone's surprise, he had turned out to have a strong move to the basket, and a good inside game. Watching him leap and feint and seemingly hover in the air before spinning a reverse layup into the net with a deft flick of his wrist, Sheba thought she had never seen anything so beautiful.

As they watched, Marianna was talking about Malthusian curves. She had with her a series of graphs showing various population cycles through time. There were rising rabbit populations, linked to a depressed cycle of foxes; and deer, linked to a similar decline in mountain lions; and so forth. In all cases there was a sharp upward climb in the curve and then an abrupt plunge as the population exceeded its resources. The last of Marianna's graphs was of world human population—one billion people, then two, and four, and projecting on out to eight and sixteen billion, the graph line still climbing. It was just matter of time, Marianna said ominously; all such curves were subject to Malthusian gravities; what went up must come down. She recommended that Sheba dig a cyclone cellar, stock it with an emergency supply of grains in five-gallon buckets, and buy a gun.

Sheba, a little bored, nodded. Marianna was nice enough, and obviously a blessing for Jack, but she could be tiresome.

"I like to think that everyone will come to their senses before it gets to that point."

"Fat chance," Marianna said. "Most people—"

She broke off, at tires squealing in the street. The two women heard a faint, almost imperceptible thump, and then, as the car sounds settled, a long, high, unearthly shriek. All the flesh of Sheba's body shrank at the sound.

"My God, my God," she said. "Let it not be Re-Bop."

But it was. They leaped to their feet and ran out into the street. The back half of the kitten's body had been crushed by the wheel; when Sheba reached her, she was writhing on the ground, trying pathetically to crawl away, and still screaming horribly. The sound was almost unbearable; it was dizzying, and Sheba stood helpless, paralyzed by it. She could no more have picked the kitten up at that point than she could have handled a live electric wire.

Just then Chris Scorich came up beside her. He still had the basketball in his hands, Sheba noted dazedly; it seemed a surreal touch. She was far enough gone to wonder if he had some weird healing purpose for it. But he tossed the ball to Jack, who was a few steps behind, and bent at once to Re-Bop. It seemed inconceivable to Sheba, like reaching into a fire and taking hold of burning wood, but he picked the kitten up and cradled her in his hands.

"Get my jacket," he told Jack. "We'll wrap her in that, for now."

"Oh, Chris, will she be all right?" Sheba said.

He glanced at her briefly, gently incredulous. Sheba began to cry. In Scorich's hands, Re-Bop had calmed and ceased to yowl. The kitten lay limply, looking up at them with eyes slightly bulged—pushed outward, Sheba could not help thinking, gruesomely, like toothpaste; and her breathing was rapid and shallow.

"This is just the kind of thing I've been talking about all along," Marianna said.

The driver of the car, a balding man in a blue-striped shirt and loosened tie, obviously on his way home from work, stood to one side, looking stricken.

"I never even saw her until she went under the wheel," he said. "She just darted out, I swear, I—"

"It's okay," Scorich told him. "It wasn't your fault. We all know that."

"Christ, I've got a cat myself," he said. "Samantha."

Jack came back with the jacket just then. They settled the kitten in it carefully, and Scorich carried her toward the house. Sheba followed, weeping.

"It's the urban environment itself that is at fault," Marianna told Jack. "It's the blight of civilization."

"For God's sake, Marianna," Jack said. "Give it a rest."

V

Rites for Re-Bop

IT TOOK RE-BOP AN HOUR AND A HALF TO DIE. SCORICH CARRIED HER TO Sheba's room and laid her, still wrapped in his jacket, on a pillow at the foot of Sheba's bed. Then he circled the room and lit incense and candles and put soft music on, moving calmly and purposefully.

Sheba settled beside Re-Bop and stroked her gently. She had stopped crying now, but she was still dazed and disbelieving. At one point she rolled one of Re-Bop's balls past her nose, as if she expected her to pounce on it as usual. The kitten's eyes tracked the ball and then returned to Sheba's face. She seemed willing enough; her look said she would have liked to please. But she was bewildered.

Jack had followed them in. It turned out that since the demise of the Institute for Health and Immortality he had been studying the *Tibetan Book of the Dead,* and to everyone's surprise he insisted now on reading the "Prayer for Help from the Buddhas and Bodhisattvas"; and after that, in proper sequence, the "Prayer for Protection from Terror in the Bardo," and the "Prayer for Deliverance from the Dangers of the Bardo," together with "The Root Verses of the Six Bardos"; reading the prayers distinctly and with proper intonation, three times each.

"O Buddhas and Bodhisattvas of the Ten Directions, Compassionate Ones, all-knowing, all-seeing, infinitely loving: you who protect all beings, bend in your compassion to come hither . . . for Re-Bop our beloved friend is passing from this world to the world beyond."

Marianna had come in as well. She stood at the far side of the room, where she seemed to freeze. She was easy to ignore, and they all did, as Re-Bop moved toward breathing her last. Only when the cat had died did Marianna gather herself and sigh; and then, to everyone's relief, she began to cry too.

Sheba cried in Scorich's arms for hours. She kept expecting him to say something wise or relevant or at least Tibetan—he had made such a study of dying, after all, and he was always talking about the bardos, the Tibetan realms of consciousness that the soul passed through on its journey between lives, and such. But when it came down to it, he just held her and cried too at times. It was Jack who read on, well into the night, talking Re-Bop through the dawning of the Clear Light, the setting face-to-face in the reality of the intermediate state and the profound doctrine of the emancipating of the consciousness by meditating upon the peaceful and wrathful deities.

Dear One, you are dying now.
As you wander alone, removed from your loved ones,
As the empty reflections of your own mind shimmer everywhere,
May the Buddhas exert their grace to aid you
And dissolve the awes and terrors of the Bardo.
As the brilliance of the five lights of widsom dawns upon you,
As the forms of the fierce and the peaceful deities appear,
O Re-Bop, noble one, may it be that you see through
   the terror and the awe,
Recognizing these forms to be yourself,
And so achieve your freedom
In the bliss of the Clear Light.

Part XVIII

Intimations of Mortality

I know you want to keep on living. You do not want to die. And you want to pass from this life into another in such a way that you will not rise again as a dead person, but fully alive and transformed. This is what you desire. This is the deepest human feeling; mysteriously, the soul itself wishes and instinctively desires it.

—St. Augustine

I

The Fragility of China

IN THE DAYS AFTER HER RETURN FROM THE EAST COAST, MARLOWE FOUND herself painting broken china, a massive study of a crashed cabinet, with shattered cups and plates and saucers strewn across a dark wood floor. The scene struck her as oddly soothing, and Marlowe dwelled on it lovingly, lavishing such minutely detailed care on every shard and fragment that the decorative pattern on the china was clearly recognizable as the one that she and Daa had registered years before to facilitate anniversary gifts.

"Better the china than the relationship," she joked to Daa, who did not smile. Daa, ever alert to early warning signs in Marlowe's work, was taking the hypervivid image of serene destruction to heart and preparing for an earthquake. She had bolted the real china cabinet to the dining room wall in six places, reinforced the sides and back from the inside, put blocks on every shelf to prevent internal slippage, and installed both locks and secondary fasteners on all the cabinet doors. As Marlowe noted, it was harder to coax a plate out of the thing now than to make a bank withdrawal. The house might collapse around it, but the china cabinet was secure.

It all seemed excessive, and a little ridiculous to Marlowe, but that was Daa's way. She was a type who fortified; and if it made her feel more safe, then as far as Marlowe was concerned, that was great. Whatever got you through the night. Daa when she felt threatened could be hell on wheels, and it seemed in general that she was in a particularly insecure phase just now. She was hanging on tight in every exchange, and they'd been fighting over the most trivial things since Marlowe got back.

It had begun almost as soon as she was home. Daa, helping her unpack after the drive in from the airport, had come upon the box with the wedding dress and veil and opened it uneasily.

"What in the world . . . ?" she'd said, holding up the big billowy veil at arm's length, as if it might attack her.

"Oh, that's my grandmother's."

"Uh-huh," Daa said dubiously.

"It's a wedding veil."

"I can see that."

"Oh, for God's sake, Daa, it's a family heirloom. It's a curiosity—it just struck me, for some reason. I may paint it."

"Of course," Daa had said, and they had left it at that; but later Daa had started crying and would not stop until Marlowe put the veil away in the box and took the box out to the storage room behind her studio. It was incomprehensible to Marlowe, but she humored Daa as she always had. Her lover of so many years, strong in countless wonderful ways, could be such a silly twit at times.

II

A Companion to Owls

IN AN ODD WAY, MARLOWE ATTRIBUTED SOME OF THE DISTANCE SHE FELT from Daa to Jackson. She was still reading his journal in small, more-or-less daily doses, like an ongoing medical treatment, and she could feel the effects in a certain sense of abstraction from the immediate life around her. She might as well have had another, absorbing relationship going; it amounted almost to a kind of affair. A strange affair, albeit—certainly it would have been tough, Marlowe thought wryly, to sort out the sexual dynamics. By now she had reached the summer of 1989, when Jackson had actually begun to face the fact that he was going to die.

July 16. Acceptance? How? And how is acceptance different from giving up?

Good question, Marlowe thought. She remembered Jackson stalled throughout that summer like a leaf in a stream, whirling in the eddy above the worst of the rapids, around and around. It had been a hellish time—*one thing after another*, as Jackson always said. He had begun to lose the sight in his right eye to an infection; sarcoma sores had crept up his legs and back; and there had been three separate hospital stays for lymph disorders and bronchial infections. His white cell count was comically low; the hearing was going in his right ear, and he had begun to fear dementia. During the second stay in the hospital, he had been supposed to die; and also during the third. His family had been called both times, but his father had refused to come. "Just as well," Jackson had said; he had not spoken to his father in seven years by then. It seemed almost like fate, to go out on such a note. But then he had not died. He had just gotten sick enough to begin half-wishing that he could.

He had read Job, Marlowe recalled—it had seemed the only sacred text with any relevance at all. Now she saw that Jackson had copied long passages into the journal, through those summer days, almost perfunctorily; coming upon them, mixed amid the other diary entries, it sometimes took Marlowe a moment to realize she was not reading a slightly melodramatic version of the daily report:

July 18. And now my soul is poured out upon me; the days of affliction have taken hold upon me.

My bones are pierced in me in the night season: and my sinews take no rest.

By the great force of my disease is my garment changed: it bindeth me about as the collar of my coat.

July 23. The hospital again. Acceptance? How? He hath cast me into the mire, and I am become like dust and ashes. I have sewed sackcloth upon my skin, and defiled my horn in the dust. My face is foul with weeping, and on my eyelids is the shadow of death. Puking all night long, fever 101.

July 27. The new oxygen bottle delivered today; the hissing keeps me awake at night and leaves me so snappish that my friends all run for cover. Trying again to meditate—what a joke. When I looked for good, then evil came unto me: and when I waited for light, there came darkness. My bowels boiled, and rested not: the days of affliction have overcome me. I am become a brother to dragons, and a companion to owls . . .

And so on, through the dog days and into September. But slowly, reading through, day by painful day, Marlowe watched the tide begin to turn. Not physically, of course—far from it. It was still one thing after another, it would be for the rest of Jackson's life. No, it was, rather, a shift in perspective, in emphasis: the Jobian harangues began to grow quieter from time to time; the sores and pains and fevers, the drugs and the hospitals and the catalog of nightmares, faded into the background. Something else was coming into the journal's pages, in occasional flashes at first like sunlight on moving water.

August 8. A sunny, quiet day. Nausea all morning and then a break just after noon, keeping some soup down. The pine tree out back had a blue jay in it, squawking—a beautiful ruckus raised amid the summer silence; and then he stopped, and a sense of peace came over me. A sense of presence. I remember feeling like that, walking with my father in the almond groves, at the end of the late summer days, all the branches sagging with nuts that were almost ripe. The air right after the evening watering seemed to hold the last of the light, and the leaves would drip, drip, drip, a sweet murmur in the settled dust. I used to think that moment was why my father really farmed. Funny, years of meditation, mantras, and lotus positions and all manner of yogas—all, I see now, just trying to get that magic back, that instant of rich stillness, and in the end it is a blue jay and not throwing up for an hour and a half. . . .

III
Sturmmacher

DAA'S UNEASINESS OVER MARLOWE'S STATE OF MIND WAS NOT DIMIN-
ished by the brief return of Marlowe's old flame Greg Sturmmacher. Sturmmacher, whose work was finally meeting with some
success, had flown into San Francisco to negotiate gallery space
for a winter show, and he gave Marlowe a call. They had dinner
at one of their old haunts in the Mission, a seedy Mexican restaurant called La Eternidad, and over nachos and margaritas they
caught up on each other's news. Sturmmacher, to Marlowe's surprise, treated her prominent pregnancy with great respect and
discretion. The baby was due within two weeks, and she felt unwieldy and vulnerable to attack, like a hobbled hippopotamus.
Her gratitude for his delicacy was matched only by her puzzle-
ment. It was uncharacteristic of Sturmmacher to let anything so
ludicrous as her condition go unscathed.

But that was only the beginning of Sturmmacher's surprises.
When the main course arrived, he proposed.

"What?" Marlowe said.

"Marry me," Sturmmacher said again, enunciating clearly. He
had reached for the hot sauce when his enchiladas verdes arrived
and was spooning a searing load over his whole plate. Marlowe
watched him heap it on, with her usual amazement.

"I can't marry you, Greg. You're twisted, sadistic, and incapable of sustained intimacy."

"But that's the human condition. That's what it means to be a
man."

"No, you've cultivated a perversity well beyond the norm."

"And sublimated it into art. I leave it all in the studio, I'm a
bland vanilla pussycat at home."

"You seem to forget that I lived with you briefly."

Sturmmacher leaned forward suddenly and took her hand. "I'm serious, Marlowe. I've changed. I've grown. I'm ready to commit."

"You've just been thrown into a weird state at the sight of me pregnant. But it's okay, Greg—really, it's okay. It's not *yours*. We haven't had sex in eight years."

"Ten. But I was going to ask you to marry me before I even knew you were pregnant. No, it's true—I swear it. I think it's the real reason I came out here."

"Nonsense. You came out here because you were afraid George Hodges was going to exhibit your work in natural light."

"All right, maybe that was the primary reason. But—"

"Look, Greg, this is all very flattering," Marlowe said, taking her hand back to attend to her chile rellenos. "Well, not flattering, actually. Insulting. Though amusing. I suppose you've gotten to a point in your career where you feel the need for a marital fiasco to deepen your general disillusionment and cynicism, and to give your hatred of women a focus. Or maybe you're just tired of going to parties alone."

"I haven't been to a party alone, I'll have you know, since 1983."

Marlowe laughed. "I do appreciate the, uh, impulse, I appreciate the whim, is what I'm trying to say, Greg. I really do. I'm glad I could figure, however bizarrely, into what appears to be the beginning of a healthy fantasy life for you. But there is no way in hell I would ever give an instant's serious thought to marrying you."

"Your child will need a decent father. A wholesome male presence. Have you thought of that?"

"I've thought of it more than you could know. It's my point, in fact. You would not be a decent father, nor a wholesome male presence."

"And Daa will?"

"Go to hell, Greg." Marlowe rose to go. Sturmmacher stood up with her and reached to keep her from walking away.

"I'm sorry, Marlowe. That was over the line."

"You spend your life over the line," Marlowe said; but she hesitated, and then sat down again. "Are you paying for this?"

"This, and the honeymoon."

"I'll have another margarita, then. Hold the honeymoon."

Sturmmacher signaled the waiter authoritatively, and the man scampered toward the bar. Sturmmacher settled back in his seat and applied more hot sauce to his food. He did have a way about him, Marlowe thought unwillingly. A certain magisterial presence, one part arrogance and one part insensitivity. But a way. And he was resilient as a cockroach, he was a survivor. Marlowe would have laid long odds, a decade ago, that Sturmmacher with all his talent and his sickness and his spite would be mad or dead by now. But he appeared to thrive.

Cockroaches thrived too, of course; it didn't mean she would marry one.

"In fact, Daa will be wonderful for the baby," she said when her drink had arrived.

"Of course she will."

"You doubt it? Daa is the most wholesome human being I know, the most nurturing, the warmest, the sanest—"

"Did I say anything to the contrary?"

"You don't have to say anything, your whole being is to the contrary."

"We used to be two of a kind, as I recall."

"You were like a childhood disease for me, Greg. I'm glad I had it then, so I don't have to have it now. Nihilism is so much more painful for adults."

Sturmmacher shrugged and attended to his food. He had added jalapeños as well, by now, and some kind of special yellow chile that would no doubt curdle the skin inside a normal mouth. His eyes streamed with tears at every bite. It was the only time Marlowe had ever seen him cry, eating Mexican food.

"I never would have pegged you for a lesbian, I guess, is what I'm trying to say," Sturmmacher said now, his mouth full of beans, his cheeks wet with mechanical tears. "No offense."

"No, of course, no offense."

"I mean, if memory serves—"

"You flatter yourself, Sturmmacher. It was a succession of men like you that converted me to women in the first place." Marlowe sipped her drink. "No offense."

Sturmmacher shrugged again, in his maddening way. He was impervious as always to conventional lines of attack; if anything, he fed on simple malice. "However you've come to rationalize it to yourself. Your extremity gives you away. You've had to make me a devil far beyond the level that any actual man could ever sustain, in order to keep your own real nature subdued."

"If you think I'm going to sit here and listen to this just for a free margarita and some soggy chile rellenos—"

"I'm not stopping you from going."

"You just did."

"Marlowe, you've never been more obvious. You're panting for a man to save you, for Prince Valiant to ride up on his white steed. You damn your girlfriend with faint praise for all her domestic virtues, and meanwhile some part of you is praying and watching, watching and praying, for a real man to come along. You were never anything but a political lesbian, a lesbian of rage and disappointment, a lesbian of reaction—"

"What *have* you been reading, Sturmmacher? Has the Misogyny Society printed a new tract?"

"—and now, more than ever, the seams are showing on your patched-together life. You've not getting any younger, your work isn't selling—"

"Oh, you've been following my career as well?"

"A lot of people in our old crowd still wonder what happened to the promising Marlowe Stewart. I tell them she's just going through a little bout of California. That she'll be back."

"Don't hold your breath, darling. California is often fatal."

"Nonsense, it's nothing a few antibiotics can't clear up."

"And anyway, our old crowd is just one more thing to make me grateful that you can't go home again."

"Who said anything about home?" Sturmmacher said, but his banter was losing steam. Marlowe was pleased; she felt that in some obscure way she had dodged a bullet. A ridiculous bullet, to be sure; but even ridiculous projectiles could be dangerous.

They ate in silence for a moment.

"Oh, speaking of our old crowd," Sturmmacher said at last, "Camilla Rondstadt died recently. Did you know?"

Marlowe lowered her fork. "Camilla? Really?"

"Cancer," Sturmmacher said, and lowered his voice. "Those breast implants, you remember, that she had while we were in art school?"

"I remember. Jesus." Camilla Rondstadt, one of her best friends in art school, had been a gifted painter, one of the most talented among them then. A redhead, Marlowe remembered—bright-eyed and vibrant, the life of every party. She had lost track of Camilla since her own move west; but she had always assumed that Camilla had married someone rich and was thriving. That had been Camilla's explicit intention, then: to marry rich, and to thrive. There had never been any doubt in Marlowe's mind that her friend would do both. She remembered going home with Camilla one holiday to see Camilla's family. Camilla, the baby of the clan, was everyone's darling, but Marlowe could still recall the way Camilla's green eyes had flitted from face to face, always seeking something, never resting. The two of them had gone for a walk in the green Connecticut woods, and Camilla had ruefully said she knew she would always be a princess, privileged and at risk. The price of such royalty was constant performance. But what she wanted, Camilla said, was a man to take her away, a man who didn't need the trained-seal act. For such a man she'd drop it all in a second. She'd be so real, Camilla said, that the world could take a hike.

The confession had been so frank, so naked, that Marlowe had been shocked into silence. She wondered now if she had failed Camilla there. But what could she have said? That she wanted such a man herself? But it hadn't proven true, obviously, for either Camilla or herself, that such a man would save the day. And the trained-seal act went on, in any case. That much Marlowe had clear.

"Something about the silicone," Sturmmacher went on. "All of a sudden, as it turns out, silicone is the worst thing in the world to have embedded in your chest. But then it was all the rage. And what breasts she had! They stood out by themselves."

"I wanted to have breasts like that," Marlowe said, a trifle unwillingly. Sturmmacher's barely subdued glee was repulsive to her. He had continued to eat, cheerfully enough, while they talked, and sweat oozed from his skin now as the salsa took effect.

"I remember. A sort of insurance policy, wouldn't it have been? You and Camilla were always both so insecure about your work."

"Fuck you, Sturmmacher."

"It's true. Camilla was afraid that no one could possibly love a flat-chested painter's work—or a flat-chested painter, for that matter. You were too, but you had that little extra edge of faith, of artistic commitment, not to say of talent."

"Actually, I was too poor to have the operation. And besides, my mother wouldn't let me. I needed her permission, as I re-call—I was only seventeen. God bless my mother. And so the moment passed."

"And now your breasts are lovely, and so full of milk." Sturm-macher leaned forward again. "Marry me, Marlowe. We'll kill the child and live with wild abandon. I'll suckle at your teat my-self."

The thought made Marlowe's nipples shrink; the familiar sense of violation that came with any prolonged exposure to Sturmma-cher had set in now completely. She wanted only to go home and grieve for Camilla Rondstadt properly, away from the man's ob-scene glibness. She set her napkin down and rose.

Sturmmacher did not move this time to stop her, but he fol-lowed her with his tiny black eyes.

"At least spend the night at my hotel. I'd love to work around that belly."

"You make it all so easy, Greg. You really do. You're such a pig." And she turned to go.

"Even a pig can unearth his bit of truth, if he roots around enough," Sturmmacher said placidly, and reached to add the remnants of her margarita to his own. As she left, Marlowe had the sense that he was content to have given it his best effort. The old art-school try.

For her part, she was ill, and after she got home she spent most of the rest of the night draped over the edge of the toilet, puking violently. Perhaps it had been the beans; in retrospect, the lard had seemed suspect. Daa was sterling, as she always was in such cases. She sympathized and joked and mopped around the edges. She could forgive anything, Daa said, to a woman whom Greg Sturmmacher made so sick.

IV

A Prayer for Camilla Rondstadt

THE NEXT DAY MARLOWE RUMMAGED THROUGH HER OLD ALBUMS UNTIL she found a photograph of Camilla Rondstadt. The picture dated from their art-school days; it had been taken perhaps a month or two before the implants. Camilla's breasts, softly rounding a light gray cashmere sweater, seemed adequate enough. She smiled at the camera in that soft, bright way she'd had, a way that seemed to Marlowe now—but was it only hindsight?—strained and a little scared. Too eager to please—Camilla had tried so hard to get everything right. She'd been that way as an artist too. Her technical skills, her capacity for sheer mimetic rendition, had been extraordinary. Camilla drew in the manner of Leonardo or Picasso or Dürer, deftly, effortlessly; she could and would paint in any style that seemed to please whomever it was important to her to please at any given moment. And she had done the same with her face, her hair, her clothes, her body—Camilla's look was always up-to-date. Marlowe remembered how she had envied her that chameleon's grace. They'd always said Camilla would do what it took to succeed.

Now Marlowe sketched her delicate face, poised to please; and the fine line of Camilla's shoulders. She hesitated; and then in the space beneath the collarbones she made an alien machine protrude, all steel and hard lines, a robotic centerfold physique on steel wheels. Camilla as twisted centaur was only the beginning of the rage before grief, she thought; but it was a beginning. With or without love, they all were dancing as fast as they could, until death came to claim them. And whether it was Sturmmacher's cynicism or Camilla's plastic breasts or Daa's bolting the china cabinet to the wall—or Prince Valiant himself guarding the door of the happy home, for that matter—death still came. No fortification, no preparation, sufficed to stave it off; no shape, not even silicone-enhanced, held up.

September 22. The equinox—no doubt my last. Now the balance tilts toward the lengthening nights. And I am going into the dark too. Odd, how sweet it can seem at times. And this is what they were all talking about, of course—all the spiritual teachers, all the hopeful saints and visionary sinners: this pure sweetness of simply being here, alive, awake, appreciative. I can smell the autumn in the air. We'll have a fire tonight ourselves—Marlowe has gathered the wood already and laid it in the grate. I had a bit of toast for lunch, the first solid food I've kept down for three days. It was delicious—I'd almost forgotten that pleasure of hunger satisfied. How have we made such a chore of living and dying? It is the easiest thing.

Easy for you to say, Marlowe thought; but of course it hadn't been. She knew that better than anyone. She even remembered that piece of toast—despite his pleasure in it, Jackson had in fact not managed to keep it down. He had taken the nausea in stride by then—one more small defeat among hundreds of small daily defeats, to be shrugged off. And he had enjoyed the fire that night, completely; they had watched the flames for hours as if they were the most absorbing movie. It was the first of a dozen such evening fires—that was the autumn of the fireplace, Marlowe recalled, and of the drives in the hills to see the changing leaves.

What she really wanted, Marlowe thought, was simply Jackson's Cheshire cat serenity, the smile that lingered even as the body faded, that effortless acceptance that held up even as every effort failed. She wanted the timeless love, the eternal moment, in front of the fire. She wanted Camilla Rondstadt happy and not crazed, wanted her unmaimed, unviolated, uninflated, wanted her healed and at peace.

It amounted to a prayer. And so she drew her friend in a second sketch, a resurrection of that sweet afternoon in the green trees. Camilla's peach-ripe skin could catch the sun in just such a way and make the world seem soft and fragrant; her hair could hold the sunlight so and make it glow like a quiet flame.

And then, almost as an afterthought, she drew the man who had loved Camilla for herself, who hadn't needed the military-industrial-complex breasts or the trained-seal act. The man, she could not help but think, who had never showed up. In the sketch, he looked a lot like Dante. The two of them walked hand in hand along the leafy path, as in a fairy tale. And it was only when she was done with her little fantasy piece that she looked at it and thought what a great Lovers card it would make, for her tarot deck.

V

A Matter of Interpretation

DAA WAS NOT PLEASED AT ALL BY THE LOVERS CARD. WHEN MARLOWE showed it to her that night when Daa got home from work, Daa looked at the painting for a long time, then set it aside.

"That's not Camilla Rondstadt, that's *you*," she told Marlowe. "Walking off into the sunset with a man."

"Oh, come on, Daa."

" 'Lovers.' Marlowe, how *could* you?"

"I don't know what you're talking about. I think it's a beautiful picture."

"*That's* what I'm talking about. We wait ten years for you to make an image of lovers, and—"

"Daa, you're making too big a deal out of this."

"Am I?"

"You're tired. You've been on your feet all day. Let me just make you some dinner, and—"

"Jesus, Marlowe, quit dodging me. Let's talk about this."

"I don't see that there's all that much to talk about. You don't like the painting. Big deal. You don't have to like every painting I do. You don't have to like *any* of them, for that matter."

Daa sighed and sat down in one of the chairs at the kitchen table. She took off the earth-brown waitress shoes she wore at the Constellation Cafe and sighed.

"This isn't about art, Marlowe. Don't get off on some weird high horse. This is about love, and what it means to you."

"You're reading way too much into this, Daa."

"And you're playing dumb. Five years ago you wouldn't have painted a card like this."

"No, I wouldn't have dared paint anything but two perfect lesbians, it's true. I would have been terrified of any image but the 'correct' one. But I've come a long way since then, I'm secure enough to risk some imagery that transcends my private situation."

"Oh?"

"Daa, the point of this painting is healing between the sexes. This is about Camilla Rondstadt, and what it would have taken for her to be happy, what kind of man she would have had to find to not distort herself into a grotesque."

"Of course. Of course it is, Marlowe. It has nothing to do with you."

"Well, it doesn't, actually."

"I'm going to take a shower," Daa said, and stood up.

"Daa—"

"A bath, actually. It's been a hell of a day."

"Daa, don't *be* like this!"

"Marlowe, you can make yourself believe what you want. But don't insult my intelligence. I can see you clearer than you can see yourself right now."

"Now you sound like Greg Sturmmacher."

"Well, maybe he was on to something. Maybe that marriage proposal of his shook you up more than you're willing to admit."

"It made me puke, if you will recall."

"So you're saying this painting of two hazy heterosexual lovers, this monument to the societal cliché, has nothing to do with you and me, or with what you want from love?"

"That's exactly what I'm saying. What I want from love is *you.*"

Daa sighed. "I think I'll take that bath."

VI

Eggs from Oya

DAA DREAMED THAT NIGHT THAT MARLOWE HAD GONE AWAY. A MAN IN expensive jeans had taken her to Puerto Vallarta. They had gone on the rumor of some healing fountain at a shrine for the Virgin Mary. This was unlikely enough, Daa recognized, even in a dream. Marlowe had a horror of bad water—and no taste for miracles either. But in the dream she drank without a qualm. The man had veiled her head in lace, which he said would make her immune. Daa's warning cries came out in bad Spanish—another dream quirk, as she didn't speak a word of the language. But she felt so ignored, so despised, so third world.

Then she was alone, and cooking eggs—three eggs, sunny-side up. Marlowe preferred hers over easy. But she was cooking for herself now, Daa thought, and she could make her eggs any damn way she pleased.

Then three priestesses of the African goddess Oya came, with three perfect egg yolks.

"Are you ready to meet the warrior queen?" they asked Daa, and she nodded in the dream.

"But you must come alone," they said.

"But I am alone," Daa said, and woke.

VII

A Dawning Sense of Loss

THE BED BESIDE HER WAS EMPTY. MARLOWE HAD RISEN EARLY, AS SHE often did, and gone off to paint. Daa lay still for quite a while, feeling the heavy pain in her chest like a cold fog. Still, the dream seemed like a sharp truth; and when she got up, Daa made an altar to the goddess Oya, with figures of Our Lady of Candelaria, St. Theresa, and St. Catherine. And that Wednesday, Oya's day, at the dark of the moon, she sang a song to the River Niger, the Amazon, and the wind; and, wearing a robe in the Goddess's colors of red, purple, brown, and burnt orange, and festooned with copper bracelets, she made herself a feast of red wine and eggplant parmigiana, with plums and purple grapes for dessert.

The next day she finally cleaned out the old hummingbird feeder she had hung the day she learned that Marlowe was pregnant by Jack. It had been empty for months, and Daa filled it now with very sweet red Kool-Aid and hung it up again. It was beautiful, shining clear red in the sunlight, and Daa sat for hours that afternoon, watching the green birds flit up to it. She had always thought of Marlowe as a hummingbird in spirit—quick, quick, quick, with a needle beak for sweetness, her mind an iridescent blur.

Quick, quick, quick, and gone, like a hummingbird, Daa thought. For she really had the sense now that Marlowe would go away.

Part XIX

The Path of Renunciation

Now that the bardo of dying dawns upon me,
I will abandon all grasping, yearning, and
*   attachment,*
Enter undistracted into clear awareness of the
*   teaching,*
And release my consciousness into the unborn
*   Ground.*
As I leave this compound body of flesh and blood
I will know it to be a transitory illusion.
                                    —Bardo Thodol

I

A Particular Shade of Blue

SHEBA'S GRIEF AT THE LOSS OF RE-BOP COLORED THE ENTIRE HOUSE. Literally: after an initial period of immobility she set about to repaint the exterior in blue. Bluish, anyway: the ill-chosen color verged on turquoise and glared unexpectedly as it acquired mass. She had picked it out on a foggy day, and it looked best beneath gray skies, where it had a cool and soothing air. But when the sun came out, the Lapidge Street house looked like a carnival tent, or a postcard Hawaiian sea. The neighbors muttered briefly about invoking a clause in the community association agreements that forbade "spectacular or outrageous decoration and displays"; but in the end they let it go.

No one in the house itself seemed to care that much. The wild new color drew only the mildest of sardonic comments from Marlowe, who was in her own world now, it seemed to Sheba, preoccupied with art and love and death and the coming of her baby. And Daa was preoccupied with Marlowe's preoccupation. Daa said the new color was lovely, if a little loud. Jack only shrugged in a world-weary way and said, "Vanity of vanities, all is vanity." He was spending all his time with Marianna Swift, who had converted him to an urgent view of the global situation. They were stockpiling food and tools for the coming worldwide disaster, and reading books on how to survive in the absence of civilization. Even their sexual noises, as broadcast through the house's ventilation system, indicated an apocalyptic fervor. Only Jack's massages seemed to give Marianna any peace. For half an hour after them she emanated a kittenish contentment, and a wry acceptance of the planet's doom. If the massage was combined with a long hot bath, she could cease to rage against the dying of the light for as long as an hour. But then she would burst forth from the waters aflame with mission again. It seemed to Sheba that Jack looked a little tired, world-weariness aside.

No one, as Sheba saw it, had taken the time to mourn Re-Bop properly, or to share her own mourning with her. Jack promised her a series of massages guaranteed to help her get in touch with her grief, as he said; but he had yet to fit any of these into his busy schedule. Jack also recommended that she see a telepathic animal counselor and channeler for deceased pets, a man named Noah, which Sheba did, for fifty dollars for a half-hour session. Noah went into a trance and told her that Re-Bop was enjoying herself in kitty heaven and would almost certainly be reborn in the human realm. In her next incarnation, Noah said, Re-Bop would bring a special message of love and peace to all the world, as a result of her profound experience of a loving relationship in her most recent life, and her sympathies with the natural order. Sheba was given a tape-recorded copy of the session's proceedings, which she found, upon reaching home, had somehow been erased, leaving only a long, edgy wailing sound.

Daa promised to go with her to get another kitten when the time was right, but otherwise she was too immersed in her Marlowe-related dramas just now to be of much comfort to Sheba.

Only Chris Scorich helped her paint the house and weep, and weep and paint the house. Apparently he was capable of seeing the two activities as aspects of her single grieving. Sheba had never been more grateful for Scorich's presence in her life. His duties at Dan Dzin's center in San Francisco still took up most of his waking hours; and his guilt over his failed celibacy, it sometimes seemed to Sheba, took up much of the rest. But more and more he found time to be with her. He was kind and sweet and supportive, attentive and unhurried. He drank wine with her in the evenings, which she knew violated his tenets. The two of them went for walks and discussed the immanence of God and held hands. Occasionally Scorich was stricken by remorse, but he didn't seem to hold it against her. He said his karma was no one's business but his own, and that if he ended up in hell as a result of this heaven, so be it. Sheba had begun to think he might really love her. The depth of his torment struck her as a hopeful sign. He was not entirely lost to purity. Some nights he even stayed with her; and then she would wake early, before dawn, to find the room aglow with candlelight. Scorich would be sitting on his woolen meditation mat at the foot of her bed, his breathing long and slow and measured, his eyes fixed on the intricate mandala he had placed on the wall behind her makeup table. You could barely see the design through the forest of creams and scents and eye-shadow containers, but Scorich said that was the way of the world. He took it as a metaphor for meditation itself.

Sheba would lie still in bed then, keeping her own breath low and quiet because she wanted him to stay forever. But she knew that he would leave as soon as he knew she was awake. He was on a mission to save all sentient beings, and he didn't really have time for a personal life.

II

A Fire Hot Enough

ONE DAY TOWARD THE END OF JUNE, HOWEVER, SCORICH UNCHARACTER-istically came by the Lapidge Street house at about ten o'clock in the morning. Sheba, high on a scaffold, painting the upper story, was amazed to see him: Scorich usually spent his mornings chanting and translating Dak Dzin Rinpoche's latest lectures from the somewhat stilted and formal Tibetan in which they were composed into very hip California English. But there he was, and with a newspaper in his hand no less. Sheba had never seen him with a newspaper before. Secular news was something that came and went without affecting Reality.

She would have clambered down from the scaffold, but Scorich motioned for her to stay, and so Sheba sat down on the plank and dangled her feet and waited for him to climb up to her.

"Escaped from the lamasery, did you?" she said teasingly when he reached her. "Should I be expecting a truckload of guys in orange robes any second, to come and haul you back?"

Scorich did not smile. He had brought the newspaper with him, she noticed, and his face seemed as gray as the print.

"It's a holiday, of sorts, at the center," he said, and handed her the paper. Sheba took it with a puzzled glance. The main headline was something about the Middle East, grim to be sure but nothing extraordinary. Her eye moved down the front page, past a Washington scandal and the death of a rock star, and found at last the smaller headline on the far left column: "Spiritual Leader Diagnosed with AIDS."

Sheba glanced at Scorich, who was looking down and would not meet her eye; then she quickly scanned the story. Dak Dzin Rinpoche had checked into Mount Zion Hospital the previous day with what had been diagnosed as AIDS-related pneumonia. His condition was serious, but stable; it appeared that he would survive this bout.

"Sources close to the Tibetan teacher said that he had been infected with the AIDS virus through a blood transfusion administered during a minor operation in 1985," the article said. "It is not immediately known how the revelation will affect the large Shivadharma American Tantro-Buddhist community, of which Dak Dzin is the spiritual leader, but at the dozens of Shivadharma centers on both coasts and across the country today, the mood was somber but upbeat.

"Hospital officials meanwhile denied that Dzin could have contracted the AIDS virus through transfusion, insisting that adequate screening procedures were already in place for donated blood at that time."

Sheba said, "I'm sorry, Chris. I know how hard this must be for you."

Scorich looked down at his hand. "You don't know the half of it, yet. Dak Dzin didn't get the virus from a transfusion."

"What?"

"Just what I said. That's a stall, a delay, a PR Band-Aid. . . . No, it's a lie, actually." Scorich met her eyes for the first time. "That's what I'm trying to say. The senior staff were up all night last night, at the hospital, trying to figure out how to break this to the world, and this is what we came up with. A flat-out lie. Five of us in that room, all longtime disciples and devotees—professionals, if you will. Almost a century of combined spiritual practice between us, decades of discipline, meditation, service, ardent surrender to the highest truth—and we couldn't come up with anything but this pathetic little lie."

"You mean . . ."

"Does it take a rocket scientist? Is it so inconceivable? Dak Dzin Rinpoche, enlightened head of the Shivadharma lineage, incarnation of the spirit of Padmasambhava, embodiment of the living truth, got the virus the way the vast majority of people on this planet get it, through unprotected sex with somebody else who had it."

Sheba looked down at her paint-stained hands and said nothing. Scorich looked outward. From the scaffold they could see over the house across the street, to the hills above Noe Valley. The last of the coastal morning fog was just receding from the crest of the ridge, sliding back toward the ocean like a retreating wave. Above the green, damp peaks the sky was pure, fresh blue.

"Through unprotected sex with a *number* of people who had it, actually," Scorich said. "It's just a matter of time before the whole story breaks. I really don't know what we hoped to accomplish with this virgin-birth version. I don't think any of us knew last night, for that matter. But there it is, on page one. A monument to our fear. And now we'll have to deal with it all, and our lies as well."

They both fell silent. Sheba toyed with the paint brush; it was drying out, and she set it into the can of rinse water. Scorich continued to look at the hills.

"Maybe it's not such a terrible thing after all," Sheba said at last. "I mean, it's a tragedy, of course. And it will be a scandal. But was has he actually *done?* So he wasn't the great celibate, so he was something of a hypocrite. He's only human, after all."

"There's more," Scorich said miserably. "He knew."

"Knew?"

"He knew, Dak Dzin has known for several years, that he was carrying the virus. And he didn't tell anyone, he continued to have unprotected sex with people anyway. Men and women. Disciples."

Sheba thought of Rebecca Tomlin, shyly twisting her dish towel in her hands at Gloria Demonde's house. "Oh my God."

"There are others. Two or three, at least, that we know of, infected with HIV through Dak Dzin."

Sheba opened her mouth once and closed it and shook her head.

"And it gets worse yet. Several of the Shivadharma board of directors knew about the whole situation months ago, knew about the lovers, knew he was recklessly endangering everyone he came into sexual contact with. And they let it go on, they didn't do a thing." Scorich put his head in his hands. "God, I don't know if I can stand this."

"You can't blame yourself, Chris."

"Actually, I can."

"No. You didn't know."

"It doesn't even matter. The thing is done, and we're all going to have to pay now. This scandal has just begun to break, the Shivadharma people are still in denial; and when the shit really hits the fan, there's no telling how it will all come out. This could sink the organization entirely. It's going to shock and disillusion thousands of devotees and followers, and it's going to keep thousands of others away entirely. It's going to smear everything Eastern with its fallout, it's going to be a blow not just to everything Dak Dzin has tried to accomplish in America but to the whole movement to introduce Eastern teachings to the West. It's going to feed every rotten image of guru trips and Eastern mumbo jumbo. It's a stink bomb, and it's about to go off, and I'm not sure what the hell I can do."

"You can leave."

Scorich laughed bitterly. "Get off the sinking ship, you mean?"

"You don't owe this man anything, Chris. He deceived you and misled you, just as he deceived and misled everyone else. This is his karma, not yours."

"No, that's just what you don't get. This is the karma of the Shivadharma lineage. When Dak Dzin dies, a regent will be named, to administer the community and to provide for the education of Dak Dzin's reincarnation—"

"His reincarnation!"

"That's how it works. A successor will be found, in the traditional manner. The chain cannot be allowed to break—no matter how weak some of its links are."

"So let it go on. You don't have to ruin your own life for it."

"Maybe I do. Dak Dzin has asked me if I would be willing to act as translator for his regent, after he dies."

Sheba exclaimed, dismayed, "Oh, Chris, no."

"No? Why not? Because it's damaged goods? I should hold out for a better offer? The day before yesterday, I was convinced that I was doing important work, that I was part of the transmission of truth to a world that desperately needs the truth. And now that the road gets a little rocky—"

"A little rocky!"

"I used to pray to be tested. Ha-ha, right? But I did. I prayed that God would bring me a fire hot enough to burn away anything that wasn't Real."

"God's already done it. Dak Dzin isn't real."

"And neither am I, for that matter, and neither are you. I take that as a given." Scorich stood up abruptly, making the scaffold sway.

"Come with me," he said. "Will you?"

"Come with you where?"

"To the desert. Things are always clearer there."

III

The Clear Light Stays

THEY DROVE EAST IN SCORICH'S BATTERED OLD DATSUN, OUT OF THE BAY Area and across the Valley, through the foothills, and over the Sierras into Nevada. On the car's cassette player, Scorich played an old tape of Dak Dzin leading a small group in a chant praising Amitabha, the Buddha of compassion, over and over again. Sheba tried a few times to make some conversation, but Scorich had settled into a grim preoccupied silence, and at last she gave it up and watched the scenery go by. They had left in such a hurry she still had paint on her hands.

Near Reno, Scorich turned north and followed the narrowing two-lane road for another hour until they reached Pyramid Lake. Here he turned right, and followed the shore around to the north side, and they bumped along a dirt road until they reached an isolated spot between the brown barren hills and the water. Scorich stopped the car and turned the engine off, and they sat in silence for a time. It was midafternoon, and the brown earth glared in the white sun. The deep blue lake was utterly still, its surface shining in patches, and the sky was white-blue and cloud-less. A single lizard scurried past the car and froze, its tongue flickering. The heat came off the sand around them in silent waves.

"I saw a sea monster here, once," Scorich said at last; and as Sheba glanced at him uncertainly, he smiled. "It's true. I came out here about twenty years ago, all angst-ridden and disgusted with the world and myself, intending to meditate until I died or became enlightened. It was about this time of year, too. I set up a little tarp for shade and sat in full lotus, in one-hundred-and-ten-degree heat, for about five days. All I had was a couple of gallons of water, and a lot of chutzpah. And along about the second or third day I started to see things—old Paiute warriors, and seagulls that spoke, and fiery wheels in the sky. And I saw a sea monster. It came right out of the lake. I just sat there, telling myself it was a projection of my own mind. It was like a dragon, only sort of chubby and awkward—blue-brown and scaly and plump, with a great mouthful of teeth. It made a tremendous splashing as it came out of the water, and then it dragged itself across the sand. It was actually breathing fire—I know that seems cliché. It came right up to me, and I could feel the heat. And I just sat there, on the verge of freaking out. I didn't know which was worse—that this thing might be real enough to eat me, or that I had gotten crazy enough to imagine something so vivid. And meanwhile it was looking at *me*, like *I* was crazy, like, 'What are *you* doing here?' "

"And what happened?"

"Nothing. After a while, it just sort of shrugged and snorted and went back into the water. It left tracks—I swear to God it left tracks in the sand. And I just kept sitting there."

"And you became enlightened?"

"No."

Sheba smiled. "You died, then."

"In a manner of speaking, I suppose. I went to India, looking for somebody who might be able to explain that sea monster to me, and also the meaning of life. And I found Dak Dzin." Scorich abruptly opened the car door and got out and walked toward the edge of the lake. Sheba followed and caught up with him as he squatted on the stony shore, looking out over the blue, still water. She squatted beside him.

"Actually, I was going to go to Japan," Scorich said. "I was seventeen, I had just dropped out of high school, and I was going to join a Zen monastery—I had been reading Suzuki and Alan Watts. But the travel agency had a special on Kashmir that week. And so I went to India." He laughed. "I've often wondered about that. Does it mean, cosmically, that I was meant to find my way to Dak Dzin in Kashmir no matter what? Was it a divine setup?

Or would I have locked onto some Zen abbot the same way I did onto Dak Dzin? I know I was *primed*—like a duckling, you know, ready to imprint on the first large moving spiritual object I came across. But Dak Dzin *was* special. I'll never forget the day I met him. He was living in a cave, an actual cave, way back in the Himalayas. It was a three-day hike to get there from the valley. I had already been wandering around Kashmir for almost two months, getting all the diseases and meeting all the main street masters, but nothing had clicked yet and I was actually starting to feel a little jaded about it all. So I was ready to get off the beaten track, and when I heard about this eccentric exiled Tibetan lama back in the hills, I was ready to go. My guide was a chubby little Muslim—we had to stop five times a day for him to pray, but otherwise he was good. He kept telling me that Dak Dzin was a madman. I said yeah, yeah. I preferred a madman by then—I'd had it with the run-of-the-mill gurus and holy men. And I was already impressed by the guy, if only by how far *away* he was. I mean, he was *way* back in the mountains—after the second day we didn't see another soul, just mountain goats and eagles.

"Two miles away from Dak Dzin's cave we got hit by a snowstorm, a blizzard, out of nowhere, in the middle of July. The guide was freaked, he said it was a sign from Allah, that Dak Dzin was not to be approached, and that we should turn back at once. But I said no way, I was going on. And damned if the guy didn't just turn around and leave me there! He said if I wanted to fuck with Allah—to 'risk His wrath,' I think is how he put it, he spoke the quaintest English—that was my business, but that he had a family to think of. And off he went, back down the mountain.

"So there I was, at fifteen thousand feet in the Himalayas, with the snow coming down so heavy I couldn't see fifty feet ahead. It was three and a half days back to town, assuming I could find my way at all; and all I knew was that somewhere up ahead of me to the north—I had no idea where, exactly—was a cave, with some guy in it I'd never met and knew nothing about except that he was a madman. If I'd had any sense at all, I suppose I would have been terrified, but you know, it was the strangest thing, I felt no fear whatsoever. I felt peaceful, in fact, serene—I was perfectly sure it would all work out. Even *now*, looking back, it's hard for me to imagine how sure I was. But I knew I wasn't fucking with God, I knew I was right where God wanted me to be, that I was in his hands. And I must have been, too, because there's no other way I would have found that tiny cave—it was tucked back into this little ravine. I went right to it like a homing pigeon and stumbled in out of the snow, and Dak Dzin was sitting there with a big smile on his face as if he'd been expecting me all along. And my mind just went blank. I dropped down and kissed his feet, and I don't know how long I was there on the floor of the cave, but after a while I looked up, and he was still smiling, just quiet and content, not making a big deal out of anything. He got up and took my backpack and tossed it out of the mouth of the cave, and then he gave me some kind of tea. All this without saying a word, but it wasn't awkward at all, it was the sweetest silence. And I felt like I had just come home, there wasn't a thought in my head, except that I'd arrived."

"And you stayed?"

"For five years. Not in the same cave, of course. That was his summer cave, as it turned out." Scorich laughed and tossed a flat stone into the water.

"Five years," Sheba marveled. "But what did you *do?*"

"Do? Nothing. I undid, I suppose."

"What do you mean?"

"Well, just *that*. Everything I thought I was supposed to do, I did, or tried to do, but every time I did, Dak Dzin would smile and shake his head. 'Nah,' he'd say. We'd go for weeks without talking—all he said was 'Nah.' It sounds strange, I know, especially now, when he's talking all the time about meditative techniques, and telling people to chant and pray and do their mantras, and to eat right and do this and that. But we didn't do any of that, then. He'd *hum*, sometimes. It was a big event when he hummed, I remember. But mostly he just sat there quietly in that cave, or just out front on the ledge. I would go get water, or wood for the fire, but I think he would have been just as happy if I hadn't. I remember the day after I got there, I kept expecting him to indicate that it was time to eat. But he never did. And there wasn't anything in the place to eat anyway. I just kept watching him all day, but he never gave a sign. Finally, I went out and got the food out of my backpack and cooked us up a meal, and he ate a little of that. And I had enough food for a week, and we lived on that, and when it ran out, I figured he would show me where to go to get more. But he never did—one day passed, two, three, and we hadn't had a bite to eat, there wasn't a crumb in the place, and at fifteen thousand feet there wasn't any vegetation or anything to gather. And part of me was going, 'Holy shit, what have I gotten myself *into* here?' But you know, after the second day I wasn't even that hungry most of the time. I drank a lot of water, and my system was clearing itself out in all kinds of ways; I'd get head-aches and little fevers and chills and sweats. After about a week, I figured I'd either starve to death or learn to live off the air, or whatever it was *he* was doing, and I just relaxed then. It was extraordinary—everything was so peaceful. It was so beautiful. And there was nothing to do. I was absolutely content."

"But what *happened?* I mean, you didn't sit there for five years without eating, right? You did *something*."

Scorich shrugged. "After a couple of weeks, some visitors showed up. They had rice, and fruit. And after that, somebody always came. Not often, and not regularly, and not the same peo-ple, but somebody would always show up eventually. They would bow and touch his feet and sit around him—disciples. They seemed a little surprised to see me at first, but then they shrugged it off. If it was okay with Dak Dzin, I guess, it was okay with them. And Dak Dzin would sit quietly with them, the same as he did with me. Only sometimes they'd ask him questions, and he would answer them. All in Tibetan, or Kashmiri dialect—that's how I learned the languages, from sessions like that, and from talking with his devotees. With me, he never talked, for years."

"I can't believe that."

"Well, it's true. And it was the best thing that ever happened to me. Although I have to admit that after the initial period of bliss it did start to get to me, it turned into a sort of hell, for quite a while. I mean, I started going *crazy*, doing nothing—I'd find my-self *seething*, thinking that he was just a phony or an idiot or that

I was a phony or an idiot, wasting my life, that I was not progressing, that I was *regressing*, degenerating. Or worse, that there was nothing to progress *to* or regress from. My mind would run wild, and at some point I would just get up and walk out. I must have walked halfway back to the valley fifty times, ready to just drop the whole thing, get a shave and a haircut, find a girl, find a McDonald's and a *New York Times*. But every time, I stopped, because anything I could imagine doing in the valley, or 'back home in civilization,' seemed at least as empty and foolish as pissing my life away in the mountains with a phony or an idiot. I was in God's hands, I was a dead duck, and I knew it, and Dak Dzin knew it. He'd known it before me, I think. Every time I came back he'd still be sitting in the same damned spot I'd left him in, and he'd smile and nod, or just do nothing more often than not, like I'd never been away. And this went on for *years.*'' Scorich chuckled and shook his head. ''Oh, I was a hard case. But, you know, when I think of that time now, it's like it all happened in the brightest sunlight, with everything in focus and peaceful—the mountains, the sky, the rocks, the water. I would just sit there with Dak Dzin when I wasn't going nuts, and it was all clear and easy. It was easy if there was food, and easy if there wasn't. It was easy if I was having visions of angels—and I did, ad nauseum—and easy if I was having visions of demons. It was all God. I really had that—*it was all God.*''

''Dak Dzin still says it's all God,'' Sheba said pointedly.

''Yes, he does, doesn't he? He's famous for it now.''

''That's what I don't understand. How . . . ?''

''Did we get from there to this morning's headlines?'' Scorich looked at her. ''I barely know myself. It's funny, but I think it may have started with a photograph. I took a bunch of shots the first week I was there in the mountains, but after I realized that I might be there the rest of my life, I gave my camera away, to one of the devotees who came to visit. Just gave it away and would never have given it another thought. But he apparently got the film in it developed, and the next time he came to the cave he brought that photograph of Dak Dzin in the lotus posture, looking very wise and serene. And Dak Dzin, to my surprise, was delighted with it. I'd never seen him like that before. 'Magazine?' he kept saying. 'You took for magazine?' I think he had some kind of idea, even then, of making it big in the West. He was ambitious. It was the weirdest thing, you'd think it was absolutely impossible that anyone who'd been doing what he had been doing for decades *could* be, but he was. At the time, of course, I just thought it was cute, a quirk. Endearing, like a kid.

"Anyway, that photograph was a popular item among the devotees too—they all wanted copies. The guy I'd given the camera to started selling prints, and pretty soon more people were coming, people we'd never seen before, who had just seen that photo of Dak Dzin on somebody's altar table and been struck by it. It started slow, but it was a definite trend—the first year I was there, we might have seen fifteen people, total, the whole year. The next year it was thirty. By the time Dak Dzin was persuaded to come down out of the mountains, it was hundreds of people, people every day, half a dozen, a dozen people a day, people from Bombay, Delhi, Australia, Pittsburgh. There were tour guides in town making a fortune off Dak Dzin excursions by then—he was a kind of local cottage industry."

"He was *persuaded*, you say, to come down? It wasn't his idea?"

"It was God's idea. You have to understand that, to understand any of this. Dak Dzin didn't *have* ideas anymore, and he didn't *do* anything. It was God. Not I, but Christ in me—that sort of thing. He was at the service of the cosmos."

"But—"

"Well, what actually happened was, one day a rich devotee offered to set him up in a monastery in town, and just like that, Dak Dzin said yes. It shocked the hell out of me—I mean, I *loved* it in the mountains by then, I would have been perfectly content to stay there the rest of my life. Even with more people coming, it was wonderful, peaceful, simple. I'd long since gotten over my restlessness, I could just sit for hours in a sort of bliss, I thought I was *done*. I laugh at that now, at my presumption, but I really believed I was a finished item. I had Dak Dzin, and Dak Dzin had God, so I had God. Pretty much all to myself, which turned out to be important.

"Anyway, all of a sudden, boom, we're off to town, and Dak Dzin is a phenomenon. *Thousands* of people came, literally thousands, a stream of them. And Dak Dzin just sat there in his chair the way he had sat there in the cave and beamed and blessed them, healed the lame, cured the sick. I saw it happen dozens of times, it was real. And he had me up there beside him, to translate, because we were getting Westerners by then, quite a few of them—somebody *had* written him up, in some U.S. magazine. And eventually some guy from L.A. suggested a visit to the States, he'd pay all expenses, he just thought it was important that Dak Dzin's wisdom reached the West. And Dak Dzin smiled and said, 'You bet.' Just like that, like he'd been waiting for it.

"I was *sick*. I suppose, even then, I knew. Certainly I had a *sense*. I said, 'Rinpoche, what are you doing? Where are you *taking* us!' And he smiled at me. God, I loved that smile of his. And he said, 'What are you talking about, with all this doing and taking? Don't you know that we're still sitting quietly in our cave in the mountains? We have gone nowhere—all of this, and all that will come, is what has come to *us*. There is nothing for us to do but watch it rise and fall away, and to dwell in God.'

"Well, I remember, I laughed at that. 'It's as if we've died, you mean?' I said. 'Like in the *Tibetan Book of the Dead?* And this is all just another bardo, a transitional state of consciousness? It's a product of our minds?'

" 'Exactly, exactly,' he said, pleased. 'It's just like that. We are going to go and read the California book of the dead.' " Scorich looked at the lake before them and shook his head. "That was ten years ago. We left for the West Coast two weeks later."

"And what *happened?*"

Scorich looked at her. "Nothing happened. Dak Dzin was right. I'm still sitting on that mountain, immersed in God, watching God rise and fall away, rise, and fall away."

"No, I mean—"

"I know what you mean. And that's what I'm trying to tell you. You can't have it both ways. All those years ago, I was ready to die for a vision of God—to be eaten by a sea monster, to die in a blizzard, to starve to death—whatever. I knew that I *had* to die to myself, to find what I was really looking for. I was callow, stupid, slick, but I knew that much, that my life as it was was worse than worthless. Unless a kernel of wheat falls onto the ground and dies . . . Well? I gave up my life, I offered it up, and I got God in return. That was the deal. Whose fault is it now if I want to re-nege, if I want my life back? Is it Dak Dzin's? Is it God's? No, it's mine." Scorich shook his head again. "Take this cup away from me—it's funny, that was always the part of Christ's story I didn't get. I mean, he was the son of God, right? God incarnate. He *knew*—and yet, for those moments, he really didn't want to go through with it. I was always sure that if it came to the same point with me, I'd be so filled with God, so secure in that vision, that I'd pick the fucking cup right up and drain it off, no questions asked. I prayed—it's crazy—I prayed to be like Jesus. Well, surprise: be careful what you pray for. I've got the whole ball of wax. And I wish to hell I didn't."

"But Dak Dzin—"

"Dak Dzin doesn't *matter*. Dak Dzin is just what he always said he was, God's convenience. As you are, and as I am. Dak Dzin is the hammer that drives this particular set of nails. That's all. The cross is mine."

"I can't accept that."

"That's okay with me."

"No, I mean—well, either he's done a terrible thing and must bear the consequences, or he hasn't. And you've admitted your-self that—"

"Oh, it's a nightmare, all right. I was trying to think as we drove out here how it could be worse. I mean, AIDS, Jesus—it's the new leprosy. Throw in homophobia, and something ap-proaching the incest taboo—we just don't want to *hear* that gurus are fucking disciples, doctors are fucking patients, parents are fucking children—and that strain in the American psyche that secretly believes in the guilt of the sexual victim as well as the sexual aggressor—well, it's a mess all right, it's about as toxic as you could want to get. It's a state-of-the-art tar baby, late-twentieth-century American version, and anybody who touches it in the least is going to get smeared." Scorich looked west, across the lake. "No, no one wants to hear it. It's all a big party back there, a joyride, take a drug, take a seminar, buy a mantra and use it for fifteen minutes to ride off into the realms of bliss. Dak Dzin was right, it's the California book of the dead, the dreamer's guide to that great gauzy land where all your spiritual fantasies come true, and angels dust you with their wings. But you've got to read the whole book. Even in the original Tibetan, the peaceful deities are followed by the wrathful ones." Scorich stood up abruptly and dusted off his hands. "And none of it means shit. The Clear Light stays—it stays, and stays. It's we who run away, we who lose it, because we can't recognize it in the forms that gross us out the most."

He started back to the car. Sheba hesitated a moment, then moved to follow. But at a splashing behind her, she stopped and whirled, her heart pounding suddenly in her chest. Scorich had gotten to her after all, she thought sheepishly, with his monster stories. But it was nothing, of course—a fish had jumped, or a turtle had surfaced. Did they have turtles in such a distant desert lake? All she could see was a dark swirl in the still surface, where whatever it was had been.

IV

Rely on Your Wisdom Mind

THEY DROVE BACK INTO THE SUNSET. SCORICH, SUDDENLY, WAS CHEER-ful; they laughed and sang the entire way, and he was more tender with her than he had ever been. By the time they arrived in the Bay Area, Sheba was certain that it would all be all right—she even joked to Scorich, as he dropped her off at the Lapidge Street house, "Just pretend that it's a dream, and everything will be fine." Scorich laughed and kissed her good-bye and drove off making the little "okay" sign with his thumb and forefinger.

In the days that followed, though, he did not call and did not return Sheba's calls to his apartment number. She followed the unfolding of the Dak Dzin scandal in the daily papers with chagrin. It was worse even than Scorich had foreseen. There was talk of criminal charges being filed. Dak Dzin had disappeared into the Shivadharma retreat center in the Sierras; the Nirmanakaya movement had split into fierce factions, one calling for Dak Dzin's immediate resignation, the other loyal to the teacher. It was not a pretty sight to watch unfold, and Sheba, knowing Scorich's fastidiousness about even the best publicity, felt for him deeply.

But still she could not reach him. When a recording told her one day that his home phone had been disconnected, she gathered up her courage and went to the San Francisco Shivadharma meditation center. He was not there, but a letter had been left for her at the desk, and she opened it eagerly.

The note was short, but not unkind. Scorich too had gone to the mountain retreat. He was fasting and meditating most of every day, he said, and could not be reached, and he would not be back in the foreseeable future. He commented on the media circus and reminded her that their first date had been to see a Tibetan puppet show. "Think of all this as something along those lines," he wrote. Sheba recognized his wry tone, and his tenderness. She barely recognized him from the picture he had enclosed, however—Scorich had shaved his head and taken the orange robes of a monk. He looked timeless and alien and absolutely awful, and she tore the picture across its face; then regretted it and gathered up the pieces to take home with her.

Scorich had enclosed in his letter a little sheet with the Buddha's "Four Reliances":

Rely on the message of the teacher, not on his personality;
Rely on the meaning, not just on the words;
Rely on the real meaning, not on the provisional one;
Rely on your wisdom mind, not on your ordinary, judgmental one.

He had also scrawled, on the outside of the envelope, a sort of postscript, which Sheba did not find until she got back to her room on Lapidge Street and began to cry in earnest. The quote was from Milarepa: "Seeing emptiness, have compassion." In the weeks that followed, she had plenty of time to try to practice that impossible advice; and time too to appreciate the irony of Scorich's renewed commitment to the monastic life. Dak Dzin's shame and failure had succeeded, apparently, in a way his decades of purity never had, in making a renunciate of his chief disciple.

Part XX

Better the China than the Relationship

In my solitude
I have seen things very clearly
that were not true.
—Antonio Machado, *Times Alone*
(translated by Robert Bly)

I

The Unexpected Presence of God

JACK FOUND TIME BETWEEN HIS PREPARATIONS FOR THE MILLENNIUM TO give Marlowe a massage one afternoon in mid-July, to relieve the tension in her swollen body. The baby was a week overdue, the Fourth of July had come and gone—"So much for dreams and precognitions," as she said—and her doctor was talking of inducing labor, an option that Marlowe resisted. She had a deep sense that the baby's own timing should prevail. And she could understand a certain hesitation, a reluctance on the child's part. It was not, after all, such an appealing world to come into.

Meanwhile she felt like an immense sack of water and potatoes, strained at every seam. No position gave relief, and she had ceased to find comfort even in the dignity of her condition. She had resolved, in fact, to dismember the next person who said she looked like an earth goddess.

Jack's soft hands, wise as ever, drained the tension off and made her feel like a human being again. He worked on her for almost two hours, smearing the vast landscape of her belly and breasts with jasmine oil, and letting his fingers and palms trace a slow-deepening web of relief. Marlowe groaned and sighed and sank into the buoying peace; she could feel her soul rising to the surface of her skin and then expanding beyond it; and then, all at once, Jackson was there, unmistakably, a presence so light and sweet and clear that there could be no doubt.

Marlowe blinked, but he did not disappear. Above her, Jack rubbed on deftly, firm and gentle, humming to himself, apparently unaware that Jackson resided in the sunlight now, and in the piano music that played on the cassette machine, in the scent of the oil and the warmth where their skin met. Marlowe stirred tentatively, torn between her fear of losing this new and vivid sense of presence and her desire to test its limits and depths. But every sensation, every thought, every movement, only fed it—he was *with* her. Marlowe began to chuckle to herself. They were all going to think she was nuts. But he was so real and present she would have to set an extra plate at every table.

"Can you feel it, Jack?" she murmured happily, certain that his sensitive hands would be quivering at this radiance, this sudden warm glow.

"What?"

"The presence of God."

"No," Jack said cheerfully. "But I'm glad that *you* can." His hands rested softly on her belly. "It's a blessing on your child."

"On our child."

Jack glanced at her, startled, then smiled. "Yeah. On our child."

"Isn't life strange? You're really the last person I would have thought of, if I'd ever given a single thought to having a baby. Even now, I marvel. I suppose I didn't think you were up to it."

"I think that all the herbs I was eating at that time made me incredibly potent," Jack said modestly.

"No need to get too esoteric about it. We're mammals, after all. The procedure is well established. I suppose that what I'm trying to say is that I'm grateful. I hated you at the time, and I know I was cruel afterward—"

"Well, not really—"

"Oh, I know, I know. But I was. Even now I can work myself into a good mean state, if I think about it too much. But I'm grateful too. Not because I feel fulfilled as a *woman*, you know. But because—oh, I don't know. Because it's so *interesting*. You know. It's so absolutely fascinating."

"Well, I just want you to know that I'll always be there, for you and the baby."

"Nonsense, darling. Don't get all caught up in your fatherhood again at this late date. It's unbecoming, and unrealistic."

"I just meant—"

"I wouldn't count on you to mail a letter. You're a flake, Jack. You're an absolute, total flake. I say that with all affection and friendship. You stick with Marianna, try your best to be there for *her*. She's a flake too."

"I'll never understand you, Marlowe," Jack said, hurt.

Marlowe smiled. She was still ensconced in an imperturbable sense of presence and peace. "Don't try, sweetheart. You just keep working on that jump shot and preparing for the end of the world." And she rose from the table and drew her robe around her unhurriedly, then padded barefoot down Jack's narrow little attic stairs. She paused at the second-floor landing, then continued on down the rest of the stairs, through the quiet kitchen and into the backyard, pausing at the tight, pale rosebuds on Sheba's great-grandmother's bush before passing into the cool sanctuary of her studio.

II

A Circle of Ecstasy

HERE SHE DREW A BATH, IN THE ANCIENT METAL TUB WITH UNICORN'S FEET that she had found at a garage sale years before. The tub had sat gathering dust for years; she had used it to keep spare paints in, until Victor Morris had taken it upon himself that spring, during the period of his furious excavations and pipe-laying in the backyard, to hook the tub up to actual running water. It had proven an immeasurable luxury and blessing, and never more so than now. Marlowe ran the water deep and hot and eased herself in. She sighed at the relief to her buoyant body. She was a whale by nature after all, she thought; she was made to give birth at sea.

Jackson lingered still; she could feel his simple ease in everything she did. The steaming water's comfort was his, the way it beaded on her still-oily skin was beautiful, and was his. Outside, she could hear sirens somewhere in the city, drawing closer, and soon the roaring arrival of the fire engines somewhere in the neighborhood; but it was peaceful where she was, and Marlowe soaked and sighed.

After some time she climbed from the tub and dried herself carefully. She rubbed some more lotion on her body, luxuriating in the smooth warmth. She hesitated over her robe, then decided not to put it on; on an impulse, she found the box where she had stashed her grandmother's wedding dress and veil and put them on instead. With her belly as it was, the satin stretched to the utmost, and she could not fasten the dress in the back. But it was beautiful. And as she drew the veil over her head, she felt that she had passed into a secret place, a white-veiled refuge from all things painful and sad. What she could see through the veil was true and real; she had been freed, by a miracle, to see what was true and real.

Marlowe took a piece of chalk and drew a careful circle around herself on the rough wood studio floor. And then she sat quietly. She was glowing, she was quite sure that she was basked in a warm internal glow. She had never felt so perfectly complete.

III

A Loving Energy Capsule

WHILE SHE WAS SITTING THERE, THE DOOR TO THE STUDIO BURST OPEN, and Dante rushed in.

"Marlowe! The house is on fire! Did you realize—"

And then he stopped. Marlowe, sitting quietly still in her perfect magic circle, smiled through the veil, though she knew he could not see her face.

"Marlowe, are you all right?"

"I'm perfect, Dante. And so are you. We're all perfect, actually, just the way we are. It's a miracle, you see."

"Uh-huh," Dante said, dubious but not entirely averse. "Marlowe, the house is on fire. There are firemen out there, and paramedics. We were afraid for a while that you had been trapped in the attic. The whole top of the house—"

"No, no, I'm all right, as you can see." Marlowe was surprised at her own continued calm. Apparently this serenity was fireproof. "I was just having a bath."

"Yeah. I'm so relieved." Dante hesitated, seemingly at a loss. "Is everyone else all right?"

"Oh, yes. It was you we were worried about."

"Well, there you go, we're all okay," Marlowe said, and stood up. The world was perfectly clear to her, through the veil. She was at peace with the nature of things. "And the house?"

"The attic is sort of burned up. But they seem to have it under control now."

"Good. Then you can stay and visit. Would you like some juice, or some wine? Or how about a loving energy capsule?"

Dante blinked. "What?"

"A loving energy capsule," Marlowe said, and crossed to her table to pick up a large brown bottle of pills. Jack had given her the capsules, some kind of concoction of flower essences and Taoist herbs, soon after she had learned of her pregnancy, to promote a nurturing emotional matrix for the baby during its time in the womb. Marlowe had taken two the first day and felt only a mild, generalized irritation; she had set them aside and given them no more thought for months, but now she took a handful of the huge pink capsules out of the bottle and lifted her veil.

"They stimulate the heart chakra, according to Jack. I'm having two." And she swallowed them with a flourish.

Still Dante hesitated.

"Oh, come on, Dante."

"Are you sure it's okay?"

"You mean, is it legal?"

"I'm very sensitive to substances."

Marlowe laughed. "It's somewhere this side of acid, sweetheart." She shook two, and then a third pill, into his hand and poured him a chaser of plum juice. Dante dutifully swallowed the capsules, then looked around the studio as if he expected the walls to crawl away.

"I don't feel anything yet."

"You will," Marlowe said. Her own heart was soaring again; the pills in fact seemed to have induced a kind of exuberance. She was filled with a sudden appreciation for Jack's weird and foolish magic, and for the intuitions of the herbalists and the ancient Chinese. Or perhaps she had just been primed for this, and the loving energy capsules were mere placebos, tricks to alert her to the truth before her eyes. Which, clearly, was love—the nature of things was love. And all the world's gyrations and spectacle were gestures of love, blind or lucid, the pulses of a single warmly beating heart.

Dante had wandered uneasily over to the boxes she had brought back from New York and found a little red-and-blue xylophone on wheels amid the baby toys. He tapped out "Twinkle Twinkle, Little Star" now, then from sheer nervous energy started in on something that sounded vaguely African, a lilting, haunting beat. Listening, Marlowe marveled, as she always did, at the beauty of what he did.

"Dante . . ." He paused and turned. "Dante, kiss me."

"What?"

"Will you kiss me?"

Dante looked startled, and then, clearly, dismayed; and her heart sank. "Oh, God, Marlowe. I—"

"Forget it," she said quickly, tearing the veil off and throwing it aside, and stepping out of the chalk circle. A fury, sharp as bile, rose in her, at her incredible stupidity; she felt chastened, as by a skid on a wet road, and a cold sobriety had instantly replaced her previous elation. What had she been *thinking?*

But she hadn't, of course, Marlowe thought bitterly. She hadn't been thinking at all. She had been relying on God. That way true madness lay. Like Icarus, her deepest intuitions were self-destructive.

"Marlowe, I—"

"Listen, Dante, please. Just forget it. If you ever cared about me, forget I said anything, and don't ever tell anyone."

"No, no, it's not that. I *want* to, Marlowe. I really do. It's just—"

"I know, I know, I *know*. Just *forget* it, will you? I was drunk, I was stoned. It must have been the flower essences, I had regressed to a more primitive level of consciousness. Really, I think we can look at it like grown-ups, don't you, and just say that I was intoxicated in some sense. Of course I know that you couldn't—I mean, that we couldn't—that *I* couldn't—I mean, *shit*, I could *never* be so incredibly foolish as to suppose—I don't know what kind of weird, sick, twisted, mechanical, happily-ever-after thing was I in the *grip* of, but—"

"*No.* No, no, Marlowe, calm down. Listen. I want to. I *want* to."

She looked at him wildly. Dante's face was clear and calm. He was so beautiful, Marlowe realized yet again. He was such a beautiful spirit. She could hear the radio crackling on the fire truck in front of the house, and the shouts of firemen.

"Want to *what?*"

"Kiss you. I want to." And he crossed to her, in a movement so uncharacteristic, so thrillingly smooth and practiced, that Marlowe thought even while he was doing it that he must have gotten it from watching movies; and he took her in his arms.

IV

No Earthquake Necessary

DAA TOOK IT BADLY. MARLOWE TOLD HER IN THE KITCHEN ABOUT HALF AN hour later. The fire in the attic had been extinguished at last; Jack's former Immortality Environment had been more or less completely destroyed. Apparently a ray of late-afternoon sunlight through one of the dangling crystals had focused to a burning point and set a curtain ablaze. A nearby shelf laden with massage oils had exploded, and one thing had led to another. No one had been hurt, but the whole house smelled of smoke, and soggy, black footprints covered all the floors, laid out in strange quasi-patterns of panic and purpose like painted dance steps. Firemen were still trooping out with their equipment, hauling hoses and axes and oxygen containers down the stairs and out of the house, across the ravaged living room. In saving the place they had inflicted an almost incomprehensible amount of peripheral damage. Chairs were smashed and vases were broken; no rug appeared to have gotten through unsoaked or unsoiled.

Daa herself was swathed in white, thick bandages on both arms. Believing that Marlowe was trapped in the attic, she had rushed up the burning stairs into the worst of the flames and sustained second-degree burns. Her hair was singed and her eyebrows were gone, and her face was bright, smooth red.

"Oh, sweetheart!" Marlowe exclaimed. "Are you all right?"

"Oh, yeah. A little doped-up, maybe, but that's nice." Daa shook her head. "God, that Jack and his stupid crystals, they almost got us all fried."

"Is everyone else okay?"

"Yeah. Even Jack, what luck."

"Good, good," Marlowe said, and took a breath. "Uh, listen, Daa, there's something I should tell you."

Daa glanced at her warily. "Oh?"

"I asked Dante to kiss me just now, out in the studio."

"You did *what?*"

"I asked Dante to kiss me. And he did." Marlowe hesitated. "And I want him to kiss me some more."

Daa was silent for a long moment, and absolutely still, the two unwieldy bundles of her gauze-wrapped hands lying inertly before her on the table like awkwardly wrapped gifts.

"It's Sturmmacher, isn't it?" she said at last. "That sleazy old boyfriend of yours. He got to you."

"Nonsense," Marlowe said, shifting in her chair. "This has nothing to do with Greg Sturmmacher." She was still wearing the wedding dress, though she felt quite foolish in it by now. The hem was already soiled from dragging it across the sooty floor. The veil sat on a chair beside her like a third in the conversation. Not Jackson anymore, though, Marlowe reflected ruefully. That vision had fled with her panic at Dante's first reaction and had not returned with his acceptance.

"He got to you, big-time," Daa asserted again. "He hit a nerve."

"No. I'm telling you, Daa, this came from strength."

"Can't you see it, Marlowe? You're reacting to some deep male voodoo, that's all. You got dosed with psychic poison and you're having emotional cramps and nausea. It will pass."

Marlowe rose from the table and went to the window. In the backyard, the broken Aphrodite fountain streamed. She had never gotten around to fixing it, she had just let it run, and the water poured from various fractures and seams, from the Goddess's cracked jaw and from the gap where her arm had been.

"You're shaken, you're unstable and scared," Daa persisted, sensing an advantage. "It's perfectly understandable. The baby coming has made you a little crazy. God knows what's happening with your *hormones.* Your father almost died and your slimeball ex-boyfriend said the magic words. You've got this damned silly dress on and it has you under its spell. But it's all just magic, sweetheart—it's Rumpelstiltskin, in different shapes. We can get through this, just like we've gotten through everything else. All we've got to do is call it what it is and get back to our love for each other."

Marlowe crossed back to the table and took the veil from the chair. As she put it on, she felt the same sudden rush of secret power. The world through the veil seemed distant and unable to touch her, and exposed in its essence. Daa looked at her sadly.

"For God's sake, Marlowe, take that damned thing off and talk to me straight."

"I do love you, Daa. I think I've been afraid that I didn't, that I couldn't. But I do. I see that now. It's just like Jackson said—"

"*Jackson.* Here we go again with—"

"I think that maybe this is how he saw the world. I think this is why I loved him so."

"Jackson was gay, Marlowe. You loved him because he was safe. Just like Dante's safe. You don't really think this thing can go anywhere, do you? *Dante?* You did a little magic, you drew a circle, you cast a spell. You put your magic bonnet on, and it all looks gauzy and right. But it's not a true thing, Marlowe. It will pass."

"I feel like I'm just *waking* from a dream, Daa. I'm sorry, I know it sounds awful, but I really do. I think we've been fooling ourselves."

"No. *You've* been fooling yourself, maybe. Certainly you're fooling yourself now. But I never wavered. I loved you then, I love you now. But if you really want to run with this crazy—"

"I think I love him, Daa. I think it might be real."

Daa, abruptly, was silent and looked at her bandaged hands again.

"Not that I love you any less, we'll always still be—"

"Don't insult me," Daa said stiffly. "Leave me that much dignity, at least, to refuse your scraps and leftovers."

Marlowe held her tongue. They were silent for a moment, and then Daa said, "I think I'd like my grandmother's ring back."

"I understand," Marlowe said, and slipped the diamond ring from her finger. She laid it in Daa's open hand, on the white surgical bandage, and Daa looked at it for a moment.

"I was so sure it was right," she said, and began to cry. "Oh, Marlowe, Jesus, I could kill you."

"I understand," Marlowe said again.

"No," Daa said fiercely. "You don't understand *shit.*" And she left the room without a backward glance.

She paused in the dining room, and Marlowe heard her fumbling with the keys to the china cabinet. And then she winced, as Daa smashed a plate to the floor. And then another.

The methodical smashing went on for almost five minutes, plenty of time for Marlowe to reflect that she'd misread her paintings in their eerie accuracy once again. No earthquake had been necessary, and no reinforcement of the cabinet would have sufficed. Daa herself was breaking every piece they had.

V

Retreat to Amazon Ranch

THE NEXT MORNING DAA PACKED TWO BAGS AND LEFT THE LAPIDGE STREET house for the Mendocino County ranch of Antoinette Lafontane and Persephone Prescott-Bowers. It had been years since she had made the drive into the mountains alone, but she knew the way like the back of her hand. It had been Daa who had found Amazon Ranch in the first place some ten years before; and she had initially wanted to buy the land herself. But then she had fallen in love with Marlowe, who had a horror of being too far from a corner store. And so that dream had passed: she and Marlowe had ended up helping Toni and Pesky build their home here instead.

Today, Daa made the difficult drive in a sort of blessed daze, up and down, and up and up and up, through the creeks and along the ridge. She parked her battered Datsun just inside the gate. She hesitated a moment, then made her way up to the house. She had determined not to cry or wail or bemoan a single thing. Toni and Pesky had been telling her for years that this might happen, and she didn't want to give them a chance to say I told you so.

Inside, she was welcomed with open arms by Persephone Prescott-Bowers, who had been in the kitchen. The whole house smelled deliciously of baking bread. Pesky was her usual happy bundle of energy, bustling about the kitchen with a Budweiser in her hand, chattering away. Daa took her own beer and sat at the table listening, dreading the moment when she would have to tell her friend that she had come seeking haven.

While she stalled, Toni drove up in the couple's old Chevy

286

pickup truck and joined them. She was thrilled and surprised to see Daa; a single glance exchanged with Pesky was enough for her to establish that Daa had yet to reveal the reason for her unannounced visit, and so Toni too opened a beer and settled in to tell the day's usual wild tales from the Tyger Lady Bar and Barbeque.

The kitchen darkened while they talked. Their conversation ranged widely, but circled like a bird at last and landed in silence. The three women sat at the table considering the dregs of their beers.

"Would you like another beer, Daa?" Pesky said. "Are you going to stay for dinner?"

Daa drew a breath. "Actually, I was wondering if I might stay, um—well, for a *while*."

"Of course," Toni said at once. "Of course, sweetheart, for as long as you like."

"It's Marlowe, isn't it?" Pesky said.

"Hush, Pesky," Toni said.

"Yes, it's Marlowe," Daa said, and began to cry. Toni and Pesky moved at once to embrace her, and she only cried harder at their sympathy. It might even have been easier, in a way, if they had said I told you so.

Part XXI

Swimming Lessons

*Whatever may be the result of this
enterprise, I am satisfide there is
more Folley in this world than I supposed
before leaving home.*
      —Hiram Pierce, of Troy, New York,
            on his way to California, 1849

I

Deep Waters

DANTE THREW HIMSELF INTO HIS NEW ROLE WITH A ZEAL THAT FIRST GRAT-
ified and then alarmed Marlowe. He began at once to work on a
series of love songs for her, lively, almost frenetic compositions
equally indebted, it appeared, to John of the Cross's *Spiritual Can-
ticle* and "I'm All Shook Up" by Elvis Presley. Dante bought books
on maleness in the nineties, love without codependence, birth
without violence, and sensitive stepfatherhood and was soon
spouting all manner of supportive jargon and earnest nonsense—
accented incongruously, to be sure, with Dante's peculiar tone,
so that what in someone else might have been superficial self-
improvement, in Dante came across simply as a role in a poorly
written play, in which he seemed miscast.

It was the same with every detail of his attempts to be a boyfriend. Having given not an instant's thought in all of his life to
the matters at hand, he was a babe in the woods with regard to
boy-girl paraphernalia, and he succumbed systematically to a
series of foolish investments. His notions of what was required
were bizarre at best. He bought a tuxedo that did not fit, and a
ring for Marlowe that in addition to being overpriced and ill-
fitting looked like something out of a Cracker Jack box. Apparently in anticipation of cohabitation, he bought a set of sheets,
in a floral pattern so grotesque they had to be returned. He purchased silverware shaped like bamboo, which would not hold
food. Despite Marlowe's insistence that they let the relationship
take its own time and find its own form, he had memorized several standard wedding ceremonies and was constantly wanting
to practice. He consulted a series of astrologers, regarding aus-

picious dates, and in general ran around like a chicken with its head cut off.

Marlowe tried to get him to relax, but there was no slowing him down. Dante apparently viewed relationship as a dangerous new element for which he must strenuously prepare: water, perhaps—he had always had a horror of water, incongruous for such a fluid personality. A fear of merging, he had joked in the past, the rivulet's terror of disappearing into the sea. Now, however, he moved against the current of his fear. He began to take swimming lessons and was soon spending hours daily at the pool, and swimming up to several miles a day. His skin paled and his hair changed color, bleached to a chlorine-tinted green. His eyes were constantly red, and his face grew hollow and haggard with exertion. And still he strained and pushed himself, swimming lap after lap. Soon he was swimming in the ocean as well, risking the terrible currents near the Golden Gate, floundering for hours out toward Alcatraz and back, and emerging from the sea chilled and trembling, with a grim air of having only begun to face the issue.

His dreams too were of deep waters, treacherous riptides, depths and tricky currents. He told Marlowe it was a blessing. He was grateful to her, Dante said, for the opportunity to face his deepest fears at last, and to master them by plunging in. He felt that he was breaking through to a new level of being. He felt that love was transforming him.

To Marlowe it seemed more likely that he was simply cracking up. But she had her own absorbing troubles. Daa continued her extended stay at Toni and Pesky's ranch in Mendocino. Her parting note to Marlowe had emphasized that they should let a good amount of time roll over things before attempting to communicate with each other again in any way. Daa appeared to feel that several centuries might do it.

It was impossible for Marlowe to imagine any amount of time sufficing; the confusion of her mixed emotions at this point seemed to know no bounds. She had burned a bridge, she felt, almost certainly foolishly; she had thrown away a decade of love and the labor of liberation. And for what? A numinous moment? A fantasy fulfilled? A kiss? Dante wasn't *that* great a kisser. He had a lot to learn, actually. All he really had going for him, Marlowe suspected at times, was the virtue of a certain undangerous familiarity, and demographics: male *enough*, he fit the bill for a heterosexual relapse.

Daa, who *was* a great kisser, a great cook, a sensitive lover, and a wise friend, had returned a great mass of mystical stones, feathers, trinkets, gifts, and found objects of historical significance to their relationship, a wholesale renunciation of mementos that broke Marlowe's heart. She left behind as well a huge pile of sketches and drawings that Marlowe had made of her over the years, and Marlowe had a number of bad hours leafing through these. The images tore at her—Daa, self-conscious and fearful at first, had grown into a wonderful model, languid, humorous, sensual, and increasingly at home in her body. All their history together was here, and Daa's progression through the years they had lived together from uncertain and edgy girl to confident woman was poignant in a way that Marlowe could hardly stand. She wept and ached, but could not bring herself to put the sketches away. Daa had her there, it seemed—it might have been Marlowe who had left, but it would always be Daa who had the edge in putting unhealthy emotions and reminders behind her. No doubt she was drinking wine with Toni and Pesky already, dismissing the decade as pearls before swine, commiserating over Marlowe's careening nature, which had been obvious from the first, and healing toward the future. When Daa closed a door, it stayed closed. While Marlowe knew that she herself felt every door to be permanently ajar.

It didn't help that her mother wasn't sure about this sudden love. Marlowe had been certain that Bernice, at least, would be thrilled by her fresh attempt at men, but it turned out that her mother had made giant strides over the years toward accepting her relationship with Daa, so much so that her first reaction at the news of the breakup was dismay. She urged Marlowe to think it through, to work it out. Apparently Bernice believed more strongly in monogamy than in heterosexuality. It was only slowly, over the course of several long tearful conversations, that she began to warm to the idea of Dante.

"Isn't he that very strange musician I met, that time I was out there a few years ago?" she asked Marlowe.

"He is *not* strange, Mother. Well, yes, I suppose he is, a little. But he is not *very* strange. He's a perfectly wonderful musician, and a sweet, sweet man."

"No doubt, no doubt."

"He's setting the *Divine Comedy* to music," Marlowe offered in the hope that this would strike a resonant note in her mother. It amazed her that she should be striving so, at this late point in her supposed adulthood, to be pleasing her mother still.

"How marvelous," Bernice said dutifully, in a tone that suggested that she wondered a little. But then she perked up and began to discuss potential showers. Two were possible now, of course—one for the baby, and one for the wedding. Bernice still felt that Millie Preston would jump at the chance to throw one or both of them.

Marlowe was relieved to note that amid all her other radical shifts she still had it clear that Millie Preston was an insipid twit. Apparently neither impending motherhood nor an affair with Dante could destroy her brain entirely.

"We don't really need any showers," she said. "Dante's already been buying a few things. And to tell you the truth, Mother, marriage is a distant dream at best."

"Well, maybe I can put something together myself," her mother said, unfazed. "I'll want to fly out there, of course, for the wedding. And the birth as well." Bernice hesitated delicately. "Do you have any idea which will—well, be *first?*"

Marlowe laughed. "The birth, dear."

Bernice's hesitation spoke volumes.

"It's all *right*, Mother. All of it. It's all right."

"If you say so, dear. I've tried to never interfere, you know, in your affairs." While Marlowe was still agape at that, she added, "Well, in any case, I love you, darling. We'll talk soon."

And Bernice hung up, leaving Marlowe with a lingering sense of frustration, of the sort she had formerly been able to dispel through griping to Daa. Now, however, she was stuck with it.

The empty china cabinet, still bolted immovably to the dining room wall, haunted her. A single cup had miraculously survived the carnage, and Marlowe drank her coffee from it in the mornings and considered her plight. What had she actually let herself in for? It all seemed unreal—boyfriend and birth, possible husband and child, it all had the air of a dream. But her years with Daa now seemed equally unreal. That was the worst danger, perhaps, of pronouncing anything dreamlike. Once you were alerted to the phenomenon, not much held up at all. Unreality was a contagion.

Only occasionally did some sense of substance flicker through. One day in his workshop, she watched all afternoon as Dante fixed an old cello. Dante made his meager living making and fixing musical instruments, tuning pianos, restoring old family violins, and giving music lessons, but Marlowe had never seen him at work before. It was, indeed, the first time she had been in his workshop. The walls were papered with charts and posters beyond her comprehension, the intervals and harmonies of the spheres, and the consonancies of the mundane monochord from Fludd's *De Musica Mundana,* as well as a graphic depiction of the fundamental relationships between the seven heavens and the seven sacred vowels from alpha to omega. Dante's basic Pythagorean leanings showed as well in half a dozen chord pyramids, vaguely Egyptian, which she knew he had used to channel higher harmonies into his breakfast toast and razor blades. With the cello, though, he was as tender as she had ever seen him, slow and contemplative and concentrated in a way that made her suspect he could have been a master craftsman had he not been such a flake. He treated his tools as a craftsman treated tools; and his work was as precise as a sonata. There was something almost medieval to him, working there in the little pool of light beneath the lamp in his cluttered shop; Marlowe felt she could have watched for hours, and she was almost sorry when he finished the job, clamping the cello carefully in a vise to let the glue dry overnight.

Later that evening they went out for a walk in the park near his apartment, and Dante surprised her with a truly authoritative kiss. One thing led to another, and soon they lay down on his sweater in the twilit grass and made out, both of them smiling over her bulk and the unfamiliarity of his caresses. But it was warm and intimate, and Marlowe, reclining on the ground with her head in the crook of Dante's arm, and looking up at the freshest sliver of new moon, had a sudden glimpse, as of a new land, of an emotional vista absolutely uncharted and unexplored. It was, it seemed, normality, sanity, and it was just coming into sight on the horizon. It was a terrifying thought.

II

A Little Holiday

NINE MONTHS AFTER HER ARRIVAL IN SAN FRANCISCO, SHEBA BEGAN TO wonder whether she should return to the East Coast. Everything in California seemed to be falling apart. The loss of Scorich, so soon after the loss of Re-Bop, was devastating. The fire at the Lapidge Street house had destroyed her new paint job, and she had no energy for another attempt. The savings that had financed her spiritual *Wanderjahre* on the West Coast were almost gone, and she would soon have to look for work. She missed Daa. She missed Scorich. She missed Marlowe, who seemed a million miles away.

She even missed Jack, who had moved out of the house to stay with friends while Victor Morris did the repairs on the attic bedroom. Sheba discussed the situation with Victor Morris one afternoon, sitting on a stack of drywall sheets while he pulled burned boards from the old attic ceiling. Victor proved surprisingly unsympathetic:

"You were the one who expected to find heaven on earth here. You were the one who thought that all you had to do was come to California and sit cross-legged for twenty minutes a day, and everyone would sprout wings and halos. And now you're all discouraged because they didn't. But it wasn't California's fault either way. Life is tough here, just like it is on the East Coast. Hell, that's what life *is*—shit happening. It's just that here they call it karma instead of shit. But anywhere you go, kittens die and fires start and people break up—"

"At least on the East Coast they break up because they don't *like* each other. I mean, here—well, what can I say, it's just crazy. It's *crazy*."

"You always knew the guy wanted to be a priest, Sheba."

"A monk."

"Whatever, same difference. Hell, I admire him. He's just about the only real thing in California, if you ask me. At least he stuck to his guns when it came down to the crunch—"

"Which guns?" Sheba said glumly.

"—unlike the rest of these bozos, who run away at the first sign of the honeymoon being over. I mean, poor *Daa*."

"Poor Daa?"

"Well, don't you think so? Ten years she's been with this woman, *ten years*. They've been in love, they've been committed to each other—"

"I always thought you disapproved of Daa and Marlowe. I thought you thought they were *sick*, actually."

"Well, what if I did? That was before I got to know them."

"Will wonders never cease."

"You could learn a thing or two from them, if you ask me. Especially Daa. Now *there's* a woman who understands how to love someone."

"Oh, for God's sake, Victor Morris, don't start in on *that* again."

"I never stopped. As far as *that* goes. But I was talking about Daa. She and Marlowe have been as good as married, and now all of a sudden Marlowe's acting like it was just a fling before she found the right man. It ain't right, if you ask me."

Sheba thought of Scorich, to whom *she* was just a fling, and began to weep. "Oh, God. Why is life so *complicated?*"

"Damned if I know," Victor said, not without sympathy, and he crossed to offer her his handkerchief.

Sheba accepted it and blew her nose. "It's *awful.*"

"It'll wear you out sometimes."

They were silent a moment, and then Victor said carefully, "You know, Sheba, I was thinking—that is, I had an idea that—well, that maybe you'd like to get away some weekend. Like this weekend, maybe."

Sheba looked at him warily. "Get away?"

"Like a vacation, I mean. A little holiday." He was monitoring her expression closely, and not wholly discouraged by what he saw there, he plunged on. "I was thinking we could drive east, into the Sierras, toward Lake Tahoe maybe, up around there. It's real pretty country, from what I hear, and—"

"Victor—"

He help up his broad hands placatingly. "I ain't suggesting it's an *in*timate holiday, now—I'm just talking about friends. A couple of friends taking a trip. Separate beds, hell, separate rooms if you want. But I just thought it would be nice, just a little holiday, get away from the city for a bit. I'm right frazzled with complications myself lately, if you want to know the truth. I could use a break." He eyed her. "Honest, Sheba, I'd be good as gold, it would just be a friendly thing. What do you say?"

Sheba hesitated, frankly considering it, surprised to find herself tempted. Scorich was part of it, she realized—she did want to get away from anything that reminded her of him. And the Lapidge Street house was such a shambles at the moment.

And then there was Victor Morris himself, who had not, she realized, been absolutely unpleasant lately. And she could handle Victor Morris.

"Well . . . When would we leave, if we did?"

"Tomorrow!" Vic said, thrilled. "Tonight! Hell, whenever you want—it's just a matter of toothbrushes and a change of clothes or two, and a hop in the truck. You really want to go?"

"Oh, it might be nice at that. To get away for a bit."

III

Bacon Double Cheeseburger

THEY LEFT ALMOST AT ONCE, OSTENSIBLY TO BEAT THE TRAFFIC BUT ACTU-
ally to spare Sheba the necessity of reconsidering. By the time the
sun began to go down, they were half an hour east of Berkeley,
driving through the rolling, summer-brown hills toward the cen-
tral Valley. Vic's truck radio, to Sheba's amusement, was still set
to a country-music station. He offered to change it—he was all
graciousness since her acquiescence—but on a whim, she had
him leave it as it was. The music of her childhood and youth had
not changed much, though it seemed to her at moments that an
element of self-consciousness, and perhaps even self-parody, jangled in the newer Nashville sounds. But the older songs surprisingly moved her, all the same old trains and rain and broken
hearts. She found herself, at one point, singing along with Victor
to some vintage Hank Williams, just as they had in high school.
She stopped herself almost at once, but the damage was done—
Vic's grin said it all, and even his failure to tease her about it was
conspicuous enough to be a sort of commentary.

He was at his most charming, humorous, and attentive. Sheba
found herself thinking of their first date, with an amused indulgence. Victor could try so hard. When they stopped for dinner at
a roadside diner on the outskirts of Sacramento, he even leaped
from the truck cab and hurried around to open the door for her,
and Sheba laughed.

"Lord, Victor, don't go overboard. You'll strain yourself."

"Just trying to treat you like a lady," he said, unabashed. "I
reckon you probably forgot what that's like."

It was as close to an explicit sally as he had come since they had left the Bay Area, and she decided to meet it head-on, to nip such things in the bud. "You promised to keep this a friendly holiday, Victor. If you really want to treat me right, you'll keep your word."

"Oh, I'm as good as my word. Nobody's ever said less of Victor Morris." And he opened the door to let her into the restaurant.

It was the kind of place she had not been in since she came to California, with a linoleum floor and red-and-white-checkered plastic tablecloths, and the neon logos and coats of arms of beer companies competing for wall space with an elk's head mounted behind the cash register. The cook was a big-bellied, balding man in a stained white T-shirt; and the cashier-hostess-waitress who greeted them as they came in was a fortyish woman painted to look twenty-five, with bouffant hair in a shade of unnatural orange and bright red lips.

"Coffee?" she said, turning the cups that were already on the table upright, and beginning to pour.

"Thanks," Vic said; "None for me, thank you—" Sheba began, but her cup was already filled.

"The chicken fried steak is good tonight," said their hostess, and with another crack of her gum, she left them with their menus.

"Nice place, huh?" Vic said.

Sheba glanced at him sharply, certain that he was being ironic, but he was sincere, and she realized in an instant the gulf that separated them. The realization brought a fierce surge of something like pity. Not just for Victor—who was, after all, just trying to show her a good time—but for herself. She felt strangely, poignantly, spoiled. She thought of Chris Scorich and wondered what he would have made of a place like this.

Vic had not noticed her emotion; it was part of the keenness of what she was feeling, that he could probably not even suspect it. Looking at his sturdy, good-natured face as he studied the menu, Sheba felt ashamed of herself. She had once been simple too, and greed had made her complex.

The waitress returned to take their orders. Sheba deferred to Vic, while she hurriedly studied her own menu. She was no longer on Jack's Immortality Diet, of course—Jack would have seen nothing here but Death—but middle America made few allowances even for casual vegetarians. Vic ordered the chicken fried steak, which came with mashed potatoes and peas; and a Budweiser. The waitress looked at Sheba.

"Uh, I'll have a salad."

"Okay," the waitress said. "And . . . ?"

Sheba hesitated.

"It's on me, kid," Vic said, misinterpreting her scruple. "Price no object."

The rough generosity, typical of him, touched her. Sheba thought suddenly that she didn't really care what Chris Scorich would have made of Dick's Hi-Way Diner, or of Vic himself. To hell with him and his neo-Tibetan niceties.

Sheba smiled at Vic and looked up at the waitress. "I'll have a bacon double cheeseburger, and fries. And make that two Buds."

IV

Better Not to Start

THEY DID NOT DRIVE MUCH FARTHER AFTER DINNER. VICTOR WANTED TO save the mountain scenery for the daylight, and so they stopped for the night at a motel in a little town in the foothills. Vic scrupulously rented two rooms for them; and Sheba, though feeling guilty at incurring him the extra expense, was grateful. Too much had happened too quickly; she was confused and overwhelmed and wanted time to sort things out. Even the bacon double cheeseburger, after the initial defiant thrill, weighed on her stomach now. She wanted only to be alone, and in bed, and after thanking Victor briefly she fled to her room and locked the door.

She fell asleep almost at once and dreamed. Scorich was dead. It was her duty to dispose of the body. He lay on the floor in the corner of Shakti Arguello's living room, looking oddly like an object in Shakti's collection of sacred art. Outside, Sheba's great-grandmother's rosebush was burning. Scorich said something about Sheba needing to take off her shoes. "But you're dead," she said, suddenly furious. "What do *you* care?"

When she woke, the sun was already well up in the sky; apparently Victor had let her sleep in. The image of the rosebush in flames was still with her. As was her anger; she continued to be furious. She dressed and went outside. Victor was outside his room, leaning on the railing of the walkway, looking up at the hills. The sight of him moved her unexpectedly. He was so solid, so steadfast.

"You should have woke me up."

Victor shrugged. "You needed your sleep."

Sheba leaned on the rail beside him. She was dressed in jeans, she realized, for the first time in months. She hadn't worn jeans since she had met Shakti Arguello. How long ago was *that?* Months, merely. It seemed lifetimes. Maybe that was what everyone meant when they talked about their past lives—all they really meant was things that had happened a few months or a few years before to someone so naive, in retrospect, as to seem like someone else. That day in Shakti's living room, the future had seemed so bright: it had all been so exciting, spiritual challenges this and soul growth that. Sheba remembered how eager she had been for the spiritual challenges to start at once. Be careful what you ask for, she thought. Who was it who said that? Scorich, of course. No doubt she had asked for *him.*

Oh, it had all been in the stars all right, Sheba thought. But it was funny how Shakti's predictions hadn't mentioned any of the things that had hurt the most.

"Are you hungry?" Victor said.

"No. That burger did me in, actually. I may never eat again." And, as he laughed: "I'm serious, Victor."

"Lord, don't I know it. You're the most serious woman I ever came across."

"Don't patronize me, goddammit."

Victor raised his hands, pleading innocence, and said nothing.

That was progress, Sheba thought. Perhaps the California experience hadn't been wasted after all.

They were silent for a moment.

"I dreamed about Chris last night," Sheba said at last.

Victor hesitated, looking perhaps a little pained, then said, "He was a damn fool to let you go."

"And you're a damn fool to still want me."

Victor conceded this with a shrug and continued to study the hills. Again Sheba was struck by his equanimity. It could be maddening of course. But there was something to be said for a stiff upper lip.

"You know what bothers me most?" she said.

"What's that?"

"I came to California to get free of all this stuff."

"What stuff is that?"

"This man-woman stuff. This country-music jamboree, this silly mindless dance of boy meets girl. I wanted to find myself, I wanted to *be* myself. And what did I do but fall right back into it in the biggest possible self-destructive, silly damned way. And now I've played the fool and put all my eggs in some man's basket again and gotten it dropped, and I'm all brokenhearted and low. I'm just another verse in a country song. I'm so demoralized, I can't even paint the house again."

"I'll help you paint the house."

"That's not what I *mean*. I mean—oh, hell, I don't know what I mean. I wanted to be a different person, you see? I wanted to be strong and brave and free and true. I wanted to be—oh, I don't know, *spiritual,* and creative, and brilliant. And I'm not, you know—I'm really just *not*. I'm just Lucy McKenzie's girl, from Indigo Falls."

"I reckon it might take a little while to become a whole different person, at that."

"God, I wish I just didn't give a damn."

"You've done pretty well with not giving a damn, as far as I'm concerned."

"Yeah, well, you make it easy," she said, and they laughed. "Oh, Victor. Take me back."

He stopped and looked at her. "Back?"

"To Indigo Falls. To Virginia. Let's just get in the truck and keep going east."

Victor glanced at her, his eyes widening slightly, then he looked away and made a great show of studying his hands. Sheba realized with a small thrill that she had surprised him completely for once. Well, she had surprised *herself*. It had just popped out of her. But she meant it, Sheba thought. She *meant* it. It was time to cut her losses.

The silence stretched on; Victor continued to examine his fingernails. At last, though, he sighed and shook his head. "Ain't life funny. You know, there was a time when I'd have been fool enough to jump for that like a dog for a phony bone."

"I'm serious, Victor."

"I don't know what you're going to do in Indigo Falls, Virginia, darlin', if a bacon double cheeseburger makes you sick."

"I don't see what that has to do with anything."

Victor shook his head and straightened. "Sheba, look, it just don't wash anymore. That's all I'm saying. You'd never forgive either of us, if we went drooping back now. You'd always wonder where you left that strong, brave, free, true, creative person you were looking for in California."

"She's a pipe dream, Victor. Just like you always said."

"I reckon it's a little soon to tell."

Sheba was silent. The brown foothills in front of them rose toward the Sierras, beneath a vast blue sky. It was the same sky, she thought: the same sky as Virginia. How had she ever thought the sky could be different?

"And anyway, it ain't me you want, even if you do decide to settle down. I admit that I was wondering, when you said you'd come along on this little jaunt. But I was thinking it over last night—"

"You're a good man, Victor. You're plenty good enough for the likes of *me*."

"I'm not disputing that. But you'd always see me as something you settled for."

Sheba opened her mouth to reply, then closed it. He was right, of course.

"I don't know what it is you want," Vic went on. "I don't know if *you* know, really. But I know you can't go back now. I suppose I was wishing you could too. I suppose I was wishing *I* could. But we've started something, gone a bit down a different road. And I guess we're stuck now, with seeing where it takes us."

"That's what Chris said."

"What's that?"

"He was talking about the spiritual path. He said, better not to start down it at all. But if you do start, better to finish it."

"I reckon he might have been right at that. Though to tell you the truth, I wouldn't know from spiritual path. I was talking about California."

"That's what I love about you, Victor." She kissed him suddenly on the cheek. "Oh, what a good and true friend you've turned out to be."

"That's me, all right," Vic said ruefully. "A good and true friend to women I would just as soon have married. I suppose I am one noble son of a bitch, at that."

V

Coming Home

THEY SPENT THE WEEKEND IN A CABIN ON THE SLOPE ABOVE THE NORTH-west shore of Lake Tahoe, and contrary to all of Sheba's expectations and suspicions, it turned out to be a wonderful time in a beautiful place. She felt freed, and blessed. The pines' fresh murmur in the summer breeze calmed something in her soul; the emerald expanse of the lake soothed her spirit. Victor cooked their meals, whistling and cursing cheerfully. They had chicken every night, and okra, and beet greens steamed just so and slathered in butter. They had hush puppies, and fresh-squeezed orange juice for breakfast. And Victor did the dishes too. Apparently he had come to California to learn how to move around a kitchen. Sheba walked along the stony beach alone both evenings as twilight passed into night and watched Venus rise above the hills on the opposite shore, followed by a waxing three-quarter moon, and it seemed to her that a miracle had occurred. Scorich had left her with her best self after all and stolen only her phony dreams. As she thought this, an owl peeled away from a low tree near her and crossed the moon with two slow swooping movements of its wings.

Sheba was so grateful to Victor Morris that she might have shared a bed with him, to prove they both were liberated beings; but Vic held his ground and stayed in the upper bunk. Which only made her more grateful.

This trip had been good for Victor as well. Sheba could see it in his jokes, and in the confident bounce of his walk. Something in him had been set free too, some ghost loosed at last to fly away to other realms. They had come to California, Sheba thought, each in a way looking for a love that could not be, and had found friendship instead. And it was good.

Meanwhile there were the moon and stars, the wind and the trees and the sky, and the vast blue summer lake in the morning with the sun filling the mist above it with gold. They frolicked, laughed and sang and swam, and when the time came to return to the Bay Area, it seemed both right and a thing to be regretted at the same time—a sweet loss, a treasured passing. They sang on the drive back too, to every corny song that came on the radio. For the sheer silliness they stopped at Dick's Hi-Way Diner for dinner again, and Sheba had the chicken fried steak.

Which also made her queasy, as it turned out. Apparently certain things had changed for good. Still, they arrived at the Lapidge Street house in high spirits, just as the moon, now almost full, cleared the East Bay hills. They came into the kitchen, laughing, to find Marlowe, Jack, and Marianna Swift all sitting grimly at the kitchen table. Marlowe's eyes were red and swollen, and Jack was holding her hand.

"What?" Sheba cried. "Is it the baby?" But she could see, even as she spoke, that Marlowe's belly was still full and round.

"No," Marlowe said miserably. "No, no, no."

"It's Dante," Jack said, and looked down at the table.

So the relationship was off. Sheba relaxed, despite herself. It made sense to her, actually. And Marlowe would see it too, in time.

"Oh, Marlowe, I'm so sorry—," she began, but Marlowe interrupted, shaking her head.

"No, *no*. You still don't get it."

"He's dead," Marianna said. "Oh, God, I could just *shit*, at the way this urban culture—"

"Dead?" Sheba said stupidly. "Dante?"

"He's dead all right," Marlowe said.

"But—how—?"

"His car went off a bridge on Highway One. It landed upside down in the creek, and he was trapped inside." Marlowe looked at her hands. "Dammit, all those swimming lessons. All those goddamned swimming lessons, and he drowned in three feet of water."

Part XXII

Setting the Comedy to Music

First there's dying,
then Union, like gnats inside the wind.
                                    —Rumi

I
Memorial

Fare well, old friend,
The setting sun
Has lit your face, has lit your face.

Dante's ashes were scattered beneath the rosebush in the Lapidge Street backyard about a week later, in a ritual attended by most of their circle. The wind, so still until the crucial moment, capriciously lifted as Sheba opened the urn and whirled the ashes twice past the startled faces of everyone present before depositing most of their gray mass in the fountain, where the churning waters beneath the broken Aphrodite mingled them irretrievably. A smaller amount of denser ash and bits of bone settled to the earth as intended beneath the roses, while a few of the last stray particles of Dante's earthly form caused several in the crowd to sneeze.

Meanwhile the Pink Flames softball-team choir, down from Mendocino for the occasion, sang on, sweetly and sadly and softly, beneath the apple tree, accompanied on acoustic instruments by Dante's grieving band, the Holy Rose Parade:

Fare well, old friend,
And journey forth,
Though I may weep, though I may weep.

Daa, who had returned from Amazon Ranch to help arrange the ceremony, circulated among those present with a handful of salt, placing a pinch on each person's tongue and saying, "My body is salt, taste the breath of death." Marianna Swift, on a strict

salt-free diet in accordance with her project of never dying, refused her pinch, as did Albert Nerdowsky, who noted that excessive sodium inhibited optimal synapse function in the brain.
Nerdo, dressed entirely in black flannel to dampen extraneous
field resonance, and sweating profusely, had set up a modulated
frequency receiver, or MFR, keyed, he said, to a wavelength
Dante in his present immaterial form would find easy to work
with. A continuous pulse of bright green sine waves showed on a
dark screen, accompanied by a high, steady tone. The device was
prepared to register the slightest Dante-induced modulation of
frequency as light and music, and a small crowd had gathered
near it to monitor his anticipated presence.

> *Fare well, old friend,*
> *Raise your sail again*
> *On a different sea, on a different sea.*

Shakti Arguello danced and prayed aloud and laid a tarot
spread that indicated that Dante's soul was faring well. Her wa-
terproof mascara was holding up through bouts of elegant tears.
She had lost ten pounds since her return from the British Isles
and gotten her tan back, and she looked radiant and fit in a flowing lavender chemise. Her new boyfriend, a Sufi dancer into chro-
motherapy, trailed her with an attentive air. His many-colored
outfit, dominated by blues and greens, was a blend calculated to
heal the deepest griefs.

Jack, at Daa's request, poured wine into plastic cups at a table
set up by the garden and circulated among the guests with a tray
of crackers, cheese, and smoked sardines. He wore a dark suit, in
accordance with his sobered state—it had been Jack who had,
with Marlowe, identified Dante's drowned body on the night of
the accident. The police had called the Lapidge Street house after
finding the number in Dante's pocket, and Jack and Marlowe had
gone down to the morgue at 2 A.M. and viewed the corpse on its
slab. Dante in death had been much like Dante in life, unbruised,
pale, and placid, his face relaxed in a cool repose—unusual, the
coroner's assistant had said, in those who had had as much time

as Dante had to watch their death approach. Hanging upside down in the half-flattened Fiat in the dirty creek, his seat belt holding fatally and both doors jammed as the car filled with water, Dante had made an obvious peace. Only his hair had been disturbed: it was flattened and wet and smeared in a pattern suggesting the Fiat's ceiling. Looking at him, Jack had expected his eyes to open any moment—it had seemed so much more likely that Dante had simply dozed, a mistake had been made, an understandable error, and that he would wake and smile. Marlowe had told the police she was his fiancée and signed the papers needed; and two days later Jack had gone with her again, to pick up the cremated remains.

The experience had affected him deeply. The next day he had gone to morning mass at St. Anne's of the Sunset and lit a candle for Dante's soul. He had attended mass on every morning since. His sudden Catholicism was inexplicable to everyone, as Jack had been raised a relatively dilute Methodist. He had also ceased to call himself Jack Slow Hands and had gone back to using the last name he had been born with, which was Wilson. Watching the NBA championship game on television, he had realized that everyone in both starting lineups was younger than he was, and he had decided to give up his basketball career. The accumulation of shifts was straining his relationship with Marianna, who viewed his moves as capitulations to a dying society's anesthetization to the fact of its mortality. But Jack said he didn't care. He said mortality *did* pain him, he wasn't afraid who knew it, and he was looking for all the anesthetization he could find.

Meanwhile, he served the drinks and offered up hors d'oeuvres to the assembled guests, his lips moving slightly as he said Hail Marys to himself. Sometimes even now he would forget the words and would refer to a little plastic-laminated card, inscribed with the text of the prayer and decorated with a vivid blue-clad Virgin, which he carried in his pocket for just such moments.

> *Fare well, old friend,*
> *Do not delay*
> *At the open gate, at the open gate.*

Marlowe sat on the top back step, her usual perch at parties, and nursed a glass of sharp red wine. She refused a refill when Jack came by with a fresh bottle, for the baby's sake, but she accepted a pinch of salt from Daa, who lingered to meet her eyes before moving on. Marlowe watched her go with a keen sense of having been unable to meet her kindly glance with warmth. Since Daa's return after Dante's death, she had been a marvel of compassion, seeing to every detail that she could, relieving Marlowe of the burdens of phone calls and answering-machine messages, cards and flower arrangements, cooking every meal, and in general making it plain by her openhanded presence that she would be there in any way that Marlowe needed. But Marlowe was unsure of what she needed, if anything, and had kept her distance, painfully, even as she felt that it was cruel. She knew that Daa would take her back in an instant, if it went that way; all would be forgiven. But that could never be again. Not because of a grief for Dante, or because as a lover he had been so supreme a revelation that her bridges to other pleasures were forever burned. Far from it—Dante, though inexorably sweet, had frequently been inept, an enthusiastic kid with a lot to learn, though eager to please. No, her failure to return went deeper—she had used Dante, she had known it even at the time, used him to get free, used him like a ladder to reach a different place. Because he had been easy to use, and because she'd felt he would be easy to throw away when the climb was made.

Now he was dead, and Marlowe's responsibility seemed obvious. All Dante's swimming lessons, the grueling preparations, the training regimen for relationship, had been a kind of cry for help, a floundering in an intimacy that was more than his simple soul could bear. She'd taken him out in waters way too deep.

Sheba crossed the yard now to sit beside her, her face flushed with weeping. Her cousin, Marlowe noted sourly, had been circulating like a widowed queen; the view remained, among their circle, that Sheba had been Dante's true and only love.

"Why do I feel that we've been here before?" Marlowe said as Sheba settled.

Sheba shook her head. "God, it's like a dream. Last time we had a party here, Dante sang those silly songs by the rosebush until three A.M. and played his guitar. Remember? I keep glancing over there, half-expecting to see him." She glanced at Marlowe and lowered her voice. "It's weird, I know, but I was sure I heard him earlier."

Marlowe shrugged; she'd heard that note a dozen times already. It seemed a common coin, touched by a thousand hands into cliché. "All I've heard is the silence of the spheres. I suppose because I'm just plain mean."

"Oh, come on, Marlowe, you're not—"

"No, no, please, allow me that much, at least, the consolations of honesty. Boil it all away, the surface and the depth, and I'm a bitch, an ice queen. I think I was corrupted early on, by the freedom of art. Now I'll never know if *any*thing is real."

"Dante was real," Sheba said, intending to comfort her.

"Real to whom? Everyone, and everything, is real to you, my dear. It's me I'm trying to please." And as her cousin looked uneasy: "Oh, don't be disconcerted by me, Sheba, it's just my raging ego. Sound and fury, signifying nothing. All of it, signifying nothing. I'm the one who's seen through everything and only found her mean little self behind the screen. I'm a curse, I'm the real ghost at the banquet. Dante's lucky to have squirmed free. I'd have withered his every dream."

"You've never been a curse to me."

"As I say, you're a special case. I've been a shit to you too, but you're impervious. And so we continue to relate."

There was a stir among the small crowd gathered near the center of the yard. Nerdo's modulated frequency receiver had registered a perturbation in the field as a short sequence of notes that sounded a little like the opening bars of "Three Blind Mice," and everyone was exclaiming.

"God, look at these people," Marlowe said. "They're clueless, absolutely clueless in paradise."

"They loved him too, Marlowe."

"If they really loved him, I don't see how they could mistake him for static on a trumped-up radio." Marlowe looked at her. "He's gone, Sheba. Gone. I killed him."

"Nonsense," Sheba said, startled.

"I did, I overloaded him. With malice aforethought. You can't imagine it, you can't even imagine thinking it, it would collapse your rose-colored view of the world even to consider that anyone could be so low. But I know that it's true, and I have to live with it. I ran a two-hundred-twenty-volt current through wiring set for one-ten and blew it out. He drove off that bridge because it was easier than being a boyfriend, and he was too kind to leave a suicide note."

"Marlowe, it was an accident. Dante loved you, he was happy, he wanted to *marry* you."

"No, he wanted to marry *you*, my dear. Because you are sweet and beautiful and forgiving, because you move in a benevolent, well-meaning haze, but most of all, I think, because you didn't want to marry *him*. He loved you like you love a sunset or a beautiful piece of music, because it felt wonderful. He didn't necessarily want it to affect his *life*. While I—I did the worst thing you can do to someone in that la-la land of love. I called his bluff, I asked him to get a little real. And it was too much for him. Humankind is not made to experience much real love."

"I don't see how you can *think* that."

"It's a career, of sorts. You've got your scientists, you've got your technicians, you've got your lawyers. And then you've got your career fuckups and Cassandras, living in the rented rooms where the wallpaper of the world wears thin and you get to see what lies beneath. Don't try this at home, folks—this woman is a trained professional." Marlowe finished off her wine and looked around. "Where the hell is Jack when you need him? Bartender!"

"I don't believe you mean a word of this."

Marlowe glanced back at Sheba. "No?"

"No. It's too easy, it's too glib. I've seen you do this before, it's your way of defending yourself."

"Spare me the analysis, Sheba. Can't you see I'm all torn up with grief?" Marlowe set aside her glass and moved to rise, and as she did, a shadow fell across them, and they both glanced up.

It was Daa, with a jar of honey and a silver spoon, making a second ritual circuit through the guests. She dipped the spoon in the honey jar and held it out to them.

"Taste the sweetness of life, sisters."

"I was hoping, actually, you'd brought more salt," Marlowe said. "All this sweetness is about to make me gag."

Daa hesitated, uncertain; as she did, Sheba reached out and took the spoon from her hand and closed her mouth over the honey. Daa glanced furtively at Marlowe's empty wineglass.

"I'm sober as a monkey, dear Daa," Marlowe said. "Too sober, I'd say. Too goddamned sober."

"I know this is hard on you," Daa said. She took the teaspoon back from Sheba and moved off with the honey; and they heard her pause beside Marianna Swift.

"Taste the sweetness of life, sister."

"Thank you, no," Marianna said. "I'm trying to eliminate empty calories, actually."

Marlowe laughed and rose to go. On the receiver near the center of the yard, Nerdo to his chagrin had locked onto the BBC, and a Beethoven sonata was playing. People were throwing coins into the fountain, in vague subscription to Dante's odyssey, as the Pink Flames continued to sing.

> Fare well, old friend,
> You'll come again
> In a different form, in a different form.

II

A Complicated Grieving

FOR A WEEK AFTER THE MEMORIAL, MARLOWE HOLED UP IN HER STUDIO, eating hot-plate soup and sleeping on the cot and cultivating her rage. The world faded; Daa stayed three long days at the Lapidge Street house, looking for a sign, then gave up and went back to

Mendocino. Sheba made casseroles and left them at the studio door, but otherwise kept out of Marlowe's way. Jack, after a few pathetic attempts to visit, sat most days in the attic, contemplating the charred remains of the Immorality Environment in a kind of quiet daze. The reconstruction had been delayed—Victor Morris had been called away to a remodeling job in San Jose and had no time to spare. Marlowe missed the hammering and crash of him at work—at least in that busy noise she'd had a focus for her rage and been able to despise the fact that the world went on in its usual heedless career. But in the silence that had settled, everything seemed to have gone away.

Not even reading Jackson's journal helped. She had expected some companionship and comfort, at least, from that quarter, a little taste of doubt, despair, the flavor of mortality resisted. But she was almost finished with the journal, she was reading through his last few months, and Jackson in the final winter of his life had been relentlessly serene. The recollection for some reason gave her little pleasure now; Marlowe realized that she had come by an unexpected route to half-resenting Jackson's achieved serenity. That calm, that deep, unwavering acceptance he had arrived at, which had once been the image of spiritual achievement for her, seemed now like a stale cliché. The irony was not lost on Marlowe: beginning the reading of his journal unable to remember Jackson's anguish, she found herself unwilling now to recall his peace. It was, she thought, as if he had cheated, somehow, in dying, when the really hard thing, obviously, was to *live*.

She was ashamed to have ever believed love mattered in the least. But she had one last responsibility as a result of her previous delusion. Jack and Victor Morris had cleaned out Dante's apartment, but they had left the clearing of his musical studio to her, assuming Marlowe would wish to take Dante's oeuvre into some special safekeeping. In fact, her initial impulse was to set it all aflame, but it was more painful to try to explain this to Jack and Victor—who were sincere and foolish and upright, scrupulous to a fault, and incapable, it seemed, of comprehending the least ambivalence—than to simply agree to dispose of Dante's musical remains. Still, she put it off from day to day.

Meanwhile she painted and repainted the Lover's card for her tarot deck. The initial version that had pleased her so, of Dante and Camilla Rondstadt strolling into a healing haze, struck her now as too eerie to bear; there seemed a weird responsibility in the fact that she had assigned Dante prematurely to a place among the beloved dead. For a version or two she cheated on the features, until the lovers were indistinguishable beings in an anonymous cheery world; but even as she tried to erase her premonition—if such it had been—she found secret clues in the gait and posture of the figures. She was painting Dante in spite of herself, and even when she tried to paint him out of the picture, he showed up in the landscape itself. Marlowe realized that her sense of guilt had gotten out of hand, and that these efforts at redemption resembled nothing so much as the last paintings of Rhonda Rose Chesterton, a teacher she'd had in art school. Rhonda Rose had believed in her later years that she'd killed her brother with a painting of the seashore marred by a power station and an ominous flight of crows. She had painted that landscape over and over, working on the shape of the clouds, and agonizing over the responsibility inherent in the depiction of a tide. She retired early from her teaching career and spent her final years in feverish attempts to get it right, laying on coat after coat of oil paint until the canvas seemed swollen, following the landscape through deep permutations and attempts, until, just before her death, she arrived at a great expanse that was mostly black, broken only by a few brightly colored fish swimming at the bottom.

Marlowe, catching a glimpse of herself in the mirror at this time, caught a glimpse of Rhonda Rose as well and felt the deep pull of those obsessive depths. There was a kind of relief in such furious pain, the release of being beyond the pale. But she was blessed in the end by a promise yet to keep. Dante's landlady called, regretfully; the place would have to be vacant by the end of the week. The woman understood the delay entirely and suggested hiring a moving company—she knew some people who would do it cheap. But Marlowe gathered herself immediately and said she'd do it herself. The Lovers' card had come around to herself and a man who looked like Dante but was not, walking hand in hand through a desert, past bleached and stunted trees. She hadn't touched it for a day and a half, the paint had dried on her palette, bleak and gray, without a hint of green, but the painted sky to the west suggested rain. And so she went on a Thursday afternoon.

III

Canto 21

DANTE'S LANDLADY, VERONICA, WAS A SLIM, EDGY WOMAN WITH bleached hair, in her late thirties, wearing a College of Marin sweatshirt and an anxious look—one of *us*, Marlowe thought immediately, as opposed to one of them. She hadn't been prepared for a landlady even marginally hip, though she recalled now that Dante had occasionally spoken of Veronica with great affection. He had said she was into past lives. She let Marlowe into the apartment near Thirty-eighth Avenue with much apology and sympathy, and an air of understanding that was slightly disconcerting. Marlowe wondered what Veronica thought she knew.

The rooms Dante had lived in were eerily vacant, and the bare wood floor smelled faintly of Murphy's wood soap. The walls had been repainted in a tasteful cream. Even the perpetually dripping kitchen faucet had been fixed—Dante had always let his leaks go, in the belief that the pulse of the universe could be spontaneously detected in such things. Sometimes late at night, indeed, he would play along with the dripping sink, letting the water set the backbeat.

It was disorienting, and vaguely disheartening, to find the place so purged and straightened. Veronica, trailing her as she moved slowly through the rooms, and still a little uncannily aware of Marlowe's state, apologized for all the improvements. She was going to raise the rent; apparently she'd been giving Dante a break for years—at least partly, she seemed to suggest, because she and Dante had weathered a difficult stretch together, as Christians during the Roman Empire. Veronica was not explicit, but Marlowe gathered that the fierce faith she'd shared with Dante then had led them both to the lions, and that it had been an ecstatic bonding experience. Marlowe, who could usually hear such things with a simple amusement, was surprised to find a glimmer of jealousy awakened in herself. It was none of her business, after all, what Dante had been doing eighteen hundred years ago.

Despite her urgency on the phone, Veronica appeared to be in no hurry. She allowed Marlowe to wander the empty rooms; she scrubbed the sink again and did a few windows; and, at length, went out for Chinese food.

"Do you like mu shu pork?" she said as she went out the door. "There's a great little take-out place just up the street, the Abode of the Ten Immortals in Heavenly Peace."

"I'm a vegetarian."

"Dante liked Mongolian beef," Veronica said with a wife's knowing air. "He'd been a Tartar too, you know. He played the Mongolian flute." And she went out, leaving Marlowe once again caught between a catty resentment and a weirdly awakened hint of grief. What Dante had really liked, she knew, was Big Macs and cheeseburgers. Why that should make her want to weep was not entirely clear.

With Veronica gone, Marlowe felt freed to make her way at last into the room she had come to clear. Here nothing had changed since her last visit to Dante a few weeks before; the combination workshop and recording studio was as strewn with tools and instruments, papers and tapes and mixing boards, as it had been the day that Dante died. The light on his cheap message machine, which played a snatch of a Hopi chant before emitting a high screech, was flashing. Marlowe hesitated, then hit the play button and listened in growing wonder to fourteen messages from all over the country, pleas from people who needed musical help or something tuned, or who'd had a glimmer of some song they wanted to share or who wanted Dante to join them for some jam or session with a band. She'd always thought of Dante as a sort of secret phenomenon, a private pleasure; but apparently not. Someone had called from Buffalo simply to chant the seventy-two names of God, though Dante's inadequate machine cut him off after thirty-three. Another woman said she'd dreamed that Dante sat at the back of her latest recital and smiled. A man in San Jose wanted to do an operatic version of the landscapes of Cézanne and seemed to believe that Dante would know what he meant. Listening, Marlowe slipped into awe at the density of Dante's weird musical web. The memorial too, she recalled now, had been crowded with people she'd never met before—some musical grapevine had spread the word to any number of students and colleagues and musicians of every persuasion, saxophonists and jazz pianists, rockers and Indian drummers, *Ein Sof* cabalists with resonating cymbals and hermetic fiddle players, Kenyan singers and violinists who believed Einstein had found the key to gravity while playing Mozart. After the chant had ceased, indeed, the ritual had quietly turned into a series of jam sessions, which gradually increased in volume as the Holy Rose Parade continued to grieve and drink. The playing had gone on late into the night, through waves and troughs of ecstasy and grief, and Marlowe had been unable to sleep. But no one, among the neighbors who usually did, had called the police. She'd thought of calling them herself, but it had seemed vaguely sacrilegious. And so the jam had gone on.

When the messages had run their course, she hit the save button and began to roam around the rest of the workshop. Along the far wall, she lingered a little greedily over a shelf of eight-track tapes and various cassettes. The Holy Rose Parade was well represented in a series of basement tapes and a few studio pieces, but Marlowe had no interest in these familiar compositions. Dante's real passion, revealed only intermittently, had been the rendering into musical form of the *Divine Comedy*. She'd heard versions of various cantos performed at parties, or as occasional pieces—when Jackson had died, for instance, Dante had been moved to play his upbeat jazz interpretation of canto 21 of the Purgatorio, in celebration of his soul's release:

> But when some soul at last is purged and whole
> And leaps to seek its higher place,
> The mountain shudders with cries of joy.

Most of what she'd heard in snatches over the years from Dante's magnum opus had been from the Inferno, though; it had been Marlowe's impression that Dante had not progressed much beyond the various regions of hell in his labors. Now she was surprised to find the tapes, clearly labeled, that indicated otherwise: on eighty-eight cassettes, in a wildly eclectic array of musical styles, Dante had made his way out through the deepest point of hell and up the mount of purgatory, well into the Paradiso. The last bit he'd recorded formally was from canto 21 in Heaven, where Beatrice ceased for a time to smile at the Pilgrim, knowing that the radiance would turn him to a heap of ash, and the heavenly chorus passed into a brief silence to spare his mortal ears. Marlowe slipped the cassette into the machine and listened as Dante's voice sang the text simply, accompanied by the rippling of a single synthesized flamenco guitar, in notes that ran like fire:

> I saw more flames
>   descending, whirling rung to rung, and they
>   grew lovelier with every whirl they made.
> Around this light they came to rest, and then,
>   in one voice all those lights let out a cry
>   the sound of which no one on earth has heard—
> Nor could I hear their words for all the thunder.

Listening, Marlowe began to weep, amazed, relieved, and grateful to be allowed at last the simple warmth of grief. She'd been in such a rage, for weeks.

While she was crying, Veronica came back, with little cartons of Chinese food. She'd taken the liberty of ordering an eight-vegetable and mushroom dish for Marlowe, who continued to cry as she ate. They listened for hours to Dante's tapes, reminiscing tentatively and drinking Chinese beer; and Marlowe didn't really cease to cry until she opened her fortune cookie, which said, "You will meet an old friend in a new way." That made her laugh. She was not above taking comfort in such things, by then, she missed him so.

IV

A Song for Beatrice

MARLOWE HAD THE BABY THREE DAYS LATER, THE LABOR TAKING MOST OF the night. While she was in the final stages, she passed beyond the pain into an odd free zone where Dante's presence was as clear as the midwife's cheap perfume. In gratitude, Marlowe named the baby Beatrice. Despite her certainty that she would confound her circle with a son, she'd brought a beautiful black-eyed girl into the world.

Jack was there for the whole ordeal, wearing a shirt of soothing green, holding her hand through the sweaty worst of it, and coaching her breathing; and by the time the little girl emerged, Marlowe could even look at him and smile and believe he understood. Daa had returned from Mendocino just in time to be there too, and she and Sheba sang sweetly, a song of welcome Dante had written just before he died, as the baby was bathed in warm rose water and laid on Marlowe's breast. The midwife thanked the Goddess and beamed. All things considered, she said, it had been a very gentle birth.

Part XXIII

The Bardo
of Rebirth

Now, to assert vehemently that things like this are really so as I've narrated them, doesn't befit any man of sense. But that this is so, or something pretty much like it, about our souls and their dwelling place, since it is clear that the soul is immortal—it is quite fitting we say that.
—Plato, *Phaedo*

I

Reboptu

SOME WEEKS LATER, A STRAY KITTEN CAME BY THE LAPIDGE STREET HOUSE while Sheba was repainting the facade in a tasteful gray. The kitten sat itself up at the base of the scaffold, peering up and mewing, until Sheba relented and fetched it a bowl of milk. She sat beside it on the porch while it lapped away, telling herself that objective criteria for ownership decisions would have to apply. The kitten was maybe six weeks old, an alert and tiny male, black and gray, with deep green eyes and a cocky air. Before the day was over it was splashed endearingly with paint, from batting at the brushes, and Sheba had surrendered all pretense and decided to keep it. She named it Re-Bop Two, or Reboptu, with a tentatively Egyptian flavor; but, perhaps inevitably, everybody called him Dante.

II

A Sacrifice of Underwear

SHEBA WAS IN A PHASE OF CLEANING OUT HER ROOM AND REPAINTING IT IN a milder shade of yellow. She'd given all but one of her dangling crystals to Jack and taken down her posters. She pruned the rose-bush back and cut her hair again and threw her accumulated cache of half-burned candles away. She felt herself to be on the verge of fierce and major renunciations, though the specifics still seemed vague. And things seemed to be going her way again. Marlowe, noticing the two rudraksha seeds in the bowl on Sheba's altar table, had given her Jackson's old mala; with its 103 rudrakshas, she now had a total of 105—three short of the Buddhist standard of 108, Sheba thought, but not bad for San Francisco.

She believed her kundalini might have awakened at last as well—a little Indian man with a big grin had touched her head lightly at a weekend seminar and a bolt of blue flame had made its way down her spine and exploded somewhere within her. At the same moment she'd heard the Rolling Stones playing "Under My Thumb." She'd returned a week later to the tiny storefront center in the Haight and the little man had given her a meditation technique, an almost embarrassingly simple attention to her breath, and told her not to eat shelled seafood for two years; now every Thursday night she went to the center and chanted Rama Sita Jai. She was dreaming of bleak, stark landscapes, of difficult purgative journeys cheerfully embraced, though the little man had told her several times not to get grim. But Dante's death had shaken Sheba deeply, and she didn't want to waste the precious deep sobriety of loss. She even gave the rosebush's pedigree, in their common great-grandmother's confident hand, to Marlowe, for fear it would get lost in the general denuding. And Marlowe surprised her by being grateful. She said she'd been wanting for years to pay more attention to their family history.

Meanwhile Sheba wished the little man would find more things to ask her to give away. Lobster and crabmeat, however tasty, didn't seem sufficient to break the worldly bonds. He smiled at her haste and said that California made everyone believe such changes could happen fast. For himself, he just wanted to learn to speak better English and keep out of trouble with the police. There were problems with his green card. Meanwhile, she should meditate and live decently.

Still, Sheba felt the need to purge herself of earthly bonds. She threw away the pretty underwear her mother had sent and wore plain cotton panties. She was prepared to go to any extreme, but she hesitated over renouncing her visiting cards. Her mother still kept traces of the old elegant ways alive and had raised her to believe that one day she would need to leave an engraved card in someone's silver tray, to indicate that she had stopped in to see them. The cards themselves, a neat box of them, were crisp and creamy and said SHEBA MARIE MCKENZIE in sterling script. "You just don't know when you might have a situation where you need to leave a calling card," Sheba's mother had said, when she gave them to her daughter on her seventeenth birthday; and even now Sheba believed it might be so. She'd kept three of the cards in her purse religiously for years and never had occasion to leave one anywhere. Now, faced with the stark end of an era, she found she hadn't the heart to throw them all away. She compromised by giving one to the little man the next time she went to see him.

He held it up to the light and squinted at it. "I see. You come from an ancient lineage. Very good." And he put the card on his altar table—miraculously, Sheba noted, in a little silver tray. It made her wish she'd kept her underwear.

III

The Vagaries of the Mail

ON THE DAY THAT JACKSON WOULD HAVE TURNED THIRTY-NINE, MAR-lowe drove to his parents' home just north of Yuba City to deliver a letter. She had finished reading Jackson's journal the week before, with an odd sense of anticlimax. The main work, it seemed, had been done; toward the end, the day-to-day diary had given way for the most part to sketches and doodles. Jackson drew the pine tree outside his window almost every day; he sketched the flowers in the bedside vase and the hummingbird at the feeder. A sketch of Marlowe moved her deeply—a tender study of her with drawn face and sunken eyes. She wondered if to Jackson's eyes she had really looked so pained.

What reflections there were on his imminent death were—not casual, Marlowe thought, but *easy*. There was a lightness, almost a joviality to the final entries. Jackson, tired out by the long succession of ailments and afflictions, had let go of his body lightly, almost gratefully; but more than that he had simply been at peace. It had, it seemed, been the little things he was most interested in—an orchid opening a week before he died got two sketches and the last page and a half of prose he managed to write, while the Tibetan schemata of the various afterlife bardos he could expect to pass through upon dying got a single line, and that a joke.

And as a last surprise, there were letters—Jackson in the last week of his life had written to practically everyone he knew, sweet, moving, honest farewell notes, short and occasionally loopy with the morphine, at points illegible, but lit with his presence. Marlowe wondered where he had found the time. The letters did not seem to be drafts, or exercises—it appeared to Marlowe that Jackson had simply never gotten around to sending them, and so she had mailed most of them off to the people they were addressed to, with cover notes explaining the delay. Call it karma, she had thought. But there was one letter it had seemed better to hand-deliver.

She had called in advance and was welcomed at the door by Jackson's mother, Trina, in the apron she apparently never bothered to take off. She gave Marlowe a warm floury hug and ushered her into the living room, where Jackson's father, Mark, sat, in the big leather easy chair Jackson had described so many times. According to Jackson it took a world event to get his father out of that chair. Marlowe, apparently, was not a world event—Mark merely nodded at her and waved one hand toward the couch. Marlowe sat down and surprised him by accepting a whisky without water and a beer chaser—the drinks of the house, as she knew perfectly well. Jackson himself, rather pointedly, had never touched anything stronger than wine, and Marlowe had gathered that over the years it had become an odd point of subterranean dispute between father and son.

What the hell, she thought; let's get a little plastered for the sake of peace.

The Jim Beam helped, actually. Mark's conversation was as rigid and shot through with empathic prejudice as she had remembered. And there were still various ordeals to be undergone, it seemed. Trina had to show her Jackson's old room, for instance; poignantly, pathetically, it had been maintained more or less unchanged since he had been in high school. There were tennis trophies and a Latin Club award, programs from the musicals he had starred in, and a greenish brass Buddha—Jackson had discovered Zen at fifteen. There was a prominent photo, almost painfully ironic, of Jackson at his junior prom with a sweet blond girl in a deep blue gown, with a corsage pinned to her breast. He had known by then that he was gay, Marlowe knew—this perfect American image might as well have been from one of the musicals he had performed in. But in his mother's historical recreation here, the six-by-eight picture got center stage.

Back in the living room, there was more Jim Beam, perhaps mercifully, and photo albums. Jackson's parents, for all their goodwill, didn't know what to do with her except show her evidence of a Jackson Marlowe had not, necessarily, known. But she *could* see him, Marlowe thought, from time to time in those old snapshots: in the smile, in the sharpness of a look, she could catch a glimpse of the man she had come to know. And it was a blessing, in a way, to see him so young and peppy, with all that naive flesh on his bones. So many of her last images of him were skeletal.

At last, though, there was nowhere left to hide and nothing else to do. Marlowe refused Trina's halfhearted invitation to stay for dinner; she had no intention of enduring dinner here. She opened her purse and handed over the letter and would gladly have fled then and there, her duty discharged; but Jackson's father wanted her to stay while he read it. He had gotten out of the chair to take the envelope from her, Marlowe noted. For that extraordinary concession alone, she felt it had been worth the trip.

Mark read the letter slowly, his lips moving a little. Several times, embarrassed, he had to ask Marlowe to decipher a word or a phrase. Jackson's handwriting had grown loose and sometimes jagged, near the end, and he had for the most part abandoned the effort of capitals and punctuation.

dear dad—

    it's funny what it takes to get us to the point where it is simple and clear. we've spent so many years in fear and anger and re-crimination. i won't say wasted—for all I know there was some profound necessity there. But whatever it was—and we could both make the obvious lists of blame and failure—it doesn't seem so relevant anymore. it seems to me to have lifted, like a fog lifts

    Remember how you used to drive me to school sometimes? the valley fog in the morning was so dense sometimes we couldn't see the trees beside the road. you always told me that if we climbed a high enough hill the sun would be out   that was inconceivable to me. i remember wrestling with that concept all through grade school—it was a notion like God or Justice or all the other things you used to talk about: impossibly abstract and, as i got older, perhaps even a little dubious, and finally i threw all those notions out because i thought that was what I had to do to be free.

    but then funny thing last week my friend Marlowe took me for a drive. i had been very sick for about a month, it was the first day i could get out of the house at all. san francisco was socked in with fog, as it so often is, so we drove north, across the golden gate, which will usually get you out of it pretty quickly but that day marin county was fogged in too; and so marlowe turned up mt. tamalpais, and we wound upward in the fog

    And suddenly, a miracle—we turned a corner and came out through the top of the fog into the brightest, clearest afternoon, blue sky and golden grass and the mountaintop above, and nothing below us but miles and miles of beautiful fluffy white, a quilt of fog and cloud as far as the eye could see   the whole bay area was buried beneath that quilt, in cold layers of gray, but there we were in the sunlight. And suddenly i remembered what you had told me about rising out of the tule fog.

i don't mean to say that i had doubted you entirely until that moment, of course i had managed to figure out some years before that you actually could pop out of the fog sometimes. i even felt i had done my share of popping out in ways you could not understand—i don't mean to open old wounds again—what i really mean to say is it was just particularly vivid that day, that you had told me the truth. and in fact the strangest thing has happened over the years— all those notions you used to harp on all the time have crept back into my life, in ways i never would have expected   Not just the revelation that any fog, however thick and seemingly infinite, is local, or that you have to change your oil every x thousand miles, but god justice beauty integrity i have discovered them all afresh, and been grateful to you every time i have come upon something else you had told me about that i had tossed away or ignored, some other landmark in some other bright clear landscape that you had told me about and i had written off as myth, or fairy tale, or one of the desperate lies we all need to tell ourselves sometimes   And now i think you must have been trying all along to tell me things that to you were as clear as the fact that if you drive up high enough on mt. tamalpais on a foggy day you will break out into sunlight, no matter how sad and cold and gray you felt, how hopeless you felt along the way

and now i think we live most of our lives in that cold tule fog, Dad—we live at best in the hope of sunlight, and the memory of it, and in the stories about it we hear   And at times we are blessed to break out into the clear, and then all the things that seemed obscure and hazy, soaked in gray, are bright and obvious like my love for you, and my gratitude   Maybe it's too late—though i can't really believe that—it seems to me so bright and clear that it can never be too late, Dad, to say I love you—and the rest of it, that long drive in the fog, it doesn't matter in the sunlight—it doesn't matter a bit from here it is all so clear

It had grown almost dark outside; it would be a long drive home, Marlowe thought unwillingly. She was going to have to stop in Yuba City for a monster cup of coffee and some aspirin. But she was glad she had stayed. Mark had ended up over by the window, his back to Marlowe, his shoulders shaking almost imperceptibly; Jackson would almost certainly have been pleased, to see his father out of that chair, for quite so long.

IV

The California Book of the Dead

TWO DAYS BEFORE THE AUTUMN EQUINOX, ON THE ANNIVERSARY OF JACKson's death, Marlowe opened a new show of her work at a little Oakland gallery called The Interior Castle, near the Rockridge BART station. She titled the show "The California Book of the Dead" and arranged her work of the last several years thematically. Taken in sequence, the pieces led one through a sort of death and rebirth experience, including a good long period in the intermediate bardos and odd domains of consciousness, purgatories and infernos, lesser heavens and lesser hells. The tarot miniatures and studies of trees were there, the series of apocalyptic mops and the smashed chinaware, the rosebush and some abstract pieces rooted in bits of Dante's music, and the halo series of her father in the hospital bed, including several angels. Jackson was there, laughing as his soul's feather was weighed by Egyptian deities; and Dante, in a land where music manifested instantly as it was conceived, as breeze and the movement of creeks; and her old art-school chum Camilla Rondstadt with perfectly natural breasts in a New York City that glimmered like Augustine's City of God. She'd even included Aumakua Parker dancing happily with Pele, and Re-Bop and Daa's grandmother Alva and a dog she'd lost when she was eight—all the dead were there, in a surreally lucid series of portraits in unreal places tentatively labeled

"Prayers of the Faithful for the Dearly Departed." One thing led into another, through a maze of screened-off display areas and labyrinth rooms, with varied eerie lighting and sound effects arranged by Albert Nerdowsky and a quiet, steady background tape playing Dante's score for the *Comedy*, from Inferno to Paradiso, all of it culminating in an abrupt way at the table where the wine was poured and the cookies were eaten, in daylight that by then seemed strange.

She'd even seen to the cookies and wine herself. The wine was from the St. Helena vineyard of a friend whose family had been making wine in one place or another since the days of Francis of Assisi, from his vintage year of 1987. The cookies were fortune cookies, custom-made with fortunes Marlowe had written herself—"Follow your star, and likely as not you will live in poverty, loneliness, and obscurity, and die unrecognized"; or "Despair makes the heart grow fonder"; or "One good turn deserves another, but more often is wasted"; and "All things come to her who waits. And then they go away again."

Both cookies and wine were having a great success and threatened at moments to overshadow the artwork itself. Still, several paintings had sold right away, and the gallery owner, Herbie Morrow, was pleased, and wanted more of the mops-head series, and more smashed china. "It's very postecofeminine," he told Marlowe over his second glass of wine. By the third he was saying it was post even that, it was postmortem, it was après-everything, it needed a whole new name. But Herbie was always that way; another glass and she would be a genius, and if he drank a bottle, it would begin to seem she had defined an era.

Daa came, with her new girlfriend, Eve, a sweet, secret-seeming, serious poet, wearing black and brown and gray—a relatively new lesbian, Marlowe discerned immediately, being initiated, in her way, by Daa. The two of them were obviously blissful, so deeply so that Daa gave Marlowe a kiss that said all was forgiven. They'd just returned from Big Sur; happiness, that universal healer, had touched Daa's life again. Eve held Daa's hand steadily and followed everything with wide gray eyes. They did not stay long—Daa still did not approve of either the mops-head series or the general morbid air of Marlowe's current phase, as she perceived it—and went off early, back to the Lapidge Street house, where Daa had moved back in, reclaiming her old bedroom as if nothing had happened. Marlowe watched them leave—they would, she knew, fall into bed and make the ventilators ring with new discoveries, then lie around eating marshmallow zingers and watching old movies. Even now, the thought could cause a pang.

Greg Sturmmacher came and lavished mean praise on everything he saw. He found the realism delightfully passé, and the abstraction "fragile, even crystalline"—meaning, Marlowe knew, weak—and he saw fresh possibilities in the Egyptian motifs. She'd always done her best work, after all, on ancient themes seen in an idiosyncratic way. He liked the cookies best, Sturmmacher said with a perfectly straight face; and he left early too, with a woman who apparently had a lot to learn.

Toni and Pesky drove all the way down from Willits in their new pickup truck, and Toni had surprising things to say about the relation of certain of Marlowe's bardo scenes to the dance work of Nijinsky. Shakti Arguello had a mystical experience somewhere near the portrait of Re-Bop and resolved to get a cat. Sheba passed through carefully, still a little tentative as to what it might mean to be walking around with an awakened kundalini, but she loosened up after some of the wine and praised the Dante portraits lavishly. She was also charmed to recognize Ellie the elephant, and the stuffed kangaroo she had given Marlowe when they both were seven, in the *Portraits of the Dearly Departed*; she even found their great-grandmother, of the rosebush legacy, in one of the mops-heads, which was news to Marlowe, who merely nodded, as she always did when someone found something in her work she hadn't seen herself.

The Tibetan gong that Daa had given Dante the previous Christmas, said to be able to summon the dead, was set up at an obscure point within the maze of paintings, in a pool of soft blue light, and people kept hitting it spontaneously as they passed. Every time the deep reverberate pulse rang through The Interior Castle, Marlowe tensed, alert to something, anything—some token of mystical presence, she supposed, of the sort she had grown to know through her long meditations on Jackson. But Dante never came, in any form she could recognize. She told herself that he was already there, through his music, but the argument felt weak.

She had a sense, in any case, that his absence was appropriate enough—the place was crowded, the people clever and loud, and the show had something of the smell of a success. It was not, when you got right down to it, Dante's kind of scene.

V

The View from the Ridge

As the show wound down, Marlowe wandered the gallery, helping Herbie gather the empty plastic wineglasses. She was prepared to take the train back to San Francisco, but at the last minute she accepted a ride from Victor Morris.

Victor had shown up toward the end, coming straight from work, in a T-shirt and jeans that were still a little dusty. Marlowe had seen him at one point standing, his noble brow furrowed earnestly, near a mops-head piece that verged on pure chaos. Later she'd noted a similar look on his face as he read his fortune cookie. He'd gone back into the labyrinth several times. As they walked now to his pickup truck, Marlowe asked him how he had liked the show.

"So much of what you paint is angry," Victor said at once, surprising her. She'd been prepared to defend the abstraction and surrealism against someone whose favorite painter was probably Grant Wood. "Angry, and pained."

"That's because I'm a realist," Marlowe said, and Victor laughed and opened the passenger door of the truck to let her in.

"And I thought it was just because you were angry and pained," he said, and closed the door after her, before she could reply.

Marlowe stewed while he circled around to the driver's side, and as soon as he climbed in, she said, "I think that art that doesn't acknowledge our deepest pain before it puts it all in perspective is just anesthesia in the service of delusion."

"I must have missed the part where you put it all in perspective."

"It was plain as the nose on your face. The basic text of every book of the dead is from Ecclesiastes—vanity of vanities. Life is short and full of foolishness, and then we die."

"Ah," Victor said, and started the truck. "And then?"

"The rest is stories that we tell ourselves, to try to deal with the anger and the pain. And if we get lucky, we make ourselves feel better for a while."

"And what's the difference between that and anesthesia in the service of delusion?"

Marlowe glanced at him. "You surprise me, Victor."

"Because I actually speak English?" He smiled and pulled the truck out into traffic.

They rode for a moment in silence, then Marlowe said, "The difference is that art is aware of the insubstantiality of the lies it tells itself. It doesn't mistake itself for reality."

"Reality being anger, and pain."

"Anger and pain are delusions too, actually. Reality is emptier than we can ever imagine."

"Your basic cheerful nature shines through more and more as I get to know you." Victor made a left turn, up toward the hills.

"Where are we going?"

"I've seen your work. I thought maybe you'd like to see mine."

"Yours?"

"This latest house I'm working on. It's in such a pretty spot."

"I've got to get home for dinner. I told the others—"

"It won't take long." He glanced at her. "Indulge me. My fortune cookie said that this would be my lucky day."

"The hell it did. I wrote every one of those things. The best you

335

could have gotten was one saying that radiation therapy has slightly less effect on life expectancy than simple wishful thinking.''

He reached into his pocket and pulled out a tiny slip of paper and handed it to her. Marlowe read, in amazement, '' 'Grace will ever find a way.' '' She looked at him. ''A cuckoo in the nest. You slipped this in yourself.''

''Not me. I took potluck like everyone else.''

''Then that goddamned little Chinese guy double-crossed me. Shit!'' Marlowe settled back in her seat. ''Well, there you go. You see how it is? You just can't win, even if you stack the deck.''

''Life is tricky that way,'' Victor agreed, and downshifted the truck with a slight crunch of the gears. The hill had steepened; concrete foundations of burned-out homes dotted the landscape, and here and there a new house under construction looked out over the brown earth. The great fire that had ravaged the Oakland hills a few years before had swept through here. Blackened trees and scorched street signs were still the only things standing for blocks at a time. A crow flew over the opposite hill like an omen, or something in a dream. Seeing it all in the settling evening light, Marlowe fell silent. It made her point, in a way, this desolate place; but she took no pleasure in the fact. As she took no pleasure at Dante's demise. It was merely the facts of the case.

''I thought you said the house was in a pretty place,'' she said at last.

''Did I? Maybe I meant that it will be, when everything grows back.'' Victor pulled the pickup over to the curb, at the bottom of a little set of concrete steps. The blackened sign at the base of the walkway read GONDO PATH, and Marlowe laughed.

''It's an allegory, right?'' she said. ''For the stations of the cross?''

''It's a construction site,'' Victor said, and got out of the truck. She followed, and they walked up the steps together. At the top, to the right, the framework of a two-story house commanded a view of the city below, and the Bay. Across the water, behind San Francisco, the setting sun was moving toward the sea.

"I've been working here for about three weeks," Victor said, leading her through the doorframe onto the bare wood flooring. Heaps of material lay in every direction, and coiled orange extension cords had been set neatly aside. He lifted a heavy box of nails from a pile of plywood sheets and brushed the sawdust off to clear a spot for her to sit down. Marlowe took the place, and he sat beside her, facing west.

"There's going to be a picture window here," he said, indicating the frame of the wall facing them.

"All the better to watch the fire approach, I suppose, the next time it burns this place down."

"Actually, the fire would come from the east," Victor said, and pulled a paper bag from a recess beside the stack of wood. "Would you like a beer?"

"You're suspiciously prepared."

"I was hoping, actually, you might come up here with me. Though I didn't realize we'd time it just right for the sunset." Victor reached into the bag and pulled out two Budweisers; he opened them and handed one to Marlowe.

"To the success of your art show."

"To everything that has burned away, that we could sit here with a view like this, on such a lovely evening," Marlowe said, and tapped his bottle with hers before she drank.

They sat in silence for a while. The lights in the city were beginning to twinkle, and the rush-hour traffic of the freeways was clearly visible. But there was no sound, and the activity below seemed placid, the vista peaceful. The western sky was aflame above a bank of fog on the horizon. Marlowe found that she was humming softly, a little piece that Dante had set to music years before. He had only played it for her twice, once the night they had met, at a party at Jackson's house; and once on a beach near the Russian River's mouth, beside a bonfire, as a drizzling rain began to fall. He had finished it even as everyone else began to run for their tents—his duty, Dante had said, to the universe. Marlowe could remember the warm, golden firelight gleaming in the droplets on his face, as he bent over the strings to play; and the way he had wiped the guitar dry, shielding it with his body as he put it back in the case, long after everyone but her had fled.

> Everything lost is found again
> In a new form, in a new way.
> Everything hurt is healed again
> In a new life, in a new day.

"That's pretty," Victor said.

"It's just a little ditty."

"By Dante?"

She glanced at him appreciatively. "The tune, yes."

Someone had left a hammer on the plywood flooring near their feet. Victor bent to pick it up and held it absently, expertly. Marlowe had a sudden flash of him putting up the frame of these walls, sawing planks, driving nails.

"I dreamed about Dante last night," she said. "The first time, since he died."

"Oh?"

"We were somewhere pretty, walking, and this old woman came up to us and asked directions. She was all wrought up, she had this long, involved story. I was ready to dismiss her right away, but Dante listened to the whole thing patiently. And at the end of the story, he pointed the way for her to go, very simply. And the woman looked at him and smiled. 'You're such a nice young man,' she said. 'Such a good *listener.'* And Dante laughed and told her, 'I'm dead.' 'Oh,' she said. 'Is *that* how you do it? Well, good for you.' And she wheeled her cart off. She was a street lady, I think." Marlowe sipped her beer. "Just a dream, of course."

"Still, it's probably nice to see him."

"It is, actually." She drank again and looked at the bottle in surprise. It was already empty. "Jesus, bartender, call a cab."

"There's more beer."

"No, I think you'd probably better take me home, before I get maudlin."

"How about dinner? I know a great little place not far from

here—Thai food. It's my great discovery. I never knew Thai food existed, until I came to California. I don't know what I thought people in Thailand *ate*.''

''No, I'm afraid I really should be getting back, Victor, thanks. Jack is sitting with the baby, he's been great about this kind of stuff, but I don't want to be away too long. And then Daa is making dinner, and I said I'd be there. Plus, to tell you the whole gory truth, I wanted to fix the toilet tonight. It's been running lately, and—''

''I could come by and fix that, if you'd like,'' Victor persisted, and Marlowe looked at him. The mechanical process of courtship had been engaged, she realized—a marriage proposal would issue from all this in due time as surely as hamburger from a meat grinder. Victor Morris only knew one way to go about things with women, and the dance had begun somehow now with her, the eight-step polka toward the movie ending.

Meanwhile, back at the house, Jack was singing lullabies to the baby, with whom he'd been spending most of his days. And Daa would have clambered out of bed with Eve by now and begun dinner. In the weeks since her return to San Francisco, she too had been spending a lot of time with Beatrice. It wasn't family, it was merely some weird California variation on domesticity that would pass like the wind, but it was the way this child was being raised at the moment, and Marlowe was more grateful than she could say. She'd never have made it through alone.

The sun, blood red, was easing spectacularly into the gray mass of fog, on one of the last days of summer. Jackson had said the year before that he wanted to die before the days got short again. That was so like Jackson, to actually follow through on an aesthetic thing like that. Dante had never expressed a preference, but she could imagine he would have liked a summer departure too. He'd practically said as much the night they had made out in the summer grass, while the July moon rose above the hills—he'd said he felt complete enough to pass away without a qualm.

The thought for some reason loosed a wave of affection in Marlowe. Would she really have traded those last days with him, his frantic swimming lessons included, for anything? She'd begun to know him in a wholly different way, and her grief was colored by his absent lips now; her body ached differently, the expectations of her senses had changed, as a fruit of that meeting of—admittedly bewildered—flesh. Her days would be forever different for having held that tentative man, beneath that absolutely certain moon.

From somewhere nearby Marlowe could smell sweetness—jasmine, she realized. Someone had already replanted, in the burnt dirt.

Beside her Victor waited patiently. He was not her type, of course; he would never do. But friendship was where you found it. And God only knew where friendship could take you.

"If you'd really fix the toilet, you can stay for dinner," she said. "It will be macaroni and cheese, I'm afraid. No one's had much energy for cooking elaborate meals lately."

"Oh, macaroni and cheese is my favorite," Victor said at once, earnestly, and Marlowe laughed. What was funniest of all, perhaps, aside from the way the twilight made his face seem like a teenager's, was that she believed him.